Naked City

ALSO EDITED BY ELLEN DATLOW

Blood Is Not Enough

Alien Sex

A Whisper of Blood

Little Deaths

Off Limits

Twists of the Tale: An Anthology of Cat Horror

Lethal Kisses

Vanishing Acts

The Dark

Inferno

The Del Rey Book of Science Fiction and Fantasy

Poe: 19 New Tales Inspired by Edgar Allan Poe

Lovecraft Unbound

Tails of Wonder and Imagination

Darkness: Two Decades of Modern Horror

Digital Domains: A Decade of Science Fiction and Fantasy

The Best Horror of the Year, Volumes One–Three

WITH TERRI WINDLING

Sirens and Other Daemon Lovers

A Wolf at the Door and Other Retold Fairy Tales

The Green Man: Tales of the Mythic Forest

Swan Sister: Fairy Tales Retold

The Faery Reel: Tales from the Twilight Realm

Salon Fantastique

The Coyote Road: Trickster Tales

The Beastly Bride and Other Tales of the Animal People

Troll's Eye View: A Book of Villainous Tales

Teeth: Vampire Tales

The Year's Best Fantasy and Horror: First through Sixteenth Annual Collections

THE ADULT FAIRY TALE SERIES

Snow White, Blood Red

Black Thorn, White Rose

Ruby Slippers, Golden Tears

Black Swan, White Raven

Silver Birch, Blood Moon

Black Heart, Ivory Bones

WITH KELLY LINK AND GAVIN J. GRANT

The Year's Best Fantasy and Horror: Seventeenth through Twenty-first Annual Collections

WITH NICK MAMATAS

Haunted Legends

Naked City

TALES OF URBAN FANTASY

EDITED BY

ELLEN DATLOW

St. Martin's Griffin
New York

These stories are works of fiction. All of the characters, organizations, and events portrayed in the stories are either products of the authors' imaginations or are used fictitiously.

Printed in the United States of America. For information, address St. Martin's Press, 175 Fifth Avenue, New York, N.Y. 10010.

www.stmartins.com

Book design by Rich Arnold

Library of Congress Cataloging-in-Publication Data

Naked city : tales of urban fantasy / edited by Ellen Datlow.—1st ed.
p. cm.
ISBN 978-0-312-60431-8 (hardcover)
ISBN 978-0-312-38524-8 (pbk.)
1. Supernatural—Fiction. 2. Fantasy fiction, American. 3. Short stories, American. I. Datlow, Ellen.
PS648.F3N35 2011
813'.087660806—dc22

2011008088

10 9 8 7 6 5 4 3 2

Copyright Acknowledgments

For my parents, Doris and Nathan Datlow, whom I love dearly

and who infected me with their love for reading.

Contents

Introduction

The term *urban fantasy* was originally applied to fantasy written in reaction to the works most popular up to the early 1980s—high-fantasy, imaginary worlds with medieval trappings. Instead, some writers began to inject magic into contemporary times and into urban areas, both real and invented. Mark Helprin set his charming novel *Winter's Tale* in New York City, and John Crowley set his classic *Little, Big* at least partially in a recognizable New York. Many of Charles de Lint's Newford stories and novels take place in a thinly disguised Toronto, while Emma Bull's *War for the Oaks* is indelibly linked to Minneapolis. Terri Windling was influential in the subgenre's "founding" by creating *Borderland,* a shared-universe original anthology series (the first two edited with Mark Arnold), set in an imaginary city in which humans and magical creatures could meet and interact.

Urban fantasy as we have come to know it today combines the often-dark edge of city living with enticing worlds of magic. Its subgenres include noir crime and paranormal romance. But the urban landscape is what's crucial.

As one who lives in and loves New York City and enjoys traveling to other cities around the world, to me, urban centers seem to seethe with an energy, cultural diversity, and creativity that is more difficult to find in suburban or rural areas. You can lose yourself in a big city or you can find yourself.

In soliciting stories for this anthology I asked writers to consider all types of locations (as long as the story takes place in a city—existing or made up). I wanted the city to be as important as anything else in the story—in other words, where the story takes place *should* matter, in some way, to the story. Perhaps the most fun of editing an anthology such as this is the sheer variety of types of stories that can fit under the rubric "urban fantasy." Some of the authors chose existing cities that are well known and easy to identify. There are several New York stories—each very different. Other stories take place in London; Berlin; New Orleans; Haifa, Israel; Chicago; Seattle; Mexico City; Las Vegas; Asbury Park, New Jersey; and Cherry Creek, Colorado. Others created imaginary cities.

Urban centers are packed with people, and this component of cities can be both a boon for gregarious types or a curse for those who are shy and reserved. It can also be utterly intimidating to newcomers, such as the pair of odd-couple immigrants in Delia Sherman's historical fantasy, or it can be an opportunity for those with bad intent, such as the protagonists in Jeffrey Ford's and Matthew Kressel's stories. A weird joyousness pervades John Crowley's story, which takes some off-the-cuff remarks by inventor, futurist, and visionary Buckminster Fuller quite literally, creating an unexpected fantasia.

Some of the greatest loneliness can be experienced when surrounded by people—such is the case for the eponymous character in Kit Reed's "Weston Walks," a recluse who ventures out only periodically; Nathan Ballingrud's displaced person, a haunted refugee from the natural disaster that took his home; and Peter S. Beagle's bitter academic hoping for a last chance of stability. Naomi Novik has written the quintessential New York story.

The Naked City was the title of a 1948 semidocumentary crime movie, inspired by the book by famous urban documentarian/crime photographer Weegee. In turn, the lauded television series *Naked City* ran in half-hour episodes 1958 to 1959, was canceled, and then was reincarnated in 1960 as an hour-long show, lasting until 1963. (An uncle of mine played a minor role in one episode, but I was too young to stay up and watch it.) The catchphrase was "There are eight million stories in the naked city. This has been one of them." The city was New York, and eight million was an approximation of the population at the time. So aside from being catchy, the title reflects the diversity of what lies between these two covers.

—Ellen Datlow

Naked City

Curses

A DRESDEN FILES SHORT STORY

BY JIM BUTCHER

Jim Butcher is the bestselling author most known for his urban fantasy series The Dresden Files. He also writes the Codex Alera series. Butcher lives in Missouri with his wife, son, and a ferocious guard dog.

Most of my cases are pretty tame. Someone loses a piece of jewelry with a lot of sentimental value, or someone comes to me because they've just moved into a new house and it's a little more haunted than the seller's disclosure indicated. Nothing Chicago's only professional wizard can't handle—but the cases don't usually rake in much money, either.

So when a man in a two-thousand-dollar suit opened my office door and came inside, he had my complete attention.

I mean, I didn't take my feet down off my desk or anything. But I paid attention.

He looked my office up and down and frowned, as though he didn't much approve of what he saw. Then he looked at me and said, "Excuse me, is this the office of—"

"Dolce," I said.

He blinked. "Excuse me."

"Your suit," I said. "Dolce and Gabbana. Silk. Very nice. You might want to consider an overcoat, though, now that it's cooling off. Paper says we're in for some rain."

He studied me intently for a moment. He was a man in his late prime. His hair was dyed too dark, and the suit looked like it probably hid a few pounds. "You must be Harry Dresden."

I inclined my head toward him. "Agent or attorney?"

"A little of both," he said, looking around my office again. "I represent a professional entertainment corporation, which wishes to remain anonymous for the time being. My name is Donovan. My sources tell me that you're the man who might be able to help us."

My office isn't anything to write home about. It's on a corner, with windows on two walls, but it's furnished for function, not style—scuffed-up wooden desks, a couple of comfortable chairs, some old metal filing cabinets, a used wooden table, and a coffeepot that is old enough to have belonged to Neanderthals. I figured Donovan was worried that he'd exposed his suit to unsavory elements, and resisted an irrational impulse to spill my half cup of cooling coffee on it.

"That depends."

"On what?"

"What you need and whether you can afford me."

Donovan fixed me with a stern look. I bore up under it as best I could. "Do you intend to gouge me for a fee, Mr. Dresden?"

"For every penny I reasonably can," I told him.

He blinked at me. "You . . . you're quite up front about it, aren't you?"

"Saves time," I said.

"What makes you think I would tolerate such a thing?"

"People don't come to me until they're pretty desperate, Mr. Donovan," I said, "especially rich people and hardly ever corporations. Besides, you come in here all intriguey and coy, not wanting to reveal who your employer is. That means that in addition to whatever else you want from me, you want my discretion, too."

"So your increased fee is a polite form of blackmail?"

"Cost of doing business. If you want this done on the down low, you make my job more difficult. You should expect to pay a little more than a conventional customer when you're asking for more than they are."

He narrowed his eyes at me. "How much are you going to cost me?"

I shrugged a shoulder. "Let's find out. What do you want me to do?"

He stood up and turned to walk to the door. He stopped before he reached it, read the words HARRY DRESDEN, WIZARD backward in the frosted glass, and eyed me over his shoulder. "I assume that you have heard of any number of curses in local folklore."

"Sure," I said.

"I suppose you'll expect me to believe in their existence."

I shrugged. "They'll exist or not exist regardless of what you believe, Mr. Donovan." I paused. "Well. Apart from the ones that *don't* exist except in someone's mind. They're only real *because* somebody believes. But that edges from the paranormal over toward psychology. I'm not licensed for that."

He grimaced and nodded. "In that case . . ."

I felt a little slow off the mark as I realized what we were talking about. "A cursed local entertainment corporation," I said. "Like maybe a sports team."

He kept a poker face on, and it was a pretty good one.

"You're talking about the Billy Goat Curse," I said.

Donovan arched an eyebrow and then gave me an almost imperceptible nod as he turned around to face me again. "What do you know about it?"

I blew out my breath and ran my fingers back through my hair. "Uh, back in 1945 or so, a tavern owner named Sianis was asked to leave a World Series game at Wrigley. Seems his pet goat was getting rained on and it smelled bad. Some of the fans were complaining. Outraged at their lack of social élan, Sianis pronounced a curse on the stadium, stating that never again would a World Series game be played there. Well, actually he said something like, 'Them Cubs, they ain't gonna win no more,' but the World Series thing is the general interpretation."

"And?" Donovan asked.

"And I think if I'd gotten kicked out of a Series game I'd been looking forward to, I might do the same thing."

"You have a goat?"

"I have a moose," I said.

He blinked at that for a second, didn't understand it, and decided to ignore it. "If you know that, then you know that many people believe that the curse has held."

"Where the Series is concerned, the Cubbies have been filled with fail and dipped in suck sauce since 1945," I acknowledged. "No matter how hard they try, just when things are looking up, something seems to go bad at the worst possible time." I paused to consider. "I can relate."

"You're a fan, then?"

"More of a kindred spirit."

He looked around my office again and gave me a small smile. "But you follow the team."

"I go to games when I can."

"That being the case," Donovan said, "you know that the team has been playing well this year."

"And the Cubs want to hire yours truly to prevent the curse from screwing things up."

Donovan shook his head. "I never said that the Cubs organization was involved."

"Hell of a story, though, if they were."

Donovan frowned severely.

"The *Sun-Times* would run it on the front page. CUBS HIRE PROFESSIONAL WIZARD TO BREAK CURSE, maybe. Rick Morrissey would have a ball with that story."

"My clients," Donovan said firmly, "have authorized me to commission your services on this matter, if it can be done quickly—and with the utmost discretion."

I swung my feet down from my desk. "Mr. Donovan," I said. "No one does discretion like me."

Two hours after I had begun my calculations, I dropped my pencil on the laboratory table and stretched my back. "Well. You're right."

"Of course I'm right," said Bob the Skull. "I'm always right."

I gave the dried, bleached human skull sitting on a shelf amidst a stack of paperback romance novels a gimlet-eye.

"For *some* values of right," he amended hastily. The words were conciliatory, but the flickering flames in the skull's eye sockets danced merrily.

My laboratory is in the subbasement under my basement apartment. It's dark, cool, and dank, essentially a concrete box that I have to enter by means of a folding staircase. It isn't a big room, but it's packed with the furnishings of one. Lots of shelves groan under the weight of books, scrolls, papers, alchemical tools, and containers filled with all manner of magical whatnot.

There's a silver summoning circle on the floor, and a tiny-scale model of the city of Chicago on a long table running down the middle of the room. The only shelf not crammed full is Bob's, and even it gets a little crowded sometimes. Bob is my more-or-less-faithful, not-so-trusty assistant, a spirit of intellect that dwells within a specially enchanted skull. I might be a wizard, but Bob's knowledge of magic makes me look like an engineering professor.

"Are you sure there's nothing you missed?" I asked.

"Nothing's certain, boss," the skull said philosophically. "But you did the equations. You know the power requirements for a spell to continue running through all those sunrises."

I grunted sourly. The cycles of time in the world degrade ongoing magic, and your average enchantment doesn't last for more than a few days. For a curse to be up and running since 1945, it would have had to begin as a malevolent enchantment powerful enough to rip a hole through the crust of the planet. Given the lack of lava in the area, it would seem that whatever the Billy Goat Curse might be, I could be confident that it wasn't a simple magical working.

"Nothing's ever simple," I complained.

"What did you expect, boss?" Bob said.

I growled. "So the single-spell theory is out."

"Yep," Bob said.

"Which means that either the curse is being powered by something that renews its energy—or else someone is refreshing the thing all the time."

"What about this Sianis guy's family?" Bob said. "Maybe they're putting out a fresh whammy every few days or something."

I shook my head. "I called records in Edinburgh. The wardens checked them out years ago when all of this first happened, and they aren't practitioners. Besides, they're Cub-friendly."

"The wardens investigated the Greek guy but not the curse?" Bob asked curiously.

"In 1945 the White Council had enough to do trying to mitigate the bad mojo from all those artifacts the Nazis stockpiled," I said. "Once they established that no one's life was in danger, they didn't really care if a bunch of guys playing a game got cursed to lose it."

"So what's your next move?"

I tapped my chin thoughtfully with one finger. "Let's go look at the stadium."

I put Bob in the mesh sack I sometimes tote him around in and, at his petulant insistence, hung it from the rearview mirror of my car, a battered old Volkswagen Beetle. He hung there, swinging back and forth and occasionally spinning one way or the other when something caught his eye.

"Look at the legs on that one!" Bob said. "And whew, check *her* out! It must be chilly tonight!"

"There's a reason we don't get out more often, Bob," I sighed. I should have known better than to drive through the club district on my way to Wrigley.

"I love the girls' pants in this century," Bob said. "I mean *look* at those jeans. One little tug and off they come."

I wasn't touching that one.

I parked the car a couple of blocks from the stadium, stuck Bob in a pocket of my black leather duster, and walked in. The Cubs were on the road, and Wrigley was closed. It was a good time to knock around inside. But since Donovan was evidently prepared to deny and disavow all knowledge, I wasn't going to be able to simply knock on the door and wander in.

So I picked a couple of locks at a delivery entrance and went inside. I didn't hit it at professional-burglar speed or anything—I knew a couple of guys who could open a lock with tools as fast as they could with a key—but I wasn't in any danger of getting a ticket for loitering, either. Once I was inside, I headed straight for the concourses. If I mucked around in the stadium's administrative areas, I would probably run afoul of a full-blown security system, and the only thing I could reliably do to that would be to shut it down completely—and most systems are smart enough to tip off their home security company when that happens.

Besides. What I was looking for wouldn't be in any office.

I took Bob out of my pocket so that the flickering golden-orange lights of his eyes illuminated the area in front of me. "All right," I murmured. I kept my voice down, on the off chance that a night watchman might be on duty and nearby. "I'm angry at the Cubbies and I'm pitching my curse at them. Where's it going to stick?"

"There's really no question about that, is there?" Bob asked me.

"Home plate," we said together.

I started forward, walking silently. Being quiet when you sneak around isn't difficult, as long as you aren't in any rush. The serious professionals can all but sprint in perfect silence, but the main thing you need isn't agility—it's patience and calm. So I moved out slowly and calmly, and it must have worked, because nobody raised a hue or a cry.

The empty, unlit stadium was . . . just wrong. I was used to seeing Wrigley blazing with sunlight or its lights, filled with fans and music and the smell of overpriced, fattening, and inexplicably gratifying food. I was used to vendors shouting, the constant sea-surge of crowd noise, and the buzz of planes passing overhead, trailing banners behind them.

Now Wrigley Field was vast and dark and empty. There was something silently sad about it—acres of seats with no one sitting, a green and beautiful field that no one was playing on, a scoreboard that didn't have anything on it to read or anyone to read it. If the gods and muses were to come down from Olympus and sculpt unfulfilled potential as a physical form, they wouldn't get any closer than that hollow house did.

I walked down the concrete steps and circled the infield until I could make my way to the seats behind home plate. Once there, I held Bob up and said, "What have we got?"

The skull's eyelights flared brighter for a second, and he snorted. "Oh, yeah. Definitely tied the curse together right there."

"What's keeping it going?" I asked. "Is there a ley line passing underneath or something?"

"That's a negative, boss," Bob said.

"How fresh is it?"

"Maybe a couple of days," the skull replied. "Maybe more. It's an awfully tight weave."

"How so?"

"This spell resists deterioration better than most mortal magic. It's efficient and solid—way niftier than you could manage."

"Gee. Thanks."

"I call 'em like I see 'em," Bob said cheerfully. "So either a more experienced member of the White Council is sponsoring this curse, and refreshing it every so often, or else . . ."

I caught on. "Or else the curse was placed here by a non-mortal being."

"Yeah," Bob said. "But that could be almost anything."

I shook my head. "Not necessarily. Remember that the curse was laid upon the stadium during a game in the 1945 World Series."

"Ah, yes," Bob said. "It would have been packed. Which means that whatever the being was, it could blend in. Either a really great veil or maybe a shapeshifter."

"Why?" I asked.

"What?"

"Why?" I repeated. "Why would this theoretical being have put out the curse on the Cubs?"

"Plenty of beings from the Nevernever really don't need a motivation."

"Sure they do," I said. "The logic behind what they do might be alien or twisted beyond belief, but it makes sense to them." I waved my hand at the stadium. "This being not only laid a curse on a nexus of human emotional power, it kept coming back week after week, year after year."

"I don't see what you're driving at, boss."

"Whoever's doing this is holding a grudge," I said thoughtfully. "This is vengeance for a genuine insult. It's personal."

"Maybe," Bob said. "But maybe the emotional state of the stadium supercharged Sianis's curse. Or maybe after the stadium evicted Sianis, who didn't have enough power to curse anybody anyhow, someone decided to make it stick."

"Or maybe . . ." My voice trailed off, and then I barked out a short bite of laughter. "Oh. Oh, that's *funny*."

Bob spun in my hand to look up at me.

"It wasn't *Sianis* who put the whammy on the Cubs," I said, grinning. "It was the *goat*."

The Llyn y Fan Fach Tavern and Inn was located down at the lakeside at the northern edge of the city. The place's exterior screamed "PUB" as if it were trying to make itself heard over the roar of brawling football hooligans. It was all white-washed walls and heavy timbers stained dark. The wooden sign hanging from a post above the door bore the tavern's name, and a painted picture of a leek and a daffodil crossed like swords.

I sidled up to the tavern and went in. The inside matched the outside, continuing the dark-stained theme on its wooden floors, walls, and furnishings. It was just after midnight, which wasn't really all that late, as bar scenes went, but the Llyn y Fan Fach Tavern was all but empty.

A big red-haired guy sitting in a chair by the door scowled at me. His biceps were thick enough to use steel-belted radials as armbands. He gave me the fisheye, which I ignored as I ambled on up to the bar.

I took a seat on a stool and nodded to the bartender. She was a pretty woman with jet-black hair and an obvious pride in her torso. Her white renaissance shirt had slipped entirely off both of her shapely shoulders and was only being held up by her dark leather bustier. She was busy wiping down the bar. The bustier was busy lifting and separating.

She glanced up at me and smiled. Her pale green eyes flicked over me, and the smile deepened. "Ah," she said, her British accent thick and from somewhere closer to Cardiff than London. "You're a tall one, aren't you?"

"Only when I'm standing up."

Her eyes twinkled with merry wickedness. "Such a crime. What are you drinking, love?"

"Do you have any cold beer?" I asked.

"None of that colonial piss here," she replied.

"Snob," I said, smiling. "Do you have any of McAnally's dark? McAnally's anything, really."

Her eyebrows went up. "Whew. For a moment, there, I thought a heathen walked amongst us." She gave me a full smile, her teeth very square and straight and white, and walked over to me before bending over and drawing a dark bottle from beneath the bar.

I appreciated her in a polite and politically correct fashion. "Is the show included in the price of the drink?"

She opened the bottle with an expert twist of her wrist and set it down in front of me with a clean mug. "I'm a generous soul, love," she said, winking. "Why charge when I can engage in selfless charity?"

She poured the beer into the mug and set it on a napkin in front of me. She slid a bowl of bar nuts down my way. "Drinking alone?"

"That depends on whether or not you'll let me buy one for you."

She laughed. "A gentleman, is it? Sir, you must think me all manner of tart if you think I'd accept a drink from a stranger."

"I'm Harry," I said.

"And so we are strangers no longer," she replied, and got out another bottle of ale. She took her time about it, and she watched me as she did it. She straightened, also slowly, and opened her bottle before putting it gently to her lips and taking a slow pull. Then she arched an eyebrow at me and said, "See anything else you like? Something tasty, perhaps?"

"I suppose I am kind of an aural guy at the moment," I said. "Got a minute to talk to me, Jill?"

Her smile faded swiftly. "I've never seen you in here before. How is it you know my name?"

I reached into my shirt and tugged out my pentacle, letting it fall down against my T-shirt. Jill studied that for a few seconds, then took a second look at me. Her mouth opened in a silent "ah" of understanding. "The wizard. Dresden, isn't it?"

"Harry," I said.

She nodded and took another, warier sip of her beer.

"Relax," I said. "I'm not here on Council business. But a friend of mine among the Fair Folk told me that you were the person to talk to about the Tylwyth Teg."

She tilted her head to one side, and smiled slightly. "I'm not sure how I could help you, Harry. I'm just a storyteller."

"But you know about the Tylwyth Teg."

"I know stories of them," she countered. "That's not the same as knowing them. Not in the way that your folk care about."

"I'm not doing politics between members of the Unseelie Accords right now," I said.

"But you're one of the magi," she said. "Surely you know what I do."

"I'm still pretty young, for a wise guy. And nobody can know everything," I said. "My knowledge of the Fair Folk pretty much begins and ends with the Winter and Summer Courts. I know that the Tylwyth Teg are an independent kingdom of the Wyld. Stories might give me what I need."

The sparkle returned to her eyes for a moment. "This is the first time a man I've flirted with told me that *stories* were what he needed."

"I could gaze longingly at your décolletage while you talk, if you like."

"Given how much trouble I go to in order to show it off, it would seem polite."

I lowered my eyes demurely to her chest for a moment. "Well. If I must."

She let out a full-bodied laugh, which made attractive things happen to her upper body. "What stories are you interested in, specifically?"

I grinned at her. "Tell me about the Tylwyth Teg and goats."

Jill nodded thoughtfully and took another sip of beer. "Well," she said. "Goats were a favored creature among them. The Tylwyth Teg, if treated with respect by a household of mortals, would often perform tasks for them. One of the most common tasks was the grooming of goats—cleaning out their fur and brushing their beards for Sunday morning."

I took a notebook from my duster's pocket and started making notes. "Uh-huh."

"The Tylwyth Teg were shapeshifters," Jill continued. "They're a small folk, only a couple of feet tall, and though they could take what form they wished, they usually changed into fairly small animals—foxes, cats, dogs, owls, hares, and—"

"And goats?"

She lifted her eyebrows. "And goats, aye. Though the stories can become very odd at times. More than one Welsh farmer who managed to capture a bride of the Tylwyth Teg found himself waking up to a goat beside him in his bed, or took his wife's hand only to feel the shape of a cloven hoof beneath his fingertips."

"Weregoats," I muttered. "Jesus."

"They're masters of deceit and trickery," Jill continued. "And we mortals are well advised to show them the proper respect, if we intrude upon them at all."

"What happens if we don't?"

Jill shook her head. "That would depend upon the offense,

and which of the Tylwyth Teg were offended. They were capable of almost anything if their pride was wounded."

"The usual Fair Folk response?" I asked. "Bad fortune, children taken, that sort of thing?"

Jill shook her head. "Harry, love, the Queens of Winter and Summer do not kill mortals, and so frown upon their followers taking such action. But the high folk of the Tylwyth Teg have no such restrictions."

"They'd kill?" I asked.

"They can, have, and will take life in acts of vengeance," Jill said seriously. "They always respond in balance—but push them too far and they will."

"Damn," I said. "Those are some hard-core faeries."

Jill sucked in a sharp breath and her eyes glittered brightly. "What did you say?"

I became suddenly aware of the massive redhead by the door rising to his feet.

I swigged a bit of beer and put the notebook back in my pocket. "I called them faeries," I drawled.

The floorboards creaked under the weight of Big Red, walking toward me.

Jill stared at me with eyes that were hard and brittle like glass. "You of all, wizard, should know that word is an insult to . . . them."

"Oh, right," I said. "*They* get real upset when you call them that." A shadow fell across me. I sipped more beer without turning around and said, "Did someone just put up a building?"

A hand the size of a Christmas ham fell onto my shoulder, and Big Red growled, "You want me to leave some marks?"

"Come on, Jill," I said. "Don't be sore. It's not as though you're trying all that hard to hide. You left plenty of clues for the game."

Jill stared at me with unreadable eyes and said nothing.

I started ticking off points on my fingers. "Llyn y Fan Fach is a lake sacred to the Tylwyth Teg over in the Old World. You don't get a lot more Welsh than that leek-and-daffodil emblem. And as for calling yourself 'Jill,' that's a pretty thin mask to cover the presence of one of the Jili Ffrwtan." I tilted my head back to indicate Big Red. "Changeling, right?"

Big Red's fingers tightened enough to hurt. I started to get a little bit concerned.

Jill held up a hand and Big Red let go of me at once. I heard the floor creaking as he retreated. She stared at me for a moment more, then smiled faintly and said, "The mask is more than sufficient when no one is looking for the face behind it. What gave us away?"

I shrugged. "Someone has to be renewing the spell laid on Wrigley Field on a regular basis. It almost had to be someone local. Once I remembered that the Fair Folk of Wales had a rather singular affinity with goats, the rest was just a matter of legwork."

She finished off the beer in a long pull, her eyes sparkling again. "And my own reaction to the insult was the cherry on top."

I drained my mug and shrugged modestly. "I apologize for speaking so crudely, lady. It was the only way I could be sure."

"Powerful, clever, *and* polite," she murmured. She leaned forward onto the bar, and it got really hard not to notice her bosom. "You and I might get along."

I winked at her and said, "You're trying to distract me, and doing it well. But I'd like to speak to someone in authority over the enchantment laid on Wrigley."

"And who says our folk are behind such a thing?"

"Your cleavage," I replied. "Otherwise, why try to distract me?"

She let out another laugh, though this one was softer and more silvery, a tinkling and unearthly tone that made my ears feel like someone with fantastic lips was blowing gently into them. "Even if they are, what makes you think that we would alter that weaving now?"

I shrugged. "Perhaps you will. Perhaps you won't. I only request, please, to speak to one with authority over the curse, to discuss what might be done about it."

She studied me through narrowed eyes for another silent moment.

"I said please," I pointed out to her. "And I did buy you that beer."

"True," she murmured, and then gave me a smile that made my skin feel like I was standing close to a bonfire. She tossed her white cloth to one side and said, toward Big Red, "Mind the store for a bit?"

He nodded at her and settled back down into his chair.

The Jili Ffrwtan came out from behind the bar, hips swaying in deliciously feminine motion. I rose and offered her my arm in my best old-fashioned courtly style. It made her smile, and she laid her hand on my forearm lightly, barely touching. "This," she said, "should be interesting."

I smiled at her again and asked, "Where are we going?"

"Why, to Annwn, my love," the Jili Ffrwtan said, pronouncing it *"ah-noon."* "We go to the land of the dead."

I followed the Jili Ffrwtan into the back room of the pub and down a narrow flight of stone stairs. The basement was all concrete walls and had a packed-earth floor. One wall of the place was stacked with an assortment of hooch. We walked past it while I admired the Jili Ffrwtan's shape and movement, and wondered if her hair felt as soft as it looked.

She gave me a sly look over one bare shoulder. "And tell me, young magus, what you know of my kind."

"That they are the high ladies of the Tylwyth Teg. And that they are surpassingly lovely, charming, and gracious, if you are any example, lady." *And that they could be psycho bitches from hell if you damaged their pride.*

She laughed again. "Base flattery," she said, clearly pleased. "But at least you do it well. You're quite articulate—for a mortal."

As we got farther from the light spilling from the staircase, the shadows grew thick, until she made a negligent gesture with one hand, and soft blue light with no apparent source filled the room around us. "Ah, here we are."

She stopped beside a ring of large brown mushrooms that grew up out of the floor. I extended my otherworldly senses toward the ring and could feel the quiver of energies moving through the air around the circle like a silent hum of high-tension electrical lines. The substance of mortal reality was thin here, easily torn. The ring of mushrooms was a doorway, a portal leading to the Nevernever, the spirit world.

I gave Jill a little bow and gestured with one hand. "After you, lady."

She smiled at me. "Oh, we must cross together, lest you get lost on the way." She slid her fingertips lightly down my forearm. Her warm fingers intertwined with mine, and the gesture felt almost obscenely intimate. My glands cut my brain out of every decision-making process they could, and it was an effort not to adjust my pants. The part of my head that was still on the job got real nervous right about then: There are way too many things in the universe that use sexual desire as a weapon, and I had to work not to jerk my hand away from the Jili Ffrwtan's.

It would be an awful idea to damage her pride with that kind of display.

And besides, my glands told me, *she looks great. And smells even better. And her skin feels amazing. And . . .*

"Quiet, you," I growled at my glands under my breath.

She arched an eyebrow at me.

I gave her a tight smile and said. "Not you. Talking with myself."

"Ah," she said. She flicked her eyes down to below my waist and back, smirking. Then she took a step forward, drawing me into the ring of mushrooms, and the basement blurred and went away, as if the shadow of an ancient mountain had fallen over us.

Then the shadow lifted, and we were elsewhere.

It's at this point that my senses pretty much broke down.

The darkness lifted away to light and motion and music like nothing I had ever seen before—and I've been to the wildest spots in Chicago and to a couple of parties that weren't even being held inside our reality.

We stood inside a ring of mushrooms and in a cave. But that doesn't really cover it. Calling the hall of the Tylwyth Teg a cave is about the same as calling the Taj Mahal a grave. It's technically accurate, but it doesn't begin to cover it.

Walls soared up around me, walls in the shape of natural stone but somehow surfaced in the polished beauty of marble, veined with threads of silver and gold and even rarer metals, lit by the same sourceless radiance the Jili Ffrwtan had summoned back in Chicago. They rose above me on every side, and since I'd just been to Wrigley, I had a fresh perspective with which to compare them: If Wrigley was any bigger, it wasn't by much.

The air was full of music. I only call it "music" because there aren't any words adequate to describe it. By comparison to any music I'd ever heard played, it was the difference between a foot-powder jingle and a symphony by Mozart, throbbing with passion, merriment, pulsing between an ancient sadness and a fierce joy. Every beat made me feel like joining in—either to weep or to dance, or possibly both at the same time.

And the dancers . . . I remember men and women and silks and velvets and jewels and more gold and silver and a grace that made me feel huge and awkward and slow.

There aren't any words.

The Jili Ffrwtan walked forward, taking me with her, and as she went she changed, each step leaving her smaller, her clothing changing as well, until she was attired as the revelers were, in a jeweled gown that left just as much of her just as attractively revealed as the previous outfit. It didn't seem strange at the time that she should grow so much smaller. I just felt like I was freakishly huge, the outsider, the intruder, hopelessly oversized for that place. We moved forward, through the dancers, who spun and flitted out of our path. My escort kept on diminishing until I was walking half hunched over, her entire hand covering about half of one of my fingers.

She led me to the far end of the hall, pausing several times to call something in a complex, musical tongue aside to one of the other Fair Folk. We walked past a miniature table laid out with a not-at-all-miniature feast, and my stomach suddenly informed me that it had never once taken in an ounce of nutrition, and that it really was about time that I finally had something. I had actually taken a couple of steps toward the table before I forced myself to swerve away from it.

"Wise," said the Jili Ffrwtan. "Unless, of course, you wish to stay."

"It smells fine," I replied, my voice hoarse. "But it's no Burger King."

She laughed again, putting the fingers of one hand to her still proportionately impressive bosom, and we passed out of the great hall and into a smaller cavern—this one only the size of a train station. There were guards there—guards armored in bejeweled mail, faces masked behind mail veils, guards who barely came up over my knee, but guards nonetheless, bearing swords and spears and bows. They stood at attention and watched me with cold, hard eyes as we passed them. My escort seemed delightedly smug about the entire affair.

I cleared my throat and asked, "Who are we going to see?"

"Why, love, the only one who has authority over the curse upon Wrigley Field," she said. "His Majesty."

I swallowed. "The king of your folk? Gwynn ap Nudd, isn't it?"

"His Majesty will do," rang out a voice in a high tenor, and I looked up to see one of the Fair Folk sitting on a throne raised up several feet above the floor of the chamber, so that my eyes were level with his. "Perhaps even, His Majesty, sir."

Gwynn ap Nudd, ruler of the Tylwyth Teg, was tall—for his folk, anyway—broad shouldered, and ruggedly handsome. Though dressed in what looked like some kind of midnight-blue fabric that had the texture of velvet but the supple sweep of silk, he had large-knuckled hands that looked rough and strong. Both his long hair and beard were streaked with fine, symmetrical lines of silver, and jewels shone on his fingers and upon his brow.

I stopped at once and bowed deeply, making sure my head went lower than the faerie king's, and I stayed there for a good long moment before rising again. "Your Majesty, sir," I said, in my politest voice. "You are both courteous and generous to grant me an audience. It speaks well of the Tylwyth Teg as a people, that such a one should lead them."

King Gwynn stared at me for a long moment before letting out a grunt that mixed disbelief with wry satisfaction. "At least they sent one with half a sense of manners this time."

"I thought you'd like that, sire," said the Jili Ffrwtan, smiling. "May I present Harry Dresden, magus, a commander of the Order of the Grey Cloak, sometime mortal Champion of Queen Mab and Esquire of the Court of Queen Titania. He begs to speak to you regarding the curse upon the Field of Wrigley in the mortal citadel of Chicago."

"We know who he is," Gwynn said testily. "And we know why he is here. Return to your post. We will see to it that he is safely returned."

The Jili Ffrwtan curtsied deeply and revealingly. "Of course, sire." Then she simply vanished into a sparkling cloud of lights.

"Guards," King Gwynn called out. "You will leave us now."

The guards looked unhappy about it, but they lined up and filed out, every movement in sync with the others. Gwynn waited until the last of them had left the hall and the doors boomed shut before he turned back to me.

"So," he said. "Who do ye like for the Series this year?"

I blinked my eyes at him several times. It wasn't one of those questions I'd been expecting. "Um. American League,

I'm kind of rooting for Tampa Bay. I'd like to see them beat out the Yankees."

"Aye," Gwynn said, nodding energetically. "Who wouldn't. Bloody Yankees."

"And in the National League," I said, "the Cubs are looking good at the moment, though I could see the Phillies pulling something out at the last minute." I shrugged. "I mean, since the Cubbies are cursed and all."

"Cursed?" Gwynn said. A fierce smile stretched his face. "Cursed, is it?"

"Or so it is widely believed," I said.

Gwynn snorted then rose and descended from his throne. "Walk with me."

The diminutive monarch walked farther back into the cavern, past his throne, and into what resembled some kind of bizarre museum. There were rows and rows of cabinets, each with shelves lined in black velvet, and walls of crystalline glass. Each cabinet had a dozen or so artifacts in it: ticket stubs were some of the most common items, though there were also baseballs here and there among them, as well as baseball cards, fan booklets, team pennants, bats, batting gloves, and fielders' gloves.

As I walked beside him, careful to keep my pace slow enough to let him dictate how fast we were walking, it dawned on me that King Gwynn ap Nudd of the Tylwyth Teg was a baseball fan—as in *fanatic*—of the original vintage.

"It was you," I said suddenly. "You were the one they threw out of the game."

"Aye," King Gwynn said. "There was business to attend, and by the time I got there the tickets were sold out. I had to find another way into the game."

"As a goat?" I asked, bemused.

"It was a team-spirit thing," Gwynn said proudly. "Sianis had made up a sign and all, proclaiming that Chicago had already gotten Detroit's goat. Then he paraded me and the sign on the field before the game—it got plenty of cheers, let me tell you. And he did pay for an extra ticket for the goat, so it wasn't as though old Wrigley's successors were being cheated the price of admission. They just didn't like it that someone argued with the ushers and won!"

Gwynn's words had taken on the heat that you can only get from an argument that someone has rehearsed to himself about a million times. Given that he must have been practicing it since 1945, I knew better than to think that anything like reason was going to get in the way. So I just nodded and asked, "What happened?"

"Before the game was anywhere near over," Gwynn continued, his voice seething with outrage, "they came to Sianis and evicted him from the park. Because, they said, his goat smelled too awful!"

Gwynn stopped in his tracks and turned to me, scowling furiously as he gestured at himself with his hands. "Hello! I was a *goat*! Goats are *supposed* to smell awful when they are rained upon!"

"They are, Your Majesty, sir," I agreed soberly.

"And I was a *flawless* goat!"

"I have no doubts on that account, King Gwynn," I said.

"What kind of justice is it to be excluded from a Series game because one has flawlessly imitated a goat!?"

"No justice at all, Your Majesty, sir," I said.

"And to say that I, Gwynn ap Nudd, I the King of Annwn, I who defeated Gwythr ap Greidawl, I the counselor and ally to gods and heroes alike, *smelled*!" His mouth twisted up in rage. "How *dare* some jumped-up mortal ape say such a thing! As though mortals smell any *better* than wet goats!"

For a moment, I considered pointing out the conflicting logic of Gwynn both being a perfect (and therefore smelly) goat and being upset that he had been cast out of the game for *being* smelly. But only for a second. Otherwise, I might have been looking at coming back to Chicago about a hundred years too late to grab a late-night meal at BK.

"I can certainly see why you were upset and offended, Your Majesty, sir."

Some of the righteous indignation seemed to drain out of him, and he waved an irritated hand at me. "We're talking about something important here, mortal," he said. "We're talking about *baseball*. Call me Gwynn."

We had stopped at the last display cabinet, which was enormous by the standards of the furnishings of that hall, which is to say, about the size of a human wardrobe. On one of its shelves was a single outfit of clothing; blue jeans, a T-shirt, a leather jacket, with socks and shoes. On all the rest were the elongated rectangles of tickets—season tickets, in fact, and hundreds of them.

But the single stack of tickets on the top shelf sat next to the only team cap I'd seen.

Both tickets and cap bore the emblem of the Cubs.

"It was certainly a serious insult," I said quietly. "And it's obvious that a balancing response was in order. But, Gwynn, the insult was given you unwittingly, by mortals whose very stupidity prevented them from knowing what they were doing. Few enough there that day are even alive now. Is it just that their children be burdened with their mistake? Surely that fact also carries some weight within the heart of a wise and generous king."

Gwynn let out a tired sigh and moved his right hand in a gesture that mimed pouring out water cupped in it. "Oh, aye, aye, Harry. The anger faded decades ago—mostly. It's the principle of the thing, these days."

"That's something I can understand," I said. "Sometimes you have to give weight to a principle to keep it from being taken away in a storm."

He glanced up at me shrewdly. "Aye. I've heard as that's something you would understand."

I spread my hands and tried to sound diffident. "There must be some way of evening the scales between the Cubs and the Tylwyth Teg," I said. "Some way to set this insult to rights and lay the matter to rest."

"Oh, aye," King Gwynn said. "It's easy as dying. All we do is nothing. The spell would fade. Matters would resume their normal course."

"But clearly you don't wish to do such a thing," I said. "It's obviously an expenditure of resources for you to keep the curse alive."

The small king suddenly smiled. "Truth be told, I stopped thinking of it as a curse years ago, lad."

I arched my eyebrows.

"How do you regard it, then?" I asked him.

"As protection," he said. "From the *real* curse of baseball."

I looked from him to the tickets and thought about that for a moment. Then I said, "I understand."

It was Gwynn's turn to arch eyebrows at me. "Do ye now?" He studied me for a time and then smiled, nodding slowly. "Aye. Aye, ye do. Wise, for one so young."

I shook my head ruefully. "Not wise enough."

"Everyone with a lick of wisdom thinks that," Gwynn replied. He regarded his tickets for a while, his hands clasped behind his back. "Now, ye've won the loyalty of some of the Wee Folk, and that is no quick or easy task. Ye've defied Sidhe queens. Ye've even stuck a thumb into the Erlking's eye, and that tickles me to no end. And ye've been clever enough to find us, which few mortals have managed, and gone out of your way to be polite, which means more from you than it would from some others."

I nodded quietly.

"So, Harry Dresden," King Gwynn said, "I'll be glad t'consider it, if ye say the Cubs wish me to cease my efforts."

I thought about it for a long time before I gave him my answer.

Mr. Donovan sat down in my office in a different ridiculously expensive suit and regarded me soberly. "Well?"

"The curse stays," I said. "Sorry."

Mr. Donovan frowned, as though trying to determine whether or not I was pulling his leg. "I would have expected you to declare it gone and collect your fee."

"I have this weird thing where I take professional ethics seriously," I said. I pushed a piece of paper at him and said, "My invoice."

He took it and turned it over. "It's blank," he said.

"Why type it up when it's just a bunch of zeroes?"

He stared at me even harder.

"Look at it this way," I said. "You haven't paused to consider the upside of the Billy Goat Curse."

"Upside?" he asked. "To losing?"

"Exactly," I said. "How many times have you heard people

complaining that professional ball wasn't about anything but money these days?"

"What does that have to do—"

"That's why everyone's so locked on the Series these days. Not necessarily because it means you're the best, because you've risen to a challenge and prevailed. The Series means millions of dollars for the club, for businesses, all kinds of money. Even the fans get obsessed with the Series, like it's the only significant thing in baseball. Don't even get me started on the stadiums all starting to be named after their corporate sponsors."

"Do you have a point?" Donovan asked.

"Yeah," I said. "Baseball is about more than money and victory. It's about facing challenges alone and on a team. It's about spending time with friends and family and neighbors in a beautiful park, watching the game unfold. It's . . ." I sighed. "It's about fun, Mr. Donovan."

"And you are contending that the curse is fun?"

"Think about it," I said. "The Cubs have the most loyal, diehard fan following in Major League ball. Those fans aren't in it to see the Cubs run rampant over other teams because they've spent more money hiring the best players. You know they aren't—because they all know about the curse. If you *know* your team isn't going to carry off the Series, then cheering them on becomes something more than yelling when they're beating someone. It's about tradition. It's about loyalty to the team and camaraderie with the other fans, and win or lose, just enjoying the damned game."

I spread my hands. "It's about *fun* again, Mr. Donovan. Wrigley Field might be the only stadium in professional ball where you can say that."

Donovan stared at me as though I'd started speaking in Welsh. "I don't understand."

I sighed again. "Yeah. I know."

My ticket was for general admission, but I thought I'd take a look around before the game got started. Carlos Zambrano was on the mound warming up when I sat down next to Gwynn ap Nudd.

Human size, he was considerably over six feet tall, and he was dressed in the same clothes I'd seen back at his baseball shrine. Other than that, he looked exactly the way I remembered him. He was talking to a couple of folks in the row behind him, animatedly relating some kind of tale that revolved around the incredible arc of a single game-deciding breaking ball. I waited until he was finished with the story, and turned back out to the field.

"Good day," Gwynn said to me.

I nodded my head just a little bit deeply. "And to you."

He watched Zambrano warming up and grinned. "They're going to fight through it eventually," he said. "There are so many mortals now. Too many players and fans want them to do it." His voice turned a little sad. "One day they will."

My equations and I had eventually come to the same conclusion. "I know."

"But you want me to do it now, I suppose," he said. "Or else why would you be here?"

I flagged down a beer vendor and bought one for myself and one for Gwynn.

He stared at me for a few seconds, his head tilted to one side.

"No business," I said, passing him one of the beers. "How about we just enjoy the game?"

Gwynn ap Nudd's handsome face broke into a wide smile, and we both settled back in our seats as the Cubs took the cursed field.

How the Pooka Came to New York City

BY DELIA SHERMAN

Delia Sherman is the author of numerous short stories, many of which are to be found in anthologies edited by Ellen Datlow and Terri Windling. Her adult novels are *Through a Brazen Mirror* and *The Porcelain Dove* (which won the Mythopoeic Fantasy Award), and, with fellow fantasist and partner Ellen Kushner, *The Fall of the Kings*. Her novels for younger readers are *Changeling, The Magic Mirror of the Mermaid Queen,* and *The Freedom Maze*. She has taught writing at the Clarion and Odyssey science fiction and fantasy workshops and at conventions. She is a founding member of the Interstitial Arts Foundation. Sherman lives in New York City, loves to travel, and writes in cafés wherever in the world she finds herself.

Early one morning in the spring of 1855, the passengers from the *Irish Maid* out of Dublin Bay trudged down the gangway of the steam lighter *Washington*. Each of them carried baggage: clothes and boots, tools and household needments, leprechauns and hobs, fleas, and the occasional ghost trailing behind like a soiled veil. Liam O'Casey, late of Ballynoe in County Down, brought a tin whistle and the collected poetry of J. J. Callanan, two shirts and three handkerchiefs rolled into a knapsack, a small leather purse containing his savings, and a great black hound he called Madra, which is nothing more remarkable than "dog" in Irish.

Liam O'Casey was a horse trainer by trade, a big, handsome man with a wealth of greasy black curls that clustered around his neat, small ears and his broad, fair temples. His eyes were blue, his shoulders wide, and he had a smile to charm a holy sister out of her cloister. He'd the look of a rogue, a scalawag, faster with a blow than a quip, with an eye to the ladies and an unquenchable thirst for strong drink.

Looks can be misleading. Liam had an artist's soul in his breast and a musician's skill in his fingers. One night in the hold of the *Irish Maid*, with the seas running high and everyone groaning and spewing out their guts, he pulled out his tin whistle to send "Molly's Lament" sighing sweetly through the fetid air. All through that long night he played, and if his music had no power to soothe the seas, it soothed the terror of those who heard it and quieted the sobbing of more than one small child.

After, the passengers of steerage were constantly at Liam to pull out his tin whistle for a slip jig or a reel. Liam was most willing to oblige, and might have been the best-loved man on board were it not for his great black dog.

Madra was a mystery. As a general rule, livestock and pets were not welcome on the tall ships that sailed between the old world and the new. They made more mouths to feed, more filth to clean up. Birds in cages were tolerated, but a tall hound black as the fabled Black Dog, with long sharp teeth and eyes yellow as piss? It was the wonder of the world he'd been let aboard. And once aboard, it was a wonder he survived the journey.

"A dog, seasick?" Liam's neighbor, a man from Cork, pulled his blanket up around his nose as Madra retched and whined. "Are you sure it's nothing catching?"

Liam stroked Madra's trembling flank. "He's a land-loving dog, I fear. I'd have left him behind if he'd have stood for being left. Perhaps he'll be easier in my hammock."

Which proved to be the case, much to the amusement of the man from Cork.

"The boy's soft, is what it is," he told his card-playing cronies.

"Leave him be," one of them said. "Fluters and fiddlers are not like you and me."

When the *Irish Maid* sailed into New York Harbor, New York Bay was wide as an inland sea to Liam's eyes, the early morning sun pouring its honey over forested hills and warehouses and riverside mansions and a myriad of ships. Islands slid past the *Washington* on both sides, some wild and bare, some bristling with buildings and docks and boats. The last of these, only a stone's throw from Manhattan itself, was occupied by a round and solid edifice, like a reservoir or a fort, that swarmed with laborers like ants on a stony hill.

The Cork man broke the awestruck silence. "Holy Mother of God," he said. "And what do you think of Dublin Bay after that?"

With all of America spread out before him like a meal on a platter and the sea birds welcoming him into port, Liam had no wish to think of Dublin Bay at all. He'd come to America to change his life, and he intended to do it thoroughly. Country bred, he was determined to live in a city, surrounded by people whose families he did not know. He'd live in a house with more than one floor, none of them dirt, and burn coal in a stove that vented through a pipe.

He'd eat meat once a week.

As the lighter slowed, the hound at his feet reared himself, with some effort, to plant his forepaws on the *Washington*'s rail and panted into the wind that blew from the shore. After a moment, he sneezed and shook his head irritably.

The Cork man laughed. "Seems your dog doesn't think much of the new world, Liam O'Casey. Better, perhaps, you should have left him in the old."

Madra bared his fangs at that, for all the world, the Cork man said, as though he spoke Gaelic like a Christian. Liam stroked the poor animal's ears while the lighter docked and the steerage passengers of the *Irish Maid* began to gather their bundles and their boxes, their ghosts and their memories and staggered down the gangway. On the pier, customs officials herded them to a shed where uniformed clerks checked their baggage and their names against the ship's manifest. These formalities concluded, the new immigrants were free to start their new lives where and when they pleased.

The lucky ones, the provident ones, embraced their families or greeted friends who had come to meet them, and moved off, chattering. A group of the less well prepared, including Liam and the man from Cork, lingered on the dock, uncertain where their next steps should take them.

With a sinking heart, Liam looked about at the piled boxes, the coils of rope, the wagons, the nets and baskets of fish, thinking he might as well have been on a wharf in Dublin. There was the same garbage and mud underfoot, the same air thick with the stink of rotting fish and salt and coal fires, the same dirty, raw-handed men loading and unloading wagons and boats and shouting to each other in a babel of strange tongues.

"That'll be you in a week or so," the Cork man said, slapping Liam on the shoulder hard enough to raise dust. "I'm for the Far West, where landlords are as rare as hen's teeth and the streams run with gold."

A new voice joined the conversation—in Irish, happily, since his audience had only a dozen English words between them. "You'll be needing a place to sleep the night, I'm thinking. Come along of me, and I'll have you suited in a fine, clean, economical boardinghouse before the cat can lick her ear."

The newcomer was better fed than the dockworkers, his frock coat only a little threadbare and his linen next door to clean. He had half a pound of pomade on his hair and a smile that would shame the sun. But when the boardinghouse runner saw Madra, his sun went behind a cloud and he kicked the dog square in the ribs.

"Hoy!" Liam roared, shocked out of his usual good humor. "What ails you to be kicking my dog?"

"Dogs are dirty creatures, as all the world knows, as thick with fleas as hairs."

"A good deal thicker," the man from Cork said, and everyone snickered, for Madra's coat after five weeks on shipboard was patchy and dull, with great sores on his flank and belly.

The boardinghouse runner grinned, flashing a golden tooth. "Just so. Mistress O'Leary'd not be thanking me for bringing such a litany of miseries and stinks into her good clean house. A doorway's good enough for the pair of you." And then he turned and herded his catch away inland.

Liam sat himself down on a crate, his knapsack and his mangy dog at his feet, and wondered where he might find a glass and a bite in this great city and how much they'd cost him.

"Yon was the villain of the world," Madra remarked. "Stinking of greed and goose fat. You're well shut of him."

“The goose fat I smelled for myself,” Liam answered. “The greed I took for granted. Still, a bed for the night and a guide through the city might have been useful. Are you feeling any better, at all, now we’ve come to shore?”

Madra growled impatiently. “I’m well enough to have kept my ears to the wind and my nose to the ground for news of where we may find a welcome warmer than yon gold-toothed cony-catcher’s.”

“And where would that be, Madra? In Dublin, perhaps? Or back home in Ballynoe, where I wish to heaven I’d never left?”

The hound sighed. “Don’t be wishing things you don’t want, not in front of me. Had I my full strength, you’d be back in Ballynoe before you’d taken another breath, and sorry enough to be there after all the trouble you were put to leaving in the first place.” He heaved himself wearily to his feet. “There’s a public house north of here, run by the kind of folk who won’t turn away a fellow countryman and his faithful hound.”

“You’re not my hound,” Liam said, shouldering his pack. “I told you back in Ballynoe. I did only what I’d do for any living creature. You owe me nothing.”

“I owe you my life.” Madra lifted his nose to sniff the air. “That way.” Moving as though his joints hurt him, Madra stalked away from the water with Liam strolling behind, gawking left and right at the great brick warehouses of the seaport of New York.

The Pooka was not happy. His eyes ran, his lungs burned, his skin galled him as if he’d been stung by a thousand bees, and the pads of his paws felt as though he’d walked across an unbanked fire. He was sick of his dog shape, sick of this mortal man he was tied to, sick of cramped quarters with no space to run and the stink of death that clung to mortals like a second skin. Most of all, he was sick, almost to dissolution, of the constant presence of cold iron.

He'd thought traveling with Liam O'Casey was bad, with the nails in his shoes and the knife in his pack, but Dublin had been worse. The weeks aboard the *Irish Maid* had been a protracted torture, which he'd survived only because Liam had given over his hammock to him. This new city was worst of all, as hostile to the Fair Folk as the most pious priest who'd ever sung a mass.

Yet in this same city, on this poisonous dock, the Pooka had just met a selkie in his man shape, hauling boxes that stank of iron as strongly as the air stank of dead fish.

The Pooka had smelled the selkie—sea air with an animal undertang of fur and musk—and followed his nose to a group of longshoremen loading crates onto a dray. As he sniffed curiously about their feet, one of them grabbed the Pooka by the slack of his neck and hauled him off behind a stack of barrels as though he'd been a puppy.

"What the devil kind of thing are you?" asked the selkie in the broadest of Scots.

"I'm a Pooka," he said, with dignity. "From County Down."

"Fresh off the boat and rotten with the iron-sickness, no doubt. Well, you're a lucky wee doggie to have found me, and that's a fact."

The Pooka's ears pricked. "You have a cure for iron-sickness?"

"Not I," the selkie said. "There's a Sidhe woman runs a lager saloon in Five Points. All the Gaelic folk who land here must go to her. It's that or die." The selkie pulled a little wooden box from his pocket and opened it. "Take a snort."

The Pooka filled his nose with a scent of thin beer, sawdust, and faerie magic. "One last question, of your kindness," he said. "Would a mortal be welcome at this Sidhe woman's saloon at all?"

The selkie replaced the box. "Maybe he will and maybe he won't. What's it to you?"

"We're by way of being companions," said the Pooka.

"Dinna tell me he knows you for what you are?" The selkie whistled. "That'd be a tale worth the hearing. Tell it me, and we'll call my help well paid."

The Pooka knew very well that his tale was a small enough price for such valuable information, but it was a price he was reluctant to pay. Stories in which he was the hero and the mortal his endlessly stupid dupe—those he told with pleasure to whoever would hear them. A story in which the stupidity had been his own was a different pair of shoes entirely. Still, a favor must be repaid.

"I will so," he said.

The selkie bared strong white teeth. "But no just now: I've work to do, and you, an Irish fay to see. Shall we say before midsummer? Ask for Iain. Everybody kens me here on the docks. Oh, and dinna fash yourself over yon mortal. The woman'll no harm him—if he keeps a civil tongue in his head."

"Oh, he's civil enough," the Pooka had answered, somewhat sourly. "He's the gentleman of the world, he is. The creature."

Which was why, as much as the Pooka resented Liam O'Casey, he could not dislike him, and why, after six months in Liam's company, he was far from home, iron-sick and mangy and too feeble to shift his shape, burdened with an unpaid blood debt and no prospect of paying it.

The Pooka had a nose as sharp as a kelpie's teeth, but lower New York was a maze of bewildering and distracting smells. The streets reeked of dung and garbage, of dogs marking their territory and the sweat of horses pulling heavy drays. The Pooka was startled out of what remained of his fur when a scrawny, half-wild sow squealed at him. Prudently, the Pooka whined and wagged his tail submissively. The sow snorted at him and trotted on.

Bowing to a pig! If the iron-sickness did not finish him, surely shame would do the job. The Pooka thought he'd like to kill Liam for bringing him here. But not until he'd saved his miserable life.

Liam had been hungry and thirsty when he got off the *Washington* at dawn. By noon, he was tired and footsore as well, and as bewildered as he'd ever been in his life. Listlessly, he watched Madra sniff the door of Maeve McDonough's Saloon, which looked no different to him than the fifty other such establishments he'd sniffed along the way, except for a sign in the window offering a free lunch. Liam read the fare on offer—cold meat, pickles, onions—and sent up a short and heartfelt prayer to the Virgin that their journey might end here. He sent a second prayer of thanks when Madra pricked his ears, raised his tail, and trotted down the filthy steps and into the dark room beyond.

Upon inquiry at the wooden counter, Liam learned that the free lunch came at the cost of two five-cent beers, which he was happy to pay, even though the beer was poor, sour stuff and the meat more gristle than fat. While he ate, a woman, well supplied with dark hair and bold eyes and an expanse of rosy-brown skin above the neck of her flowered gown, cuddled up, giving him an excellent view of her breasts and a noseful of her musky scent.

"Like what you see, boyo? I can arrange for a closer look."

Head swimming, he was on the point of agreeing when another woman's voice spoke, tuneful and sweet as a silver bell. The whore hissed, showing teeth a thought too long and pointed for beauty, and slid back into the crowd of drinkers.

Startled, Liam looked up into the face of the tall, redheaded woman on the other side of the bar. She'd a faded-green woolen shawl tied across her bosom and a look about her he was coming to recognize after six months in the Pooka's company: a luminous look, as though her skin were fairer, her hair more lustrous, her eyes more lambent, her whole person altogether more light-filled than an ordinary woman's. It was not a look he'd expected to see in the new world.

"Welcome to Five Points," said the woman. "There's a fine dog you have."

Liam looked down to see Madra sitting by his leg, panting cryptically. "Oh, he's not mine," he said. "Not in the way of ownership. Our paths lie together for a while, that's all it is."

The woman's smile broadened. Liam noted, with relief, that her teeth were remarkable only in being uncommonly white and even. "A good answer, young man. You may call me Maeve McDonough. I am the proprietress of this place. You are welcome to drink here. Should you be looking for a place to lay your head this night, I've beds above, twenty cents a night or four dollars a month, to be paid up front, if you please."

Liam laid the silver coins in Maeve's hand with a bow that made her laugh like a stream over rocks, then recklessly ordered another beer and carried it toward a knot of Irishmen who looked as though they'd been in New York a week or two longer than he.

The Pooka yawned nervously and licked at a sore on his flank. It seemed to him that it, like everything else in this forsaken place, tasted of iron. How many nails were in this building? How many iron bands around the barrels of beer? He could sense a stove, too, and most of the customers, unless he was much mistaken, were armed with steel knives. Some even carried pistols. It was almost unbearable.

It *was* unbearable, and the Pooka was beginning to realize that there was nowhere in this city where he might escape from the pain that gnawed at his bones. Hemmed in by mortals, surrounded by iron, with more mortals and iron outside on the street, the Pooka was ready to bite everyone around him and keep on biting until he died or the pain went away, whatever came first.

A cool hand touched his head. A fresh scent, as of spring fields after a rain, soothed his hot nose and cleared the red mists from his brain. The Pooka looked up into the amused green eyes of a Sidhe woman.

"I am called Maeve," she said. "Follow me."

The room Maeve led the Pooka to was, if anything, darker and hotter than the saloon itself. Stacked beer barrels lined the walls, and a complex apparatus of glass and tin on a table smelled strongly of raw spirits.

"A Pooka," Maeve said, setting down her lantern. "I've not seen your like before on this side of the wide ocean. A word for you, my heart. The city's no place for a creature of the bogs and wilds."

"Yet here I am," the Pooka said irritably. "On the point of paying with my life for the privilege, too."

"Well, perhaps it needn't be as costly as that." Maeve regarded him gravely. "What is your life worth, Pooka?"

"I haven't much to give you," the Pooka said. "Would you accept my everlasting gratitude?"

Maeve laughed. "What a joy it is to have a trickster to bargain with, even one half dead. I'd save you for the pure pleasure of your company, but that would be bad business. Come, give me a dozen hairs from your tail, that I may call upon you at my need."

"Good will is good business, lady. Three hairs will buy you my respect and affection as well as my service."

"Seven hairs I'll take, and no less. Unless you're willing to give the mortal over to my hands, to do with as I will."

The Pooka hesitated. "Much as it galls me to admit it, there's a small matter of a blood debt beween us." He sighed heavily. "Seven times I'll come to you, then. You drive a hard bargain, missus."

"Sure, and it's a hard city for the Fair Folk to live in." Then Maeve went to a shelf and brought back a charm, which she wove into the thick fur of the Pooka's ruff.

The charm bit like flies and nettles. The Pooka whined and scratched at his neck.

"It won't help you if you get rid of it," Maeve said mildly. "It's tear it off and die, or endure it and live. It becomes less irksome with time."

"I'll endure it," said the Pooka.

Out in the saloon, Liam was learning a number of facts.

Item: Work, although possible to come by, was not as plentiful in New York as poor men eager to do it.

Item: What work there was stretched from dawn to dusk, taxed a man's back more than his mind, and paid barely enough to keep body and soul together.

Item: Not all the poor men looking for work in New York were mortal.

Among Liam's new drinking companions were a midget in a bottle-green coat, sporting a pair of coppery sideburns to rival Prince Albert's, a boyo in threadbare moleskin with black curls hanging down around his ears, and a shortish man with curly golden hair and a clay pipe between his teeth.

Mindful of his purse, Liam refused a bet on a race between a horse and a pig and an opportunity to invest his savings in a sure moneymaking business. But when the golden-haired man pressed him for his name and county, Liam bethought him that his purse was not the only thing in danger here.

He made a dive for his knapsack and withdrew his tin whistle. "Anybody for a tune?"

The midget brightened. "D'ye know 'Whiskey Before Breakfast'?"

"Do I not?" said Liam, and began to play. If he hadn't been tipsy and perhaps a little more than tipsy, it's likely he'd have made a pig's ear of it, with his heart thundering in his breast and the spit dry in his mouth. As it was, "Whiskey Before Breakfast" came pouring out of his tin whistle as clear and clean as a May morning in Ballynoe, with all the birds singing.

The midget tapped his tiny, beautifully shod feet. The boyo hooked his elbows over the shelf nailed along the wall and sighed. The small man laid down his clay pipe and clapped time. "Whiskey Before Breakfast" rippled out over the room, until the whole saloon was listening to the bright notes skip through the rafters and ring against the stone bottles ranged behind the bar.

After playing the air three times through, Liam dropped the tin whistle from his lips and opened his eyes.

"Another," the midget said hoarsely.

Liam gave them "The Witch of the Glen" and "The Lady's Pantaloons" and "I Buried My Wife and Danced on Top of Her," which jig had them dancing as they roared out the words. And then he segued, without thinking about it, into an air he'd made before he'd decided to make his fortune in America.

When he was done, the boyo embraced him, dripping salt tears on the top of his head.

"All hail the fluter!" the midget shouted, and lifted his tankard.

"The fluter!" the others echoed.

A tankard appeared at his hand. When he'd drained it, another took its place. Liam wet his mouth and played again.

By and by, Liam felt a nudge at his knee and looked down to see Madra, looking, if possible, more miserable than he'd looked before, with a great mat of twigs and mud tangled in the fur at his neck and a wild look in his piss-yellow eyes.

Liam tucked the whistle away and knelt. "Is it well with you, Madra, my dear?"

"It is not so," said Madra, irritably. "How do you think it makes me feel, responsible for you as I am, to see you hob-nobbing with leprechauns and cluricans and gancanagh and other such scrapings from the depths of the faerie barrel? And me no more fit to protect you than a day-old puppy?"

Liam laughed. "Is that what they are? Well, they seem to like my music well enough. They'll not harm me, I'm thinking, as long as I play for them."

"Very likely," said Madra dryly.

Liam felt a hand upon his shoulder and looked up to see Maeve McDonough herself smiling down at him.

"My thanks, sir, for the entertainment. You've put a thirst on my customers the like of which I've not seen since I came to these shores. I've sold enough drink this night to pay for your dinner—yes, and your dog's, too, if he's a stomach for a bit of meat. Come eat it in the back room, away from this moither, and then you'd best take yourself off to bed before they suck you dry entirely."

Left to himself, Liam might have taken the dinner and forgone the bed, so flown was he on beer and praise and his own dancing music. But he'd Madra to think of, and Madra looked to be on his last legs. So Liam followed Maeve into the back room, where he absorbed a bowl of quite reasonable stew, as well as Madra's portion, which the poor beast was far too ill to eat.

Indeed, the Pooka could not have been worse. The charm Maeve had given him to counteract the iron-sickness bit into his neck like a wolf. His muscles trembled, his vision blurred, and he'd a mighty thirst on him that water did nothing to assuage. In all the long years of his existence, he'd never suffered so—not even when he'd stumbled into a steel trap set for poachers, which he'd been saved from by a stale-drunk horse trainer named Liam O'Casey.

By the time Liam had eaten, the Pooka was too weak and sore even to stand. Clucking, Liam scooped him up in his arms and carried him bodily up the rickety stairs.

The state of Maeve's saloon had given Liam a tolerably accurate notion of the accommodations she had to offer.

It was a dismal enough apartment, low ceilinged and airless, with a door at each end. The side walls were lined with wooden shelves upon which Maeve's boarders were stacked four high and two deep. Liam found an unclaimed space on the lowest shelf, near the far door and right over the piss pot, and tucked Madra into it. He fit himself as best he could around the dog's burning, shivering body and fell asleep.

Thanks to the excitement of the day and the number of five-cent beers he'd downed, Liam slept heavily. He woke once when his fellow boarders retired, drunk and stumbling on the rickety ladders to the upper sleeping shelves. He woke once again when someone trod on his hand climbing down to use the piss pot. The third time he woke, it was to the piteous whines of a dog in agony.

Liam opened his eyes to see a dozen tiny, glowing creatures. Their gauzy wings whirred as they hovered about Madra, pulling at his ears and whiskers and the small hairs about his eyes. Liam shooed them away like bees, and like bees they turned upon him and pinched at his face with sharp little fingers. Owning himself defeated, Liam gathered Madra in his arms and bore him carefully down the stairs to the saloon. And there the pair of them spent the balance of the night, curled on a floor only a little fouler than the sleeping shelf above.

In the gray dawn, the Pooka woke to the toe of a boot in his ribs and Maeve's face looking down at him. "The top of the morning to you, trickster," she said. "And how are you finding yourself this lovely spring day?"

The Pooka levered himself to his feet. His body was sore but no longer wracked with pain, and the burning glede upon his neck had cooled a degree or perhaps more. He yawned hugely and shook himself from ears to tail. "I'm alive," he said. "Which comes as a pleasant surprise. As to the rest, I wish I were back in Erin, deep in a nice bog, and a rainy night descending."

"And so do I, trickster. So do I." For a moment, Maeve allowed her true face to show through the glamour, gaunt and fierce as a mewed hawk. "Now wake your mortal, trickster. I've the floor to sweep and the charms to make for any iron-sick Folk who chance to wash up at my door the day."

So the Pooka nudged Liam O'Casey with his nose and gave him to know it was time to be up and about.

Liam awoke with a foul mouth, a griping in his belly, and an aching head. Dunking his head in a barrel of stale water did something to resign him to a new day. A five-cent beer and a slice of soda bread hot from the oven did more. Thus fortified, Liam O'Casey set out into the April morning in search of employment.

Madra came with him.

Left to his own devices, Liam might have stopped to pass the time of day with someone, preferably a mortal like himself, who might give him advice a mortal could use. As it was, he could only follow Madra, trying not to get knocked down by a heavily laden cart or trip over a feral pig or run into a pushcart or one of the hundreds of gray-faced men on their way to work. He was hot and out of breath when Madra stopped in front of a big square clapboard warehouse.

Liam looked up at the sign: GREEN'S FINE FURNITURE. EST. 1840. EBENEZER GREEN, PROP.

"No doubt it's slipped your mind that I'm a horseman, Madra, not a carpenter."

Madra heaved a sigh. "There's a stable behind, you great idiot—I can smell it. Go on in now; it can't hurt to ask."

Liam brushed down his jacket, straightened his cap, and walked into the warehouse. The place was busy as an ant's nest, with an army of roughly dressed men running about with raw lumber and finished furniture, while a burly man in a loud silk waistcoat over his shirtsleeves and a porkpie hat shouted orders. Presuming this to be Ebenezer Green, Liam approached and greeted him in his best English.

Mr. Green turned a pig-eyed glare on him. "Speak American, Paddy, or git out. Better yet, do both. This is a know-nothing shop. We don't do business with Micks and such-like trash."

The man's voice was flat and loud, his accent unfamiliar. His tone and look, however, were as clear as the finest glass goblet.

"I'll be bidding you good day, then," Liam said. "Mr. Know-Nothing, sir." Then he turned on his heel and marched out.

"It seems a strange thing to be bragging of," he said as he and Madra left Green's Fine Furniture behind them.

"He certainly knows nothing about horses," Madra said. "Did you see his nags? Like harrows they were, draped in moth-eaten hides. You're well out of there."

The next stable Madra found was attached to a hauling company near the docks. It was run by Cornelius Vanderhoof, who, like all Dutchmen, didn't care which language a man spoke as long as he was willing to take a dollar in payment for ten hours of work.

"I've no need of a stableman," he told Liam kindly enough. "I have two horse boys, and that's all I need."

"All boys are good for is to feed and water and muck out," Liam said. "I'd care for them like children, I would."

Mr. Vanderhoof shook his head. "Come back in May. I might have work for you, if you can handle a team."

And so it went all the weary day. One livery stable proprietor had just hired someone. Another offered Liam fifty cents to shovel muck. Another shook his head before Liam even opened his mouth.

"It's April," he said. "Nobody will be hiring until summer. You're Irish, right? Why not carry bricks or dig foundations like the rest of your countrymen?"

"I'm a horse trainer," Liam said, hating the pleading note in his voice.

"I don't care if you're the king of County Down," the livery man said. "Ostlers are a dime a dozen in these parts. You want to work with horses, take a train west."

As they emerged from the livery stable, Madra broke the heavy silence. "It's getting on toward dusk. Shall we be heading home?"

Liam looked at the heavy carts piled high with crates and boxes lumbering over the rutted streets, at the ragged, gray-faced men plodding homeward in the fading light, at the street children, dirty and barefoot, lingering by pushcarts in hopes of a dropped apple or an unwatched cabbage. His ears rang with the rumble of wheels, the squeak of unoiled axles, the shouting and swearing and laughter.

"I have no home," he said. "Just now it seems to me I'll never have a home again."

He waited for Madra to call him a pitiful squinter or prescribe a pint or a song to clear his mind. But Madra just plodded down the street, head down and tail adroop, as tired and discouraged as Liam himself.

Being immortal, Folk do not commonly find time hanging heavy on their hands. A day is but an eyeblink in their lives; a month can pass in the drawing of a breath. The Pooka had never imagined being as aware of the arc of the sun across the sky or the length of time separating one meal from the next as he had been since his life had been linked to Liam's.

Today had been a weary length indeed.

At first, the Pooka had simply been glad to be alive and reasonably well. Maeve's charm itched, but it was a healing itch, and he felt some strength return to his limbs. He kept running up to railings and barrels and iron-shod wheels just to touch them and sniff them and prove once again that they had no power to hurt him.

The encounter with Ebenezer Green shook him. Had he been on his game, the Pooka would have nosed out what manner of man Green was before they'd even crossed the threshold.

But the Pooka was not on his game. A whole day on the town, and he hadn't tricked so much as the price of a drink out of a living soul. The fear grew on him that Maeve's charm had cured his iron-sickness at the expense of his magic. What he needed was something to knock him loose from the limited round of mortal concerns he'd been treading since Liam had freed him from the poacher's trap. He needed a bet or a challenge or a trick. Something tried and true, for preference not too dangerous, that would put him on his mettle and bring Liam a bit of silver.

"Liam," he said. "I have an idea. Tomorrow, as soon as it's light, we'll take ourselves up out of this sty to wherever it is the rich folk live. You shall sell me as a ratter for the best price you can get."

"Shall I so?" asked Liam wearily. "And what if no man needs a ratter or will not buy an Irish one?"

"There's always a man wants to buy a dog," the Pooka said confidently.

Liam shook his head. "I will not, and there's an end. What kind of man do you take me for, to sell a friend for silver money?"

"Oh, I'd not stay sold," the Pooka assured him. "I'd run away and meet you at Maeve's before the cat can lick her ear."

"And if you can't escape? What then? Will I steal you back again? It's stark mad you are, Madra. The city's gone to your head."

The Pooka was charmed with his plan and argued it with cunning and passion. Yet Liam would not be moved. It was illegal, he said, immoral, and dangerous, and that was an end on it. All of which confirmed the Pooka in his opinion that Liam was no more suited for city life than a wild deer. Were the Pooka not there to look after him, he'd surely have been stripped of his savings and left to starve in a ditch before he'd so much as fully exhaled the ship's air from his lungs.

West, the Pooka thought. *He'd like it out west. Tomorrow I'll think about getting him on a train.*

A furious squeal interrupted the Pooka's planning. Hackles rising, he turned to find himself nose to bristly snout with a big, ugly, foul-breathed sow.

A fight's as good as a trick for clearing the mind.

The Pooka bared his teeth and growled. The sow's amber eye glittered madly, and she wheeled and trotted back for the charge. The Pooka spared a glance at Liam, saw him surrounded by a handful of half-grown shoats, squealing and shoving at his legs. Liam was laying about him with his knapsack, cursing and trying to keep his feet in the mired street. If he were to fall, they'd trample him sure as taxes, and possibly eat him where he lay.

Fury rose in the Pooka's breast, then, pure and mighty. Ducking the sow's charge, he leaped into the melee around Liam, landing square on the largest of the shoats. The pig threw him off, but not before the Pooka had nipped a chunk out of its ear. Spitting that out, he fastened his teeth into the nearest ham. The shoat it belonged to squealed and bolted, leaving only four and their dam for the Pooka to fight.

He'd not endured a battle so furious since St. Patrick drove the snakes into the sea and the Fair Folk under hill. This fight he intended to win.

At home on his own turf, the Pooka would have made short work of the pigs. At home, even in his dog shape there, he was faster than a bee, mighty as a bull, and tireless as the tide. But weeks of iron-sickness and short commons, stuck in one shape like a chick in its shell, had sapped his strength.

The Pooka slipped in the slurry of mud and dung; a sharp trotter caught him a glancing blow. He felt the bright blood run burning down his flank, and a wave of pain and terror washed through and through him. Immortals cannot die, but they can be killed.

Instinct told the Pooka that he must shift to save himself. Fear whispered that he could not shift, that he'd lost the knack, that he'd been a dog so long, he'd forgotten what it felt like to have hooves or horns or two legs and a coat he could take off.

Seeing her enemy falter, the sow took heart and charged, squealing like a rusty hinge, her tusks aimed like twin spears straight at the Pooka's soft belly.

Instinct triumphed.

Tossing his streaming mane, the Pooka screamed and aimed

his heavy, unshod hooves at the sow's spine. Quick as he was, she was quicker yet, scrambling out from under his feet at the last instant. The Pooka turned upon the shoats around Liam like an angry sea, striking with hoof and tooth.

The sow, seeing her shoats threatened, charged again, barreling toward the Pooka like a storm full of lightning. Wheeling, the Pooka reared again. This time, his hooves crushed the sow into the mud.

The Pooka stood over the bodies of his enemies and trumpeted his victory into the evening air.

An arm snaked across his withers and clung there. Liam's voice, shaky with relief, breathed in his ear. "Oh, my heart, my beauty, my champion of champions. That was a battle to be put in songs, and I shall do so. Just as soon as my legs will bear me and my heart climbs down from my throat."

The Pooka arched his neck proudly and pawed at the corpses piled at his feet. A shoat, recovering from its swoon, heaved up on its trotters and staggered away down the street, straight into the path of a bay gelding harnessed to a shiny black buggy driven by a man in a stovepipe hat.

Bruised and shaken as he was, Liam was no more able to leave a horse in difficulties than swim home to Eire. No sooner did he see the shoat run between the bay's feet and the bay shy and startle and kick its traces, than he ran to its head and grabbed its harness.

The bay tossed him to and fro like a terrier with a rat, but Liam hung on, murmuring soothing inanities in Irish and English, until the gelding's terror calmed and it stood silent and shivering.

Liam stroked the bay's nose and looked around him.

The street was a shambles, with the corpses of his late assailants bleeding into the mud. A crowd of day laborers stood all around, goggling with their mouths at half cock. Off to one side, Madra the hound was licking the blood from a gash on his flank.

The gelding's driver climbed down from the buggy, his cheeks as white as his snowy shirtfront.

"Thank you." His voice, though flatly American, was kind. "That was bravely done. I take it you know something about horses?"

Liam touched his forehead with his knuckle. "I do so, sir."

"Ostler?" the gentleman asked.

"Back in my own country, I was a trainer. Racehorses."

The gentleman looked startled. "A horse trainer? I'll be blowed! Do you mind if I ask your name?"

"It's Liam O'Casey, if it please your honor."

The gentleman laughed, showing strong teeth. "Honor me no honors, Mr. O'Casey. I'm plain William Graves, and I breed horses." Mr. Graves produced a pasteboard card. "Here's my card. I've a little farm up past the orphan asylum—Eighty-fifth Street, more or less. If you care to come there tomorrow, it may be that we'll find something to talk about."

Mr. Graves shook Liam's nerveless hand, climbed back up into his buggy, collected the reins, and drove off.

"Well, that was a piece of luck and no mistake."

It was Madra's voice, but when Liam turned, he saw no dog beside him but a tall man in a black-skirted coat as filthy as it was out of fashion. His skin was pale, his crow-black hair was tied with a strip of leather, and his narrow eyes were set on an upward tilt, with his black brows flying above them like wings.

"You can be shutting your jaw now, Liam O'Casey," the Pooka said. "I'm not such a sore sight as that, surely."

"Madra?"

"For shame, and me standing before you on my two legs as fine a figure of a man as you are yourself." The Pooka linked his arm through Liam's and propelled him down the street. "Come away to Maeve McDonough's and stand yourself a whiskey for a good day's work well done. You may stand me to one as well."

Looking back over his shoulder, Liam saw a pair of cart horses in thick collars pulling a piano in a wagon over the broken bodies of the swine. "My knapsack," he said sadly. "My tin whistle."

"The works of the late lamented J. J. Callanan were beyond saving," the Pooka said. "The tin whistle, on the other hand . . ." He held it out to Liam, dented, but whole. "I saved your purse, too."

"And my life." Liam stopped in the street and offered the Pooka his hand. "I'm forever in your debt."

The Pooka looked alarmed. "What are you after saying, Liam O'Casey? There's no question of debt between us. Favor for favor. Life for life. We're quits now."

"Will you be leaving me, then?" asked Liam, and the Pooka could not for the life of him tell whether it was with hope or dread he asked it.

"Not before I've had my drink," he said, and was ridiculously pleased to feel the arm in his relax its tension. "I'll see you safe up to Mr. Graves's farm first."

"Do you think he's prepared to employ me?"

"Of a certainty. And give you his daughter's hand in marriage, I shouldn't wonder."

Liam laughed aloud. "He's not much older than I, Madra. His daughter would be an infant, presuming he had one at all. This is the real world we're in, after all, not a fairy tale."

"Are we not?" They'd reached Maeve McDonough's by now and descended into the hot and noisy saloon. "And here am I, thinking there's room enough for both in a city the size of this. New York's got life in it, my friend. I'm minded to stay awhile. As long as you come down from the country from time to time and give us a tune. There's no joy in a city where you cannot hear 'Whiskey Before Breakfast.'"

On the Slide

BY RICHARD BOWES

Richard Bowes has published five novels, two collections of short fiction, and fifty stories. He has won two World Fantasy Awards and the Lambda, International Horror Guild, and Million Writers Awards. Recent and forthcoming stories appear in *The Magazine of Fantasy & Science Fiction,* and the anthologies *Digital Domains, The Beastly Bride, Wilde Stories 2010: The Year's Best Gay Speculative Fiction, Haunted Legends, Best Gay Stories 2010, Nebula Awards Showcase 2011, Supernatural Noir,* and *Blood and Other Cravings*. Several of these stories are chapters in his novel in progress, *Dust Devil: My Life in Speculative Fiction.*

The author's home page is www.rickbowes.com.

Sean Quinlan caught the 6:30 wake-up call almost before his cell phone began its first ring. He murmured, "Thanks," glanced at Adrianne La Farice, who wore only a soft, lovely smile and barely stirred in her sleep, thrust the phone aside, slipped from the bed in the pearly morning light, and padded quietly out of the room.

He wasn't awake so much as in a place where the line between work and dreams had been erased. In the ample living room he flicked on the DVD player, keeping the sound way down. In the kitchen he started the coffee. Back in the living room he sat in his shorts on the arm of the couch and watched the opening scene in an episode of the old *Naked City* TV show.

Grainy black-and-white detectives in suits and hats chased a gunman over the roofs of early 1960s New York. Sun through the apartment windows made the gray figures look like ghosts, and Quinlan liked that effect.

The gunman turned to fire, and the detectives ducked behind a chimney. An actor playing a uniformed cop fell, shot. The fugitive fled down a fire escape with the two detectives firing after him.

Quinlan turned up the sound half a notch to catch the voice of the old character actor who played the hard-bitten police lieutenant in the series. "Wounded in the hunt, with the law on his trail, the fugitive returns to his final lair, his first home, the old neighborhood." The trumpets played the city-at-dawn theme music, which mixed nicely with early rush-hour street noise from downtown Manhattan fifty years later.

The episode was set in a neighborhood of five-story tenements that Quinlan didn't quite recognize. It had probably been torn down and turned into high-rises. When coffee smells spread, he stood and discovered Adrianne in a floor-length robe, with her eyes barely open, leaning in the doorway and watching him. Her smile was gone.

"More detectives," she mumbled. "You never stop working, do you, Sean?"

"My granddad and his friends used to make fun of what they called 'twenty-four-hour-a-day cops'—guys who were always on duty," he said. "Now it's like I've become one. Can I offer you some of your own coffee?"

"Yes, please." She made her way to the bathroom saying, "When we were kids, I remember guys backing off from confronting you because they just *knew* you were the law."

Adrianne La Farice had been Adie Jacobson when they were in their early twenties and she waited tables while he took care of the door at Club Red Light over in the Meatpacking District back in the now-legendary early nineties.

She returned saying, "I don't need to be up this early. I don't need to be up at all. With business the way it is, I could spend the day in bed, and I think I will." She uttered some variation on that every morning and never followed through.

His divorce had left him broke. Adie's divorce from Henry La Farice, the designer, was much more successful, leaving her with this renovated condo and a partnership in a prosperous real estate business. Sadly, like everything else in New York, that was now in the tank.

Over the last several years they'd made it their pleasant habit to get together like this each time he'd been in New York on a job. And it was in Quinlan's mind to see if they could turn this into something more permanent.

When he brought Adie the coffee and half a bialy, she was sitting up in bed reading e-mail on her laptop. "No apartment in Manhattan's going to be sold today. Everybody who owns one remembers when it was worth two million dollars. Anyone who wants one will offer a quarter of that and then either can't get financing or can't explain where they got the cash."

Quinlan took a jacket and slacks out of the corner of the closet that he'd been assigned, and got socks and underwear from the rolling suitcase in which he'd brought them.

In the bathroom he stared through the steam at the

serviceable face he was shaving, the short hair with almost no gray. "The family face, anonymous and perfect for stakeout work," his grandfather "Black Jack" Quinlan had said. Jack Quinlan had made detective lieutenant on the job. He'd died almost thirty years back, when Sean was barely thirteen. He thought about the old man almost every day.

Sean looked in the mirror and smiled just a bit. Lately he'd had occasion to notice that the Quinlan face was also perfect for a man on the run. He put on a jacket and shirt but no tie because suddenly there wasn't time. On the way to the bedroom he picked up the brown snap-brim that he'd been wearing for practice and put it on his head with just enough tilt.

When he kissed her Adie said, "Brazil! I've got a Brazilian with money interested in a penthouse, and with that trade agreement he doesn't even have to explain where he got the cash."

Then she looked up and said, "You are beyond retro, mister. You disappear and I'll start believing in Sliders."

"People talk about Sliders. Have you ever known one?"

"It's escapism, not reality. I think they took the name from some old TV show nobody watched. I know a woman who described her teenage son as a perfect 1969 hippie. He had the clothes and the hair; his room was papered with old posters, and he hardly ever left it. One morning he disappeared, and she thinks he slid back there, claims she found notes from him written on old yellow paper and telling her he was OK. Of course, she's also delusional enough to think the Dow will hit sixteen thousand some fine day."

Turning to go he said, "Remember the Peggy McHugh party tonight."

Adie nodded and pointed to a set of handcuffs attached to one of the brass rods on the headboard. "Can you hide those before you go? The cleaning lady's coming today."

Outside on Rivington Street, it was still early enough that Quinlan got a cab with no problem. This Lower East Side drug pit of his youth had gotten gentrified and hip beyond measure. But times like this, on mornings with bright, merciless sun shining on empty shop windows, it had started to look a bit shabby again.

As the cab rolled across Houston Street into the East Village, he noticed people setting up folding tables on the widened sidewalks, opening for business in the big informal flea market that had grown up there.

Portable dressing rooms lined Avenue B. On Tenth Street police barricades blocked traffic onto that side street. Miss Rheingold posters and ads for Pall Malls covered over the Mexican restaurant and reflexology parlor signs. Extras were ready to stand on the corner in greaser haircuts or lean out of first-floor windows in housecoats and hairnets. Down the block, lights brighter than the sun illuminated a tenement.

Getting out of the cab Quinlan was spotted by a couple of the film crew. "Morning, officer," one said, and they all laughed.

For their amusement and his own he did an imitation of the old cop he'd heard on TV. "This is my once and future city. My life consists of long periods of waiting and brief flashes of action and violence. My name's Sean Quinlan. And when I can get the work, I'm an actor."

Big parts of Quinlan's life were in a condition he didn't want to think about. But he had a good part in a medium-sized film. Nothing else would matter for the next few hours.

At 9:22 one day in the spring of 1960 New York Police Detective Pete McDevitt climbs out of an unmarked Buick, flicks his half-smoked cigarette away, and steps into East Tenth Street. His suit is gray and his shirt is blue to match his eyes. His tie is bloodred and his hat is tilted back a tad to give full value to his face. Detective Pat Roark exits from the driver's side wearing brown with a white shirt and blue tie, as befits a steady backup man and faithful partner.

McDevitt was played by Zach Terry, star of *Like '60,* a Hollywood production currently shooting exteriors on the streets of NYC. Detective Roark was Sean Quinlan's role. As a featured player it was his duty to exit on the far side of the car and step smoothly into his proper place one pace behind and two feet to the left of the star.

Pete McDevitt keeps his eyes fastened on an upper floor of the tenement opposite. But Pat Roark gives a quick scan over his shoulder, to see if anyone is watching them.

Quinlan planted that gesture in rehearsal and put it in each of the takes, wanting it there to emphasize that his character was the competent by-the-book cop. No one has commented one way or the other.

What he kept in his mind was a street full of guys and women setting out dressed for work, kids going to school on a spring day more than fifty years before. He blocked out what he actually saw—the trucks, the crew, the commissary table, the lights, and the crowd of gawkers.

Sean Quinlan felt a bit dizzy, like he was about to fall or maybe fly and wondered if this was how the start of a Slide felt. He had created a background for his character. Roark and McDevitt were supposed to pick up Jimmy Nails, a two-bit thug suspected of having ambitions above his station, for questioning. Roark was a ten-year veteran of the force, a guy with a wife and two kids who was talking about moving to the suburbs. He would not be bouncing on his toes on an ordinary morning on a routine assignment.

A sound crew moved with them just out of camera range as the two cops continued a conversation that the audience would just have heard them have in the car. That scene got filmed in California a couple of weeks back.

> "Definitely it's spring, Pat, my boy," says McDevitt and comes to a halt. Roark's expression is mildly amused, a bit bored until he follows the other's gaze.

Without looking, Quinlan knew Terry was wearing the trademark same half-bemused, half-aroused little grin he had used at least once in every episode of *Angel House*.

> Then Roark sees what McDevitt sees, and his jaw drops just a bit. They hold the pose.

"Cut!" said Mitchell Graham, the director. "I think we may have it." Crew members moved; traffic began to flow. Zach Terry looked Sean Quinlan up and down for a moment before the two of them stepped apart.

The actors had worked together once a couple of years before, when Quinlan appeared in an episode of *Angel House*. That's the HBO series featuring a law office whose partners are angels but not necessarily good ones—an amusing show, Quinlan thought, once you accepted the premise. Terry was one of the stars.

Quinlan had played a quirky hit man who didn't happen

to be guilty of the killing with which he'd been charged. Their two scenes together had gone well, and Quinlan hoped the look just then didn't mean some kind of tension.

On the way back to his dressing room he passed a girl, maybe twenty, in pedal pushers, teased hair, and pumps. She smiled and he turned to watch her walk away.

A production assistant saw him look and said, "That kid has all the moves. This location is a magnet for Sliders. They think if they dress in period and hang around sites like this they'll wake up in 1960. One told me that the trick was *not* to think about Sliding back while you did all that."

The kid had a nice ass but not enough to make his head spin like it did. In his dressing room Quinlan did relaxation exercises, sipped iced tea, sat silently for a few minutes, and finally listened to his calls. Arroyo, the lawyer, was first.

"Sean. I assume everything you wanted to keep is already out of the condo. As of today it's repossessed. Second, my colleague who's handling your case up in San Bernardino says there's no word from the DA's office. We don't know if an indictment is coming down. But as we discussed, an indictment is just their way of getting you to testify. I'm wondering if you got my bill."

Quinlan had gotten the bill. The condo was one more casualty of his divorce and bankruptcy. When he could have sold, he couldn't bring himself to do it. When he had to sell, there were no buyers.

Everyone had consoled him about the divorce, like he'd suffered a death in the family or been laid off from work. Monica Celeste had the better career, was a major presence on daytime TV. Quinlan told himself that if the situation had been reversed he wouldn't have dumped her. But all that was in the past.

The San Bernardino matter was current. A runaway grand jury led by a self-righteous young DA was investigating collection-agency practices. Some debtors apparently testified that a few years before, Quinlan had led them to believe he was a cop. So far nothing had gotten out to the media.

That time just after the divorce was still a jumble in his mind. One thing he was sure of was that testifying meant implicating his former employers, which would be very unwise. Another thing about which he was positive was that lawyers had eaten up his *Like '60* pay.

Adie was at the office and in full business mode when she left a message. "For the Peggy McHugh thing, we can meet at Ormolu at eight. I mentioned that to a prospective client and he knew all about it. So we may meet him there."

The last call was a voice from deep in a disreputable past. Rollins said, "You asked around about me. Here I am. I know where to find you." Quinlan was a bit amused.

When they knocked on his door to say he had ten minutes, Quinlan thought about his character for a few moments. Roark had the usual problems trying to raise a family on a cop's salary. His wife and he had disagreements. But she was a cop's wife and understood what that meant. A steady guy was Roark, a good partner.

Detectives McDevitt and Roark hold the same poses as at the end of the previous scene. The audience has just watched a sequence shot two weeks before on a sound stage in California. It shows what the two cops are watching—a nude woman standing behind gauze curtains.

The viewers see a reverse strip, as she hooks her bra, pulls up her panties, draws on nylons, wriggles into a slip, a blouse, and a skirt. She bends slowly to put on her shoes.

Suddenly McDevitt shakes himself awake. "Decoy!" he says. "She's letting him get away." The pair of them run for the front door of the building.

Locations had found an untouched and ungentrified tenement. Props had filled the dented cans in front with in-period trash—a partly crushed Wheaties box, a broken Coke bottle, a striped pillow leaking feathers.

A little old lady with a wheeled shopping cart gets in their way. The stoop is worn and paint is peeling on the railing. As they run up the steps the front door opens.

And there stands Laura Chante, the first time the audience gets a good look at her. Laura is the girlfriend of a very wrong guy, hard but soft, bad but good. She wears high heels, a black sheath skirt, and a jacket open to reveal a pale, shimmering blouse. A scarf with a streak of scarlet covers most of her blond hair. "You boys looking for someone?" she asks with an innocent expression.

Laura was played by the young London actress Moira Tell. Her posture, her accent, her attitude were impeccable.

Peggy McHugh still had a sassy smile. Back in the 1950s and 60s she had made a career playing bright young girlfriends and wisecracking best pals of too-sweet heroines. She was the young detective's fiancée in the *Naked City* TV series.

At eighty she played tough old broads with a regular role on *As the World Turns* and a girlfriend thirty years her junior. In a nod to nostalgia she'd been cast as Detective Pete McDevitt's hip, utterly unsentimental grandmother in this movie.

It was her birthday, and Mitchell Graham, the director, along with the movie's producers threw a little party for her at Ormolu's on Union Square and invited the press.

Ms. McHugh had already knocked back a Jameson on the rocks and was swirling champagne in her glass when Quinlan came up and hugged her.

"How are you doing, you old witch?" he asked.

"Sean! Thought I'd see more of you on this shoot. How's your mother? Still living in New Mexico with what's-his-name?"

Peggy McHugh and Quinlan's mother, the former Julie Morris, had been pals back when his mother was acting, back when she married his father, Detective Jim Quinlan.

"Arizona. Lou Hagan is the current husband. Nice guy—retired broker. She's fine. Sends her love."

"Your mother was gorgeous. She and your father, when they met, were more like a movie than any movie I've been in." And having taken the conversation to a place where Quinlan didn't want to go, Peggy caught sight of someone else and said, "Bella! So wonderful of you to come!"

Quinlan stepped away, went to the bar, sipped a Scotch, and looked around the room. Ormolu's tin ceiling had been polished to a fine shine; the wood paneling looked rich as chocolate. The place had been a dump twenty years before when it was a rock club called Ladders. Long before that it had been an Italian wedding hall.

Sean's parents were quite a story—the young actress and

the young cop who got himself quite dirty trying to keep her in style. Jim Quinlan shot himself when the shit came down. Sean had been three when that happened and found it out in bits and pieces.

Once when he was small his grandfather had explained how it was growing up in the Irish New York of the twenties and thirties. "Kids who got in trouble, which was most of us, got let off with a warning if we had cops in the family. Those without a relative on the force got a criminal record. Simple justice and nothing less."

Out of nowhere Quinlan had asked about the father whom he barely remembered and knew almost nothing. "Did my dad get into trouble?"

He never forgot the grief on the old man's face as he said, "Your father got more than a couple of warnings."

Adie was across the room talking intently to a thin man wearing thousands of dollars' worth of suit and a long, dark ponytail.

Where Quinlan was standing he could hear Mitchell Graham say, "Sometimes acting is beside the point and it's the physical presence you want. Someone walks on camera unannounced and the audience knows he's a killer."

Quinlan shifted slightly and saw that the director was talking to Moira Tell and a reporter. "In America, real Mafiosi go to jail, get involved in the prison drama group, get out, and go into business playing Mafiosi on stage and screen. When Friedkin shot *Sorcerer* down in Latin America he hired a couple of Sing Sing School of Drama graduates to play the thugs. The two stopped off on the way down there and helped pull a robbery. This delayed them and held up the shooting. When they showed up, Roy Scheider, the star, said, 'I was told we were waiting for actors—these are just gangsters.' Supposedly, the two were deeply hurt that their artistic bona fides were being questioned."

Moira Tell laughed and moved toward the bar. On her way she noticed Quinlan. "You are very good," she told him.

"Sing Sing School of Drama."

"Oh, he was *not* talking about you. Graham admires what you're doing, the presence you bring. He believes all that nonsense about inner-emotion-American versus exterior-detail-English acting."

"You were great this afternoon."

"It's wonderful to visit a past that has nothing to do with me at all."

From across the room they heard Peggy McHugh in full voice speaking to a cable interviewer: "Back when the economy was first going down the toilet, someone asked me if I'd like to go back sixty years. I thought they meant would I like to be young again. Instead they just meant me going just as I was. 'Before heart bypasses, before air conditioning?' I asked them. 'You're out of your mind,' I said. Sweetheart, we lived like dogs back then."

Adie said as they were leaving a bit later, "The one I was talking to is the Brazilian from this morning. He wants to buy a penthouse. He's loaded." Somehow money had not really come up in all the years they'd known each other.

The ferry boat called the *Queen of Union City* disembarks passengers onto a Hudson River pier in the West Twenties. A woman wearing a veiled hat leads a small boy in an Eton cap and a girl in a straw boater by their hands. A tall man in a three-piece suit and a topcoat follows them. An old slat-sided truck piled with crates of live chickens rolls onto the pier past a large sign reading ERIE LACKAWANNA FERRY COMPANY.

Under that in smaller letters is "Departures from Manhattan on the hour and the half hour, 4 A.M. to 8 P.M."

Detectives Pete McDevitt and Pat Roark stand under a clock that says 2:25, poised, alert and ready to step out from behind the makeshift ferry shed. Then McDevitt says, "Now," and moves to his right. Roark at the same moment moves to his left.

Roark served a year in Korea. Firemen are navy; cops are army. Quinlan knows this. The next line is his:

"Okay Nails, freeze."

"Cut!"

The truck with the chickens went into reverse and parked next to a mint-condition 1955 Oldsmobile and an old-fashioned ambulance the size and shape of a station wagon.

Before the first take Mitchell Graham had said, "Sean, you're so perfectly in period that I feel like I should film you in black-and-white."

As McDevitt that day, Zach Terry wore his hat at the same great angle as Quinlan did. Graham noticed that. After the first take he told Quinlan, "It's distracting to have both of you with your hats alike. Could you straighten yours?"

The game was called protecting the star. Sean knew that game. McDevitt's hat was an important prop today. He shifted his own fedora.

"Perfect," said the director.

A featured player yields gracefully in the hope that a director will remember when casting in the future. Quinlan wondered how many movies Graham would direct after this one. He wondered what his own career would look like if an indictment came down in California.

Crews were setting up for the next scene, which would be shot in front of an old three-story building just across from the piers. For the movie a sign had been erected on the front that read MURPHY'S FINE FOOD AND DRINK. ROOMS BY THE DAY OR WEEK.

Once this had actually been a waterfront tavern with rooms rented to sailors on the upper floors. For a while after the waterfront shut down it had been a notorious gay bar called the Wrong Box.

Carter Boyce, the actor playing Jimmy Nails, was in costume and taking a practice walk toward the ferry shed. Carter Boyce was a nice guy who happened to have a mug two feet wide with bad news written all over it.

In the next scene, Jimmy Nails was supposed to have just come down the wooden exterior stairs that led from the second floor of Murphy's. He had an overcoat on his arm and carried a satchel.

The scene of Nails on those stairs had been completed the day before through the miracle of second-unit work.

Detectives McDevitt and Roark stand exactly where they were at the end of the last shot. In the background as they start to move toward Murphy's, the Oldsmobile and the chicken truck roll off the dock in one direction, a red Studebaker station wagon goes by in the other.

Twenty feet away from them Jimmy Nails drops his

luggage and overcoat and swings a double-barrel shotgun their way. McDevitt, acting instinctively, whips off his fedora and flings it at Nails's face in one gesture. Jimmy, his eyes rolling like a trapped beast, is a creature of instinct and empties a barrel at the hat. Roark's gun jumps into his hand and he fires three times. Jimmy Nails goes down firing the second barrel into the ground.

The hat flying through the air and getting blasted into felt confetti was being shot that same week by a special-effects outfit in California.

"Thanks," Roark says.

"That hat cost me seven bucks at Rothman's," says his partner, his buddy.

"Cut. Let's put Zach and Sean about a foot farther apart," said Graham. "And Sean, slower on the reaction. Let the hat surprise you as much as it does Carter. Sean, are you with us?"

Quinlan nodded. For a moment he'd felt like the back draft of the vintage vehicles was pulling him away from this time and place.

Over several takes the vintage Studebaker blew a tire and the wind and the sun played hell with Mr. Terry's hair. Half a dozen people surrounded him, spraying his chestnut locks.

"Exposure to the elements . . ."

"It's not, of course, but the light makes it look thin."

". . . lighting adjustment . . ."

This Quinlan knew was also about protecting the star, as was the scene they kept enacting. McDevitt needed to save

Roark's life to mitigate, for the audience, the fact that his misjudgment was going to cost Roark his life.

As they prepared for what turned out to be the last take, Quinlan couldn't stop thinking, each time he looked at Zach Terry, that this was the bastard who was going to get him killed.

At some point during the last couple of takes, Sean Quinlan became aware of a figure from his disreputable past. Rollins stood across the street dark and sharp in a navy blue suede jacket and soft leather shoes and watched everything that went on.

When they were finished with *Like '60* for the day, he and Rollins went down the avenue to what had been a nouveau-chic diner and now seemed to be slipping into just being a diner with a liquor license.

"We had some rare adventures, you and I," Rollins remarked, when they settled into a back booth, "a pair of theater students out looking for adventure."

"And not caring where they found it."

"Always on the right side of the law, though."

"Not as I remember. There was the time we unloaded the Quaaludes those crazy guys from NYU manufactured in their chemistry lab."

"We weren't caught. That's being on the right side of the law, as far as I'm concerned. Glad you got in touch. I've been following your career. Sorry about the divorce. Monica Celeste must be loaded."

Quinlan shrugged. "I see you're still the Well-Dressed Passerby," he said. "That routine keeps working for you?"

"In any large city there are always the lost, the confused, and the lonely that need an assist from a passing stranger." Rollins gave a charming smile. "Actually, though, I've gone legit. I'm in the tourist business—tours of various old New Yorks. You heard about that?

"We have people taking daytrips to 1890s New York. Out in Brooklyn in a couple of spots you can walk down a street and almost think it's a hundred and twenty-five years ago. Any decade you can think of, people want to see the remains."

Rollins smiled. "It's an amazing confluence, you being back in town and making this movie. *Like '60* is on the cusp of the hottest boom in this dying town. Your movie is going to be porno for the ones who go for fifties New York. That ferryboat sliding up to the dock and that truckload of chickens and you and your pal in those hats and padded-shoulder suits will make them cum in their Dacron/rayon pants."

Sean gave a grin. "In tough times people want to go elsewhere," Rollins said. "With every corner of the planet going down the drain, the places they favor are in the past. Some lunatics even want to go back to the Great Depression. Like this one isn't bad enough for them. But I don't ask questions; I just set up the tours. Who would have guessed that a master's degree in history from Columbia would stand me in such good stead?"

"Especially since you never went there."

Rollins shrugged. "What makes it all weird and twisted and thus makes it my kind of enterprise is that some of the clients believe that if they can find a place with enough artifacts that evoke a certain time, they'll get a jolt and wind up there.

"Most of them want to go back to the seventies, the sixties, the fifties. They figure things would be comfortable enough. ID requirements were still loose back then. Sliders know enough about those times that they could make a nice living betting on the World Series and buying Xerox stock. One said that if he could get back to 1950 he'd have almost sixty years before stuff got really screwy."

"You've heard them talk all this out? Ever help any of them do it?"

"None of my clients and no one else I've ever known has actually managed the Slide. They've all heard about someone going back in time. They know someone who found a message from someone who disappeared saying he's living like a king in 1946. Psychiatrists say it's delusional. People can't deal with bad times."

"You believe the shrinks know what they're talking about?"

"They diagnosed me as a sociopath back when I was in high school. It sounded good and I went with it. If you're looking for a guide to the Slide you're out of luck. If you want a job leading 1950s nostalgia tours, I'd be happy to hire you."

"Thanks, but I have other plans." Quinlan rose and put a ten down on the table. "Nice talking to you, Rollo."

For a moment Rollins looked hurt. Then he said, "Sorry to break your heart, Quinlan. It's nice that you figured if anyone in New York knew how to Slide it would be me. You've been in and out of the city over the years without ever trying to get in contact, so I wondered what you wanted. Somehow I didn't think of this. Either you got stupid out in California or you got very desperate."

In the early morning light, stepping carefully along a tenement fire escape just off Tenth Avenue in Hell's Kitchen, Detective Roark edges forward, revolver in hand. Up ahead is Figs Figueroa's window. In another moment his partner will knock on the door of the apartment and Figueroa will be on the move. Roark curses the stupidity that led him into this. Backup is on its way and they could have waited. But the lieutenant is not happy with the way they'd bobbled Jimmy Nails's arrest the other morning or the way they'd then made him too dead to talk. McDevitt thinks the two of them need some redemption.

As Roark inches forward, the window right behind him opens. He drops to a crouch, revolver at the ready, turns, and sees the terrified face of an old woman about to hang a basket of wet laundry on her wash line. When Roark turns back, Figueroa stands on the fire escape with an automatic leveled on him.

"Cut."

On the roof just above Quinlan were an assistant director, the script girl, the cameraman, and the director himself. "We need this one more time," said Graham. "Just do what you've done before." He looked closely at Quinlan and said, "Get this man some coffee."

It was late in the morning and Quinlan had already gone up this fire escape six times. He guessed this particular building got cast for the part because of this fire escape, which was as black and labyrinthine as the stairways of a Piranesi prison. People fussed with his clothes and his makeup. He'd lain awake all night next to Adie, who slept soundly. Somebody brought him coffee.

This scene was his best moment in *Like '60*. By coincidence, it and the one they'd shoot immediately afterward were his last ones in the film. His work in New York was over.

If someone asked him what *Like '60* was about, Quinlan

would have said it was the story of a cop who was an ordinary guy wanting the ordinary things and living in a simpler and not very enlightened time. This man is pulled by circumstance and human weakness into a situation where his life is on the line.

Again he climbs the stairs and inches forward. Again the window opens and, revolver at the ready, he stares into the terrified face and looks up too late to see his killer.

This morning, it seemed as if Rollins was right about the Slide being a delusion. Quinlan felt no distant hum of past times. His stomach was tight, his shoulders tense.

In his dressing room he looked at his messages. Adie had called from her office to say she had a meeting with a client and would have to miss the wrap party. This morning she had asked him—gently, indirectly, not like he was being evicted yet—if everything was OK for him back in LA. She hadn't mentioned the Brazilian, but he was an invisible presence.

As Quinlan sat absorbing this, Arroyo, the lawyer, called. "My associate in San Bernardino says the grand jury will hand down indictments in an intimidation/extortion scheme this afternoon at around six P.M. New York time. You're accused of impersonating a law officer. One alleged victim says you showed him a badge, threatened to run him in on false charges if he didn't come up with his payment."

"That's a lie." Sean said that automatically, but the only memory the accusation evoked was an appearance he'd made as a rogue cop on *NYPD Blue* many years before, in which he'd flashed a shield.

"Sean, they're not interested in you. They want the ones who hired you."

"Speaking those names means I'll be dead or in witness protection," he said. "I'll get back to you."

Quinlan remembered when he turned thirteen and decided that instead of becoming a cop, which was all he'd wanted up until then, he was going to be an actor. His grandfather had said, "Tough luck, kid; you drew your father's face and your mother's brains."

He jumped when a woman from props knocked on the door and came in to put him into a bloody shirt.

Pat Roark lies sprawled face up in the alley with the gun still clasped in his lifeless hand, his hat beside his head, his dead eyes staring at the sky.

The scene is shot from above. The camera looks down as a dozen extras—kids carrying schoolbooks, women in curlers and housedresses, guys in work clothes, idlers, and honest citizens—suddenly converge from all directions to see the dead man who has fallen from the sky.

The computer imaging of Roark falling backward off the fire escape and slamming into the asphalt had been completed before he left Los Angeles.

"What was he doing up there?" a woman with a Spanish accent wanted to know.

"He's a cop," said a wise-ass kid. "See that police special."

As the sirens wail and echo off the alley walls, Pete

McDevitt runs down the fire escape, yelling, "Pat! Jesus, no!" His voice breaks into a sob.

Quinlan couldn't tell if he used the dippy smile. The shot of Pat Roark dead in the alley would be used repeatedly in the film as a motive for Zach Terry's Peter McDevitt in his quest for the killer and the ones behind the killer, who, it turned out, reached all the way to the commissioner's office.

The old stage actor Denny Wallace, whose father was a Polish Jew and whose mother was a French ballet dancer, played Lieutenant O'Grady.

Standing over the corpse, he delivers Roark's epitaph. "He was worth twenty of you. I'll have your badge and your gun for this, boyo."

Quinlan heard applause on the set, which meant this was probably the last take. There was comfort in lying dead in an alleyway, killed in the line of duty in a time when that meant something. This was the part of his life that actually made sense.

The applause faded and died. Smell was the first thing he noticed, tobacco smoke and garbage and exhaust. Sirens sounded on the avenue. Quinlan focused his eyes on a kid with bat-wing ears, a crew cut, and jeans so stiff they could stand up by themselves. A bunch of scruffy street rats stared down at him.

"It's a cop!"

"How'd he get here?" The city accents were thick enough to cut.

He closed his hand on his prop gun, and they all stepped

back. "You been shot, mister. You need a doctor?" Quinlan remembered the prop blood on his shirt front. No one, he noticed, talked about calling the cops.

"He's a fuckin' actor. Look at the makeup," said an old lady with way too much lipstick, peering into the alley.

All Sean wondered as he got up was how long it would take Graham and the rest to notice he was gone. He dusted himself off, buttoned his jacket to hide the dye on his shirt front, and wiped his face clean with a pocket handkerchief.

It was a five-story city, and the sun shone directly from across the Hudson. Everyone got out of his way as he walked down the alley. He stuffed the gun in his pocket.

"Anyone follows me . . ." He gestured to it. He doubted that anyone in Hell's Kitchen was going to call the police. But he moved quickly, got on Tenth Avenue, and started walking.

Cars and clothes gave only a hint of the year. A corner newsstand had a big display of papers dated May 19, 1957.

His father would be about half his age and still in the army in Germany. His mother would not have moved here from Buffalo. His grandfather and grandmother lived up on Fordham Road in the Bronx. The avenue was lined with pawnshops. The gun was a prop, but he figured it would be worth a buck or two.

"Black Jack" Quinlan and he would be about the same age. If he was here. He had to be here. Once he explained things, once he showed this face, Sean Quinlan couldn't imagine them denying this fugitive a welcome.

The Duke of Riverside

BY ELLEN KUSHNER

Ellen Kushner's first novel, *Swordspoint,* was hailed as the progenitor of the "mannerpunk" or "fantasy of manners" style. Its eventual sequel, *The Privilege of the Sword,* won the Locus Award and was a Nebula nominee and a Tiptree Honor book. A third novel, *The Fall of the Kings,* set in the same unnamed city, was cowritten with Delia Sherman and explores the fate of the city and its people in the next generation. "The Duke of Riverside" is set shortly before and after the events of *Swordspoint.*

Ellen Kushner is also the host of the long-running public radio series PRI's *Sound & Spirit* and a cofounder of the Interstitial Arts Foundation. Her original spoken-word performances include *Esther: The Feast of Masks* and *The Golden Dreydl: A Klezmer "Nutcracker" for Chanukah* (with Shirim Klezmer Orchestra, on Rykodisc CD). A popular speaker and teacher, she lives in New York City with Delia Sherman and no cats whatsoever.

That kid never belonged here. We all knew that from the moment he walked through the door, looking nervous and madder than hell. Bad combination. Everyone figured he had a weapon, because people like that usually do. The drinkers stopped drinking, the barmaids stopped serving, and the dicers held up their dice mid-roll. Sukey moved a little closer to Annie, as the girls like to protect each other when they can.

Rosalie stepped forward. It is her bar, after all. "What can I get you?" she asked.

"What can you get me?" His voice told everyone that was the stupidest question he'd ever been asked. "What can you get me?" All sneer. And that snooty Hill accent. Definitely not from around here. "Do you happen to have Ludlow's treatise, *On the Causes of Nature*? Oh, no, they banned it. How about a roast peacock, then? Or a cup of really strong poison?"

Rosalie rolled her eyes. "I'll go see," she said. Like she'd already taken his measure and decided he wasn't dangerous after all, just nuts. She turned her back on him, and the whole room relaxed.

He was a scholar, clearly. He had that long student hair, tied back with a piece of string. And that long black robe they all wear, hanging off his bony shoulders like laundry, only it hadn't been washed for a while. But pissed-off scholars don't usually come down to Riverside. Hell, they don't even come here to get pissed. They know it's a place you're likely to get rolled, rolled and then maybe killed. Nobody drinks here who doesn't have to.

Red Sukey sidled up to him. She'd been holding on to Annie, but when Rosalie turned her back, Sukey grabbed her chance. "Buy me a drink?"

He looked down at her. He was incredibly tall. "What for? Are you thirsty?"

She's not very old. Not much experience there. "No." She

moved a little closer to him, to show him what she had. "I'd be nice to you."

He got it then. "For a drink? Are you serious?"

We all waited to see if he had any money. Most men, you mention money, their hand goes automatically to where they keep their purse, just for an instant. But his hand didn't even go to his belt. Nothing, then; or he was smarter than he looked. I, myself, was willing to wait and see.

And then Nimble Willie stuck his head in through the doorway gasping, "Fight! Fight!" and we forgot all about the bony scholar and headed for the street to see. Poor Archer Fink had finally gotten St. Vier to take his challenge, god knows how. Richard St. Vier was too good to fight a newbie like Archer, and if Archer didn't know it, we all did. Probably it was that girl of his, the blonde, egging Fink on to show his stuff. Maybe she even thought he really had a chance.

We're used to seeing them come and go, these young swordsmen. They fight like stags in autumn, to prove who's best. Only, being swordsmen, they tend to kill each other off. That's how you get good jobs in the city, not to mention respect here in Riverside.

That day my money was on St. Vier, but so was everyone else's. I only won eighteen brass minnows.

It was done in a minute—barely time to make our bets. St. Vier lunged quick and hard, Archer Fink grunted and wheezed, and it was all over, blood shooting up after the tip of the sword when St. Vier pulled it out.

The student was right there. He was standing very still; he didn't even put up his hand to keep the blood from hitting him. His black robe was spattered with shiny black drops. He stared at the body like he'd never seen one before.

St. Vier walked away from the fight and into the tavern.

Rosalie brought him a drink. She loved that he drank at her place. It brought her custom. When the nobles from the Hill were looking for a swordsman to hire, they sent their servants down to Rosalie's to find him. She loved that, too.

The scholar followed him in. "I'll have one, too," he said to Rosalie.

She said, "First, let me see your money."

"You didn't ask *him* for money."

Rosalie snorted. "St. Vier, I know. Who the hell are you?"

"I'm no one," he said fiercely. "Forget it."

"Who are you?" Rosalie said again, in that tone of voice that always gets her cash on the barrel.

He turned his head and looked down at her. It was a long damn way. "Alec," he said.

"Is that all?"

"Just Alec."

The swordsman was ignoring the whole thing. He was leaning on the bar, knocking down his thirst with his back to them both—though one hand never left the sword at his side.

"St. Vier," the kid said aloud. He pushed loose hair back from his face, not even noticing the smear of blood he left there. The air around him started to feel dangerous again. Maybe it was his voice, the way he said the name. "St. Vier," he said again, long and low. I've heard nobles use that voice, up on the Hill, when they're telling a servant they want something done. Yeah. I did some work up there once. But just once. They talk real slow, like they have all the time in the world. Which they do.

The swordsman heard it, too. He turned his head. "Yes?"

"You're Richard St. Vier?"

The swordsman nodded.

"And you kill people."

St. Vier looked him up and down. It stretched his neck some; the kid was a real beanpole. He must've seen what we all saw: young, skinny, hungry, poor, bad-tempered, and out of place.

"Sometimes I do."

"Do you ever kill them just because they're no earthly use to anyone at all?"

"No. No, I don't think I've ever done that."

"Well." The kid stepped back, putting a sword's length between them. "That is disappointing. What do you do it for, then?"

"Sometimes just for practice."

"Like now, for instance? Was that just for practice?"

St. Vier's eyes darted over to where Archer's girl had begun a horrible racket in the corner, weeping and wailing. Sukey and Annie were trying to keep her quiet with cheap brandy. For a swordsman, St. Vier is pretty easygoing. But he never likes a lot of noise.

"In a way."

"It must be very tiring, killing all those people."

"Not very."

"You'll do it again, then. Soon."

The swordsman looked at him again. St. Vier was popular on the Hill those days, fighting for the nobles at their parties and stuff. Demo matches only: First Blood, hardly ever to the Death. No wonder he liked to practice in Riverside. Nobles can be pretty squeamish. But it's a good bet St. Vier would know that voice pretty well by now, the low, purring voice this ragged guy was using. "Look," St. Vier said, "do you have a job for me? Is that what this is about?"

The student tugged his frayed cuff down. "A job? Me? I don't even have the price of a beer."

"Then what do you want?"

"I don't suppose you'd kill me for free."

A smile forced its way onto the swordsman's face. "No."

"For practice, then?"

"Can you fight?"

The scholar opened his robe to show nothing hung on his belt, not even a knife. "Not particularly, no."

"That's no good, then. I like a challenge."

"Oh." The young scholar turned away. "Maybe later, then. But remember," he said over his shoulder, "you had your chance."

Richard St. Vier watched the tall man walk out of the bar alone. Sometimes nobles came down to Riverside in disguise, looking for kicks or for connection. Some disguise. He wasn't just ragged, he was dirty. His face was young but thin and hollow like hunger. A starving nobleman? A jumped-up servant? A tutor in disgrace?

Richard shook his head. Poor kid. Whatever he was doing in Riverside, he was going to have an interesting time while he lasted. Maybe he should have bought him a beer, for a sort of welcome. The first day was always hard, here.

I, myself, did not expect to see that Alec again.

But then I kept hearing about him. Wandering Riverside like a lost soul, trying not to get laid but to get killed, near as I could tell. It should have been easy. He was going about it exactly the right way—insulting people, asking stupid questions. . . . The thing is, he was unarmed. He had no money. Sometimes he made people laugh, saying things no one else would dare to. No one really wanted to be the one to off him. He was probably crazy. That's a different kind of dangerous.

I saw him again at Rosalie's a few days later. I was looking over some very fine silver spoons that Hal had managed to find in a house uptown, and in walks the skinny kid, right up to where Rosalie is ladling out stew for Fabian Greenspan.

"Is that food?" he says to her. "Or are you trying to get rid of old wash water?"

"You could use a little of both," Rosalie retorted.

Fabian sniggered. Some of the soup he was eating came out his nose.

"Oh, look," the kid said. "It's medicinal, too."

Fabian had the shakes. It was early in the day for him—just past noon—and Rosalie wanted to feed him before he started drinking and she'd have to throw him out. He couldn't handle it at either end.

"Hungry?" Rosalie asked Alec.

"Hardly. I *like* rotten pears and cast-off cheese mold. And I've found the best place for getting them. You should try it. Slenderizing."

"Hey," Fabian protested. He had a soft spot for Rosalie.

The boy looked down his long nose. "Well, you do get thicker as you get older, don't you?"

"Hey!" Fabian roared feebly, and went for the kid.

"Hey," said another voice, a calmer voice. The swordsman St. Vier was peeling Fabian off that Alec character.

"Hey, Richard," Rosalie said calmly. "Want some stew?" If she doesn't like you, she just ignores you.

The young scholar was standing very stiff. I guess he'd never been attacked by a guy with the shakes before. Or he wasn't used to being ignored.

"Richard St. Vier," he drawled. "You're off your game."

"No," St. Vier said; "I ate already." He was always polite, even to drunks.

"You're a disappointment," the scholar went on.

The swordsman turned to him, giving him his full attention. "How so?"

A swordsman's full attention is not something you really want on you. It gave me a chill. The tall kid's eyes glittered hard, like he was fevered, but his skin was pale, like he was casting his final throw.

"It's been three days, now. You haven't killed a soul. Don't think I haven't noticed. You haven't even stepped on a bug. I think you're vastly overrated. What's the matter, have you lost your nerve?"

The swordsman stood up. "Come with me."

This is it, we thought. *Good-bye, scholar.*

The scholar's hands were shaking; I was close enough to see that. But he thrust his pale face forward and followed St. Vier out of the tavern.

It wasn't going to be a pretty death. St. Vier wouldn't waste good swordsmanship on an unarmed man. But I had a bet on with Hal, so we followed them out there.

The scholar was standing against a wall, very white in the face against his black robe and the crummy stone. "Remember," he was saying, fast and breathy, "one blow to the heart. They say you're quick."

Young men can be real fools. Not just the scholar, but the young swordsman we all called Dapper Dan, who must have taken a bad notion to impress St. Vier. Guys like that think being a swordsman's all about risks and big gestures, and he made one now.

"Allow me," I heard him say, as he drew his blade.

St. Vier was St. Vier. Dan should never have shown cold

steel around him. Someone with slower reflexes might have taken the time to notice that the blade wasn't coming in his direction. But Richard St. Vier moved fast.

You have to love the guy. He drew and slashed right across Dan from the side, a gorgeous twist nobody else could have made in time. Dan squawked and fell, and St. Vier said, "Damn," when he realized what he'd done.

The scholar hadn't even had time to move out of the way. He stared down at poor Dan.

"You should have let him," he said.

"It wasn't his business," said St. Vier. But I was out there, and I saw: He hadn't drawn until Dan did. Whatever he was planning to do with the scholar, it wasn't the long cold kiss of steel, as the poets say. "Would you like a drink?"

They walked back into Rosalie's tavern together, and that was that. From then on, you never saw them apart.

Nobody bet on when they started sleeping together, because there was no way of finding out for sure. Their landlady, Marie, the whore and laundress who lets out rooms above the courtyard of the old place with the well where she washes, is usually a pretty good egg, but she got all prissy with, "Master St. Vier's business is his own, and at least he pays his rent on time most months, not like some. . . ." But why else did St. Vier make it clear over and over that anyone who laid a finger on his crazy student would have him to answer to? More than one bully, pimp, and bravo fell that year when they tried it anyway. As far as St. Vier was concerned, there was one rule: Don't Mess with Alec, no matter what.

I guess Lord Horn didn't know about St. Vier's Alec rule. How could he, when he lived way up on the Hill with the rest of them? What some old noble wanted Alec for was anybody's guess, but not everyone was sorry when Alec disappeared for a while. It made the swordsman jumpy as hell, though. He made some inquiries, killed a few hired toughs who should have known not to mess with Riversiders, got Alec back, all right—and then he went after Lord Horn and took care of him, too.

Well, what else could he do? He had his point to make. But the city didn't see it that way. Brought St. Vier up on murder charges, threw him in the Chop. Nobody liked it, but what could we do? We don't ask anyone in the city to do us any favors. We look after our own, no squealers; but if you're taken, good luck to you.

Alec broke that rule. For St. Vier, see. Of course, we didn't know it at the time. We thought Alec had left again because he was bored or lonely or scared shitless. Fabian Greenspan swore he'd seen him lying with his throat slit off Fuller's Way. But Fabian doesn't always see so clearly. Red Sukey said he'd thrown himself from the Bridge because of the tragedy of his eternal love. But Sukey likes theatre. Then Nimble Willie came back from plying his trade over by the Council Hall, claiming Alec had passed him riding in a carriage with the Duchess Tremontaine's crest on it, all decked out in green velvet and gold lace. That was a little startling, because Willie's pretty reliable, but not nearly as startling as when St. Vier turns up again the next day, and Alec a day or so later, hair cut short but wearing the same old black robe, rattier than ever. So we couldn't help ragging on Willie with, "So where's the gold and velvet, Willie?"

No velvet—and no money, either. Maybe he spent it all to spring St. Vier. I know that Alec is broke again because I try touching him for five in silver against my next lucky job uptown and he gives me one of those speeches that basically translates as "Get away from me or I'll get St. Vier to rip your balls off." Nice to know they're still such excellent friends. Everything back to normal. Except word trickles down from people with legitimate jobs up in the city (meaning Riversiders who just couldn't hack it any more, gone up there to scrub floors and dishes) that Alec is in fact a very close relative of the duchess. So maybe he's lying about the money. But, then, why doesn't he buy himself some decent clothes?

Alec came storming out of the bedroom in their rooms at Marie's, shoving his hair back behind his ears. Richard stopped practicing long enough to get out of his way. Alec never really knew where his body was in relation to anything around him.

"Have you seen my boots?" Alec demanded. "I took them off last night, and they've vanished. I think someone ate them. I'm going to the market. Please don't consume anything else useful while I'm gone. The shad are in, and they sell out fast. I'll bring some home. Where are my boots?"

"Behind the bed."

"I've looked there."

"Look again."

Alec emerged fully shod, clutching his robe to his throat. "I've lost my cloak pin."

"It's here." Richard picked it up off the mantel, careful not to dislodge Alec's small collection of precious books. "Do you want me to come with you?"

"To protect me from murderous fishwives?"

Alec shoved his hair back behind his ears again, and shook his head with annoyance as it fell forward.

"There's nothing you can do about it," Richard said. "Just wait. It grows when it grows."

"How philosophical," Alec drawled sarcastically. "How

very like the wise old farmer in the tutelary readers for young people."

"How long did it take you to grow it out the first time?"

"Years," Alec growled. "And everyone still laughed at me when I got to university because I looked like a new boy. It had just gotten good and long when I left. The one thing I finally got right. And then I had to go and cut it, just to make a nice impression on the Council for the duchess."

"Well, it worked," Richard said.

"Not that it wasn't worth it," Alec added. "She nearly died when she saw me all cleaned up."

The hair would grow long again; meanwhile, there was still enough for Richard to sink his fingers into, and he did.

Nobody knows who owns most of Riverside, but it's probably Alec's relatives, and they've probably buried the deeds, because who really wants their very own piece of this crumbling rabbit warren? Like there's that crazy cat-lady at the top of that old pile on Ferrian Alley. You'd pay *not* to own that house.

Young guys always believe in luck. Most of them never get old. And some, like that Alec, have it all, even if they may not look it at first.

Richard wasn't looking for the letters, but the swordsman had a very good sense for what was around him. He always knew where things stood in a room, and he knew when anything changed. The letters were hidden all over the place: under the mattress, behind Alec's books on the mantelpiece, even in an old pair of winter boots gathering dust in the corner because they needed resoling but no one could ever remember to take them out.

Richard knew Alec would never burn the letters, because there was writing only on one side, and Alec was terrifically cheap. Richard could see that it was good paper—thick and heavy laid, the ink on it crisp and clean. He had no idea what the writing spelt out. But he did recognize the seals, heavy with wax that Alec would probably melt down sooner or later to reuse:

Tremontaine

I was there at Rosalie's the day the news came.

"Tremontaine!" Willie called, breathless, across the tavern. But Alec wouldn't look up from his dice. He was losing, as usual, but as usual refusing to quit and cut his losses.

"Hey, Alec, listen up!" Nimble Willie finally reached the table where Alec was dicing with Hal and Fat Rodge. "Hey!" he panted. Really, he could hardly breathe. "Didn't you hear me calling you?"

"I heard you calling *someone*. What is it, Willie? You're dripping like a cheap candle and you stink worse than my luck."

"I've got news."

Alec's fingers tightened on the side of the table, and could you blame him? *News* could always be St. Vier lying somewhere bleeding his guts out. "Well, spit it out. We're in the middle of a game, here."

"Your granny's gone."

"My 'granny'? Which 'granny' would that be, Willie?"

"You know what I mean. It's the duchess. The Duchess Tremontaine. She's dead. Last night. I came to tell you."

"Oh, re-ally?"

He lifted the dice and looked at them for a long time.

"Snake eyes," he said, and threw.

We all stared at the two perfect spots there in the middle of the table. Then Alec got up and left the tavern. No one saw him again for days. But Hal kept his money for him, down to the last brass minnow, tied up in a handkerchief. You didn't want to piss off St. Vier. And clearly, Alec's luck had turned.

"Aren't you going to see her off?" Richard asked. He was practicing in their rooms with a blunt-tipped sword, stretching and exercising against the wall, which was pitted with the marks of other practice bouts. Alec had steel of his own, a darning needle he'd learned to use in his time at university. It, too, was blunt-tipped, which was good, considering the uses to which Alec put sharp objects.

"I avoided her while she was alive. It seems hypocritical to pursue her now."

"I heard there might be fireworks. You love fireworks."

"They had fireworks last year for Lord Galing. It cheered everyone up. I'm sure the late Duchess Tremontaine would want us all to be as miserable as possible. There will probably be a choir."

Richard knew he was treading on dangerous ground, but he was genuinely curious. "They're not expecting you, then?"

Alec stabbed at the sock. "Oh, they're expecting me, Richard. The show won't be complete without the idiot grandson parading with his savage swordsman."

"Wear your scholar's robe," Richard said cheerfully. "It's black. It will give them fits."

"Shall I put a silver chain around your neck and lead you in the procession?"

Richard winced. "That bad, eh?"

The needle fell still in Alec's hands. "Bad? Oh, so you'd actually mind? I was beginning to think you liked the idea."

Alec hated people knowing anything about him. Even Richard. And now it was out. All over the city. All over Riverside.

"If you wanted to go, I'd come with you, that's all."

Richard went back to practicing, striking his sword rhythmically against the wall, careful not to look at Alec but hearing his acid, honey voice:

"By all means, let's go to the Tremontaine funeral and join the solemn procession of important people showing off just how important they really are. They're expecting us, after all. We wouldn't want to disappoint them. And then we can poke holes in a few. That, they will not be expecting. Think what a thrill it will give the assembled mourners. It will be the talk of the town. The duchess will be utterly forgotten." Alec jabbed at the sock's hole, which was not getting any smaller. "Not that she won't be forgotten soon, anyway. She's got no power anymore, has she? These people are no longer interested. They'll pay their respects, because everyone's watching, and then they'll go right back to trying to figure out who's giving the most important dinner parties now that she's gone. She never liked me, you know. I'm rotten at dinner parties. No conversation. And I slouch. She likes people who are good at things. You impressed her. She'd like it if you went. Did you ever work for her?"

"Never. You know that."

"Go now, then. Go up to the Hill, and show everyone you know how to behave properly. Just because I'm a disgrace doesn't mean you have to be."

"Why would I want to go there without you?"

"Why would you want to go there *with* me?"

Richard put his hands on Alec's shoulders. "Let's not," he said, "go anywhere at all." He could feel the tension radiating along his arms.

"How blissful," Alec drawled. "How domestic."

Richard reached down to uncover Alec's palm. The marks that scored it were vivid red, but the skin unbroken. It was only a darning needle. Richard raised the hand to his lips. The palm was hot and burning.

So it looked like everybody was going to the Duchess Tremontaine's funeral except Alec. And he was probably the only one actually invited. The rest of Riverside was just going to turn up along the route, which would run from her big house on the Hill to the Stone City outside of town. The nobles would ride in procession behind, and everyone would line up to watch them, which was just fine with us. Nothing better for pickpockets than a good colorful procession—and nothing makes a man want a whore faster than being reminded of mortality.

If Alec wanted to hide the letters that kept coming, Richard wasn't going to say anything. If Alec wanted to stop crossing the river into the city, wanted to give up excursions to the booksellers and the theater, well, he got that way sometimes. The books were all too old, Alec claimed, and the theater played nothing but comedies. He detested comedies. Alec was drinking all the time. It made him loose-limbed and clumsy, quarrelsome and fanciful. It didn't mean anything, Richard thought.

Then, on their way home from the market, there was a strange swordsman fixed at the end of the alley, blocking their way. The stranger's sword was sheathed, but loudly and clearly he spoke: "I bear challenge to David Alexander Tielman Campion, Duke Tremontaine—"

For a moment, Richard didn't even understand the words. "What the hell?"

"Just kill him," Alec said.

Richard drew his sword. "I'll take the challenge."

The other man drew and saluted.

"Is it to the Death?"

"I hope so," said Alec. "They can hardly expect me to give up the Duchy of Tremontaine for First Blood."

It was all over town. Alec was heir to Tremontaine. And on either side of the river, people were waiting to kill him before they'd let him into Tremontaine House. Lucky for him he had the greatest swordsman in the city at his side day and night to defend him. The rules were the rules. As long as St. Vier was there to take the challenge, honor was satisfied. The nobles had laid out those rules themselves, to keep them from killing each other off when there were better men to die for them. All St. Vier had to do was always be there—and never lose.

By the third challenge, Richard was getting curious.

"Is this usual when people inherit?" he asked, stepping around the dead man in the street to clean his sword.

Alec wiped his sleeve across his face. He'd barely had time to register the challenge before Richard struck the final blow. "No, it's my goddamned relatives. Contesting the succession."

"What's to contest? Weren't you always her heir?"

Alec scraped something off the sole of his boot against a corner of a wall. "No, Richard. Did you think I was holding out on you all this time?"

He had, actually.

What everyone wanted to know was *Why?* Why this crazy guy, who didn't have enough sense to get out of Riverside when he could, and take his famous boyfriend with him? Was it some kind of a joke? If he didn't want to be a duke, couldn't he just say so?

Not that we didn't enjoy the challenges. Nervous swordsmen from the Hill paid good money to find out where his young lordship might be. We told them where he *might* be. But never where he really was.

"So who was it, then?" Richard sheathed his sword, but kept his hand on the pommel as he walked.

"No one. She wouldn't name an heir while she lived. Maybe she thought it would make her immortal. Maybe she just couldn't decide."

Climbing the dark, narrow stairs to their rooms, Richard watched with extra caution for signs of intruders. He opened the door first and waited until it was shut behind them to say, "So she died without naming an heir, and it automatically goes to you?"

"No, Richard." Alec flung his robe down on their only chair

and said with entirely unjustified elaborate patience, "Haven't you been listening? She did name me. Finally. At the end."

He fished behind *On Human Understanding* and pulled out a letter, heavy with seals.

"See? It's all very official. Chosen, chosen, chosen. Like a prize rosebush at the fair. By a dying woman they probably nagged to death until she just gave them a name to shut them up."

Richard admired the elaborate writing, heavy and black, looped and angled. "So you are now the Duke Tremontaine?"

It was the first time he'd said it aloud. It sounded very strange.

Alec snapped the paper shut, using the seals as ballast.

"Well, that depends, doesn't it?"

"On what?"

"On whether I live to the end of the trial period."

"There's a trial period?"

"Oh, yes. It's open season on me until the thirty days of mourning have passed."

"And then?" he dared to ask.

"It's over. We're safe. I just have to last that long. Then it's not my problem anymore. Or yours."

"But if you don't want the duchy—"

"Who says I don't want it?"

"*Do* you?"

"I want," Alec said, untying Richard's shirt, "to make them sweat. Don't you?"

It was a little harder when they started sending down guys we knew. Steffi's kid, Luxe, who'd been so proud when that fancy uptown swordmaster took him on, and then Steffi never shut up about how her kid had finally gotten himself an important job as some noble's own house swordsman, and that's why her boy never came to see her anymore. When Luxe showed up at Rosalie's, she was thrilled. I have to admit he looked good, well fed and strong, dressed in new clothes. They were not any noble's colors, though. We thought he was off duty, but he wasn't. He bought a round for everyone, and then he said, "So what's new?" or "What's happening around here?" or something.

We all looked at each other. He had to know.

"Looking for St. Vier?" Rosalie said bluntly. She'd never liked Luxe that much.

Luxe grinned. He had good teeth. "Why shouldn't I?"

"No reason. Everyone else is. But you just got lucky."

In they came, St. Vier and Alec, walking close together. Alec's head was up, and he was laughing. St. Vier had that half smile, listening to him.

Everyone got quiet, not even trying to pretend they hadn't been talking about them.

St. Vier's polite. He nodded to the room. Actually, he was checking it out—and as Alec stepped up to the counter and ordered a beer, St. Vier grabbed him by the elbow and steered him back.

"Again?" said Alec.

"Again," his friend said.

Luxe smiled. "St. Vier."

Steffi moved in, all tits and curls. "You remember my boy Luxe, Richard, right? Here he is, come to pay us a visit."

Luxe didn't even do her the courtesy of telling her to shut up. He just kept on talking. "Will you take my challenge?"

"On behalf of his lordship, here?" St. Vier asked. "Because if you're just showing off, I'd rather not."

Luxe straightened up, and you saw the nobleman's house

servant that he'd learned to be. "I bear challenge. To the Tremontaine heir." He nodded at Alec, who was busy picking at a loose thread on his cuff. "That him?"

St. Vier shifted his weight, cutting Luxe off from Alec just a little more. "Don't try."

"Guard, then." Luxe drew. There was sweat on his upper lip already. He had good form, though. People spread out, and the bets got going. I was taking as many as I could, so I missed some of the action. Then Steffi was moaning, "No no no no no no no," and Rosalie had her arms wrapped around her. St. Vier had Luxe pinned to the floor, sweating, his blade at his throat. The throat, not the heart.

St. Vier said, "Alec?"

Alec was sweating, too, pushing hair back from his face. "What?"

"Ask him. Ask him who sent him."

We couldn't believe it. If there's one thing swordsmen don't do, it's ask that question. The patron pays, the patron calls the shots and protects whoever's working for him, so you keep your mouth shut. That's the rules.

"I don't care who sent him! They can all go to hell."

"So do I kill him, then?"

Steffi screamed.

"Hell, no," Alec said. "What for?" And turned away.

He walked on out of the tavern, and St. Vier followed him. We all stood staring at the man on the floor.

"Shit," Luxe said. He was shaking and he wouldn't get up. "Oh, shit."

The next day, I had my great idea. I waited for Alec on the street, not in Rosalie's, where everyone would see us. I waited til I saw him out with his basket to do his marketing, and I went up to him and I said, "Look, here's the thing."

He looked down his long nose at me. Way down. I can't help if I'm short. "Yes," he said, "I can see that."

I ignored the dig. You just have to. I said, "You want a message to someone? Someone up on the Hill, maybe? Something you want to say but not write down?"

He just looked at me. But not in that sneery way. His chin went down a little, listening. He had the weirdest eyes.

"You can trust me." I tried not to talk too fast, which is something people say I sometimes do. But it was hard with those eyes and him not saying anything back. "Say you make them an offer. A hundred royals, a thousand, I dunno; what's it worth to them?" He snorted. "Look, you don't want it; they do. So why not benefit? You save everyone a lot of grief and make a profit. Good for them, good for you, and everyone gets what they want."

He said slowly, "I hadn't thought of that."

Well, of course he hadn't.

"Just say the word," I told him. "I'm your man."

"Are you?"

The way he looked at me then . . . If I'd ever doubted he was really one of them, I didn't anymore. It wasn't just his eyes, it was his voice. Something curious and measuring, like he was checking me out for position of third footman on the left or something. *I'm your man.*

That's not how I'd meant it, either. I just meant it the regular way.

"I know you're a fair-minded guy, so I won't even name a price. I just—well, you know where to find me."

He nodded, turned, and walked away.

Richard met Alec on the stairs coming up. It was too dark for Alec to see how bloody the swordsman's shirt was, but he could smell it.

"Don't go up," Richard said. "There's a dead man in there."

"In *there*?" Alec pointed with his chin to their door at the top of the stairs. He was carrying a basket of fruit. The first cherries were in from the country, and he'd spent far too much on them.

"It's a mess," Richard said. He walked Alec back down the narrow stairs. "I'll tell Marie to clean it up."

Down in the courtyard, Alec could see the corners of the swordsman's mouth were white. "I'll tell her."

Marie was white, too. "I didn't," she said. "I swear."

"Didn't let the poor bastard in? I should think not."

"We know you hate cleaning up blood, Marie. It's all right."

"But who?" she said. "Who told them where you live?"

"Everyone knows where we live," Alec drawled. "It's a wonder they didn't try it before. Maybe they did and got sick of waiting last time. Don't worry about it."

"How much longer?" Richard asked, when she'd gone upstairs with her pail and some rags and sent a boy to find someone to remove the body.

"Seven days," Alec said. "And then they'll stop sending you new toys to play with."

"I don't like them messing up the house."

"Neither does Marie. I'll draw her another bucket of water. She appreciates these little gestures."

"I think," St. Vier said, "we'll sleep at Rosalie's tonight."

What was I doing out that night? Trying to earn a living, same as everyone else. The job finished early, and I was headed to Rosalie's for a drink. I wasn't trying to spy on anybody. But I saw that guy Alec come out Rosalie's back door, the one nobody uses, alone. He had a lantern. The moon was good enough for me. Alec was moving fast, but a moment later I saw St. Vier come out the same door. He didn't have a light, and I thought he'd catch up to Alec soon enough. But he didn't. St. Vier wasn't really dressed, either—shirt unlaced, jacket unbuttoned—though he did have his sword in his hand. He strapped it on as he walked, slowly and quietly, following the man with the lantern.

It didn't take a wizard to know something was up. I should've turned around and gone straight into the tavern, maybe. But I thought, *Who knows? Maybe they'll need backup.* So I followed them.

Alec went to the river, across from the University. *Good,* I thought. *He's finally going back to where he came from!* But he just stood on the bank, looking over. St. Vier stayed in the shadows, looking at Alec. When Alec moved closer to the water, St. Vier got tense, like he was thinking the beanpole might throw himself in. But then Alec moved on, walking along the embankment, trailing his hand along the low wall like it was some giant pet.

When the wall petered out he swung back into Riverside, passing through the old market, which was pretty much empty except for a few people who'd built themselves a fire to keep out the chill and the spooks til dawn. They glanced up when Alec passed, trying to make themselves small, not to be noticed. He didn't even look. St. Vier walked right by them, too, a moment later. I figured it wouldn't hurt to say hello and see if it was anyone I knew, but they weren't too friendly.

It was harder in the little streets to keep behind them. Alec was moving slower. Like it was a bright spring day and he had all the time in the world to get from Rosalie's tavern to his own lodgings. I heard St. Vier had killed a man there today.

They didn't go in. Alec leaned his head against the crumbling stone archway to the courtyard. His arm was up over his head, and his fist was clenched. He spread his fingers out slowly, ran them down the outer wall. He backed away slowly from the house, like he didn't want to let go. Even slower he walked down the street, where it was so dark we both would have lost him without the lantern.

Did he know St. Vier was following him? How could he not? How could he think he'd get so far in the night alone? And did St. Vier know it was me behind him? He must have. Or maybe not. Maybe everyone was out taking a little midnight walk that just happened to go all around Riverside. All around the places the two of them liked to eat and drink and buy things, make trouble and get out of it, kill and get talked about. All of them. Like a farewell tour.

Alec crossed Riverside, all the way to the Bridge—the good bridge, the big stone one that takes you to the side of the city with all the nice stuff: the excellent shops and pretty little houses, the wide paths by the river, where people go walking under the trees, until you climb all the way up to the Hill, where the nobles in their mansions can enjoy fresh breezes and a really good view. There are some nasty bits, too, with nasty people in them who don't care who your boyfriend is or codes of honor or anything. If Alec was planning to sneak up to Tremontaine House with his lantern in the dark, he'd better be careful.

But the dark was a little less dark now. You could see his bony, ragged form against the sky behind him. He went up to the Bridge, but didn't cross it—didn't even set one foot on it. He just stood there, staring at the city. Then he held his lantern up high, high over his head, like he was showing it to the river, or showing the whole world where he stood. And he goes and throws the whole thing far out into the water.

Alec turned around, then, back to Riverside, back to us. I couldn't see his face, but I heard his voice. "Richard?" he asked, into the graying light.

The funny thing was, he was looking in the wrong direction.

St. Vier stepped out of the shadows. "Let's go home."

They walked right past me.

Most people in Riverside lock their doors if they own anything of value, but Richard St. Vier had gotten out of the habit. This morning, though, he found the door to their rooms locked tight. They had to go back down to Marie's to get her key.

She handed them the cold old iron. "You'll want to keep this. I'll put a gate over the courtyard entry, too, maybe. Should I?"

"Not yet."

Their rooms were spotless, the old elmwood floor scrubbed almost white. "Like the pages of a book," said Alec. He took a burnt stick from the hearth and wrote something on the floor with it, then scuffed it out with his foot, leaving a charcoal smear.

Richard stood in the middle of the room. The furniture was off. It had been knocked around during the fight, of course, and then Marie had moved it to do the floor and not put it back exactly right. She'd missed a spot of blood on the wall. He pulled the chaise longue back to its place between the window and the fireplace. The inlaid table Alec had pawned his velvet coat for should be closer to the wall. He remembered the day Alec had reappeared in Riverside, fresh from his last fight with the duchess, groceries in hand and tiny shards of glass still glittering on the shoulders of that coat.

Alec flung himself into their ratty old chaise longue. Stuffing oozed. He twisted uncomfortably, got up, took a book from the pile on the mantelpiece—which Marie had dusted and straightened—and tried the chaise again.

Richard went into the next room, where his opponent had been hiding, waiting. It looked all right, but he hated knowing anyone had been in there. He opened his sword chest. Everything seemed in place. He took out a practice sword and went back to the front room to work. For a while, the room was quiet except for the rhythmic thud of his feet on the floor, the sword on the wall.

Then Alec looked up from the book he hadn't been reading. "Richard," he said, "let's go to Tremontaine House."

"All right." Richard put the sword up. "When?"

"How long will it take you to change your shirt?"

"And you? Are you going to change?"

Alec considered his own frayed cuffs. "No. No, I don't think so."

He pulled on his scholar's robe and then went out the door and down the stairs without looking back.

Richard did not stop to change his shirt; he grabbed the nearest decent sword and followed Alec down the narrow stairs, catching up with him on the landing. Alec didn't say anything; he just kept walking. Walking toward the Bridge. He walked down the narrow lanes where the old houses practically touched each other in perpetual twilight. He walked along the streets where the gutters overflowed, past the lion fountain with the broken nose where women were washing linens.

And then it turned into a story. That's the only way he could describe it.

"Where are you going?" asked Lucy Diver, and when Alec answered "Tremontaine House," Lucy put down her washing and said, "Oh, yeah? Mind if I come, too?" Alec shrugged, *Why not?* and Lucy did.

They walked through the Market Square, and people looked up from their trading in fresh-caught fish and stolen watches.

"Hey, Alec!" Toothless John called out. "I got good trout for you today!"

But Alec didn't stop.

"Where are you going?" John asked, and Lucy answered, "Tremontaine House!" and John fell in with them.

They came upon Fat Rodge and Hal, and "Where are you going?" they asked, and John answered, "Up the Hill," and they came along, too.

They picked up three or four more this way, and after that people just started joining because it was a crowd, and it was a nice day to be going somewhere new.

I was one of the ones who marched that day, the day that funny kid Alec became the Duke Tremontaine.

A whole big bunch of us parading through Riverside, drunk and sober, some at the end of their day and some just starting out, because everyone likes to be in on the action. The girls were waving ribbons in the air, and everyone was singing something different. St. Vier was guarding all of us, like some crazy wedding procession, and other swordsmen joined in, too, making a very nice appearance.

For a guy with a mouth like that on him, Alec was awful quiet. In fact, I don't think he ever said a word. Just kept on walking, a beanpole in black, paying no attention to anyone around him, just walking like he knew if he stopped the whole thing would fall apart. Sometimes we even had to run to keep up with him.

When we got to the Bridge, we kept right on going. We marched through the city, past all the shops and the fancy houses, singing and carrying on, laughing as people fell back out of our way, and we heard them shouting and screaming and calling to each other to run away or to come and see. Some even lined up, cheering. I heard "Riverside!" and "Tremontaine!" and a whole lot else, besides. But we didn't stop. We marched all the way up the broad streets to the Hill, past all those high walls and gold-and-iron gates, until we came to the biggest and fanciest, the one that was Alec's, and they had to let him in.

We lifted him up on our shoulders and carried him all the way there—over the Bridge, all the way up the Hill to Tremontaine House.

After all, he was one of ours.

Oblivion by Calvin Klein

BY CHRISTOPHER FOWLER

Christopher Fowler has written more than thirty novels and volumes of short stories, including *Roofworld, Spanky, Psychoville,* and *Calabash*. He lives in King's Cross, London.

His work divides into black comedy, horror, satire, mystery, and sets of tales unclassifiable enough to have publishers tearing their hair out. He is now writing the Bryant & May series, a set of classic mystery novels featuring two elderly, argumentative London detectives. In 2009 his autobiography, *Paperboy,* was published.

About this story, he says, "I had been planning a novel about a shopaholic housewife-turned-vigilante for some while, and it proved to be one of those books everyone seems to love but no one manages to publish—indeed, it recently got to page proofs before the last publishing house collapsed. So with the character still in my head, I freewheeled an urban fantasy around her to create something entirely new. My visions of cities are always happiest in their decline, so it was important to have an exotic, apocalyptic feel to this tale. It's about a fracture in the consumption cycle that might just turn out to be a good thing. . . ."

On the dankest, most miserable Saturday afternoon in September, Helen Abbott went shopping in London with a Derringer .25 sub-compact pistol in her handbag.

The term *shopping* hardly seemed adequate. What Helen did was blast through Selfridges department store like an armed witch on a mission. Spending money was an intimate thing for her, so she made sure she knew the entire history of the places where she shopped, just as it was a point of honor to memorize the names of all the assistants who offered her their services. She was such a familiar face in Selfridges that the store detectives kept an eye on her, thinking she must be part of some long-term thieving reconnaissance party. She did not look poor, of course, so they suspected her less. She always dressed for shopping as if going on a date: smart beige patent-leather heels and a sleek chocolate-toned skirt, never jeans or trainers, because she was anxious to be noticed and treated with respect.

It was not a good idea to shop in a highly emotional state. On that day, frenzied by the latest proof of her husband's infidelity (a used Durex Fetherlite condom tossed carelessly onto the back seat of his Mercedes—worse than last time, when it was just a gold earring), she was one thin step away from sitting down in the middle of the street and screaming. Convinced that shopping in quantity released pheromones, she ticktacked at a furious speed across the marble floors, ankles flashing back and forth, charm bracelet jangling, begging the buzz to kick in.

The remains of the summer season fashions had been left on the shelves like hard centers discarded in a ravaged chocolate box, the sales staff as listless and fractious as children trapped in class. As she circumnavigated the territory, a hunter-gatherer on a search for hangered prey, she pushed ever deeper into the undergrowth of her desires.

It was a good way to spend the day.

Lately Helen Abbott had become fascinated with the textures of fashion fabrics, and as she walked she mentally alphabetized them into alpaca, astrakhan, batiste, brocade, cotton, calico, cambric, cheviot, chiffon, chenille, crepe de chine, cretonne, and corduroy. By the time she arrived at damask, denim, and dimity she had already made her first purchase and lost her place in the lexicon of luxury.

Helen had given up on her marriage and her dreams, and only the thought of finding new ways to spite her husband kept her from slitting her own throat. She hated Graham and all of his relatives with an intensity that frightened her. The best way to remain calm, she had found, was to fight through every inch of the day. That was why she booked sessions of yoga, pilates, step classes, aerobics, rowing, and weight training. Six months ago her husband tried to strangle her in a restaurant, and she broke his wrist. The fitness kick was wearing off, though. Last week she had been thrown out of her local spa's flotation tank for smoking in it.

Helen used to work for a small publishing company in the West End, where she became a kind of hero figure because of her inventive rudeness to men, but they took away her job when she got pregnant, and couldn't restore it to her when she lost the baby, because it would have looked too obvious. Now she worked for a media company where nothing discernible was produced. A photograph of her office would have offered no clues to her purpose in the world. She was paid an astonishing amount of money to send pointless e-mails and sit in meetings saying nothing. Voicing an opinion was a good way to get fired. When people asked what she did for a living—not that they ever did—she told them that she showed up for work.

Helen never watched TV, because TV was for poor people. Besides, the news was all bad. She never went for a walk, because the streets were unthinkable. So she shopped, passing through the outdoor part of her world as quickly and quietly as possible. Shopping at Selfridges was warm rain on bare skin. The cyclamen zephyrs that drifted over her from the perfumery inflamed her membranes. She loved the way ice-blue counters underlit the ceramic faces of the cosmetic clerks, turning them into mannequins. Their frozen tableaux set her pulse racing. They drifted about her with testers and face brushes as if wielding sacrificial tools in some arcane, forgotten rite.

In housewares, the hanging crescendos of copper pots tightened Helen's chest muscles until she could barely breathe. There were no stains in these stage kitchens, because no food was ever cooked. Sometimes she pulled open the counter drawers and breathed in their emptiness. She studied the beds covered with purple-beaded casbah cushions, the pastel French cotton sheets imprisoned in plastic as smooth as plate glass, the polished maple dining tables laid for guests who would never ruin everything by turning up. When she touched the smokily elegant vases too slender to hold grocery store flowers but perfectly designed for a single arum lily, she felt safe in the arms of manufacturers.

After shopping, she always wanted a cigarette and a soapy wash, because the entire process was about sex. Buying an inappropriate dress was the equivalent to a thoughtless one-night stand, whereas designer shoes constituted a long-term commitment filled with recrimination and at least one decent orgasm. She hadn't been penetrated for over eighteen months. At first the dull ache of desire would not go away, but after a while it no longer bothered her. These days her clitoris was located somewhere near Harrods.

As she swept through Oxford Street's great cathedral of expenditure, she pondered on the verb *to spend.* It had a sexual connotation, of course, to empty the juices, to flush out, but she wondered why people talked about "spending days," as though everything was currency. She felt spent. The world felt spent.

Helen really wanted a cigarette. She smoked because it annoyed her husband to find cigarette butts left in egg yolks, coffee cups, toilets, and beds. She sunbathed naked in the garden because it annoyed the neighbors, took ages at supermarket tills because it annoyed the staff, and lit up in restaurants just to watch the look of horror on diners' faces. These days nonsmokers reacted to cigarette smoke as if they had just been involved in a Sarin gas attack. Sometimes they actually screamed.

Fuck 'em, thought Helen. There are bigger things to worry about; we just pretend there aren't. How well we all pretend.

Everyone agreed that Graham Abbott was an absolute sweetheart who doted on his wife, but the gentler and kinder he was, the more she detested him and the more he fucked around. He sold false ceilings and had a number of gastric disorders that required him to pick at small amounts of food all day so that she never needed to cook for him at night, which was just as well because the only thing she could do was eggs, an egg being the one food source you actually have to damage to eat.

Helen insolently tapped her gold card against capped teeth as she considered different sweater designs. The staff prowled after her like hungry dogs.

There was always an adrenaline rush when she bought something really expensive, a race of blood cells to the brain and heart as she pressed her card into the reader and watched the assistant delicately folding tissue as if packing a rare dead insect for a long voyage by steamer trunk.

On she went, past the TV monitors of starved catwalk girls dipping at the turn of the runway, up into menswear, a square acre of wood, chrome, and marble where everything smelled of citrus, musk, and leather—all the things she had never smelled on her husband, who only smelled of cigarettes and computers. Soon she was carrying so many purchases that the bag ropes left Japanese-prisoner-of-war marks on her arms.

Through the food hall with its aged ham hocks hanging like the thighs of long-dead chorus girls, past rows of shocked fish arranged on ice like jeweled purses, past the jars of exotic pickles as mysterious as fetuses in a medical museum, to the perfume counters patrolled by women like bony cats, where she stood paralyzed, breathing deep the smell of frangipani, honeysuckle, gardenia, jasmine, lavender, carnation, eucalyptus, lemon, sandalwood, and ambergris. The atomizers, sprays, sachets, pomanders, powders, potpourris, balms, gels, oils, soaps, lotions, sticks, and fixatives pumped such a sweet cacophony into the air that the hall shimmered and slipped in her vision.

She breathed deeper.

In fact, she breathed so deeply that she passed out, like an art lover suffering from Stendhal syndrome.

Helen Abbott regained consciousness to find a gold-braided attendant leisurely picking his nose while peering into her shopping bags and evaluating the contents. As she revived, he mimed such an extravagant show of helping her to her feet that he attracted a crowd, which he was then able to disperse by imperiously waving his gloved hands about like a policeman on point duty until she could gather her purchases and make a break for the exit.

Sometimes Helen shoplifted. Today she stuck her hand into her skirt pocket and closed pearlized nails around a pair of earrings. They were golden yellow sunflowers, bright, cheerful, fake looking. She owned a lot of plastic jewelery because there were wonderful colors in plastic that you couldn't find in nature. Whenever she flew on a shopping raid over the West End, she bought something for her charm bracelet. On this trip it was a 22-carat gold teddy bear with a tiny secret compartment in its stomach, an object of such utter vacuity that it actually defied you to find a use for it.

Helen Abbott understood a fundamental principle, that shopping was the one thing you could do without ever having to be frightened. It was a sacred rite that had become her strength and guidance. Conventional religion offered salvation in the afterlife, but shopping provided immediate absolution. It had the power to heal, to save and restore. Helen felt she would make a fantastic worshipper in a cargo cult.

She stroked the barrel of the gun in her purse and stepped into the street.

As she exited from the main entrance of Selfridges, she felt as though she were leaving the shelter of the church. The edges of Oxford Street were crusted with rough sleepers, like calcium deposits around a drain. Along the tops of the Victorian buildings, running indiscriminately over the once-graceful roofs and windows, were red dot-matrix reports filled with news so bad that no one read them anymore. She passed a Gap store, and the irony of its name did not escape her. The only gap here was the one between rich and poor. She rushed home as if passing through the atmosphere of a hostile planet.

Helen started chain-smoking when outdoors and drinking hard liquor from ten in the morning. There were two blenders in her kitchen—one for her husband's fruit shakes (he had high cholesterol) and the other for banana daiquiris. The house was empty from 8:00 A.M. to 8:00 P.M. six days a week, so on her days off Helen was able to spend the day alone, peering through the heavily barred windows, honing her bitterness. At her fitness center she repented with leg weights every morning, but then she came home and sinned again, hitting the drinks cabinet with a level of vengeful punishment that was usually only found among nuns.

That week, while the rainy gales of a London summer scoured the increasingly derelict suburban streets, Helen's house grew so cold that only her startling bursts of anger could heat it back to life. Her husband stayed out late, then stopped coming home at all.

On the last fishtank-gray Saturday afternoon of the month, Helen headed for a less-exclusive shopping mall on the outskirts of town. Its neon corridors were populated by taut-faced teenaged girls with hoop earrings and bare midriffs, their ponytails threaded through diamanté baseball caps, their plastic push-chairs imprisoning stupefied tots. Consumers drifted in stately distance like Seurat figures. There were nearly a dozen megastores linked by a central car park. With her pupils widened and her tubes unblocked by so many glittering second-rate retail opportunities, Helen set off to smack up her American Express card.

First of all she bought shoes, not real ones for walking in, but a pair for slowly crossing her legs on a bar stool and sending young men into inarticulate conflictions of desire. The sight of the gaudy heels sparkling on a black velvet dais like some rediscovered Peruvian artifact overrode the genetic defenses that governed her ability to think logically. They were so obscenely expensive that she had to screw up her eyes to look at the bill.

Then it was time to hit Inhabit, a furniture shop where she unthinkingly purchased a spindle-legged Regencia table nest, a Locarno foldaway lounge serving unit, a carriage clock, a dozen silver-trimmed tablemats depicting scenes from the Crimean War, and a huge china statue of a leopard scratching its claws on a tree. She arranged to have them delivered and gave a false address: Helen Blimpton, 666 Dingley Dell, Bombokoland. Nobody questioned the delivery instructions. They merely loaded them into the computer with a holding smile and printed out her receipts.

In Petland, she put a deposit on a Borzoi puppy and an inbred hairless cat that you had to wipe down all the time. By the time she reached Sparkles, the discount jewelry outlet, she was being trailed by a suspicious security guard. The assistant refused to let her open an account there because she had become confused about her fake home address and foolishly presented the girl with three options, each of them more ridiculous than the one before.

When Helen surveyed a rack of Diamonique "Catherine the Great" choker necklaces, the strange gleam in her eye made the security guard wonder whether she was on day release, or at least coming off medication. Either way, he watched as she slipped a three-band-clasp wristlet into her jacket pocket on the way to the exit. Seconds later, he pinned her over a display case of rather desirable handbags. The police were called and the manager sent for. When the cops showed up they seemed more interested in discussing the previous night's football.

The manager of Sparkles was a slender Asian man with thrust-up hair and a permanently surprised look on his face, as though he had just walked away from a car accident. He spoke with the guard, and when he recognized Helen, his expression became even more surprised.

"You know this lady?" asked one of the cops.

"She's a regular customer. Please let her sit down."

Helen collapsed on a divan as the manager explained that it was probably just an unfortunate mistake and that he would not press charges. She felt sure he knew she was guilty, but he let her go, preferring to protect someone he considered to be a long-term investment. She would return, he hoped, to gratefully spend a fortune in his store the next time she was afflicted with a shopping brain-cloud.

She needed to clear her head and start thinking straight, so she shared a mug of coffee with the manager, who politely suggested that she might like to arrange twenty-four-month payment plans with him. She agreed so enthusiastically that she felt guilty about climbing out of the window of the ladies' toilet and legging it across the car park to the next store.

In World of Washrooms, her MasterCard (such a manly, sadistic name) appeared for fresh purchases. Above her, "Material Girl" played from hidden speakers at just the right volume required to send people mad. This particular corporate CD of shopping's greatest hits had been rescored for bongos, Moog and theremin, making Helen feel as if she had wandered into an old science fiction film.

For the sheer hell of it, she bought a freestanding chrome towel rack, two Rhapsody molded-ceramic toothbrush sconces, an onyx soap holder shaped like buttocks, the Comfort luxury Dralon candlewick pedestal mat available in avocado or pink martini, and a LadyPore magnifying mirror with built-in makeup tray. The staff nearly had to pull her off the shag-covered faux-bamboo laundry hamper and combi-heated towel rail.

She reached the end of the chrome-railed floor and snapped a vacant sales assistant from her reverie. The girl asked her how she would like to pay. With a gunslinger's wrist-flick Helen withdrew the MasterCard and placked it onto the counter with a sound as satisfying as the snap of her husband's condom coming off. The assistant rang everything up, then zipped the card through her credit link. While she waited, she stared into the middle distance and touched the edges of her lacquered hair as if gingerly reading braille. When she checked the readout, her cheeks crinkled very slightly, as though she had just experienced the misery of trapped wind.

"I'm afraid this one is invalid," she explained, returning it. "There might be a fault with the card." She didn't believe it for a second and wanted Helen to know that she didn't, despite the necessity of maintaining the store's politeness policy. Helen knew her type. She could read more nuances into the guarded smiles of service personnel than Marcel Proust.

Sudden insolvency was an unusual and unpleasant experience. She casually riffled through her purse and submitted a less-scorched card, and when that didn't work, a third. In a mounting state of mortification, she went through seven more, but none of them registered. She could feel sweat forming in the small of her back. She had no checkbook anymore—who did?—and had no other way of paying. Finally the assistant jealously took back her products, like a peep-show manager deciding that her viewing time was up.

Helen could tell that the assistant was disappointed with her, a teacher marking an F on her favorite pupil's work. Her customer respect vanished as she desecrated the freshly packed treasures. Helen could not bear it; watching her tear open the tissue wrappings was like watching someone rip orchids apart. She had been cheated of her shopping climax. It wasn't as though she'd been looking forward to taking everything home—that part of the process was a post-coital duty, like remaking the bed—so she mumbled some excuse about having accidentally demagnetized her strips and fled.

Outside on the street, she felt shockingly exposed. The nonshoppers around her all seemed drunk, stoned, or mad. A fat man with a shaved ginger head was being copiously sick into an octagonal concrete litter bin filled with McDonald's boxes. Her fingers closed over the Derringer in her bag, warming it. Another man passed her with blood pouring down the center of his face, as if his head had been split in two. The poor always seemed to be fighting each other instead of going after someone rich. They shot up schools instead of storming into financial institutions.

There were no buses in sight. The sky was a strange color. Helen felt unusual.

Her purse yielded seven pounds fifty, not enough for a taxi. She hated the thought of being packed like pencils on a filthy train and arriving home in a sticky sheen of sweat, to sit in the kitchen staring at the spot where her crisp white cardboard bags should be standing. She knew Graham had canceled her cards in revenge for being exposed once more as an adulterer. He was authorized to do that; he played golf with her bank manager.

She needed a drink. She had stopped keeping vodka and orange premixed in a bleach container under the sink after swigging from the wrong bottle. Shopping bred a discontent that could only be assuaged by more spending. Drug addiction would have been a healthier option; at least she wouldn't have to monitor her weight and would get regular sex from strangers.

Beneath clouds the color of rancid liver, she walked to the nearest vehicle in the car park, a crapped-up blue Renault Megan.

The driver was surprised but made no attempt to take the gun from her. The Derringer was welded to her hand, its steel casing matched to her body temperature. She waggled it at him, opened the passenger door, and slipped inside. She noticed his eyes, brown with black lashes, dirty curls over a single dark eyebrow.

"What do you want?" he asked, genuinely puzzled.

"What's your name?"

"Nathan. Who are you?"

"Helen." She slapped the dashboard with her free hand. "Drive."

Nathan insisted she should keep the gun pointed toward the floor while they were inside the car, which turned out to be a good move, because the handle was so slick with sweat that she dropped it under the seat when they hit the first traffic-calming chicane. They rode like this for a while, past burned-out homes that backed right up against luxury stores.

"Pull in here."

"Now what?" he asked, calmly putting the gearshift into park.

"I shop for clothes and you pay for everything."

"How is this going to work?" asked Nathan. They were walking toward the bright glass entrance of another mall. "How are you going to try on dresses in a cubicle while keeping a gun trained on me?"

"I won't have to try anything on. I'm just going to buy things. I know my size in seventeen different countries of manufacture, so I'll only have to use a fitting room if I see something I like from Estonia or Portugal."

"You're a retail opportunist."

"And you're on my territory now," Helen warned him. "If shopping was a university course, I'd have a chair at Oxford." She wondered if she had gone too far this time. Her condition seemed to be getting out of hand.

"I think you've got a problem."

"Nothing I can't handle. In here."

They walked into DKNY half an hour before the store was due to shut. Helen kept her eyes on her hostage. Nathan seemed vaguely amused by her behavior.

She swept up a whole new wardrobe: jumpers, jackets, belts, and pairs of jeans from the racks. Whenever Nathan turned around to complain or to ask where they were going next, she allowed the gleaming barrel of the gun to become visible behind her bag, like a flasher exposing himself to a child. She picked up a trouser suit and a pair of rhinestone evening sandals from Dolce & Gabbana, then pushed Nathan in the direction of Marks & Spencer. She no longer cared whether the CCTV could see her.

"What do you think, the gray or the blue?" she asked, holding different brassieres against her breasts.

"I don't know, I really don't care," her hostage replied sulkily.

She let him see the muzzle of the gun. "Make a decision."

"The blue. This is like being married." Nathan shoved his hands into his pockets. "Do you want me to sit down over there and leaf through magazines while you rob the till?" He was sexy in a degenerate way, probably about the same age as her but more worn in. He seemed less concerned about being shot than being embarrassed.

She changed her clothes in the cubicle with Nathan

standing on the other side and the gun trained through the door. Balancing on one leg like an armed flamingo was not an easy thing to do. Shopping had been her drug of choice, and she had gone for one final overdose, hoping it would now be out of her system. She applied some lipstick while targeting Nathan in the makeup mirror, Annie Oakley attempting a trick shot. As she did so, she caught sight of a cashier peering at them around a rack of remaindered skirts, but when she looked back, the girl had vanished.

"Just stay close enough for me to kill you if I have to." She piled her hostage high and aimed him at the checkout.

On the way, Nathan's mobile rang. She nudged him with the gun barrel. "Answer it."

He listened for a moment. "Hi. No, I'm not going to be able to get there." He covered the phone. "It's my mother. She wants to know where I am. Where am I?" He took a look around. "Marks & Spencers. We're in mixed separates, but I think we're heading for knickers and pantyhose. No, I haven't met someone."

They waited awkwardly by the counter as a listless cashier detagged the items and folded them into carrier bags. Helen felt the burning panic that had been roaring about inside her receding as each purchase received its tissue-paper prepuce. Nathan withdrew a platinum AmEx card and handed it to the cashier. She almost fell in love with him.

"What's next?" Nathan asked as they moved toward the exit. Overhead, a soothing voice told them the stores were closing and reminded customers to remain security-conscious as they made their way to the car park. Helen was disappointed because there was a Cartier concession on the first floor and she'd have liked a platinum love-bracelet. Nathan had gotten off lightly.

"Give me a minute," she told him. "I'll think of something."

"You're a very unusual woman."

"Call me Helen."

"So, what do you want to do now, Helen?" he asked. "Dinner? Arson? Blackmail? When you abduct someone, it's a good idea to have a plan."

She had no answer for him. Now that she had shopped, the familiar thrill was fading to postcoital guilt. They reached the car with a trolley full of purchases, and he began loading them onto the rear seat.

"You don't know, do you?" He pushed. "Look in the back of the car, all the clothes you don't want. People get so restless they don't know what to do with themselves. You have to figure this out. What the hell is it you want?"

"I don't know how I turned into this horrible person," she said, trying not to let her face twitch. "We're given too much and it's not enough."

"So go and find yourself."

"I don't want to find myself; I want to find someone else."

"What, you want me to feel sorry for you? I have to go to work. You can come with me, but put the fucking gun away."

Nathan ran a soup-and-sandwich van for the homeless, under a dripping railway arch. The services were dying out, he said. They had become unfashionable and could no longer find sponsors. He recited the facts, a sermon he had delivered too many times: The average life expectancy of those below the poverty line was forty; two paupers died on the London streets every day; the homeless could stand three weeks of sleeping rough before long-term problems set in; a simple state of divorce was enough to force you into the open air. Perhaps a speech was required before the doling out of food, she thought, like a Victorian lecture.

Helen remembered a mauve cotton sweater, a purchase on

her last spree. It had been carefully folded into white tissue with its arms crossed like a mummy carapace, then placed into a stout blue box with a diagonal purple ribbon knotted at one corner. It had cost nearly seven hundred pounds. She watched Nathan serving free day-old cheese sandwiches, donated to make the difference between getting by and going hungry.

A young man in a fur hood leaned against the wall of the arch, noisily pissing. When he realized she was standing nearby he braked in mid-flow.

"Don't let me stop you," she said, raising a hand and averting her eyes.

"You're in my bathroom, lady." The young man buttoned his fly and spat at her legs.

She waited in the cold as Nathan handed out sandwiches to a line that showed no sign of diminishing. A little after midnight, he closed the van and drove her to the edge of the Thames. They walked across a litter-strewn concourse as bare as a disused runway, to a yellow metal ship's container butted up against a beech tree. Nathan slipped into a diagonal shadow. Helen hesitated.

Nathan beckoned. "Not everyone is out to hurt you."

He opened a padlock on a dented steel panel and shoved the door back with a ferrous scrape. "Wait." He disappeared inside.

A match flared, and gradually the interior of the oblong box was illuminated. The container was constructed of flat steel panels without windows, but it had been decorated like the Bosphorus *selamlik* of a Turkish pasha. Rolls of handmade silk in sharp shades of purple, yellow, and blue swathed the walls. A carved Emery-wood table was covered in copper bowls and fat stone jugs. A divan covered in crushed crimson velvet stood on a tattered Persian rug. Cupboards were rubbed-down river driftwood, bleached white. A black cat with yellow eyes stretched itself across a pile of cushions.

"It's all stuff people have chucked away. Have a glass of wine. I doubt it's what you're used to. Your skin's so pale. Is it as soft as it looks?" He teased out the words with his hands.

"You live here when you're not at the sandwich van?"

"I spend most of my time on building sites. I'm working on the electrics at the mall." He pulled up his T-shirt to reveal a belt lined with different drill bits, like gun cartridges. His stomach was flat and brown.

"But you have a platinum credit card."

"It belongs to a dead guy. I found his body in one of the offices this morning. It'll run out soon."

"And the car?"

"That belongs to my mother. What do you do?"

"I spend."

"Is that all?"

"Pretty much."

"Where did you get the gun?"

"I bought it. I had a fantasy of using it for target practice in Selfridges homewares department. Not on people, on soft furnishings."

"I thought you loved all that shit."

"It's complicated. The things I own usually end up owning me. My signature scent has its own Web site, for God's sake."

Nathan smiled. "There's nothing to be afraid of. This is just what happens when the world collapses. It's a perfectly natural thing. Gounod said, 'Our houses are not in the street any more; the street is in our houses.'"

"What happens after that?"

"Oh, both the streets and the houses disappear and we start all over again. I think you're helping to speed up the process." He filled two scratched blue tumblers with wine from a box. They touched glasses and drank. Nathan watched her with amusement.

"You say there's nothing to be afraid of. I've been afraid all my life. You don't seem afraid."

"Do you know about the legend of the Green Man? It's a pagan myth that exists in almost every history of England, but you can find him in many churches. There are sixty depictions of the Green Man in Exeter Cathedral alone. He goes back far beyond Christian legends."

"Who is he?"

"A forest creature that destroys dying cities and returns them to nature. The result of mixing sex and soil. He's benign and terrifying. He has a leafy face and tendrils sprouting from his mouth and nose. His hair is made from grass; his body is made from roots and flowers and branches. He is both cruel and gentle. He's coming back to turn the cities into forests."

"How do you know he's coming back?"

"He lives inside everyone."

"Including you?"

"Including me. And you."

"I think I should go."

Nathan suddenly leaned forward and kissed her, pushing hard. His right hand slipped across her stomach and up to her breasts. The left supported her in the small of her back. It seemed a good idea to lie down on the velvet divan, especially as his mouth was still glued to hers and was gently forcing her in that direction. He weighed almost nothing; she could hardly feel him straddled across her. Instead, she felt the warmth of his thighs where they touched her hips, his forearms against the sides of her chest, a wide tongue reaching into the back of her mouth for what seemed like days.

At some point later—she could not remember when—his shirt came off, and she heard buttons bouncing on the floor. His dark, soft skin smelled of sandalwood and underarm sweat that lingered on her fingers. The base of his erection pressed a denim-clad post against her crotch as he unpinned her arms and guided her hands around his hard buttocks. His chest hair formed a perfect black trapezoid, a ladder of tiny curls tracing to his navel and into the low waistband of his loosened jeans. The wide dry palm of his hand covered her pubic bone as he slipped his fingers inside her pants. The shock of a young man's cool bare hand over her sex was extraordinary; she could not recall the last time someone had cupped her so gently, opening her lightly with the tips of his fingers.

Helen sank deep into the cushions, her chocolate skirt sliding from her legs. For so long she had been constricted by the curse of propriety, strapped into a sensible brassiere and expected to behave as if she were shocked and disapproving all the time, but what was all the respectability for? What had the city given her back, apart from a wider choice of fabric patterns?

She knew she wanted him inside her, and allowed him to push her deeper into musky warm darkness, the muscles in his slim brown arms lifting and widening as he raised his body over hers, each firmly guided stroke burying a hot dark beam farther and farther into her flesh, until she could feel his stomach tense and their raised pelvic bones grate hard against each other, a cauterizing molten center to their joined bodies that could light up the little cabin and provide enough electrical power for most of the shops in Oxford Street.

It was a seduction conducted backward, starting with the

fierce, hard culmination, his eyes never leaving hers, his body pulling back and pushing in with decreasing connection, penetrate and withdraw, gentler and gentler, resolving to a faint and tender kiss.

Some minutes later, she realized he was sitting beside her, smoking. She dressed slowly and carelessly.

"Come back if you like," he said over his shoulder. "I'll be here." She could not see his smile, but knew it was wide and white and dangerous. She didn't care how much he had practiced it on other women; she liked the idea of being one of the other women. It made her feel normal somehow, involved, part of something powerful.

Rising carefully to her feet and testing the ground to stop it from swaying, she tried not to lose her balance. She smoothed her hair back behind her ears in an attempt to look vaguely sensible and in control, and pulled the container door open a crack as Nathan refastened his jeans and took a slug of wine.

Outside, she drew a deep breath of dank river air, trying to work out exactly what had just happened. Although it was still night, a warm gray nimbus of never-darkness profiled the skyline of the embankment. In contrast, Nathan's cabin was a black silhouette. In the center of one of the most overcrowded cities in the world, it could have been a chateau in rural France, beset by cawing crows and claw-branched trees, shunned by villagers, abandoned to old gods.

Her lurid yellow shopping bags lay scattered around the cabin like votive offerings of giant sweets. A stray cat emerged from one of them and yowled.

She looked up at the swirling sky. Something had changed. The air was alive with small insects. She thought she could hear the roots of trees crackling like scalded ice as they meandered beneath the softening tarmac of the road.

Helen Abbott breathed deeply. With each passing second she felt darker than the night and brighter than the stars. Something was kindling and catching within her. She could smell it in her nostrils, a freshness stronger and sharper than Clarins Sheer Citrus Moisturizing Mist or Coco De Mer Bitter Chocolate Body Butter.

In fact, when she tried to think of all those spot-lit branded jars and bottles lined up on the store shelves, she could only conjure images of exploding glass and splattering ointments. Rack after rack of skimpy garments, bursting into flame, shriveling and browning in the heat. Packets of tights spitting droplets of molten plastic. A Plexiglas bathroom shelf unit held up by plastic mermaids, shattering into a million blunt shards. A Devonshire buffalo-grain boudoir chair blasted into scraps and springs and stuffing. A thousand sizzling pairs of nearly identical trainers, a million rugs and glasses, vases and table lamps and coffee machines and computer keyboards all catching alight and melting, lifting and rolling and blowing away.

Each department store flared up in turn with a sudden *whump* like indoor lightning, followed by the popping of lightbulbs and the gentle bubbling of gilt paintwork. They glowed fiercely and soon burned themselves out into blackened shells.

The city was now dark and dead and windy, washed with the stinging baptism of rainfall, the streets split apart by emerald offshoots springing from the sap of rapidly rising trees.

Helen shook the visions from her head. Her cheeks, breasts, buttocks, legs were burning. She dug into her bag, checked that the gun was loaded, aimed it high and fired a single bullet into the sky. Then she hurled the Derringer as hard as she could in the direction of the river and headed home.

Her high heels were starting to pinch her, so she took them off and walked barefoot across the concrete toward the station. In the warmth left by her departing soles, grass sprouted up through the cracks in the pavement.

Fairy Gifts

BY PATRICIA BRIGGS

Patricia Briggs is the number-one *New York Times* bestselling author of the Mercy Thompson and the Alpha and Omega series as well as a number of traditional fantasy novels. She was born and raised in Butte, Montana, a city steeped in stories and storytellers—and the odd hobgoblin or two. She currently lives in eastern Washington State with her husband, children, and various and numerous animals.

Butte, Montana, present day, mid-December

Cold didn't bother him anymore, but he *remembered* how it felt: the sharp bite of winter on toes, fingers, nose, and ears. Even with modern adaptations, ten degrees below zero wouldn't be pleasant. Neither the temperature nor falling snow kept people out of the streets for the Christmas stroll, however. Hot apple cider, freshly made sausages, and abundant cookies under the streetlights strove to make up for the nasty weather—none of which were useful sustenance for him. He passed them by with scarcely a glance.

Well, then, he thought, impatient with himself, *what* are *you doing here?* He had no more answer now than he'd had two nights ago when he'd arrived.

The people who lived in the old mining town had always known how to party. In a hundred years that hadn't changed. Brutal climate, hard and dangerous work brought a certain clarity to the need for pleasure.

His Chinese face garnered a few looks—curiosity, no more. A century ago, Butte had had a large Chinese population. Then, the looks he'd garnered had been dismissive up on the street level but full of eagerness or fear down in his father's opium den in the mining tunnels where Thomas had been both guide and enforcer.

It was not just the looks that had changed. The streets were not cobbled, there were no trolleys, no horses. Steep streets had been somewhat tamed, and the town—once a bustling place—had a desolate air, despite the festive decorations. Buildings he remembered were abandoned or gone altogether, replaced by parking lots or parks. The few restored or well-kept buildings only made the rest look worse.

Some of the changes were vast improvements. The smelters and ore-processing plants now long closed meant that the sulfurous fog that had made it difficult to see across the street was gone. The air was immensely more pleasant to breath. The night was free of the constant noise of the machinery that churned day and night.

The crowd that moved beside him on the sidewalks was a respectable size, though much smaller than those that had filled the streets of his memories. He hadn't decided to count that on the good side or the bad side of the changes.

He put his hands in front of his mouth and blew, a gesture

to blend in, no more. Even had his hands been frozen, his breath wouldn't warm them.

He didn't know why he'd come back here. Just in time for the Christmas stroll, no less. He wasn't a Christian, despite the nuns who had ensured he could read and write: an education for her children was the only thing his quiet, obedient mother had ever stood up to his father for.

If . . . *if* he did believe, he'd have to believe he was damned, and had been since his father had brought him to the old man.

Butte, Montana, 1892, April

"*Here* is the son," his father said, his voice less clear than usual. It was hard to talk with a mouth that had been hit so many times.

Last night his father had been set upon by a group of miners who wanted opium and had not wanted to pay for it. They had beaten Father and tied him up. It had been Thomas's day to protect the shop; his older brother, Tao, was away on other business. Thomas had been shot in the arm, and while he tried to stanch the blood, one of the miners had cracked his skull with a beer bottle.

When Thomas awoke, his mother had bandaged his hurts and was crying silently as she sometimes did. From Tao, because his father would not look at him nor talk to him, he learned that his father had given the men what they wanted and more: Arsenic in the opium would ensure that they thieved from no one again. But despite the ultimate victory in the fight, his father felt that his honor and that of his family had been impinged. He made it clear that he blamed Thomas for the shame.

The next morning his father had left Tao in charge of the laundry and gone out to speak with friends. He'd been gone most of the day, and Thomas had worked hard despite his aching arm, seeking to assuage his disgrace with diligence. His uncles, his father's brothers, had stopped in with gifts of herbs, whiskey, and his grandmother's ginger cookies. They spoke to his mother in hushed whispers.

His father returned after the sun was down and the laundry storefront was closed. He hadn't said anything to the rest of the family gathered there. He'd only looked at Thomas.

"You," he'd said in English, which was the language he used when he was displeased with Thomas, because, to his father's horror, Thomas, born in America, was as fluent in English as in Cantonese. "You come."

According to his brother Tao, when Thomas was born a few weeks after his family had come to the New World, his father had given him an American name in a fit of optimism. It must have been true, but Thomas could never imagine his father being optimistic or excited about anything American.

Obediently, Thomas followed his father up the steep streets to a single-story house nestled between two new apartment buildings. There was a dead tree in the yard. Maybe it had been planted in a fit of optimism.

His father entered the unpainted door without knocking and left it to Thomas to close it behind them. The incense burning on a small table didn't quite cover a sour, charnelhouse smell. Thomas followed his father through a partially furnished front room and down the narrow and uneven stairs to the basement, where the odor of dead things was replaced by the scent of the dynamite that had been used to blast the basement into the granite that underlay the hillside.

The stairs ended in a small room lit only by a small beeswax candle. The floor beneath his feet was polished and well laid, a light-colored wood ringed by a pattern of darker. It seemed an expensive luxury to find in a basement room of a nondescript little house.

While he'd been looking at the floor, his father had continued on through a doorway, and he hurried to follow. There was something odd about this place that made his stomach clench and the hair on the back of his neck stand up. He didn't want to be left alone here.

He darted through the doorway and almost bumped into his father, who had stopped at a small entryway that dropped down a single stair and then opened up to a cavernous room. It too had only a single candle lighting it. Thomas couldn't make out the face of the man ensconced in some sort of big chair.

His father bent over with a pained grunt and set three twenty-dollar gold pieces on the floor.

"Here is the son," he said.

He put the flat of his hand on Thomas's back and thrust him toward the other man.

Not expecting the push, Thomas stumbled down the step then turned to look at his father—only to see his sandaled feet disappear up the stairway.

"The son," said the man he'd been left with. His accent was Eastern European—Slavic, Thomas thought. The Slavs were the among the latest immigrant wave that had washed over the mining town since Thomas Edison's electricity had made copper king. "Pretty boy. Come here."

Butte, Montana, present day

Though the sounds of the Christmas carols were pleasant enough, Thomas felt restless, impatient—the same feeling that had sent him driving here from San Francisco when he'd intended only an evening's drive.

Something was calling him here, and it certainly wasn't nostalgia. There wasn't much left of the town of his childhood. The last of the old whorehouses in the red-light district was falling down, and only a few buildings were left of the Chinatown where he'd grown up and died and been reborn a monster. No, he wasn't nostalgic for Butte.

This wasn't his home. He had a condo in San Francisco and another in Boston. None of his family remained here. There was nothing here for him—so why had it seemed so imperative to come?

"Hello, Tom."

He froze. It had been almost a century since he'd been in Butte. There weren't that many people who lived eighty years and still sounded so hail and hearty.

Fae.

That's why he'd had to come. He'd been called here by magic. If he hadn't been walking in the middle of a crowd, he would have snarled.

He didn't see anyone who looked familiar; the fae were like that. But he did find someone who was looking at him.

Leaning up against an empty storefront where a tobacco shop had once been was a balding man with an oddly fragile air about him. He was several inches shorter than Thomas—who wasn't exactly tall himself. The man's forehead was too large for the rest of him in the manner of some people who were born simple. Young blue eyes smiled at Thomas out of an old face.

He wore new winter boots, red mittens and scarf, and a thick down jacket.

A couple, passing by, noticed Thomas's interest and stopped.

"Nick?" The woman half ducked her head toward the little man. "Are you warm enough? There are cookies and hot chocolate in the old Miner's Bank building at the end of the block."

The male half of the couple glared suspiciously at Thomas.

"I have good new gloves," said Nick in the voice of a man but with a child's intonations. "I'm warm. I had cookies. I think I'm going to talk with my friend, Tom." He darted across the sidewalk and took Thomas's hand.

Thomas managed not to hiss or jerk his hand free. Nick, was it? His scent—at this close range—told Thomas that Nick was a hobgoblin.

"Do you live here? Or are you just visiting?" asked the man suspiciously.

"I'm visiting," said Thomas. He could have lied. Butte was smaller than it used to be, but, according to the lady who checked him into his hotel, it still had thirty thousand people living here.

His answer didn't please the man. "Nick's one of ours," he said, rocking forward on the balls of his feet like a man who'd been in a few real fights. "We watch out for him."

Ah, Tom thought. Butte's ties to Ireland had always been strong. In his day, the Irish here had set out cream in saucers outside their back doors to appease the fairies. Apparently the traditions of taking care of the Little People, changelings, and those who might be changelings were adhered to still—even if, as they clearly believed, the one they watched over was entirely human, just simpleminded.

"This is Ron," Nick the Hobgoblin said to Thomas. "He gives me rides in his yellow truck. I like yellow."

Ron who drove a yellow truck narrowed his eyes at Thomas, clearly telling him to go away, something Thomas was happy to comply with. He started to free himself.

"Tom likes tea," Nick informed them, his eyes as innocent as he was not. Not if he were a hobgoblin. "Tom likes the nighttime." He paused and with a sly smile added, "Tom likes Maggie."

Thomas's hand clenched on Nick's at hearing her name. He gave the hobgoblin a sharp look. How did the little man know about Margaret? Was *Margaret* the reason he'd been called here?

"Does he?" said the woman, with a sharp glance at Thomas. "Nick, why don't you come with us to see the singer at the old YMCA?"

Margaret.

Thomas decided that he would see what the hobgoblin wanted—and to that end, he'd have to allay the suspicions of Nick's protectors. He inclined his head respectfully toward Ron.

"Nick and I know one another," he said. "I went to school here." A long, long time ago.

"Oh," said the woman, relaxing. "Not a tourist then."

The man looked down at his watch. "If you want to catch your brother's performance, we'd better go."

As soon as those two were gone, Thomas pulled his hand away from the hobgoblin's. Mindful of the watchful glances of the people around him—the couple weren't the only ones watching out for Nick—he was gentle about it.

"Tell me, hobgoblin," he said with soft menace. "What do you know about Margaret Flanagan?"

Butte, Montana, 1900

He escorted the men through the tunnels, keeping to the front of the group so that the lanterns they carried wouldn't damage his night vision. And also because it scared them that he didn't need a lantern to find his way.

The current location of his father's opium den was a few hundred feet from where they'd started, though he'd led them through alternate routes that had added a half mile and more to the trip. It was imperative that they—mostly experienced miners, though one was a merchant's son—not be able to find their way here without a guide. First, payment was made before they entered the mines, and anyone who made it to the den was assumed to have paid their fee. Second, it made it difficult for the police to find. To ensure the location remained a secret, the den was moved every couple of weeks.

Thomas took a final turn and opened the makeshift door in invitation. The light from a dozen lanterns inside illuminated the smoky haze within. It looked like the hell the nuns had promised him.

"Tap her light, Tommy," said one of the men he'd escorted, giving him the traditional farewell wishes of a miner: When forcing a stick of explosive into a drilled hole in the granite, a miner wanted to be very careful tapping it in with his hammer.

It caught Thomas by surprise, and he took a better look at the man's face. Juhani. He'd been a Finnish boy whose father worked with the timber crews when they'd gone to school together once upon a time—twenty years and more ago. Now they were both damned—Thomas as his father's monster, Juhani Koskinen as an opium addict.

For a moment they stared at each other, then Juhani

stepped through the door into the den, followed by the rest of the men.

"Don't know why you talk to him, Johnny, my boyo," said one of them in a thick Irish lilt as Thomas closed the door, sealing them in. "He don't never talk."

Not since he'd returned from the Master as his father's new slave. What was there to say? Who would talk to him?

Even before his mother's brother, a famous scholar from a family of scholars, rescued his mother from his father's care, she had not looked upon his face if she could help it—not since he had become a monster. She had taken her other children with her when she returned to China with her brother. Thomas had been left behind.

For his father he had no words. Not that his father cared. He gave orders—and took him to the Master once a week to feed and be fed upon.

Thomas hoped his father regretted his bargain, regretted at least the necessity of the once-a-week twenty-dollar gold piece that was more than his father paid any of his workers, either in the laundry or in the opium den hidden down in the mine.

Alone, without a light of any kind, Thomas headed out deeper into the mines. The tunnels under the town were the labyrinthine result of more than three decades of every-day, round-the-clock mining. Above ground, the gallows frames of the elevators that took men down and lifted them up again when their shifts were done clearly marked the different mines. Below ground, all of the mines interconnected.

He'd heard that there were thousands of miles of tunnels and it wouldn't surprise him if that were so. The other two men who ran dens sometimes took their nonpaying customers deep into the tunnels and left them in the maze of tunnels out of which they never found their way. His father's customers all paid ahead of time or they didn't get in.

He had always been good at finding his way around the mines. Since he'd been turned, he'd gotten a lot better.

He didn't need light, didn't need to see at all. He could feel the tunnel stretch around him—and the ones above, below, and beside him, too. He could sense the areas where miners were actively digging and the ones where no one had been for a very long time. He could tell north from south, up from down, and he knew where he was in relation to the city over his head.

He never got lost in the tunnels.

It was near three in the morning. His father had gone to sleep—the men Thomas had escorted in were the very last—and Thomas was free for the rest of the night. There were boys in the den whose job it would be to rouse their customers and escort them to the surface. Thomas never had to work in the den anymore: He scared the customers. He wasn't sure if they feared him because his father used him to hurt the ones who displeased him, or if some atavistic sense warned them that he was a dangerous predator.

Thomas walked to the nearest elevator shaft—he was safely between shifts, so he didn't have to worry about the elevator cars—and began climbing down.

The darkness soothed him, as did the growing heat. It was always hot in the lower levels. He didn't need heat to survive anymore, but it had been such a luxury for him . . . before . . . that he always took pleasure in it. He climbed down until it suited him to stop a few levels above where they were actively mining. Descending the shaft pushed even his strength and abilities; he enjoyed it.

He was always alone, but somehow, deep in the heart of

the earth, with none but himself for company, he felt less so. Walking down tunnels that might not have seen people for decades, he felt comfortable in his skin and he relished it, even though it made it difficult to deny his growing hunger. Tomorrow he would have to feed.

He dreaded the feeding time. Afterward, his Master renewed his orders and made certain his fledgling understood his place. Someday, Thomas was certain, someday he would be free. But for nearly twenty years he had been slave to his father and the demon-thing that had, over a whole long year, turned him into what he was now.

He put out his hand and touched the damp earth. There was water here, underground. A huge lake, he'd been told, and streams that ran just as the creeks aboveground did. He couldn't feel the water the way he felt the earth, which spoke to his bones.

Somewhere in the darkness in front of him chains rattled.

"Please?"

A woman's voice, and Irish.

He froze where he stood. Maybe she was one of the ones who did not pay for her opium—though usually those were left much higher than this. No one but he wandered alone down here. He couldn't believe that either Mr. Wong or Mr. Luk would waste money on chains for a nonpaying customer.

"Please, help me?"

He hadn't been walking particularly quietly. She knew he was there.

The boy he'd been, Thomas Hao, would have run to the rescue. But that boy had died a long time ago and left a monster in his place.

"What would you do for me in return?" he said, breathing

in for the first time in a long time. He didn't have to, especially since he didn't speak. It made his father nervous when he didn't breathe, so he made a habit of letting his lungs sit empty.

He hadn't sensed her as he did the miners, and it bothered him. He'd assumed he could sense everyone in the tunnels, in his realm.

The chains rattled hard, agitated, as if the woman had not really believed there was someone else in the mine. "O lords and ladies, you are there," she said. "Please. My father is the Flanagan. The old one of high court. His element is fire. And I am accounted a power in my own right. Our gratitude will be yours, my word on it."

Fae. That's why he hadn't felt her. Now that he knew she was here he could sense her, but she felt so close to the sighs and groans of the earth that it was no wonder he hadn't noticed her before she'd spoken.

He avoided the fae when he could, and when he could not . . . well, the fae, unlike humans, knew exactly what he was, and they despised the monster almost as much as he despised himself.

"Please," she said.

If she were fae, chained down here, no human had done it, not this deep under the hill. He had no desire to find himself in the middle of a fae dispute.

"Sir?"

He could feel her listening. But he made no noise. This close to feeding day his heart only beat if he made it.

"You have nothing I want," he said, the words coming out hoarse and strange. He turned to go back the way he had come.

"Vampire."

He paused.

"They say there is a vampire who walks deep beneath the hill."

They must be the fae, because the humans didn't know. He didn't hunt: the Master forbade it. As a fledgling he could only take nourishment from another vampire, anyway. Taking the blood of humans did him no good at all. Every week the Master had him try it. The Master himself was agoraphobic, unable to leave his basement.

"Vampire," said the fae woman. "What do you wish most? I can grant you that."

Freedom, he thought. *If only the freedom to die.* The bleak knowledge that no one would be able to give that freedom to him until long after the remnants of Thomas Hao had been thoroughly eradicated, and there was nothing to free, made him angry with a rage that did not cloak his despair.

The sun. It had been so long since he'd walked in daylight that the hunger for it nearly eclipsed his growing thirst.

"I have power," she said. "Just tell me what you want?"

What I want, you cannot give me. And in the hopelessness of the thought, he found that he wanted her equally trapped, equally frantic, if only for a little while.

"You could feed me," he told her, his long-unused voice sharp and bitter. "I'm hungry."

"Come then," she said. "Come and drink."

No hunting, was the command. *No unwilling victims.* Sometimes the Master forgot things or did not word things carefully enough. Maybe he'd never conceived that Thomas would find a willing victim.

If he intended to stay out of fae conflicts he should walk away—but a small part of him made him hesitate. It wasn't the hunger. It was the boy he had been who wanted the woman freed. He found he couldn't ignore the boy's necessities any more than he'd ever been able to ignore the Master's. It made the monster angry.

He gave her no chance to adjust, to brace herself. He dropped beside her, gripping her head and chin. He jerked her until her neck stretched out and bit down, sinking his fangs deep. He could have made it pleasant for her; his master insisted upon it being pleasant. But he wanted her to struggle, which would force him to stop and give him an excuse not to save her, to be the monster they—the Master and his father—had made him.

Other than a gasp as he struck, though, she was silent and still against him.

Her blood tasted nothing like the Master's. It reminded him of the taffy he'd eaten when he was human. Not in the flavor, but in the feeling of richness, of self-indulgence and satisfaction.

Feeding with the Master was *carnal* in its most profane sense—pleasure and pain. When it was over, it sent his senses into a stupor and left him feeling desperate for the bath that never really cleaned the stain from his soul no matter how hard he scrubbed.

This feeding was . . . as he imagined feeding from a dragon might be—sharp and not altogether comfortable, but rich with the bottomless power of fire and earth. The fire cleansed him, the earth restored him, leaving him raw and off balance—but not filthy.

It was the first time he'd fed from someone other than the Master, and it was hard to stop. *One more pull,* he thought, *just one more.* And one more became . . . He remembered the eyes of his old Finnish friend as he headed into the opium den. It gave him the strength to stop.

She was limp and unresponsive in his hold. He sealed the wounds he'd made, regretting the roughness of his attack and wondering if he had stopped too late. He lay beside her and listened to her heart beat.

When it continued past the first few minutes, he decided that she'd survive. His hands told him that they'd only chained her feet. He slipped his fingers inside the cuffs and broke them, one at a time. The flesh beneath was blistered, and her feet were bare. His clever hands told him also that she was young, far younger than she'd sounded—thirteen or fourteen, he thought, and clad in her nightdress. They'd taken her from her bed.

Poor thing.

He picked her up and carried her to the elevator shaft. She didn't wake up until he fed her sweet tea in his father's dark laundry. She drank two cups before she said anything, her big gray eyes looking at the face of the monster he was.

He felt ashamed, and at the same time better than he had any time these past twenty years or more, as if she had saved him, instead of the other way around.

He was not hungry at all.

"What is your name?" she asked. "I'm Margaret Flanagan. Maggie." Her voice sounded composed, but her hands were shaking so badly.

He was pretty sure she was scared of him. He had put his arm around her to brace her while he fed her tea. He expected his nearness made it worse, but he also expected that if he backed away from her right now, she'd fall off the stool.

For all that she was fae, she was a child.

He told himself that her fear didn't make him sad. He was confused and hid it behind his usual emotionless mask.

"I am Hao's monster," he told her abruptly. "Where is your father? I will take you home."

She tilted her head. She closed her eyes for one breath,

heaved a sigh of heartfelt relief. When she looked up at him, she smiled, her face as bright as the sun he hadn't seen in years.

"He's coming," she said. "He'll be right here."

"Good," said Thomas, though he didn't know if that were true. If she'd had such power as he'd felt as he drank from her—earth and fire in abundance—then her father likely had more.

"Very true," said a man's voice, answering his thoughts—because Thomas had not spoken.

It took all of Thomas's considerable control not to show his surprise.

"Papa," said Margaret Flanagan, sounding for the first time as young as she looked. She pulled away from him and ran across the room to the arms of the man who stood in Hao's Laundry in a flannel shirt and dungarees, though the door was locked and the room had been empty when Thomas had carried her here.

The Flanagan didn't look imposing—only a few inches taller than Thomas, which made him short by the standards of the Irish in Butte. He didn't have the shoulders of a miner, though his hands showed the calluses of hard work.

"Vampire," he said, over his daughter's head. "I could destroy you, you're right. Fire is mine, and your kind are particularly vulnerable to it."

"Yes," acknowledged Thomas coolly. He might have been frightened, he thought, if he had really been afraid of death. Hell wasn't a pleasant thought, but then neither was a lifetime, possibly a hundred lifetimes, tied to the depraved thing that was his Master.

If a monster had taken advantage of someone he loved the way he had taken advantage of Margaret Flanagan, he would have killed that one and never felt regret. The wounds on her neck were closed, but his attack had been brutal and it would be a while before the red marks on her skin faded. The Flanagan stayed where he was.

Margaret turned her head until she could see Thomas.

"You have it now," she told him. "What will you do with it?"

"Have what?" asked Thomas.

"Freedom," she told him, and then collapsed in her father's arms.

He hadn't understood what she had done at first, not when he'd let her and her father out and relocked the laundry's door, not when he'd gone into the cupboard where he died for the day, not even when what had come to him had been sleep rather than death. He'd awakened and followed his father up the hill to the Master's house.

Hao Xun took him down the stairs to the basement as he always did, leaving Thomas with a gold coin at his feet.

"Pretty boy," said his Master. "Come here to me."

Obediently, Thomas stepped down the single stair. Above them, he heard his father walk out the door and shut it behind him.

"Give us a kiss, my sweet thing," the vampire told Thomas.

Thomas bent down to kiss his Master's cheek, one side and then the other. As he did, he reached out with one hand to grasp the long, wooden candlestick that always sat on the little table beside the wing chair though the candle it held was seldom lit.

"I'm so hungry for your blood," whispered his Master as Thomas pulled back.

As I hunger for yours, Thomas thought, thrusting the candlestick through the soft beeswax candle and into the old one's heart. He took two steps back, amazed that at long last he'd been able to do such a thing.

The old vampire leaned forward and smiled at him.

"Pretty boy," he said—and collapsed into himself.

Only then, staring at the dust that had been his Master, did Thomas understand the gift he'd been given.

Butte, Montana, present day

Freedom, Thomas thought, following the hobgoblin up the hill to wherever Nick wanted him to go. He'd spoken to her with his lips, and Margaret had heard his heart.

Thomas had left Butte that very night, with his father's twenty-dollar gold piece in his pocket. He could not wait for Hao Xun to come and get him, because he didn't want to kill the man who had sired his human self the way he'd killed the thing that had sired his current flesh. If he'd seen his father again, he wasn't certain he could have helped himself.

He had never seen either of the two fae again either, but unlike any of the vampires he'd met since then, he saw the sun every day and it did not burn him. He no longer needed to feed from a vampire in order to survive. Margaret had given him everything he'd desired as well as the feeding he'd asked for.

Nick stopped at a small well-kept house near the base of Big Butte, the hill that had given its name to the town—despite not being a butte at all. He let himself in the front door.

Thomas stopped on the porch. "If you want me inside," he told the hobgoblin, "you have to invite me in."

The little fellow stopped where he was and looked up at Thomas. "You mean no harm to me and mine, you will swear it."

"I'm not fae. Oaths have no power over me, Nick," he told the fae. "What I am is already damned."

The hobgoblin hissed and dismissed that with one hand.

"Don't throw Christian gobbledygook at me," he said. "Margaret told me you would come, told me you would help. You are here, so that is the first, but I wonder if the second is true. Vampire. I served her father most of my life. I can't afford to get this wrong."

The fae didn't like vampires. Thomas would have left because, with one exception, he didn't like the fae, either. But it hadn't been Nick who had brought him here; it had been Margaret. For her, he would do what he could.

"I owe Margaret Flanagan," said Thomas, who was better educated about fae than he'd been a hundred years ago. He knew what he was admitting—and that the fae would take it very seriously. "What she did for me was far more than what little I managed for her. I swear I mean no harm to her or hers."

"Come in and be welcome," said Nick after a pause, and turned to lead the way into his home.

There were four other people in the little man's living room, waiting for them, along with a blazing fire in the fireplace that gave out more light than heat.

One of the people, a big blond man, looked familiar, as though Thomas might have known him a long time ago. They were none of them human, and given that they were in a hobgoblin's house, Thomas was certain they were fae.

As soon as he entered the room on Nick's heels, everyone stood up—almost everyone. The kid on the piano bench just relaxed a little more. Thomas judged him the biggest threat: The really powerful ones often disguised themselves as something soft and helpless.

"Vampire," said the only woman. She was tall and muscular and spoke with a Finnish accent. "Is this the one?"

The big man's nose wrinkled as if he smelled something foul.

There was an old man—or one who looked old, since the fae could adopt any appearance that suited them. He peered at Thomas with nonjudgmental interest, which Thomas returned.

"It is him," said the boy on the piano bench. He was a beautiful young man, draped between the bench and the piano, his elbows on the cover that protected the keys. "Who else could it be? How many Chinese vampires do you think there are in Butte?"

"This is Thomas Hao," said Nick. "It is he who will find our Margaret."

He didn't introduce the others—hardly surprising, as names were odd things for the fae. Even a nickname, if held long enough, had power.

"Why does Margaret need finding?" Thomas asked.

The woman and the big man dropped their eyes and looked uncomfortable. Silence hung in the air for a moment.

"It is a long story," said Nick. "Will you take a seat?"

Thomas might be a vampire, but he had no way to judge the people in the room and was reluctant to sit down and put himself at a disadvantage.

The boy's smile widened as he slid off the bench and onto the floor. "Sit down, vampire, do—and the rest of you, too. Nick'll give him the rundown and then we'll see if she's right about the vampire."

The piano bench was hard and easy to rise from, unlike the overstuffed furniture in the rest of the room. It was acceptable—and it told Thomas something about the boy that he understood that.

Thomas sat on the bench. Once he was down, the fae took

their seats. Nick sat on the floor opposite Thomas, though there was an empty chair.

"Let me begin this tale in its proper place—with the Flanagan," he said. "He was high-court fae. Do you know what that means, Tom?"

"Powerful," replied Thomas. "Though there is no high court any longer. There are only the Gray Lords, who rule all of the fae."

"Aye," agreed Nick. "Powerful. Also old—and smart. A person didn't survive long in the high court if he weren't smart." The little man looked down at his hands.

"That's not really where the story starts," said the boy sitting at Thomas's feet. "It starts with Butte. With fae who came here hiding among the humans. It probably won't surprise you to learn that all the fae don't get along together, will it, Mr. Hao?"

"We vampires are the soul of brotherly love," Thomas responded dryly. "I assumed that the fae were the same."

The boy laughed until tears ran out of his eyes.

"It was not as funny as all that," said the woman.

"Brotherly love," repeated the boy. "Ayah. I'll remember that. Anyway, the fae came. From northern Europe and the British Isles mostly, like the people. Norwegians, Swedes, Finns, Cornish, and Irish—they all came."

Italian, too, thought Thomas. *The Serbians, the Czech, the Ukrainians.*

The boy sat up straight now, his eyes on the woman and the big man, turned slightly away from Thomas. "Once upon a time, the Irish fae would have squashed them all, but then came the ironmongers and their Christ and they bound the old places. Left us crippled and weak."

"It didn't hurt as badly," said the woman softly. "We have more iron-kissed among us, we Finns and Nordic folk."

"Iron-kissed?" asked Thomas.

"Those who work metals: dwarves, hiisi—some of them anyway, metal mages. So for thirty years we controlled the land here, and among us was one, a hiisi, who . . . was not kind to the other fae."

The boy laughed as if he thought she were funny, too.

She looked at him. "Most of us were too afraid to object." It wasn't an apology . . . not quite. "He had a talent for finding what you held dear, and then using it to make you do his bidding."

"Yes," the boy said dryly. "You suffered too, didn't you, you poor things."

She bit her lip and turned away. Apparently she was ashamed.

"And then came the Flanagan," said the old man. He might look fragile and aged, but his voice told a different story. It rumbled in Thomas's ears—British with a hint of Welsh or Cornish.

"I knew we'd get to him sooner or later," said Nick. "Flanagan changed things."

"For the better," rumbled the giant. "Even we could see that."

The woman snorted inelegantly. "He pushed the hiisi—this was an old and powerful hiisi—into summing the Iku-Tursas. The Flanagan could have worked something out, but he pushed and pushed and would not compromise."

Thomas frowned. Iku-Tursas. The name sounded familiar. He'd had some friends in school: Juhani Koskinen, Matti Makela, and another boy who was also Finnish. They told him a story once.

"The dragon," Thomas said. "But I thought it was a sea serpent."

The fae looked at him in surprise, except for the woman, who smiled and sat back. "Most people don't know Finnish stories."

"They didn't grow up here," said Thomas.

"The Tursas is a little more than a mere sea dragon, vampire," said the boy coolly. "It can take many forms. It attacked the Flanagan when he was down in the mines."

"No," said the big man at the same time the old man did. The bench under Thomas slid forward a little bit in eagerness, as if it wanted to go to the old man. Forest fae of some sort, he thought, setting his feet down a little firmer.

"It attacked the miners," said Nick. "Playing with them a little. The place where they'd be working would start leaking water. It was the Speculator Mine—the one Flanagan was working for as a mining engineer. Modern, safe, well ventilated—the Flanagan insisted upon it."

"High-court fae always did love the silly humans," murmured the boy as if to himself.

The woman snorted again and reached out with a boot to nudge him hard. "I've heard you might come from high court yourself," she said.

He jumped up, fierce with indignation. "You take it back! You take that back right now."

She smiled at him. "Of course, I never believed it. Too much stupid, not enough looks."

He shook himself like a wet cat. "Damned piru," he snapped.

"Easy prey," she purred.

Piru, thought Thomas. Finnish fae, he remembered. But was it one of the witty demons prone to games of wit, or one of the air ladies who hung out and looked beautiful until something ticked them off? He looked at the woman and decided for the clever demon; she looked a little too substantial to be floating around.

"It picked groups of miners with fae among them to frighten," said Nick, picking up his story from where he'd left off. "Eventually one of them figured out that the water they'd been hitting wasn't just an accident of geology. He took the tale to the Flanagan."

"He was supposed to charge off to confront the Finnish fae who was tormenting his people," said the old man. "He would have, too, if a certain people hadn't gone to him and told him that what he faced wasn't just any fae."

"There was betrayal on both sides," said the woman. "Some did not think that the Flanagan was strong enough to keep his promises and it would be the less powerful fae who would suffer. Others looked to him for justice and a way out from under the hiisi's thumb." She rubbed absently at the fabric of the couch where she sat. "It didn't matter. He went anyway."

"Aye," said the big man. "As he had to, being who he was. But he went armed and ready instead of oblivious. The Flanagan, he wouldn't back down for Tursas."

"Wait," said Thomas. "The Speculator. The Granite Mountain fire? This was the mining disaster, during World War One."

"1917," said Nick. "When the fire broke out, we knew he'd won."

"In true Germanic fashion," said the giant morosely, "I suppose he had."

"He never came out," Nick told Thomas. "When the fires went out, we pulled out the bodies. Some of them were fae, most were human; some you couldn't tell. We didn't find the Tursas or the Flanagan."

"Afterward," said the woman, "we met. All of us. Summoning the Tursas from its exile, as if he were a dog to come to his master. If the Flanagan hadn't . . . hadn't done whatever he did it might have eaten the world."

She believed that, Thomas thought.

"The fae killed him," rumbled the old man. "That hiisi who summoned the Tursas. He'd used so much power to do it, he was vulnerable. Even his allies turned on him. All the fae that were here: Cornish, Irish, Finn, German, Norwegian, Slav, and that little guy from Italy. We killed that hiisi who thought that his power was more important than the survival of all."

"We thought that was the end of it," the woman said. "Time passed. The city started to die, people left, and most of us left, too. Just a few stayed."

"But that hiisi had taken the Flanagan's daughter to make certain of his victory if the Flanagan, by some miracle, had destroyed the Iku-Tursas," the boy said. "Searches were made but . . . there are thousands of miles of tunnels. We thought her long dead. Then two years ago, she started to talk to us," said the boy. "A high-court trick, that, getting into your head. Unpleasant."

Thomas remembered.

"She's quite mad," whispered Nick. "Quite mad from all those years trapped in the earth."

"So what do you need me for?" Thomas asked.

"We need you to find her and kill her," said the big man.

"It is what she wants," said the boy, answering Thomas's raised eyebrow. "She tells me so, over and over. I've looked and looked and I can't find her anywhere."

"She's in the mines." Nick's voice was pensive. "We don't have an earth or iron-kissed fae left here to find her—not that they had much success when they looked before."

"And even if we did, she has a haltija." The woman looked out the window, and Thomas noted absently that the fae needed to replace the double-paned window because ice had formed around the edges of the inside of the glass.

"A what?" he asked.

She waved a hand. "A guard. This one is a kalman väki, we think—a dead man's spirit. He was probably killed and set to guard her when she was taken."

"A kalman väki," Thomas said slowly. "How do you know that, since you can't find her."

"She told us." The big man glanced at Thomas searchingly and then looked away. Thomas knew he wouldn't read anything but mild interest in his face.

"We'd have to destroy it to get to her." The woman closed her eyes. "Even if we could find her, we could not get by that. A kalman väki holds the power of mortification: It kills with a touch; not even the immortal are immune. But you aren't exactly immortal, are you?"

"The mines were mostly filled when the company shut them down." The old man pulled his beard lightly. "The old timbers were rotting through and the tunnels collapsing. Was a time you could take a step off your back porch in the morning to find a hole four or five hundred feet down that hadn't been in your backyard when you went to bed. One tunnel collapsing on top of another, on top of another. Was quite the thing to fill them—expensive and time-consuming both. But some of it is left, where the tunnels were cut into granite mostly."

"So," said Thomas. "You want me—a vampire—to go looking in the old mines to find Margaret Flanagan, who has been trapped down there for a century. Because vampires are so good at . . . what? Dissolving into mist and sinking through the earth? I think you've been watching too many bad horror movies."

"She was never the same after she met you," Nick said.

"She had such a touch with the earth: It came to her call and did as she bid. She had a little of her father's gift for fire, but it was the earth that knew her. She was able to call you here. If she can do that, she should be able to guide you to her down in the mines, where her power is greater."

"Hello, vampire," said the big man softly—and his American accent turned lilting and softened. Thomas had only talked to Margaret for a few hours, one day out of the many years he'd lived, but he recognized her intonations in the man's deep voice.

The other fae moved away from the big man, but they didn't look startled. He knew that they would not perceive his surprise; his father had taught him well.

"Or ill," the big man said, proving that her gift of reading thoughts that Thomas did not speak was still hers. The fae's clear blue eyes were not quite the same shade as Margaret's.

"They think I can find you," Thomas said carefully. "That because you called me here, you can lead me through the tunnels."

"Like to like," she answered him. *"I don't know why you heard my call, just that you did. I could not have given you your wish if you had not been earth-touched."*

He knew what she meant. How could he not? He remembered that sense he'd had of how she was a part of the earth that had held them together in its maw. He'd sensed it because the earth spoke to him, too.

Vampires develop abilities, the Master had told him. The Master could make humans do as he wanted even before a blood exchange—a rare gift, and useful.

Thomas's mother's family were scholars, back as far as their family history went—all the way, the stories said, to the dragon scholar who knew everything that dragons knew and turned into a man to see what men knew. Thomas's mother had told him that her family was founded by a *dilong*, an earth dragon. "Only a story," his father had said, rolling his eyes. He had never cared for anything that reminded him that his wife's family had higher status than his.

Thomas looked at the assembled fae. "Why do you say that she is mad?" he asked.

"My father's blood runs in the earth," the big man whispered in Margaret's voice. *"His fire consumes me. When I emerge I will burn them all to dust and beyond."*

"We think the Flanagan died two years ago," said the woman in subdued tones. She did not look at the man who sat next to her and spoke with Margaret's voice. "That he gave her his last strength so she could call out and find someone to help, so she could be saved, but it was too late."

"What would you expect of her?" asked the boy. "Alone for nearly a century. Trapped with only the dead for company, under the earth. Chained, without food or water. Neither dying nor living. And now she has the power of her father, who killed the Iku-Tursas." He shivered and hugged himself. "She will kill us all."

"No," said Thomas, coming at last to his feet. "I shall not allow it. The girl I knew would not want your deaths on her conscience." She had rescued him, a vampire who had hurt her, and still she rescued him. She did not need the blood of these fae on her hands.

It took him four days to find a way to the place she'd been kept. As the old man had promised, many of the tunnels he'd known were collapsed or filled, but his sense of the ways beneath the mining town was as good as it had ever been. He found a path.

As before, though, that earth sense he had did not betray her to him. It was the blood he'd taken from her. *Like calls to like,* she'd told him. While all the fae around her thought she was talking about her magic.

He rose in the absolute darkness and felt the shape of the last obstacle that stood between him and his goal. It was not just winter's chill, it was colder than that. He found himself wishing for a light to see the väki, but he'd never needed a light down here, so he hadn't brought one.

"Why come you smelling so of death?" It was a woman's voice; he hadn't expected her to be a woman.

"I am vampire," he told the kalman väki. "I bring death with me."

"Mine is the power of illness, of mortification of living flesh," she said. "But I would keep my charge though I have no power over the dead."

"No more than I do," he said gently. "I mean her no harm, guardian spirit. I killed those who did."

He'd killed them, her father's betrayers, so that Margaret wouldn't have to. They hadn't expected it, and he'd been careful to take out the boy first. Then the big man who could—Thomas was pretty sure—pick and chose how much Margaret could say through his lips.

He was a vampire, and these fae had believed he was their dog to do their bidding. They hadn't expected a monster, despite knowing what he was. Killing them had not taken him long.

Thomas had been raised in Butte, among the Irish, Finns, and all the other races who had come to pull the treasures of the Richest Hill on Earth. He might wear the face of a Chinese man, but he came from a family of scholars and lived among the people here for all of his childhood.

A väki of whatever kind was a protector of the treasure it guarded. No one would set such a creature to keep a prisoner in. Only a fae would think that a *vampire* would assume a väki of the grave would be an evil thing. Her father or perhaps the Finnish fae who had first warned the Flanagan of the dragon must have sent it to protect her. If they meant his Margaret no harm, the väki would not have prevented them from reaching her.

If Margaret had remained powerless in the heart of the earth, they would have left her there to rot. When her father's power came to her—or whatever had happened that she could tell their thoughts and return her own—she could finally take action against them; they had decided they had to kill her.

Somehow they'd discovered that she'd called him for help—perhaps she'd taunted them with it—that she *had* someone she could call for help. It didn't matter. What do you send against the spirit of the dead? A vampire. They had the weapon they needed; they just had to point it in the right direction. Once Thomas had dealt with the väki, they would have killed Thomas and Margaret both.

But Margaret hadn't told them everything about him. They assumed she could summon him because of the wish she'd granted him, that it had given her some sort of magical power over him. But it had been the blood. If she had trusted them—as they implied—she would have told them about that part. Telling him about the väki had been their first mistake. Not knowing that he'd bitten her and taken her blood had been the second.

Nick, who had served her father *almost* all his life, would have known a vampire saved her. But neither Margaret nor her father had told Nick the whole story.

The final, and greatest, mistake had been implying that Margaret had been driven insane, imprisoned in the earth. What was it Nick had said? "She's quite mad." A subtle word was *mad*. Nick had used it to imply one thing without a lie crossing his lips. Thomas would have been angry, too, imprisoned by his enemies. The earth was her element; it nurtured her and sustained her.

If he was wrong, if they had been innocent of all he suspected . . . ? Well, then, he was a vampire, after all—and they were fae. He would not regret their deaths.

But he had not been wrong, because he could feel the guardian move out of his path, satisfied by his answer. He slipped by it and found the fragile thing he searched for, little more than bones in chains.

"Please," she said, her voice as quiet as the whisper of the spring wind.

He broke the iron shackles first, throwing them as far from her as the confines of the tunnel allowed. He pulled a blanket out of the pack he carried and carefully, gently put her upon it.

"What would you do for me in return?" he said, raising her up and touching a damp cloth to her face. She pressed her face against it, sucking on the moisture. It would take her a long time to get water that way—and it would be slow enough not to make her sick from it.

When he pulled the cloth away and soaked it in water from his canteen again, she said, her voice hoarse, "Anything. My gratitude you have."

"Yes?" he said, pressing the cloth against her face again.

"You gave me such a gift last time. Gratitude is a poor substitute. Perhaps I should give your gift back to you, shall I?" He picked her up, and she was such a light burden, lighter even than she'd been the first time he'd carried her out of the mine tunnels.

"Oh, yes," she sighed, understanding what he didn't say, as she had before. "I should love to see the sun again."

Picking Up the Pieces

BY PAT CADIGAN

Pat Cadigan has twice won the Arthur C. Clarke Award for her novels *Synners* and *Fools* and has been nominated many times for just about every other award. Although primarily known as a science fiction writer (and as one of the original cyberpunks), she also writes fantasy and horror, which can be found in her collections *Patterns, Dirty Work,* and *Home by the Sea*. Her work has been translated into many languages, including Polish, Russian, Italian, French, Spanish, German, Portuguese, Czech, and Japanese (also Pirate and Swedish Chef via Google, which doesn't count as official publication, but she gets a kick out of it anyway). The author of fifteen books, including two nonfiction titles and one young adult novel, she currently has two new novels in progress.

She lives in gritty, urban North London with her husband, the Original Chris Fowler, and her son, Rob, and their minder, Miss Kitty Calgary, Queen of the Cats.

I don't think I've ever quite forgiven 1989. It was one of those years when everything started looking up.

OK, not *everything*. But even after Tiananmen Square, the developments in Eastern Europe were enough to make a person think the world was actually becoming a better place.

All right, then, just me. *I* wondered. I was thirty-six—theoretically old enough to know better but young enough to drop everything and fly halfway around the world for my crazy sister Quinn.

Dammit, everything goes to hell around that girl, my father used to grumble. Actually, it was more like chaos, which, now that I think of it, *was* hell for my father, a man who envisioned his daughters as swans and instead got—well, us. And Quinn, in that order. The first four (of which I was the last) made his head spin. Then when I was sixteen, Quinn arrived, unintended, unpredicted, unexpected, and made everything spin. My sister, the thrill ride. If there is such a thing as reincarnation, she'll probably come back as a Tilt-a-Whirl. Or a Wild Octopus.

Maybe a rocket, seeing as how she was born the day after the first moon landing. But it would have to be a rocket that never came down: She wasn't manic-depressive; there was no depression, just manic and more manic. Although to be honest, it wasn't mania in the clinical sense, just high energy and no brakes. Two separate therapists diagnosed her as a borderline personality. I had to look that one up. Some things seemed to fit, some didn't, and the rest I wasn't sure about, but it all sounded pretty bad.

In the end, I decided the diagnosis creeped me out, not my sister. Quinn could be frivolous and silly, the grasshopper to everyone else's ant; she could be self-centered and even insensitive, with the attention span of a gnat and poor impulse control, but she had never been mean or spiteful. Most of the time she was good-natured, slow to anger, and quick to kiss and make up. And more than anything else, generous.

My mother never missed a chance to point out Quinn's good qualities. *There's no malice in her. She's got a good heart. She never goes out of her way to hurt anyone. She'd give you the shirt off her back.* What my mother didn't mention, however, was that when Quinn ran out of shirts, she'd expect you to volunteer yours. Her tendency to presume wasn't as attractive as her thick, curly black hair or her silvery gray eyes or her smile, features that could usually persuade the susceptible to overlook her flaws.

It didn't always work to her advantage, of course. Because she was a child, she had a hard time telling the difference between *excitement* and *trouble.* I'm not sure she even knew there *was* a difference. *Because there's no malice in her,* my mother said. *Because she's got a good heart.*

In November of 1989, Quinn went to Berlin with her good heart, which had been captured by a tall, rangy blond man with blue eyes, cheekbones like the white cliffs of Dover, and snake hips. It was a package that would have held my attention even without the German accent. With it, everything he said sounded exotic and even a bit mysterious, at least to my tin American ear. Especially after a few glasses of red wine.

And very good red wine it was, too, a French Bordeaux that actually tasted as good as the label looked. He brought two bottles when he and Quinn turned up at our parents' house for the annual your-father-won't-celebrate-his-birthday dinner in early September. Only Kath, Lisa, and I were not-celebrating with our parents. Our oldest sister, Marie, and her wife were stuck in Toronto seeing their twins through chicken pox, and as far as any of us knew, Quinn was *traveling*—the family euphemism for that period beginning with the last time anyone had heard from her and ending when she finally called one or more of us to say she was OK and hint she needed a small loan. Unpredicted and unexpected again. Surprise, everybody, and oh, hey, meet Martin.

The not-a-birthday dinner immediately turned into the Quinn Show, with special guest. Quinn was bubbly, vivacious, and entertaining, Martin was personable, witty, and utterly covetworthy, and everyone enjoyed themselves. Though Kath, Lisa, and I sneaked commiserating looks at each other even as we did; sometimes it was hard not to feel drab around our baby sister.

But if we felt drab next to Quinn, we were positively lackluster compared to Martin. Originally from East Berlin, he was barely more than a toddler when his parents had given him over to some trusted friends who had smuggled him through the Berlin Wall and taken him to live with them in London. Since then, he had heard precious little of his family: All he had was a blurry photo of his parents with the two younger sisters and a brother he had never met. My mother teared up. This embarrassed Martin, who apologized. Quinn, however, sat back with a faint smile, and I knew she was pleased to have brought us someone to prick our social conscience—very much a Quinn thing to do.

She and Martin didn't stay long after that. "And there they go," Kath sighed as we stood on the front steps watching Martin's sports car pull out of the driveway. "Back to life among those more beautiful and exciting than us." Her gaze swiveled to Lisa, the grammar Nazi of the family.

For once, Lisa wasn't taking the bait. "What color do you suppose the sky is on that planet?" she asked wistfully.

"Dunno," I said. "Our eyes are probably too ordinary to see it."

"Don't be silly, Jean." Kath elbowed me. "It'll be gold lamé. With real gold."

"Girls." Mom was right on cue. "There's no malice in her. She's got a good heart."

Dad gave a small *hmph.* “I hope this Martin doesn’t break it.”

My sisters and I looked at each other, knowing immediately he would.

Quinn’s call came on one of those rare nights when I had a few friends from work over for drinks and hors d’oeuvres. The conversation was mostly about East European politics. Was this really the beginning of the end for Communism, and, if so, did that mean changes for China after all, despite Tiananmen Square? Current events along with Martin’s brief visit had me thinking more about politics than I ever had before, although he and my sister were the furthest things from my mind when the phone rang.

She was talking so fast that I couldn’t understand a word she was saying. I couldn’t even tell whether she was happy, angry, or scared. I tried calming her down so I could call her back after everyone left; instead, I ended up mouthing apologies at my guests while they showed themselves out. Eventually Quinn wound down enough so that I could get in a few questions.

Martin had gone back to London in mid-October, promising to return in a week, ten days at the most. There’d been two brief phone calls from him—one the day he’d arrived in London to let her know he’d arrived safely, the other two weeks later to say he had the flu and was too sick to fly. And after that, nothing—no calls and only the answering machine when she called him. She went on phoning at all hours of the day and night until she’d finally gotten an answer—not Martin but the neighbor who said she was watering his plants while he was in West Berlin. No, she didn’t know when Martin was coming back, big things were happening. He hadn't told her much before he left, just something about people coming through the Berlin Wall, which would be very exciting if it were true, wouldn't it. Quinn managed to wheedle the name and number of the hotel where Martin was staying out of her, then decided to take more direct action.

So here she was in Berlin, at the hotel where Martin had supposedly been staying. Only he wasn't there now, and she had been running all over West Berlin for days trying to find him. And now she'd heard about people who had gotten out of East Berlin going back through the wall and getting stuck, unable to get out again even if they had passports from the UK or West Germany or even America.

That didn't sound right to me. Could any country, even East Germany, prevent a foreign national from leaving? I thought of what I'd seen on the news about Hungary's relaxed border with Austria allowing East Germans to escape to the west. Maybe East Germany was tightening its own borders with everyone else to counter this, making travel problems for everyone, regardless of nationality? It didn't seem likely, but I just didn't know. Stranger things had happened.

"Maybe the best thing to do is get on the first flight out of there," I said the next time she stopped for breath. "Come home, wait for Martin to call you."

"Absolutely *not,*" she said. "Martin needs my help, I just *know* it. He's one of those people who went back through the wall and can't get out again. I can feel it in my bones."

"What makes you think that?" I asked.

"I just *told* you, I can feel it in my bones," Quinn said, as if I had questioned the existence of gravity. "Haven't you ever felt that way, like you just *know* something?"

It was on the tip of my tongue to say, *Yeah, but I've always been wrong unless it was something bad that I was in denial about,* but she was talking again.

"A lot of the people here think something's about to happen, but they don't know if it's going to be something good, like more travel restrictions being eased, or something bad, like Czechoslovakia in 1968—"

"Do you even know what happened in Czechoslovakia in 1968?" I asked, amazed.

"Tanks," she said vaguely. "But whatever happens, I can't leave Martin to face it alone."

I sighed. "Quinn, honey, I think you've got it backward. I think *Martin* left *you.*"

"He wouldn't. I know it in my heart. We have a bond."

There's no arguing with what someone knows in their heart or feels in their bones, but that's never stopped me from trying. It was especially counterproductive in this case, because the more I argued against it, the surer she was about Martin and the more determined she became to help him.

"I'll go get him myself," she said finally. "I'll go through the wall and find him and bring him out again."

"You just said you heard people from other countries were having trouble getting out. What if you can't get out again yourself?"

"Then we'll be stuck there together," she said nobly, making me wince.

"And what if he's *not* there? What if he's in West Berlin? Or what if he's already gone back to London—or even the U.S.? What if he's been calling your apartment to tell you when to pick him up at the airport?"

"He isn't. I told you, I can feel it in my bones. He's in trouble. He needs *me.*"

We argued for another half hour before I could finally

make her promise she wouldn't go near the wall before I got to West Berlin. I couldn't always count on Quinn's word, but, all told, she had kept more promises than she had broken and there was a very good chance she'd keep this one. She'd made a passing mention of maxed-out credit cards before I hung up.

When the plane touched down at Berlin Tegel, jet lag hit as if someone had dropped a heavy blanket on me. I managed to drag myself through customs and the baggage claim and finally through the entrance gate and straight into bedlam.

I was caught in a sea of utterly joyful people, hugging, kissing, laughing, calling to each other in German but also several other languages, occasionally even English. At least three people kissed me on both cheeks, and more tried. The hugs were harder to avoid—arms came out of the crowd to embrace me while I tried to find the city bus, which my travel agent had told me to take to Am Zoo, the hotel where Quinn was staying. If she was still there.

I didn't have to wait long at the stop, but more people had jammed themselves onto the bus than I'd have thought possible. Nonetheless, several near the door pulled me and my one small bag up into their midst, ignoring my protests that there was no room.

"You're North American? U.S. or Canadian?" a woman asked in a heavy German accent.

"Uh, U.S." I felt awkward. We were pressed up against each other so tightly I could feel her breath against my face. She had been drinking beer. So had everyone else around me.

"I'll go there one day. I never thought I would, but now I know I will!" Her wide blue eyes, already red from crying, welled up and spilled over. With great difficulty, she maneuvered one hand into the shopping bag she was holding and came up with a piece of toilet paper. I looked down; the bag was bulging. Besides toilet paper, I could see bananas, marmalade, peanut butter, face cream, shampoo, and, on top, CDs by Duran Duran and Cyndi Lauper.

"Soft enough to wipe your eyes," the woman said as she did so. "Nothing will ever be the same. My mother dreamed of this. She saw the wall go up. I only wish she had lived to see it come down again."

"It's not down yet," a man said. "Not all the way."

"It will be!" said someone else, and everyone around me cheered.

As the bus lumbered along, I found out from the people around me what had happened while I was still in transit. The party secretary in East Germany had announced there would be no more restrictions on travel to the west, effective immediately. Thousands of East Berliners, on foot or in cars, promptly made a beeline for the wall, papers in hand, demanding to cross into West Berlin. They were met by bewildered guards who, unsure of their orders, refused to let them through. In a few hours, thousands became tens of thousands, until the guards finally gave in and opened the border. But some brave souls had decided to break through the wall literally, using sledgehammers and power saws. West Berliners who gathered on the other side greeted them with champagne, embraces, even money. There was music and people were dancing on top of the Berlin Wall. The whole city was caught up in the spirit; it was the biggest street party ever.

By the time the bus reached Ku'damm, I was feeling quite a lot of that spirit myself. I was no longer tired, my face hurt from smiling, and in spite of myself, my own eyes were welling up.

But as I struggled through the heaving masses on the street looking for the hotel, I wanted to kill my sister.

Quinn had added my name to the hotel room. The people at the Am Zoo front desk were delighted to see me, or rather, my credit card, which Quinn had assured them would take care of the bill, incidentals included. I made a hopeful joke about discounts for historical events but suddenly no one understood English well enough to get it.

The room was nice enough, though I wasn't sure it was really worth the small fortune I would be paying for it. I was relieved to see my sister's things very much in evidence—it meant she hadn't gone—although she was out. Of course. Probably dancing in the streets with everyone else in West Berlin. Crisis or no crisis, she never could resist a party.

I looked out the window at the teeming streets, and jet lag hit again. Even if I'd known my way around the city, I had no energy to elbow my way through all those people. I lay down on the bed and passed out.

The next thing I knew, Quinn was shaking me like a rag doll.

"Come on, Jean, you've got to wake up!"

Squinting against the bright overhead light, I tried to pull away from her. "Stop—you're gonna give me brain damage!"

Apparently she thought I was talking in my sleep; I had to use a self-defense move to get away from her. It worked but I almost dislocated an elbow. Then instead of standing back so I could get up, she actually went for me again. I rolled away, got tangled in the duvet, and landed on the floor.

"Don't touch me; I'm awake already!" I yelled as she loomed over me.

"I was just going to help you up," she said, looking offended. "What's the matter with you?"

"Somebody shook me out of a sound sleep. What's *your* excuse?" I used the bed to pull myself up to a sitting position.

"The Berlin Wall is coming down," she said. "It's history, happening right here, right now, before our very eyes."

My very eyes still hurt from the bright light in the room: I glared up at her murderously. "And that's why you couldn't wake me up in a more civilized fashion?"

"I tried. You were dead to the world."

"I'm jet-lagged. I spent the night not sleeping in a transatlantic sardine can."

"Well, perk up, 'cause you *have* to see this; it's amazing! The East Berlin guards are trading hats with the West Berlin ones; they've got their arms around each other and they're *singing*."

I struggled to my feet, batting away the hand she offered to help. "Then Martin isn't trapped anymore, and he and his family can see each other whenever they want. Our work here is done."

Quinn blinked at me, baffled. "What work?"

"Democracy. *Liberté, egalité, fraternité.* Free at last, free at last, thank God Almighty, they're free at last. Martin and his family included. Right now, he's probably bonding with the sisters and brother he's never met in between hugging his parents. That's your cue to slip away quietly with *your* sister and go home and hug *your* parents. I'll help you pack."

"There aren't any flights out now," she said.

"How do you know?"

"Who'd want to leave? Jean, you slept the day away; there wouldn't be any flights now even if it weren't the most incredible day in recent German history."

I almost laughed; being all of twenty, my sister's idea of recent history was last Christmas. "Fine. Let's pack your stuff. I've got one little bag I haven't even opened. Then we'll be all ready to fly out tomorrow morning."

Quinn shook her head so vigorously her curls flew. "No, we're here *now*. It's happening *right now*. Every second is history. Twenty years from now, do you want to have to tell everyone that you were in Berlin when the wall came down and *you watched it on TV in your hotel room*?"

I gave in and put on my shoes.

As soon as we waded into the crowds on the street, I realized I wasn't just hungry but famished. I hadn't eaten since before the plane had landed and that hadn't been much—a small cup of yogurt and a roll so stale it had mutated into Styrofoam. Quinn didn't mind putting off our eyewitnessing history in favor of food, but then with her credit cards maxed out, she'd probably missed a few meals herself.

The problem was the crowds, not just in the streets but anywhere and everywhere food was served. "See, they don't get any of that stuff in East Berlin," Quinn told me, pointing at a smiling man loaded down with two cases of Coke. Next to him, his family were eating out of large bags from a fast-food joint. "They take their kids into stores and the kids think they're in fairyland. What we take for granted is incredible luxury to them." She sounded practically authoritative, as if she knew all about the privations suffered by people in East Germany.

That would be Martin, of course. She was parroting Martin, probably right down his tone of voice. And then it hit me: She was trying to find him. I was along to cover expenses.

I wanted to be wrong, but there she was, up on tiptoe, stretching her neck like a meerkat, scanning the crowd. Irritated, I dragged her around a couple grinning at each other as they hefted boxes of stereo equipment, through a group of young guys with enough junk food and beer for six weekend toga parties, and down a side street, where I found what was probably the only restaurant in West Berlin without a line of people a block long waiting to get in. When I saw the prices, I understood why, but I was past caring.

"You're looking for him, aren't you?" I said as we sat at a table waiting to order. "Don't deny it; I'm not a moron. But *you* are. If he's back on this side of the wall, he's probably with his family. Can't you just leave him alone with them for a while? Give him some space?" The last sentence replayed itself in my head. Had I actually said that? I wanted to bite my tongue off.

"You're being silly, Jean. It's like a tidal wave of people pouring through from East Berlin. It's impossible to find anyone." But she wouldn't look at me; instead, she studied the menu as if the secret of life were printed on it. Or Martin's current location. I started to say something else but she talked over me. "Let's just eat, okay? I don't know about you, but I'm almost light-headed with hunger."

That's what happens when you max out your credit cards, I managed not to say out loud. At this point I was too hungry to deal with anything, much less Quinn's foolishness. A relentlessly happy waitress took our orders and then brought us two pint glasses of beer we hadn't asked for, dancing away before we could tell her we wanted soft drinks instead. While the restaurant celebrated around us, Quinn and I ate our overpriced steaks in silence. Every so often, I stole a glance at her to find her doing the same; it wasn't until I'd finished a little over half the meal that I could find a little humor in the situation—the immediate situation, that was. There wasn't going to be a whole lot of hilarity in getting my sister home.

"You're twenty years old." The words were out before I realized I'd spoken.

Quinn gave a faint, puzzled laugh. "And you're thirty-six. *And?*"

"Ever think about going back to college?"

"Not *this* again." She sawed a piece off her steak. "As I told Mom and Dad and Marie and Kath *and* Lisa *and* you *and* everybody *and* their mother, I'm not the academic type. Studying isn't my thing."

"So what *is* your thing—chasing some guy halfway around the world?"

Now she looked offended. "Martin isn't just *some guy*. He's more—so much more."

"Okay, he's got quite a history, I'll give you that. Being a refugee from behind the Iron Curtain, growing up without his parents—definitely not your average man on the street. But that doesn't mean he hasn't dumped you."

"Doesn't mean he has." Quinn chewed stolidly and took a sip of beer. "You have no sense of anything that isn't *ordinary*. To you, it's all just people shifting around like, I don't know, little blocks. Legos. Martin and I aren't Legos. We have something more profound than you could ever know."

"How long were you with him?" I asked. "Two months? Three?"

"Almost four." Quinn looked smug. *So there.*

"Almost four profound months, eh? What's his middle name?"

My sister looked startled for a fraction of a second, then covered with a laugh. "Nosy, aren't you?"

"Can't say you know anyone if you don't know their middle name," I said.

"I don't like to pry. Unlike *some* people."

"I didn't know Eddie's middle name was Erasmus til after we got engaged. Turned out that wasn't the only thing I didn't know about him, and we'd been together for over a year. Good thing I found out before I did something stupid like marry him."

"You didn't break up with Eddie because his middle name was Erasmus," Quinn said. "I was only ten but I knew that."

"Correct. I broke up with him because he'd been hiding things from me."

"Martin never hid anything from me."

"You don't know that. Four months isn't long enough to know—"

"Fine," Quinn said flatly, her eyes hard. "Then I'll give him a little longer." She dragged her napkin back and forth across her mouth before dropping it on the table. "You really don't know, Jean. There's a lot more to life than you think. There really is an unseen world. I know—Martin showed it to me."

My heart sank. "Oh, no, Quinn, not like the guru."

"He wasn't a guru, he was a *swami*."

"He was a con man and he saw you coming."

"It's not like that!" she said hotly. "This isn't America where everything happened ten minutes ago. This is the Old World. Time is measured in millennia here, and everything isn't always nice and neat and easily explained. Martin opened my eyes to so much. I'm not going to just abandon him."

"You're going to have to learn the hard way *again*, aren't you?" I said before I could tell myself to shut up.

Quinn didn't take offense. Laughing, she toasted me with her beer. "We'll just see who learns what the hard way—me or my older and supposedly wiser sister."

In the course of my misspent youth, I joined the 1971 antiwar demonstrations in Washington, D.C.; some years later, I went to pre-Katrina New Orleans for Mardi Gras. Both times I thought I'd been in big crowds; this beat them by several magnitudes.

There was no place not filled with people—happy people, dancing, singing, shouting—while music played and fireworks went off. I held on to Quinn's arm, determined not to lose her—or let her lose me—but invariably someone would come between us to hug her or me or both and I'd lose my grip on her. Fortunately, I always found her again, although a few times I would grab for what I thought was her arm only to discover I was manhandling a stranger. Quinn's face would pop up several feet away, looking amused as I swam through the crowd to get to her.

"We should have tied ourselves together with rope," I said as we squeezed through the masses. Disoriented, I had no idea where we were. There seemed to be only two directions—toward the wall or away from it—and only two locations—one side of the wall or the other. Correction: There was a third location—on top of the wall. People dancing on it were reaching down to hoist others up to dance with them. Was Quinn's errant boyfriend up there? I wondered. As we got closer, I could hear, below the singing and music and general uproar, tapping noises, metal on stone in various rhythms. Hammers chipping away at the wall? It would take a hell of a lot of hammers to punch through. They needed sledgehammers or better yet, wrecking balls.

Abruptly, I heard a loud buzzing whine; on top of the wall, a cascade of sparks erupted as someone attacked it with a power saw. People cheered, and I found myself spontaneously cheering with them, which earned me another amused look from Quinn. But only very briefly—she was scanning the mass of people in front of her with more urgency.

The buzz-saw whine cut off, and I heard a new sound, the chatter of a small engine working too hard. I looked to my left, and through a break in the crowd, I saw a small car exuding a cloud of exhaust. As it inched forward, people lunged out of the crowd to pound their fists on it, startling the driver and his passengers. For a moment, I was afraid I was about to see a mob drag them out of the car and attack them. But no, the crowd was laughing. A woman shoved a bottle of champagne through the driver's side window and kissed the wide-eyed driver, while a couple of teenagers stuck flowers in the front bumper.

"What's that about?" I asked my sister.

"Trabi thumping," she said. "They've been doing it all day. Trabants are really awful cars, but that's all they have over there."

Another rattletrap car crept along behind it and was given the same treatment. I turned to ask Quinn how our being out in an enormous crowd watching people dent cars would accomplish anything, but she was gone. The arm I was holding on to belonged to a middle-aged man with a mustache; he was grinning at me with delight.

He went on grinning as I apologized and disengaged, feeling like an idiot, and a drunken idiot at that. I hadn't had much beer, but it didn't take much combined with jet lag and mass celebratory hysteria. People kept hugging me as I struggled through the crush; I stopped trying to fight them off. It was faster just to go along with it and keep moving. After a while I realized *I* was automatically hugging everyone I passed. When in Rome . . . or West Berlin.

Working my way through the crowd, I began hearing snatches of English. When I looked around, though, I couldn't see who was speaking. I listened in vain for Quinn's voice. Then all the voices were drowned out by the sound of fireworks. Multicolored lights blossomed overhead, briefly turning the night as bright as day. None of the joy-filled, upturned faces around me belonged to Quinn. I kept pushing toward the wall, calling out her name.

More fireworks streaked skyward and exploded. Suddenly a new light hit my eyes, blinding me for a couple of seconds before it slid away and rippled over the crowd: Someone on top of the wall was wielding a spotlight like a searchlight. The bright circle moved back and forth, pausing here and there; the people caught in it waved their arms and cheered.

Trying to blink away the dark patches of afterimage, I kept pushing toward the wall, calling out my sister's name. More lights appeared high up now, large banks of them, sending faint multiple shadows from the people on top of the wall over the crowd below. I put one hand up to try to shield my eyes, watering madly now from the cold. Or maybe I was so caught up in the moment I was crying with happiness like everyone else in Berlin; I honestly didn't know anymore and I was starting to feel a little scared. Not just by that but by the fact that the crowd was getting so thick that sometimes my feet didn't touch the ground.

Abruptly, I fetched up against something hard and rough and cold. I'd reached the infamous Berlin Wall, where people had died making a break for freedom, machine-gunned by East Berlin guards—and where it seemed I was going to be crushed to death, squashed by the entire happy population of West Berlin celebrating its symbolic fall.

With great effort, I pushed myself back so I could turn around, just as something hit the stone inches from my right eye. I had a glimpse of a grinning male face and then flinched as a large hammer came at me. Chips and dust flew against the side of my face.

"Watch it, you moron!" I yelled, startled and angry. "I got that in my eye!" I had one hand pressed to my eye and I didn't actually know if that were true, but it would have been just my luck to be blinded by fragments from the destruction of the Berlin Wall. Where the *hell* was Quinn? Blind or not, I was going to kill her.

"Here—a special souvenir!" Someone shoved something into my other hand and closed my fingers around it.

After a bit of careful blinking, I determined that my eye was all right even if I was still in danger of being mashed to pulp against the wall, then I turned to see the grinning face again. He was using a hammer and chisel on the wall but at a safer, lower level.

"What are you doing?" I asked, forgetting I was mad at him.

"Getting pieces of the wall," he said happily. "Special souvenirs! I gave you one!" He jerked his chin at my closed hand. I opened my fingers to see a jagged chunk of stone sitting on my palm. "See? Piece of the real Berlin Wall, the night it came down! Have to get it while we can, before it's gone!"

In spite of everything, I had to laugh. Yeah, the Berlin Wall was most definitely down. In a year's time, there'd be chunks of broken stone and brick for sale in every hotel and airport gift shop, attached to key chains, set in snow globes and paperweights and framed boxes, with or without an accompanying historic photo—Pieces of the True Wall, for sale along with toilet paper, shampoo, and CDs by Duran Duran and Cyndi Lauper. The people behind the Iron Curtain had no idea what was about to hit them.

"You want some more?" the guy asked me, pausing with the chisel against the wall. There were lots of craters where bits had just been chipped away.

I dropped the fragment in my coat pocket and shook my head. "Nah. Save some for the East Berliners. They'll need the income."

He frowned. "I *am* from East Berlin," he said.

I nodded and started to push my way past him when he grabbed my arm.

"Wait!" He fumbled in his coat pocket and came up with a compact camera. It looked brand new. "Please, could you take my picture?"

I looked at the people crowded around us. "I can try."

He posed, smiling, holding up his hammer and chisel in one hand and a large chunk of stone in the other.

"Say 'cheese.' "

"No, say '*freeeeeeedom!*' " someone shouted, to the delight of everyone in earshot. The guy did so but then had to wait an extra second while I found the right button for the shutter, which probably made his smile look just a bit strained. Not that it mattered: He now had photographic evidence to prove his rubble was really from the wall and not just something he picked up off the ground somewhere.

"There you go," I said, passing the camera back to him. "That'll take care of the provenance."

He thanked me, looking puzzled, and went on chipping away. As I kept moving along the wall, I saw that he wasn't the only souvenir hunter. Lots of people were doing the same thing, some of them filling plastic bags with chunks of history. There was one woman, however, who was actually fussy about the pieces she chipped out of the wall. She would work on a small area very carefully, doing her best to get a chunk at least as large as the palm of her hand. Once she did that, she would hold it for a few seconds, head bowed and eyes closed. Then she would either discard it and look for another section of wall or kiss it and drop it into the large cloth bag slung diagonally across her front.

I was curious but more concerned about finding Quinn. I tried calling out her name again, and this time, the sound of my American accent generated a new and unexpected response.

"American!" "Yay, American!" "USA . . . USA . . . USA!"

Suddenly, everyone in my immediate vicinity loved me. And I mean, *loved.* They rushed me all at once, pressing me into the cold stone, grabbing me, kissing my arms, my hands, whatever they could get at. This was it, I thought as I gasped for air; I was going to die of love at the Berlin Wall.

Then I felt my feet leave the ground. Oh, good, I thought giddily, I was going to crowd surf. That was so much better than getting crushed to death, I wouldn't even mind if someone groped my butt. A small price to pay . . .

But I kept rising higher and higher, and before I knew what was really happening, I was already on top of the wall amid a group of laughing, dancing people who also seemed to love me a lot, while the crowd below cheered.

The only coherent thought I had was *Omigod,* as my sense

of balance disappeared and left me teetering among strangers who might not notice I was about to fall to my death. Then my balance returned as abruptly as it had vanished and I was fine. Better than fine—it was the perfect vantage point for looking for Quinn.

I hollered as loud as I could between my cupped hands. People heard me: I saw them turn to look up at me curiously and then go on with their hugging and kissing and dancing and drinking champagne. Getting a bit more used to where I was, I started slowly sidling along the wall, stopping only for the occasional hug and kiss. Flashlights played over the sea of people. A flashlight was exactly what I needed, I thought; maybe everyone loved everyone so much up here that I could persuade somebody to loan me one.

A tall woman with spiky red hair was only too happy to let me use hers on the crowd, first demonstrating zigzags and figure eights and other patterns. I obliged briefly and then began searching methodically among the people closest to the wall. The light was already dimming in my hands, probably after hours of zigzags and figure eights. *Just my luck,* I thought—

Then I saw a head of shiny black curls directly below me; I might not have been sure except for the shiny blond head with her.

"Quinn!" I screamed.

She and Martin looked up at me along with at least thirty other people. Quinn was surprised, as if she had forgotten I was even here. Martin's expression was a mix of dismay and vague puzzlement. He didn't recognize me, I realized.

"Quinn, we have to go home *now*!" I hollered.

She made an annoyed face before turning away to argue with Martin. He wasn't having any: He kept interrupting her and gesturing at me, all the while shaking his head emphatically. No, no, a thousand times no.

"Quinn, he said no; now let's go home!" My throat was getting raw. I had to get down. But how? I tried to talk to the people around me to ask them to help me down, lower me down or something, but no one was listening now. They'd just hug me or kiss me and go on dancing or cheering. I crouched down, trying to estimate by sight how long the drop would be if I were to hang by my hands and let my feet dangle. Too far not to get hurt, I decided. Assuming I actually *could* have dangled my own body weight by my hands for longer than an eighth of a second.

Martin gestured at me again—no, not me, the wall—and pushed Quinn back a couple of feet. She tried to move toward him, but the people directly behind her grabbed her and held her back. Not roughly, but firmly, so that she could barely move. Were all those people *with* Martin? Who were they? I couldn't see their faces very well at this angle but some of them had the same shade of blond hair.

Martin's family? Then they'd gotten through from East Berlin. Or *some* of them had gotten through and they were here at the wall waiting for the rest? But why *here*? Why not at one of the actual gates, where people were coming through on foot or in their cars so the West Berliners could pound dents into them?

All at once there was an incredibly loud buzzing whine that startled me so much I nearly fell. Several feet to my right, I saw a fountain of sparks—another power saw. The hell with rubble; grab some power tools and cut yourself a whole panel. People on top of the wall and below were cheering. Except for Martin and the people with him, I saw; they actually looked scared.

Quinn was still struggling to get free. Martin seemed to be telling the people who had her to hold her tighter. Then he turned to face the wall and put both hands on the stone.

I could actually hear my sister screaming above the power saw as Martin moved closer to the wall in tiny, shuffling steps. The angle made it impossible to see what he was doing; for that matter, I couldn't even see him anymore. There was no way to lean forward without taking a header off the top. I lay down on my stomach so I could see what was directly below me.

The people holding Quinn hadn't moved, and Quinn still twisted in their grip, but I couldn't see Martin. I inched forward, scanning the people on either side of the spot where he had been standing, but he wasn't among them. And the spot where he had been remained clear: No one crowded in, almost as if an unseen barrier were keeping them back.

Quinn lifted her tearful face to look at me. I was trying to think of something to say to her, when Martin came through the wall.

The actual movement itself seemed so normal that I almost ignored it. Then I did what I can only describe as a mental double take. By that time, Martin was standing in front of the wall embracing an older woman shaking as she sobbed in his arms.

They came through the wall. They came through the Berlin Wall. Except, I remembered, some people had trouble getting through the wall. Some people got stuck. . . .

My rational mind was telling me I was tripping on the atmosphere, jet lag, beer, and possibly something my beer had been spiked with. But my rational mind was very small and very, very far away. What I was seeing told me that I had to get Quinn out of the way before she screwed things up.

"Quinn!" I bellowed. "We have to leave! *We're in the way!*"

Martin, the woman who I figured was his mother, and everyone else looked up at me. I got up and moved down several feet, trying to show them in sign language what I wanted to do. Even finally getting some help from the people up on the wall with me, however, I couldn't get close enough to the ground to jump without hurting myself. Then a few of the people holding Quinn gave her over briefly to Martin, who tolerated her clinging to him for the time it took for them to catch me. Still, it wasn't fun: the fall knocked the breath out of me.

Martin's people probably were family; close up, the resemblance was very strong. They didn't have much English but enough to make it clear that I had to catch my breath quickly and take my sister away. I wasn't sure I'd actually be able to do that, considering it had taken four of them to hang on to her, all of whom looked a lot stronger than I was. But I guess all the struggling had tired her out. I didn't need much help to peel her off Martin, and once I got her back into the thick of the crowd, she wouldn't be able to push her way through them to get back to Martin.

"Thank you," he said to me in a voice that was somehow both formal and warm. "It takes all of us to will it. I can't take her, too. We'd never get out, we'd die in there. I'm sorry, Quinn, I am." He bent to kiss her. "Go. This isn't for you."

"No, I *can* help," Quinn wailed. I turned her around, grabbed her waist, and pushed her into the crowd ahead of me. "Jean, don't, I love him—"

"Just stay out of it," I growled, wincing at the growing soreness in my throat. I'd been shouting so much I was going to lose my voice. "This isn't *your* fight. Not this part."

"You saw it, though, right?" She twisted out of my grip and turned to face me. "You saw; now you know!"

"Yeah, I saw, I know, and tomorrow I'll fall out of bed and it'll all be a dream. Cliché ending, but if it works, it works. Let's go."

"No, I want to be there for him, I want to help! I want to be part of it!" Quinn tried to push past me, but I'd been right: She had no strength left now.

"You can't," I rasped. "You're not part of it, you can't be, you never could have been. They're them and we're us."

"But he showed me—"

"His mistake. People make mistakes when they think they're all alone."

"That's not it—"

"*Quinn!* That *is* it. Now we have to let him get the rest of his family out." The image of the woman I'd seen chipping pieces out of the wall popped into my mind, tossing some pieces away, keeping others, kissing them before she put them in her bag. Because she couldn't get her own people out? Why not?

Because they had died in there. The answer came unbidden and with a certainty I couldn't justify. I shoved the thought aside, telling myself that when I woke up tomorrow, I'd have forgotten all about it

"I can help!" she insisted, trying to lunge past me again.

"You can't!" I pushed her back hard. "You don't belong with them; you're not special, you have no place in any unseen world; you're like me and the rest of *our* family. Get used to it!"

She looked at me like I'd slapped her.

"Oh, *sorry*," I said, feeling equally stung by her reaction. "It's hell being ordinary, but that's the human condition."

All the fight went out of her then, and she let me take her back to the Am Zoo.

The next morning I paid the horrendous bill and we flew back to the United States. Quinn wouldn't talk to me for most of the trip home, which didn't bother me much. I was too busy sleeping. The more time I could spend unconscious after that, the less real it seemed and the saner I felt.

Quinn eventually started speaking to me again but never about that night in Berlin. From time to time, I've been tempted to bring it up but I know that would just be asking for trouble.

I'm much more curious about what happened with Martin and his family—if he got them all out, where they are now. I'm pretty sure Quinn never heard anything from him. I don't know for certain but I'd bet money that she tried to find him again after we got home. And it wouldn't surprise me if she Googles his name now and then or looks at footage from that night on YouTube. I've looked myself and never seen anything unusual.

I've never gotten back to Berlin, but one of my friends from work went to Germany for the first time a few years ago on her honeymoon. She came back and gave us all these little bottles about three inches tall, filled with fragments of brick and stone.

"Pieces of the old Berlin Wall," she said. "You can buy them everywhere. It doesn't look like much but it's history, I guess. A little bit of history in a three-inch bottle."

I took mine home and emptied it out on a saucer. It really didn't look like anything at all. It certainly didn't *feel* like anything special. But instead of putting it back in the bottle, I dumped it outside in the backyard. Maybe it was just debris from some demolished building, or maybe it was a collection of pieces of the true wall. On the off chance it was the latter, I left it to blow away freely in the wind. It just seemed right.

Underbridge

BY PETER S. BEAGLE

Peter S. Beagle was born in Manhattan in 1939, on the same night that Billie Holliday was recording "Strange Fruit" and "Fine and Mellow" just a few blocks away. Raised in the Bronx, Peter originally proclaimed he would be a writer when ten years old. Today he is acknowledged as an American fantasy icon, and to the delight of his millions of fans around the world he is now publishing more than ever.

In addition to being an acclaimed novelist and writer of short stories and nonfiction, Peter has also written numerous plays, teleplays, and screenplays, and is a gifted poet, librettist, lyricist, and singer/songwriter. To learn more about *The Last Unicorn, A Fine and Private Place, Summerlong, I'm Afraid You've Got Dragons, I See By My Outfit,* "Two Hearts," and all the rest of his extraordinary body of work, please visit www.peterbeagle.com.

The Seattle position came through just in time.

It was a near thing, even for Richardson. As an untenured professor of children's literature he was bitterly used to cutting it close, but now, with nothing in the wings to follow his MSSU gig but Jake Riskin's offer to sub remedial English in the Joplin high schools, life was officially the bleakest Richardson could remember. Easy enough to blink through grad school dreaming of life as a Matthew Arnold–esque scholar-gypsy; harder to slog through decades of futureless jobs in second-rank college towns, never being offered the cozy sinecure he had once assumed inevitable. What about professional respect and privileges? What about medical insurance, teaching assistants, preferred parking? What about *sabbaticals*?

Rescue found him shopping in the West 7th Street Save-A-Lot. His cell phone rang, and wondrously, instead of Jake pushing for a decision, the call was from a secretary at the University of Washington English department. Would he, she wondered, be free to take over classes for a professor who had just been awarded a sizable grant to spend eighteen months at Cambridge, producing a study of the life and works of Joan Aiken?

He said yes, of course, then took a brief time settling the details, which were neither many nor complicated. At no time did he show the slightest degree of unprofessional emotion. But after he snapped his phone shut he stood very still and whispered "*Saved* . . ." to himself, and when he left the store there were red baby potatoes ($2.40 a pound!) in his bag instead of 34-cent russets.

Most especially was he grateful at being able to take over the Queen Anne Hill apartment of the traveling professor. It was snug—the man lived alone, except for an old cat, whom Richardson, who disliked cats, had dourly agreed to care for—but also well appointed, including cable television, washer and dryer, microwave and dishwasher, a handsome fireplace, and a one-car garage, with a cord of split wood for the winter neatly stacked at the far end. The rent was manageable, as was the drive to the UW; and his classes were surprisingly enjoyable, containing as they did a fair number of students who actually wanted to be there. Richardson could have done decidedly worse, and most often had.

He had been welcomed to the school with impersonal warmth by the chairman of the English department, who was younger than Richardson and looked it. The chairman's name was Philip Austin Watkins IV, but he preferred to be called "Aussie," though he had never been to Australia. He assured Richardson earnestly on their first meeting, "I want you to know, I'm really happy to have you on board, and I'll do everything I can to get you extended here if possible. That's a promise." Richardson, who knew much better at fifty-one than to believe this, believed.

His students generally seemed to like him—at least they paid attention, worked hard on their assignments, didn't mock his serious manner, and often brought up intelligent questions about Milne and Greene, Erich Kästner, Hugh Lofting, Astrid Lindgren, or his own beloved E. Nesbit. But they never took him into their confidence, even during his office hours—never wept or broke down, confessing anxieties or sins or dreams (which would have terrified him), never came to him merely to visit. Nor did he make any significant connections with his fellows on the faculty. He knew well enough that he made friends with difficulty and wasn't good at keeping them, being naturally formal in his style and uncomfortable in his body, so that he appeared to be forever leaning away from people even when he was making an earnest effort to be close to them. With women, his lifelong awkwardness became worse in the terminally friendly Seattle atmosphere. Once, younger, he had wished to be different; now he no longer believed it possible.

The legendary rain of the Pacific Northwest was not an issue; if anything, he discovered that he enjoyed it. Having studied the data on the Seattle climate carefully, once he knew he was going there, he understood that many areas of both coasts get notably more rain, in terms of inches, and endure distinctly colder winters. And the year-round greenness and lack of air pollution more than made up for the mildew, as far as Richardson was concerned. Damp or not, it beat Joplin. Or Hobbs, New Mexico. Or Enterprise, Alabama.

What the greenness did *not* make up for was the near-perpetual overcast. Seattle's sky was dazzlingly, exaltingly, shockingly blue when it chose to be so; but there was a reason that the city consumed more than its share of vitamin D and was the first marketplace for various full-spectrum lightbulbs. Seattle introduced Richardson to an entirely new understanding of the word *overcast,* sometimes going two months and more without seeing either clear skies or an honest raindrop. He had not been prepared for this.

Many things that shrink from sunlight gain power in fog and murk. Richardson began to find himself reluctant enough to leave the atmosphere of the UW campus that he often stayed on after work, attending lectures that bored him, going to showings of films he didn't understand—even once dropping in on a faculty meeting, though this was not required of him. The main subject under discussion was the urgent need to replace a particular TA, who for six years had been covering most of the undergraduate classes of professors far too occupied with important matters to deal with actual students. Another year would have required granting him a tenure-track assistant professorship, which was, of course, out of the question. Sitting uncomfortably in the back, saying nothing, Richardson felt he was somehow attending his own autopsy.

And when Richardson finally went home in darkness to the warm, comfortable apartment that was not his own, and the company of the sour-smelling old gray cat, he frequently went out again to walk aimlessly on steep, silent Queen Anne Hill and beyond, watching the lights go out in window after window. If rain did not fall, he might well wander until three or four in the morning, as he had never before done in his life.

But it was in daylight that Richardson first saw the Troll.

He had walked across the blue-and-orange drawbridge at the foot of Queen Anne Hill into Fremont, which had become a favorite weekend ramble of his, though the quirky, rakish little pocket always made him nervous and wistful at the same time. He wished he were the sort of person who could fit comfortably into a neighborhood that could proclaim itself "The Center of the Universe," hold a nude bicycle parade as part of a solstice celebration, and put up signs advising visitors to throw their watches away. He would have liked to be able to imagine living in Fremont.

Richardson had read about the Fremont Bridge Troll online while preparing to leave Joplin. He knew that it was not actually located under the Fremont Bridge, but under the north end of the nearby Aurora Avenue Bridge; and that the Troll was made of concrete, had been created by a team of four artists, weighed four thousand pounds, was more than eighteen feet high, had one staring eye made of an automobile hubcap, and was crushing a cement-spattered Volkswagen Beetle in its left hand. As beloved a tourist photo op as the Space Needle, it had the inestimable further advantages of being free, unique, and something no lover of children's books could ignore.

It took Richardson a while to come face-to-face with the Troll, because the day was blue and brisk, and the families were out in force, shoving up to the statue to take pictures, posing small children and puzzled-looking babies within the Troll's embrace, or actually placing them on its shoulder. Richardson made no effort to approach until the crowd had thinned to a few teenagers with cell-phone cameras; then he went close enough to see his distorted reflection in the battered aluminum eye. He said nothing but stayed there until a couple of the teenagers pushed past him to be photographed kissing and snuggling in the shadow of the Troll. Then he went on home.

Two weeks later, driven by increasing insomnia, he crossed the Fremont Bridge again and eventually found himself facing the glowering concrete monster where it crouched in its streetside cave. Alone in darkness, with no fond throng to warm and humanize it, the hubcap eye now seemed to be sizing him up as a tender improvement on a VW Beetle. *Grendel,* Richardson thought, *this is what Grendel looked like.* Aloud, he said, "Hello. Off for the night?"

The Troll made no answer. Richardson went a few steps closer, fascinated by the expression and personality it was possible to impose on two tons of concrete. He asked it, "Do you ever get tired of tourists gaping at you every day? *I* would." For some reason, he wanted the Troll to know that he was a sympathetic, understanding person. He said, "My name's Richardson."

A roupy old voice behind him said, "Don't you get too close. He's mean."

Richardson turned to see a black rain slicker, which appeared to be almost entirely inhabited by a huge gray beard. The hood of the slicker was pulled close around the old man's face, so that only the beard and a pair of bright, bloodshot gray eyes were visible as he squatted on the sidewalk that approached the underpass, with four shopping bags arranged around him. Richardson took them at first for the man's worldly possessions; only later, back in the apartment, did he recall glimpsing a long Italian salami, a wine bottle, and a French baguette in one of them.

The old man coughed—a long, rattling, machine-gun burst—then growled, "I'd back off a little ways, was I you. He gets mean at night."

Richardson played along with the joke. "Oh, I don't know. He put up so nicely with all those tourists today."

"Daytime," the old man grunted. "Sun goes down, he gets around. . . ." He belched mightily, leaned back against the guardrail, and closed his eyes.

"Well," Richardson said, chuckling to keep the conversation reasonable. "Well, but you're here, taking a nap right within his grasp. You're not afraid of him."

The old man did not open his eyes. "I got on his good side a long time ago. Go away, man. You don't want to be here." The last words grumbled into a snore.

Richardson stood looking back and forth at the Troll and the old man in the black rain slicker, whose snoring mouth hung open, a red-black wound in the vast gray beard. Finally he said politely to the Troll, "You have curious friends," and walked quickly away. The old man never stirred as Richardson passed him.

He had no trouble sleeping that night, but he did dream of the Troll. They were talking quite earnestly, under the bridge, but he remembered not even a fragment of their conversation; only that the Troll was wearing a Smokey Bear hat and kept biting pieces off the Volkswagen, chewing them like gum and spitting them out. In the dream, Richardson accepted this as perfectly normal: The flavor probably didn't last very long.

He didn't go back to see the Troll at night for a month. Once or twice in the daytime, yes, but he found such visits unsatisfying. During daylight hours the tourist buses were constantly stopping, and families were likely to push baby carriages close between the Troll's hands for photographs. The familiarity, the chattering gaiety, was almost offensive to him, as though the people were savages out of bad movies, and the Troll their trapped and stoic prisoner.

He never saw the old man there. Presumably he was off doing whatever homeless people did during the day, even those who bought French baguettes with their beggings.

Richardson's own routine was as drearily predictable as ever. Over the years he had become intensely aware of the arc of each passing contract, from eager launch through trembling zenith to the unavoidable day when he packed his battered Subaru and drove off to whatever job might come next. He was now at the halfway point of his stay at the UW: Each time he opened his office door was one twisting turn closer to the last, each paycheck a countdown, in reverse, to the end of his temporary security. Richardson's students and colleagues saw no change in his tone or behavior—he was most careful about that—but in his own ears he heard a gently rising scream.

His silent night walks began to fill with imagined conversations. Some of these were with his parents, both long deceased but still reproving. Others were with distantly remembered college acquaintances or with characters out of his favorite books. But the ones that Richardson enjoyed most were his one-sided exchanges with the Troll, whose vast, unresponsive silence Richardson found endlessly encouraging.

As he wandered through the darkness, hands uncharacteristically in his hip pockets, he found he could speak to the Troll as though they had been friends long enough that there was no point in hiding anything from one another. He had never known that sort of friendship.

"I am never going to be anything more than I am already," he said to the Troll-haunted air. "Forget the fellowships and grants, never mind the articles in *The New Yorker, Smithsonian, Harper's,* never mind the Modern Language Association, PEN. . . . None of it is ever going to happen, Troll. I know this. My life is exactly like yours—set in stone and meaningless."

Without realizing it, or ever putting it into words, Richardson came to think of the concrete Troll as his only real friend in Seattle, just as he began resenting the old man in the rain slicker for his privileged position on the Troll's "good side," and himself for his own futility. In the middle of one class—a lecture on the period political references hidden within Lewis Carroll's underappreciated *Sylvie and Bruno*—Richardson heard his own voice abruptly say, "To hell with *that*!" He had to stop and look around the hall for a moment, puzzling his students, before he realized that he hadn't actually said the words out loud.

On the damp and moonless night that Richardson finally returned to the end of the Aurora Avenue Bridge, the old man wasn't there. Neither was the Troll. Only the concrete-slathered Volkswagen was still in place, its curved roof and sides indented where the Troll's great fingers had previously rested.

Sun goes down, he gets around. . . . Richardson remembered what he had assumed was a joke, and shook his head sharply. He felt the urge to run away, as if the *absence* of the Troll somehow constituted an almost cellular rebuke to his carefully manicured sense of the rational.

Richardson heard the sound then, distant yet, but numbingly clear: the long, dragging scrape of stone over asphalt. He turned and walked a little way to look east, toward Fremont Street—saw the hunched shadow rising into view—turned again, and bolted back across the bridge, the one leading him to Queen Anne Hill, a door he could close and lock, and a smelly gray cat wailing angrily over an empty food dish. He sat up the rest of the night, watching the QVC channel for company, seeing nothing. Near dawn he fell asleep on the living-room couch, with the television set still selling Select Comfort beds and amethyst jewelry.

In the morning, before he went to the university, he drove down into Fremont, double-parking at 36th and Winslow to make sure of what he already knew. The Troll was back in its place with no smallest deviation from its four creators' positioning and no indication that it had ever moved at all. Even its grip on the old VW was displayed exactly as it had been, crushing finger for finger, bulging knuckle for knuckle, splayed right-hand fingers digging at the earth for purchase.

Richardson had a headache. He stepped graciously aside for children already swarming up to pose with the Troll for their parents, hurried back to his car, and drove away. His usual parking space was taken when he got to the UW, and finding another made him late to class.

For more than two weeks Richardson not only avoided the Aurora Bridge but stayed out of Fremont altogether. Even so, whether by day or night, strolling the campus, shopping in the University District, or walking a silent waterfront street under the Viaduct, he would often stand very still, listening for the slow, terribly slow, grinding of concrete feet somewhere near.

The fact that he could not quite hear it did not make it go away.

Eventually, out of a kind of wintry lassitude, he began drifting down Fourth Avenue North again, at first no farther than the drawbridge, whose raisings and lowerings he found oddly soothing. He seemed to be at a curious remove from himself during that time, watching himself watching the boats waiting to pass the bridge, watching the rain on the water.

When he finally did cross the bridge, however, he did so without hesitation and on the hunt.

"Fuck off," Cut'n-Shoot said. "Just fuck off and go away and leave me alone."

"Not a chance."

"I have to get *ready*. I have to *be* there."

"Then *tell* me. All you have to do is tell me!"

Richardson had found the bearded old man asleep—noisily asleep, his throat a sporadic bullroarer—under a tree in the Gas Works Park, near the shore of Lake Union. He was still wearing the same clothes and black rain slicker, now with the hood down, and there was an empty bottle of orange schnapps clutched in his filthy hand. Bits of greasy foie gras speckled his whiskers like dirty snow. When glaring him awake didn't work, Richardson had moved on to kicking the cracked leather soles of the man's old boots, which did.

It also got him a deep bruise on his forearm, from blocking an angrily thrown schnapps bottle. Their subsequent conversation had been unproductive. So far, the only useful thing he had uncovered was that the old man called himself "Cut'n-Shoot," after the small town in Texas where he'd been born. That was the end of anything significant, aside from the man's obvious agitation and impatience as evening darkened toward night.

"Goddamn you, somebody gets hurt, it's going to be all your fault! Let me go!" Cut'n-Shoot's bellow was broken by a coughing spasm that almost brought him to his knees. He leaned forward, spitting and dribbling, hands braced on his thighs.

"I'm not stopping you," Richardson said. "I just want answers. I know you weren't making that up, about the Troll moving at night. I've seen it."

"Yah?" Cut'n-Shoot hawked up one last monster wad. "So what? Price of fish cakes. Ain't *your* job."

"I'm a professor of children's literature, a *full* professor"—for some reason he felt compelled to lie to the old man—"at the University of Washington. I could quote you troll stories from here to next September. And one thing I knew for certain—until I met *you*—was that they don't exist."

Cut'n-Shoot glared at him out of one rheumy eye, the other one closed and twitching. "You think you know trolls?" He snorted. "Goddamn useless punk . . . you don't know shit."

"Show me."

The old man stared hard for a moment more, then smiled, revealing a sprinkling of brown teeth. It was not a friendly expression. "Might be I will, then. Maybe teach you a lesson. But we're gonna pick up some things first, and you're buyin'. Come on."

Cut'n-Shoot led him a little over three-quarters of a mile from the park, along Northlake Way, under the high overpass of the Aurora Avenue Bridge and the low one at Fourth Avenue, then right on Evanston. Richardson tried asking more questions but got nothing but growls and snorts for his trouble.

Best to save his breath, anyway—he was surprised at how fast the old man could move in a syncopated crab-scuttle that favored his right leg and made the rain slicker snap like a geisha's fan. At the corner of 34th Street Cut'n-Shoot ignored the parallel white stripes of the crosswalk and angled straight across the street to the doors of the Fremont PCC. He strode through them like Alexander entering a conquered city.

The bag clerk nearest the entry waved as they came in. "Hey, Cut! Little late tonight."

Cut'n-Shoot didn't pause, cocking one thumb back over his shoulder at Richardson as he swept up a plastic shopping basket and continued deeper into the store. "Not my fault. Professor here's got the rag on."

When they finally left—having rung up $213.62 of luxury items on Richardson's MasterCard, including multiple cuts of Eel River organic beef and a $55 bottle of 2006 Cadence Camerata Cabernet Sauvignon—it was a docile, baffled Richardson, grocery bags in hand, who trudged after the old man down the mostly empty neighborhood streets. Cut'n-Shoot had made his selections with the demanding eye of a lifelong connoisseur, assessing things on some qualitative scale of measurement Richardson couldn't begin to comprehend. That he and his wallet were being taken advantage of was self-evident; but the inborn curiosity that had first led him to books as a child, that insatiable need to get to the end of each new unfolding story, was now completely engaged. Rambling concrete trolls weren't the only mystery in Fremont.

Cut'n-Shoot led him east along 34th Street to where Troll Avenue started, a narrow road rising between the grand columns that supported the Aurora Avenue Bridge. High on the bridge itself cars hissed by like ghosts, while down on the ground it was quiet as the sea bottom, and the sparse lights from lakeside boats and local apartment buildings only served to make the path up to the Troll darker than Richardson liked.

"Stupid ratfucks throw a big party up there every October," Cut'n-Shoot said. "Call it 'Trolloween.' *People.* Batshit stupid."

"Well, Fremont's that kind of place," Richardson responded. "I mean, the Solstice Parade, Oktoberfest, the crazy rocket with 'Freedom to Be Peculiar' written on it in Latin—"

"Don't care about all that crap. Just wish they wouldn't rile *him* so much. Job's hard enough as it is."

"And what job would that be, exactly, anyway?"

"You'll see."

At the top of the road the bridge merged with the hillside, forming the space that held the Troll, with stairs running up the hill on either side. Tonight the Troll looked exactly as it had the first time he saw it. It was impossible to imagine this crudely hewn mound of ferroconcrete in motion, even knowing what he knew. Cut'n-Shoot made him put the grocery bags on the ground at the base of the eastern stair, then gestured brusquely for him to stand aside. When he did, the old man got down heavily on one knee—not the right one, Richardson noticed—and started searching through them.

"That's the thing, see. People never know what they're doing. Best place to sleep in town and they had to go fuck everything up."

"It's concrete and wire and rebar," Richardson responded. "I read about it. They had a contest back in 1990; this design won. There used to be a time capsule with Elvis memorabilia in the car, for Christ's sake. It's not *real.*"

"Sure, sure. Like a troll cares what it's made of, starting out. Hah. That ain't the point. Point is, they did *too good a job.*"

Cut'n-Shoot struggled to his feet, unbalanced by the pair of brown packages he was holding—two large roasts in their taped-up butcher wrapping. "Here," he said, holding out one of them to Richardson. "Get this shit off. He won't be able to smell 'em through the paper."

"You *feed* him?"

"Told you I was on his good side, didn't I?"

Grinning fiercely through his beard now, the old man marched straight to the hulking stone brute and slapped the bloody roast down on the ground in front of it. "There!" he said. "First snack of the night. Better than your usual, too, and don't you know it! *Ummm-mmm,* that's gonna be good." He looked back at Richardson just as a car passed, its headlights making the Troll's hubcap eye seem to flicker and spin. "Well, come on—you wanted this, didn't you? Just do like me, make it friendly."

Richardson was holding the larger unwrapped roast in front of him like a doily, pinching the thick slab of meat between the thumb and forefinger of each hand. It was slippery, and the blood dripping from it made him queasy. As he stepped forward with the offering, an old Norse poem suddenly came to him, the earliest relevant reference his magpie mind could dredge up. *"They call me Troll,"* he recited. *"Gnawer of the Moon, Giant of the Gale-blasts, Curse of the rain-hall . . ."*

Cut'n-Shoot looked at him approvingly, nodding him on.

"Companion of the Sibyl, Nightroaming hag, Swallower of the loaf of heaven.

What is a Troll but that?"

Richardson laid his roast down gently beside Cut'n-Shoot's, took a deep breath, and backed away without looking up, not knowing as he did so whether this obeisance was for the Troll's benefit, Cut'n-Shoot's, or his own.

The old man's grating chuckle came to him. "That's the good side, all right. That's the way, that's the way." Richardson looked up. Cut'n-Shoot had pushed back the hood of his rain slicker, and was scratching his head through hair like furnace ashes. "But he likes *lively* a sight better. You get the chance, you remember."

"Nothing's happening," Richardson started to say—and then something was.

One by one the fingers of the Troll's right hand were coming free of the ground. Richardson realized that the whole forearm was lifting up, twisting from the elbow, dust and dirt sifting off as it rose. The giant hand turned with the motion, dead-gray fingers coming together with a sound of cracking bricks. Then—like a child grabbing for jacks before the ball comes down, and just as fast—the Troll's hand swept up the two roasts in one great swinging motion and carried them to its suddenly open mouth. The ponderous jaw moved up and down three times before it settled back into place, and Richardson tried to imagine what could possibly be going on inside. A moment later the Troll's hand and arm returned to their original position, fingers wriggling their way back into the soil and once more becoming motionless.

There was no moon, and no more cars went by, but the hubcap continued to twinkle with a brightly chilling malice, and even—so it seemed to Richardson—to wink. He was still staring at the Troll when Cut'n-Shoot finally clapped his palms together with satisfaction.

"Well! Old sumbitch settled *right* down. Think he liked that fancy talk. Know any more?"

"Sure."

"My lucky day," the old man said. "Now lemme show you what the wine's for."

Richardson woke the next morning hung over, stiff backed, and with a runny nose. He was late to class again; and that evening, when he returned to Fremont, he brought lamb chops.

From then on he never came to the bridge without bringing some tribute for the Troll. Most often it came in the form of slabs of raw meat; though now and again, this being Seattle, he would present the statue with a whole salmon, usually purchased down at the ferry dock from a fisherman's wife. Once—only once—he tried offering a bag of fresh crab cakes, but Cut'n-Shoot informed him tersely, "Don't give him none of that touristy shit," and made him go back to the Fremont PCC for an entire Diestel Family turkey.

Richardson also read to the Troll most evenings, working his way up from obvious fare to selections from the *Bland Tomtar och Troll* series, voiced dramatically in his best stab at phonetic Swedish. He had no idea whether the Troll understood, but the expressions on his own face as he dealt with the unfamiliar orthography made Cut'n-Shoot howl.

It didn't always go easily. By day the Troll was changeless, an eternally crude concrete figure with one dull aluminum eye, a vacantly malevolent expression, and bad hair. At night its temperament was as unpredictably irritable as a wasp's. Richardson began to measure his visits on a scale marked in feet, yards, and furlongs, assessing the difference between *this* Tuesday and *that* Saturday by precisely how far the Troll stirred from its den. In that way he came to understand—as Cut'n-Shoot never bothered to explain—that the old man's task wasn't to feed the Troll at all, but rather to distract it, to confuse it, to short-circuit its unfocused instinct to go off unimpeded about its trollish business, whatever that might be. Food was a means to that end; as now was Richardson's cheerfully garbled Swedish. Even so there were nights when it would not yield, and lumbered half a mile or more before they could tempt and coax it—like two Pekingese herding a mastiff—back under the bridge. On those nights, nothing would do but "the lively," usually in the form of a writhing rat or pigeon. Cut'n-Shoot never told Richardson how—or with what—he caught them.

The months passed, and the weather turned relatively mild and notably dry. On campus this was generally spoken of as a function of global warming and greeted with definite anxiety. Richardson paid little attention to climate crises, having his own worries. His temporary tenure at the university was coming to an end with the summer quarter, and thoughts of the department chair's vague early promises moved in his heart like schooling fish: Instead of calling up job listings and sending out inquiries, he found himself manufacturing excuses to go by Aussie's office or sit near him in the faculty dining hall, hoping that mere proximity might make the man offer him work he couldn't possibly ask for.

He also began to drink, at first in pretended sociability with Cut'n-Shoot, but later with the devotion of a convert. It was not an area in which he had any sort of previous expertise. He could neither tell good champagne from bad nor upper-shelf vodka from potato-peel swill; only that in each case the latter was distinctly cheaper. It all invariably left him with a hammering headache the next morning, which seemed to be how you could tell you were doing it right.

Having no one to drink with in comfort and understanding, he came to spend the early part of many evenings drinking with the gray cat, for whom he had conceived an increasing dislike. Not only did it smell bad, it had taken to urinating on the floor outside its box and knocking down the clothes hamper to tear and scratch at Richardson's dirty clothes. Richardson, who had never hated an animal in his life, no more than he had ever loved one, brooded increasingly and extensively about the gray cat.

Nothing would probably have come of this growing fixation had he not already been drunk on the evening he discovered that the cat had peed in his only pair of carpet slippers. Having noticed a pet-transport cage in one of the closets, he pounced on the unwary animal and forced it into the cage, threw on his coat, and stalked down the hill toward Fremont, muttering in counterpoint to the cat's furious wails, as the cage banged against the side of his left knee. "Lively. Right, lively it is. Lively it bloody is."

Cut'n-Shoot said nothing when Richardson set the cage down facing the Troll, shouted "Lively!" and walked quickly away, paying no heed to the cat's redoubled howling. He did look back once, but cage and bridge were both out of sight by then.

In the morning, between the expected headache and the forgotten pre-finals lecture summarizing works intended for children from A.D. 1000 to 1850, he remembered the cat only as he was locking the apartment door. There was no time to check on the cage just then; but all day long he could concentrate on almost nothing else. Along with trying to invent something to tell the cat's owner, he became obsessed with the notion that the Humane Society would be waiting for him at the bridge with a charge of felony animal abuse—and quite possibly littering.

That evening he found the remains of the empty cage between two of the Troll's huge fingers. The door had been ripped clean away, as had most of the front of the cage, and the rest of it had been pounded almost shapeless, as though by a hammer or a great fist. There was fur.

Richardson just made it to the bushes before he was very sick. It took him a long time to empty his stomach, and he was shaking and coughing when he was done, barely able to stand erect. His throat and mouth tasted of chewed tinfoil.

When he finally forced himself to turn back toward the statue, he saw Cut'n-Shoot grinning derisively at him from the shadow of the bridge. "One thing when I do it, another when you do, hah?"

"You could have stopped it. You had other food there. I saw it. You could have let the cat out of that thing, let it go." His stomach contracted, and he thought he was going to be sick again, but there was nothing left to vomit.

"Waste not, want not," Cut'n-Shoot chuckled. "'Sides, now you really *do* know trolls."

With a mean cunning that he would not have suspected himself of possessing, Richardson designed an advertisement for a lost gray cat—even including the name he had never once called it—had a hundred copies xeroxed, and mounted them in sheltered places up and down Queen Anne Hill. Thus, when the owner returned from that enviable, *enviable* sabbatical in England, he would see that Richardson had done everything possible to track down his unfortunately vanished cat.

Would have died soon anyway, old and incontinent as it was. He surely wouldn't have wanted the poor thing peeing all over his nice condo.

The next morning he went to a pet shop in the Wallingford district, and bought two carrier cages, the first identical to the one he had found in the apartment. The second was a bit larger, since one never knew. With the latter in his hand, he continued his nightly routine, the only differences being that his rounds were now somewhat more purposeful, and that with purpose came a reduction in his drinking. He often whistled as he walked, which was unusual for him.

It astonished him to realize how many animals—strays and otherwise—were running loose on the streets of Seattle. Cats and the smaller dogs were the easiest to capture, though he felt a certain amount of guilt over the ones that came trustingly to his leather-gloved hands. But he learned that people make pets out of the most unlikely animals: He caught escaped ferrets on two or three occasions, lab rats and mice with surprising frequency, and once even a tame crow with clipped wings. He was going to set the crow free—it had a vocabulary of several words, and a way of cocking its head to consider him—but then he thought that its inability to fly would make it easy prey for any cat, and changed his mind.

He did go through cages rather often; there was no way to avoid that, given the Troll's impetuous manner of opening them.

Feeding the Troll distracted him only somewhat from his terror of impending joblessness. It was now much too late to expect reprieve: All the best positions at even the worst colleges and universities had long since been snapped up without him ever applying, the community colleges were full, and thanks to Seattle's highly educated population there were thirty people ahead of him in line for any on-call substituting, even assuming someone would have the human decency to come down ill. Meanwhile the ever-smiling Aussie had turned evasive Trappist. Richardson stopped sliding by his door.

He had no idea that he was going mad with fear, frustration, and weariness. Most people don't; and most—frightened academic gypsies included—go on functioning fairly well. He remained faithful to his classes and his office hours; and if he was more terse with his students, and often more sharp tongued, still he fulfilled the function for which he was yet being paid as conscientiously as he knew how, because he still loved it. And love will keep you reasonably sane for a long time.

Then came the bright and breezy day when word began circulating through the department—a whisper only, at first, the merest of hints—that the Tenured Prodigal was not coming home.

At 9:30 P.M. a resurrected Richardson was thinking furiously as he knocked back half a bottle of Scotch and picked at his Indian takeout. This late in the game it would surely be impossible for Aussie to fill the Prodigal's slot; he would *have* to extend Richardson now. And if God could create concrete Trolls that moved and miracles as plain as this one, why, He might yet manage a way to make this change permanent.

Richardson had no plans to go out, not even to round up a stray dog or cat (which had been growing more difficult in recent weeks, as Queen Anne residents had been keeping closer track of their pets, blaming coyotes for the recent disappearances). Considering what to say to Aussie in the morning was paramount. But eventually he could not bear to sit still and found his legs carrying him to Fremont after all. Something special was clearly called for, a little libation to luck, so at the PCC he bought more of the Eel River beef for the Troll, and for himself and Cut'n-Shoot a half gallon of a unique coconut-and-molasses ice cream he had found nowhere else.

He left the grocery grinning, turned left—and saw, a block up 34th Street, walking away, Dr. Philip Austin Watkins IV.

The Scotch proved stronger than good judgment. "Aussie!" he shouted. Then louder: "Aussie!" Bag swinging wildly, he began to run.

The department head had dined out late with friends, imbibing one too many himself as the evening wore on. "You've never been screwed until you've been screwed by the British," he'd said, and meant it. Thank heavens he'd had foresight enough to lay contingency plans.

It took him a moment to realize that his name was being called, and a troubling moment more when he turned around to recognize who it was. His apprehension should perhaps have lasted longer: Instead of a simple greeting, followed by meaningless chat, Richardson slammed full tilt into the issue of the job opening. "Aussie, I heard about Brubaker. And you promised. You *did* promise."

"I promised to do everything I could to help you," Aussie countered. "And I did, but obviously it wasn't enough. I'm sorry."

"You can't leave the slot open, and it's too late—"

"Mr. Richardson. You knew you were a fill-in, just as I

knew from the beginning that the Aiken grant was a recruiting hook in disguise. If the fish had bitten later I might have had to keep you on. As it happens, he did it while my own preferred replacement was still sitting by the phone at Kansas State, waiting for my call, exactly where he's been since I first talked to him last April. The *slot,* as you call it, is already filled."

"Oh." Without thought, Richardson removed the frozen half gallon of coconut-molasses ice cream from his grocery bag and smashed Aussie in the head with it just as hard as he could. The man was insensible when he hit the ground, but not dead. Richardson was particularly glad of that.

"That was satisfactory," Richardson said aloud, as though he were judging a presentation in class. He heard his voice echoing in his head, which interested him. Looking around quickly and seeing no one close enough to notice what he was doing, or to interfere with it, Richardson got Aussie—who was not a small person—on his feet, hooked an arm around his waist, and draped one of the chairman's arms around his own neck, saying loudly and frequently, "*Told* you, Aussie; you can't say I didn't tell you. *Sip* the Calvados, I said, don't *guzzle* it. Ah, come on, Aussie, *help* me a little bit here."

Ordinarily, the walk to the Aurora Bridge would have taken Richardson a few minutes at most; dragging the unconscious Aussie, it took months, and by the time he came near the Troll's overpass he was panting and sweating heavily. "The last lively!" he called out in a louder, different voice. "Here you *go*! Compliments of the chef."

A hoarse, frantic voice behind him demanded, "What you doing? What the *hell* you doing?" Richardson let go of Aussie and turned to see Cut'n-Shoot gaping at him, his bleared eyes as wild as those of a horse in a burning barn. "What the hell you think you doing?"

"Tidying up," Richardson said. His voice sounded as far away as the old man's, and the echoes in his head were growing louder.

"You dumb shit," Cut'n-Shoot whispered. He was plainly sober, if he hadn't been a moment before, and wishing he weren't. "You crazy dumb shit, you fucking killed him."

Richardson looked briefly down, shaking his head. "Oh, let's hope not. He's twitched a couple of times."

Cut'n-Shoot was neither listening to him nor looking directly at him. "I'm out of here; I ain't in this mess. I'm calling the cops."

Richardson did not take the statement seriously. "Oh, please. Can you stand there and tell me our friend's always lived on warm puppies? Nothing like this has ever, ever happened before?"

"Not like this, not never like this." Cut'n-Shoot was beginning to back away, looking small and cold, hugging himself. "I got to call the cops. See if he got a cell phone or something."

"Ah, no cops," Richardson said. He was fascinated by his own detachment; by his strange lightheartedness in the midst of what he knew ought to be a nightmare. He took hold of Cut'n-Shoot's black slicker, which felt like slimy tissue paper in his hand. "You have *got* to get yourself a new raincoat," he told the old man sternly. "Promise me you'll get a new coat this winter." Cut'n-Shoot stared blankly at him, and Richardson shook him hard. "*Promise,* damn it!"

Richardson heard the long scraping rumble before he could turn, still keeping his grip on the struggling, babbling Cut'n-Shoot. The Troll was moving, emerging from its lair under the bridge, the disproportionate length of its body giving the effect of a great worm, even a dragon. In the open, it braced itself on its knuckles for some moments, like a gorilla, before rising to its full height. The hubcap eye was alight as Richardson had never seen it—a whipping-forest-fire red-orange that had nothing to do with the thin, wan crescent on the horizon. He thought, madly and absurdly, not of Grendel, but of the Cyclops Polyphemus.

The Troll crouched hugely over Aussie, prodding him experimentally with the same hand that perpetually crushed the Volkswagen. The man moaned softly, and Richardson said as the Troll looked up, "See? Lively."

For the first time in Richardson's memory the Troll made a sound. It was neither a growl nor a snarl, nor were there any more words in it than there were words in Richardson to describe it. Long ago he had spent three-quarters of a year teaching at a branch of the University of Alaska, and what he most remembered about that strange land was the *sense* of the pack ice breaking up in the spring, much too distant for him to have heard it or even felt the vibration in his bones; but like everyone else, he, foreigner or not, knew absolutely that it was happening. So it was with the sound that reached him now—not from the Troll's mouth or throat or monstrous body, but from its entire preposterous existence.

"Saying grace?" Richardson asked. The Troll made the sound again, and his head descended, jaws opening wider than Richardson had ever seen. Cut'n-Shoot screamed, and kept on screaming. Richardson kept a tight grip on him, but the old man's utter panic set the echoes roaring in Richardson's head. He said, "*Quit* it—come *on,* relax, enjoy a little dinner theater," but one of Cut'n-Shoot's flailing arms caught him hard enough on a cheekbone that his eyes watered and went out of focus for a moment. "*Ow,*" he said; and then, "Okay, then. Okay."

Very little of Aussie was still visible. Richardson took a firmer hold of Cut'n-Shoot, lifted him partly off the ground, and half-hurled, half-shoved him at the Troll. The old man actually tripped over a concrete forearm; he fell directly against the Troll's chest, snuggling grotesquely. He opened his mouth to scream again, but nothing came out.

"How about a taste of the guardian?" Richardson demanded. He hardly recognized his own voice: It was loud and frayed and hurt him coming out. "How about a piece of the one who's always there to make sure you behave? Wouldn't that be nice, after all this time?"

When the Troll's mouth opened over Cut'n-Shoot, Richardson began to laugh in delighted hysteria. Not only did the great gray jaws seem to hinge at the back, exactly like a waffle iron, but they matched perfectly, hammer and anvil, when the mouth slammed shut.

After the jaws finally stopped moving, the Troll stretched toward the sky again, and Richardson realized that it was somehow different now—taller and straighter, its rough edges softening, sinking into themselves, becoming more fluid. Becoming more *real.* It stared down at Richardson and made a different sound this time.

Like a troll cares what it's made of, starting out, he thought, and somehow the echoes in his head and Cut'n-Shoot's crazy laughter were one and the same.

"Well, shit," he said. "That meal sure agreed with you."

He was just turning to run when the thing's hand, no longer concrete but just as hard, just as vast and heavy, fell on his shoulder, breaking it. Richardson was shrieking as the Troll lifted him into the air, tucked him clumsily under one arm, and began squeezing back into the lair under the Aurora Bridge. Crumpled against the monster's side—clothing shredded, skin lacerated, his ribs going—Richardson heard the tolling of an impossible heart.

Priced to Sell

BY NAOMI NOVIK

Naomi Novik was born in New York in 1973, a first-generation American, and raised on Polish fairy tales, Baba Yaga, and Tolkien. She studied English literature at Brown University and did graduate work in computer science at Columbia University before leaving to participate in the design and development of the computer game *Neverwinter Nights: Shadows of Undrentide*.

Her first novel, *His Majesty's Dragon,* was published in 2006, along with *Throne of Jade* and *Black Powder War,* and has been translated into twenty-three languages. She has won the John W. Campbell Award for Best New Writer, the Compton Crook Award for Best First Novel, and the Locus Award for Best First Novel. The fourth volume of the Temeraire series, *Empire of Ivory,* published in September 2007, was a *New York Times* bestseller.

She lives in New York City with her husband and eight computers.

"I'm over getting offended," the vampire said despondently. "I just want to stop wasting my time. If the board isn't going to let me in, I don't care how much they smile and how polite they are. I'd rather they just tell me up front there's no chance."

"I know, it's terrible," Jennifer said. No co-op board was going to say anything like that, of course; it was asking for a Fair Housing lawsuit. "Have you thought about a townhouse?"

"Yeah, sure, because of course I've got a trust fund built on long-term compound interest," he said bitterly. "I'm only fifty-four."

He didn't look a day over twenty-five, with that stylish look vampires got if they didn't feed that often—pale and glamorous and hungry—staring into his Starbucks like it was nowhere near what he actually wanted. Jennifer wasn't too surprised he was getting turned down. Right now she was feeling pretty excellent about the garlic salt she'd put on the quick slice of pizza that had been lunch.

"Well," Jennifer said, "maybe a property in Brooklyn?"

"Brooklyn?" the vampire said, like she'd suggested a beach vacation in Florida.

It took him five minutes wrapping up to leave the café: coat, gloves, hat, veil, scarf, and a cape over all that; Jennifer was so not envying him the rush-hour subway ride home on the Lexington Avenue line.

She walked the five blocks uptown and poked her head into Doug's office to report. The vampire had been bounced over to their team from a broker at Black Thomas Phillips, with blessings, after getting rejected by a second co-op board.

"Try him on some of the new condo developments, where the developer is still controlling the building," Doug said. "What's his budget?"

"A million two," Jennifer said.

“And he wants a three bedroom?” Doug said. She winced and nodded. “Not a chance. Show him some convertible twos and see if the amenities make him happy.”

“I was thinking maybe if we could shake something loose in the Victorian, on Seventy-sixth?” she said. “I could send around postcards to the current owners.”

“Keep it in your back pocket, but I wouldn’t start there,” Doug said. “The board there won’t mind he’s a vampire, but they’ll mind that he’s less than a hundred years old.”

Tom knocked on the door and looked in. “Doug, sorry to interrupt, but you’ve got that two-fifteen with the new client at their place on Thirty-second and First.”

Doug didn’t really know the building; it was a rental, and not a good one: near the Midtown Tunnel traffic, no views, and only an aggressive goblin minding the door, who scowled when Doug asked for 6B. “Six *B*?”

“Yes?” Doug said.

“You . . . friend?” the goblin asked, even more suspiciously.

“He’s expecting me,” Doug said diplomatically: Some tenants didn’t want their landlord knowing they were apartment hunting.

Unbelievably, the goblin went ahead and poked a foot at the watchcat sleeping under the front hall table. It raised its head and sniffed at Doug and said in a disgruntled voice, “What do you want from me, it’s just a real estate broker.”

“Broker?” the goblin said, brightening. “Broker, huh? He moving?”

“You’d have to ask him,” Doug said, but that wasn’t a good sign. Bad landlord references could sink a board application quicker than vampirism. He was starting to get doubts about the client anyway. Anyone who really had a $3-million budget, living here?

The IKEA furniture filling the apartment didn't give him a lot of added confidence, but the client said, "Oh, it's . . . it's in a trust fund," blinking at him myopically from behind small, thick-glassed, round John Lennon specs. Henry Kell didn't seem like a candidate to piss off goblins: He was a skinny five foot six and talked softly enough that Doug had to lean forward to hear him. "I don't like to spend it, and . . . and I don't have very many needs, you know. Only . . . well . . . I think it would be best if, if we had our own property, and I think he's come around to the notion."

"Okay, so we're looking for a place for you and your . . . partner?" Doug said. "Should I meet him, too?"

"Er," Mr. Kell said. He took his glasses off and wiped them with a cloth. "You very likely will, at some point, I would expect. But perhaps we could begin just the two of us?"

Kell didn't care about prewar or postwar, didn't care about a view. "Although I would prefer," he said, "not to look directly into other apartments"—and only shrugged when Doug asked about neighborhoods.

"Okay," Doug said, giving up. He figured he was going to have to take Kell around a little to get some sense of the guy's taste. "I can show you some places tomorrow, if you have time?"

"That would be splendid," Kell said, and the next morning he set Doug's new personal-best record by walking into the first place he was shown, looking around for a total of ten minutes, and coming back to say he'd take it for the asking price.

Not that Doug had a deep aversion to getting paid more for less work, but he felt like he wasn't doing his job. "Are you sure you don't want to see anything else?" he said.

"Honestly—the ask here is a little high, the place has only been on the market a week."

"No, I . . ." Kell said, "I think I would prefer, really, to tie everything up as quickly as possible. The apartment is quite excellent."

Not a lot of people would have called it that: It was an estate sale, the kitchen and the bathrooms were original, and the late owner had committed crimes against architecture with a pile of ugly built-ins. But nobody could deny it met Kell's criteria for privacy—three rooms facing into blank walls, another one into a courtyard, and the bedroom had a little slice of a view into Riverside Park. The neighborhood was quiet—the elves at Riverside kept it that way—and it was a condo.

"How soon can we sign a contract?" Kell asked.

"I'll get your lawyer in touch with the seller's lawyer," Doug said, and called Tom to cancel the rest of the viewings, shrugging a little helplessly to himself.

"Wow," Tom said, when Doug got back into the office.

"Yeah, that was really something," Doug said. "I think I get bragging rights for easiest commission ever made on this one. How did it go at Tudor City?"

Tom shook his head glumly. The Tudor City apartment was a beautiful place—view of the UN, formal dining room and two bedrooms, renovated kitchen, new subway-tile bathrooms, and priced to move. Unfortunately, it had come on the market as part of a divorce settlement, and before moving out the owners had gotten into a knock-down, drag-out screaming fight that had ended in dueling curses in the living room.

People weren't even getting to the master suite. They came in, stuck their heads into the big entry closet, walked into the living room, saw the long wall swarming over with huge black bugs, and turned around and went right out. Sometimes they screamed, even though Doug always warned their brokers beforehand. But it was a tough market right now, and no one wanted to give up a chance for a sale.

The potential buyer this afternoon hadn't screamed: She was a herpetologist, and Tom had really thought that was going to be perfect. He'd pitched it to her as free food supply for her snakes. "But apparently they don't eat beetles," he said.

"Well, you win some, you lose some," Doug said. "Let's see if we can get the clients to put up the fee for another eradicator. It's breaking my heart to see that place list for half a million under market."

The real estate market in Manhattan was always an adventure: everyone wanted to live somewhere in the city. The elves fought tooth and nail with Wall Street wizards over Gramercy Park townhouses and Fifth Avenue co-ops; developers tried to pry brownies out of abandoned industrial buildings in Greenwich Village so they could build loft conversions for rock stars and advertising execs; college students squeezed in four to a one-bedroom with actors and alchemists trying for their big break.

Doug had slogged through the dark days of the early nineties, when there'd been seven years of inventory on the market and nothing selling. The immortals were the worst: unless you had a co-op with a limit on how long you could sublet, good luck getting a rakshasa or a vampire to lower their asking price no matter how bad the market was. It was always, "I'll hang in there another decade and see how things go."

Even then, he'd liked the challenge of finding the perfect match of buyer and seller that moved Manhattan real estate, and he liked it a lot more now that he had his own offices tucked into a corner of the Richard Merriman, Inc., corporate headquarters, handling the clients with his own team and farming out the boring overhead to the firm.

Right now, though, it was getting a bit more challenging than he liked. Just last week, a $6-million deal for one of his exclusives—down from an ask of $7.1 million at peak, and happy to get it—had fallen through after an accepted offer. The buyer had lost a quarter of her net worth in the huge Ponzi scheme that had just gotten busted, as though there wasn't enough bad news out there.

"Oh, it was brilliant," she'd said grimly, calling to tell him why the deal was off. "They put all these zombie investors on the books, paid them out of our money, then the zombies fell apart and their accounts went to the animators, who turn out to be working for a firm owned by the partners in the fund."

"Can you get any of the money back?" Doug asked.

"Ask me in five years after I finish paying the lawyers," she said.

It made every sale twice as important and ten times as fragile. He was a little surprised they'd gotten the vampire from Black Thomas Phillips, actually, even with the two co-op rejections.

Speaking of which, he sat down to make a few phone calls to people he knew with condo exclusives, but before he got the phone off the hook, it was ringing under his hand.

"What the hell kind of crazy buyer are you bringing me?" Rina Lazar said, without so much as a hello. She was the selling broker on the Riverside apartment.

"Oh, boy," Doug said. "What happened? Did Kell back out?" That would be great; two new records—quickest sale, quickest flameout.

"Ohhh, no," Rina said. "Backing out, backing out would have been fantastic. He got my sellers' number, don't ask me how, called them up and told them, quote, their bleeping apartment was a bleeping pile of bleep, the built-ins were a disgrace, and the place smelled like dead old lady—I am not kidding you here—and nobody in their right mind would pay more than one million for the wreck, take it or leave it, end quote. The daughter just called me up in tears!"

"Oh, my God," Doug said.

"Plan on sending me a financial sheet on anyone you want to bring to any of my exclusives from now on," she said, and banged the phone down hard enough to make him wince.

"Oh, dear," Henry Kell said, when Doug called. "I gather that this means the deal is off . . . ?"

"Uh, *yeah,* the deal is off," Doug said. "Mr. Kell, maybe I need to explain this, since you're a first-time buyer. Once you make an offer, you can't just—"

"No, no, I perfectly understand," Kell said. "I assure you, I had no second thoughts myself. It must have been . . . he must have had strong feelings on the subject, I can't think why—"

"Is this your partner we're talking about?" Doug said. "Mr. Kell, if you aren't the sole purchaser here—"

"Well, I am, legally speaking," Kell said. "Only, er, he can make his opinion felt in . . . in other ways, as you see."

Doug rubbed his forehead and looked at the balance sheet on the open laptop in front of him, although he really didn't need to; he could keep track of all the contracts he had out right now in his head. "Mr. Kell, I'm sure we can find a place that will make both of you completely happy," he said. "But I really am going to need to speak to your partner, too."

"Oh, dear," Mr. Kell said.

"Wow, they're a super-interesting touch; very Kafka-esque," the art dealer said, considering the bug swarm on the wall.

"It's definitely a unique feature," Tom said, trying not to look at the wall too hard himself. The bugs made a low raspy sound climbing over each other, which he could hear even though he'd cracked the windows to let in some of the noise of the First Avenue traffic outside.

The buyer's broker—she was backed into the far corner of the living room—looked at him with raised eyebrows as her client went to poke around in the kitchen. Tom shrugged at her a little. What was he going to do?

"I do like the details," the art dealer said, coming back out. "There's something special in the contradiction between the formal style of the classic six, the stained-glass windows and the wood paneling, and the raw brutality of the insect swarm."

"Oh?" Tom said. "That is—yes, absolutely. The clients are very negotiable," he added, with a faint stirring of hope.

The art dealer stood looking around the apartment a little more, and then shook his head. "It's a really tough call, but I don't think so. The apartment is great, but, you know, Tudor City. It's so . . . stuffy. I just can't see it. It would be almost like living on the Upper East Side. But tell the sellers I love their style," he added.

"Why is the maintenance so high?" the vampire said suspiciously, reading the offering sheet for the Battery Park apartment.

"Well," the selling broker said, and then he admitted that

it was a land-lease, meaning the co-op didn't actually own the ground underneath the building, and also the lease was running out in fifteen years and no one had any idea what the term renewal was going to be. "But we've got a brownie super, and there's a fantastic sundeck on the—" He stopped at the look Jennifer shot him.

Waiting in the lobby as the vampire dispiritedly bundled himself up again, Jennifer said, "I've got a few condos lined up that we could take a look at this weekend."

"I don't want to live in a condo," the vampire said, muffled, as he wrapped a scarf around his head. "Those places let anyone in."

Jennifer opened and shut her mouth. "Okay," she said, after a moment. "Okay, a co-op it is. You know what—could I maybe get you to send me your last board application?"

"I've got the money!" the vampire said, offended, his eyes glowing briefly red from behind the scarf.

"No, I'm sure you do!" Jennifer said, not fumbling for the little crucifix she'd worn under her blouse. "I don't even really need the financials; I'm just thinking maybe there's something we could do to . . . polish it up a little extra for a board. It might be worth getting an early start on it."

"Oh," the vampire said, mollified. "All right; I'll have my last broker send it to you. I guess it couldn't hurt."

Oh, but it could. One of his three personal reference letters was from his *mother.*

"I thought it was sweet," the vampire protested. "Shows I haven't lost touch with my mortal life."

"She's ninety-six and lives in Arizona," Jennifer said. "When was the last time you saw her?"

The vampire looked guilty. "I call every day," he muttered.

The other two letters were from a pooka—just the kind of

guest everyone wanted visiting their neighbor, especially in horse form and snorting flames—and a necromancer.

"But she's in-house at Goldman Sachs, with the lost-wealth research division," the vampire said.

"Okay, see, that's excellent," Jennifer said. "Let's maybe ask her to revise this letter to focus on that, and let's just skip mentioning the necromancer part. Now, about the pooka—"

"He's a biotech entrepreneur!" the vampire said.

"Let's see if there's someone else we can get, okay?" Jennifer said.

The goblin doorman let Doug up without any hassle this time, even doing a good goblin impression of beaming. It took some effort not to glare at him. No wonder he was so happy Kell and his partner were looking for a new place, if the other guy was some kind of nut.

Kell was in the apartment alone, looking even smaller and hunched in a large shapeless sweater, and he twisted his hands anxiously as he let Doug in. "I suppose," he said, "I suppose there's no way to reopen the deal? I'd be willing to pay more—"

"Not a chance," Doug said. "Mr. Kell, I don't think you get it. If you or your partner does something, uh, *unusual,* you look unreliable, and that scares sellers. Closing can take two or three months. Even if you pay more, it's not worth having a sale fall through at the last second."

"Oh," Kell said, dismally.

"Honestly, the solution here is to find a place that your partner will be happy with, too," Doug said. "Is he here? I really do need to meet him."

Kell sighed and said, "Just a moment." He went to a cabinet and opened it and took out a bottle of whiskey and a glass. He brought them over to the table and poured a glass.

Doug had seen a lot weirder things than a client needing a drink, but it did take him by surprise when Kell slid the glass over to him instead of downing it. "Thanks, but—"

"No," Kell said. "You'll want it in a moment."

Doug started to ask, except Kell wasn't talking anymore. He'd fallen back onto the couch, and he was doubled over with his face in his hands, and something weird was happening to him. He seemed to be . . . growing.

"Uh," Doug said, and then Kell lifted his face out of his hands, and it wasn't Kell anymore. The eyes were the same color but bloodshot and wider apart in a broader face, with a flattened nose and a jaw that looked like it had been carved out of rock. His neck was thickening even while Doug watched.

"Well, fucking finally," not-Kell said, straightening up even more. The couch creaked under him. "So you're the broker who took him to that shithole?"

Doug paused and said, "And you're . . . ?"

Not-Kell was coughing a little bit, thumping himself on the chest as he finished growing. He would have made about two of Kell with some leftovers. He belched loudly and bared his teeth in what you could've called a grin, if by grin you meant a mouth full of more shining white teeth than anybody should've had. "Call me Hyde."

"Okay," Doug said, after a second. "So that would make him . . ."

Hyde snorted. "I know. He changed the name when he moved here. Fucking pathetic." He pointed to the drink. "Are you going to have that?"

Doug looked at the glass, then slid it back across the table.

"So, Mr. Hyde," he said, "can you tell me what you're looking for in an apartment?"

The eradicator stepped back from the wall of bugs and shook his head slowly and lugubriously.

"Really? Nothing?" Tom said, heart sinking.

"Sorry," the eradicator said. "These people, they lived here like twenty years or something. They put down roots. This," he waved a hand at the bugs, "this goes way, way down. I could charge you ten grand and strip off the top layers of the curse, wipe the bugs out, but they'd be back in two months. Might be even worse—millipedes or something. I hate those things." The eradicator shuddered his shoulders up and down expressively. "Anyway, you're not getting this out for good until you rip down the whole building."

He stopped and thought about it, and after a moment added, "Or you could get the two sellers back in and get them to make up. That can clear stuff like this up sometimes."

Tom looked at him. "The sellers' divorce took two years to finish, and they're still in court on some issues."

The eradicator shrugged. "Do they want to sell their apartment or not?"

Tom sighed. Then he paused and said, "So, wait, if you tried to take off the whole curse, the bugs might get worse?"

"Right," the eradicator said.

"If you *didn't* try that," Tom said, "could you maybe . . . do something else with them?"

"What did you have in mind?" the eradicator asked.

The vampire's application was still pretty disheartening, especially when Jennifer compared it to the one she was putting the final touches on that afternoon. She didn't like to jinx things, but kitsune or not, it was pretty much guaranteed Mei Shinagawa would be a shoo-in at the no-dogs-allowed Berkeley. Six letters of reference, terrific financials, and she'd even tucked in tiny origami cranes to be included with the copies of the application, one for each of the board members. The vampire's 2008 tax return, on the other hand, had a suspicious reddish-brown stain on the front.

To make the day complete, after she'd gotten off the phone with the vampire, Jennifer's phone went off with another all-caps CALL ME!! text message from one of their former buyers, a lawyer who'd bought into the top-drawer Oryx co-op for the panoramic views from the twenty-fourth-floor apartment. Now those were about to go away, thanks to a new development, and she was having fits.

"If the Landmarks Commission has approved the renovation, and there's nothing in the zoning to stop it . . ." Jennifer said apologetically. She felt bad, but what could you do? That was Manhattan: you put one building up, somebody else put a bigger one up next door.

"My view was supposed to be protected!" Angela said. "It faces onto a freaking landmarked church!"

"I'm sorry. They're going to preserve the exterior shell and put up a new building on the inside, mimicking the facade and carvings all the way up," Jennifer said. "We could look for a new place for you, if you want?"

"How can I afford a new place with this millstone around my neck? Who is going to pay two million for a one bedroom with a view of a brick wall accessorized by carvings of smiley angels or whatever these guys are putting on their monstrosity?" Angela said. "No one, that's who! Oh, my god, why did I buy at peak? I knew better!"

Of course, she hadn't known better; nobody knew better; that was why it was peak. Jennifer said some comforting things with half a mind while she collated pages of the kitsune's application, and got off the phone; then she stopped and picked the phone up again and called back. "Angela? Can you get a picture of the facade and e-mail it to me?"

"Granite countertops!" Hyde said. "I want some granite fucking countertops. None of this cheap Formica shit."

"Okay," Doug said, adding that to the list under *high ceilings, Sub-Zero fridge, central AC,* and *hardwood floors.* The list was getting pretty long. "Any particular neighborhoods?"

"That's another thing, I want someplace where there's a little goddamn fucking *life,* you understand me?" Hyde said. "I mean, what the hell was he thinking, Riverside Park. Yeah, because I want to live next to a bunch of elves singing 'Kumbaya' to the sun every morning. Not unless I get to pick 'em off with a shotgun."

"That wouldn't be such a great idea," Doug said.

"Fun, though," Hyde said, sort of wistfully.

"So," Doug said, getting off that subject, "can you tell me anything about what your, er . . . what Mr. Kell wants? He hasn't been all that clear—"

"That asshole just wants to crawl under a rock and read books," Hyde said. "Look at this—" He pointed to the particle-board bookshelves, sagging with hardbacks. "All this IKEA crap everywhere—Jesus. And this is a dream compared to what he had in here before those. Purple fucking built-ins! I had to take a sledgehammer to the whole pile of shit."

He glared at the bookshelves and then abruptly heaved himself up off the whimpering couch and headed for them with his fists clenching and unclenching, like he couldn't handle looking at them a second longer.

"So, you know," Doug said hastily, "I do have a place I'd like you to take a look at . . ."

Hyde paused before reaching the bookcases, distracted. "Yeah? What the hell, let's go now."

"I don't know if I can reach the broker—" Doug started.

"We can look at the outside," Hyde said.

The vampire called her up less than a minute after Jennifer forwarded on the e-mail. "What the hell was that!" he yelled. "I almost dropped my iPhone in the gutter!"

"Really?" Jennifer said. "So—that actually hurt?"

"It was a picture of five million crosses!"

"Fantastic," Jennifer said. "Can you meet me at Seventy-fifth and Third in half an hour?"

Getting Hyde into a taxi involved waiting fifteen minutes for one of the minivan ones to come by empty, but Doug was just fine with that: He spent the time frantically texting back and forth with Tom to get the selling broker down to the apartment in time to meet them. He didn't completely trust Hyde not to just knock down the front door and go inside, otherwise.

He got a call back from the broker while they were heading

downtown. "I just want to make sure you realize—" the guy said.

"Yes, I know," Doug said. "It's completely mint inside, though, right?"

"Oh, absolutely," the broker said. "Architect-designed gut renovation."

They got out in front of Marble Cemetery. One of the wispy, sad-eyed apparitions paused by the iron railing to watch as Hyde climbed out of the cab, which almost bounced as he finally stepped out. It looked up at him. Hyde glared down at it. "You want something, Casper?" he said. The apparition prudently whisked away.

"So Bowery is two blocks that way, and the Hells Angels club is on the next street over," Doug said, leading the way to the townhouse next door.

"Looks small," Hyde said, and he did have to duck his head to get through the front door, but inside the ceilings were ten feet. He stamped his foot experimentally. "What is this stuff?"

"Brazilian hardwood," the selling broker said faintly, staring up at Hyde with rabbit-wide eyes.

"Maybe let's take a look at the kitchen," Doug said encouragingly. "Do you have an offering sheet?"

"Uh, yeah," the broker said, still staring as he backed up slowly. "Right . . . this way . . ."

"All right, now this is fucking something," Hyde said approvingly, coming into the kitchen. There was a long magnetic strip mounted on the wall with five or so chef's knives stuck onto it. He picked off a cleaver and tossed it casually in his hand as the broker edged around him, pointing out the Miele appliances.

"And granite countertops, as requested," Doug added.

"Let's see the bathroom," Hyde said. He didn't leave the cleaver behind.

The master bath on the second floor had a big soaking tub and another small apparition hanging around outside the window, staring in with miserable empty eyes that spoke of endless despair and horrors beyond the grave. "Get lost," Hyde told it, and it disappeared.

"So, the uh, the third-floor ceilings," the broker said, stumbling over his words as they came out back to the staircase, "—a little lower, I'm not sure—"

"Maybe we could have Mr. Kell take a look?" Doug suggested to Hyde. "Assuming that you like the place so far."

Hyde looked around and said, "Yeah, this is decent. But make sure that asshole doesn't try to negotiate." He gave his toothy grin to the selling broker, who shrank away. "I'll handle that part."

"Sure," Doug said, and Hyde's smile and shoulders curled in on themselves, and Kell was there, wobbling a little in his suddenly too-large clothing.

He looked around uncertainly and said, "I . . . I'm not sure. The front windows, on the street—anyone could see inside—"

"Why don't we go upstairs?" Doug said, shepherding him onto the third floor.

Kell paused about halfway up, as the built-in bookcases came into view, before continuing up. "Well, those are nice," he said.

"And the windows look on the cemetery back here," Doug said. "Of course, I realize it's a little inconvenient," he added, and Kell looked at him. "Since Mr. Hyde won't be able to get up to this floor."

"Oh," Kell said. "*Oh.*"

Doug shook the selling broker's hand as they left the house. "Will you be around later?" he said.

"Um," the broker said, "could you . . . maybe not give my number to . . ."

"Don't worry about it," Doug said. "I'll handle going between."

The other broker looked relieved. "The seller is totally negotiable," he added, throwing a look at the cemetery. A gardener was busy nearby, spraying a thin, clutching, revenant hand that was struggling out of an old grave.

"Who *is* the seller?" Doug asked, watching.

"Investment banker," the broker said.

Doug dropped Kell off and took the cab the rest of the way back to the office. Tom had just gotten back, beaming, with celebratory lattes. "What's this for?" Doug said.

"We need to order new photos for Tudor City," Tom said, and showed them the little video clip off his camera phone. Doug squinted at it. The wall was still moving, but—

"Are those *butterflies*?" Jennifer said.

"Twenty-three varieties, some of them endangered," Tom said. "I used the catalog from the exhibit at the Museum of Natural History."

"Wow," Doug said. "Tom, this doesn't call for new photos; this calls for a relisting."

They clinked latte cups, then Jennifer shrugged into her coat. "I have to get to Hunter College. Community Board Eight is having a review meeting for a proposed new building next to the Oryx."

"Is Angela still yelling at you about that?" Doug said. "You want me to talk to her? We told her before she bought, there's pretty much no such thing as a protected view."

"No worries," Jennifer said. "We're getting a Fair Housing protest in. There's a sponsor apartment on the thirteenth floor that would be facing the new development; they're selling it to the vampire. They'll have to keep the new building below that height."

She stopped short with her hand on the door, though, as a thundering knock hit, and then another. She glanced back at Doug and Tom, then shrugged and pulled it open.

A giant horse was standing outside in the hall gazing down at them, nostrils flaring, a thin trail of smoke rising from them. Glowing red flames shone in its eyes. There was a dent in the office door where it had knocked with a front hoof. People were sticking their heads out of other offices down the hall to watch.

"Hi," the pooka said. "Marvin said you could help me."

"Marvin?" Tom said, under his breath.

"The vampire," Jennifer said.

The pooka nodded, mane flopping. "I'm looking for an apartment."

They all stood and considered. Jennifer suggested after a moment, "Maybe a ground-floor unit?"

Tom said, "Or a place with a good freight elevator? There's the Atlantica. . . ."

Doug eyed the hooves. Parquet and hardwood were definitely out. Marble tile, maybe. He looked up at the pooka. "So, tell me, how do you feel about Trump buildings?"

The Bricks of Gelecek

BY MATTHEW KRESSEL

Matthew Kressel's fiction has appeared in *Interzone, Electric Velocipede, Abyss & Apex, Apex Science Fiction and Horror Digest, Andromeda Spaceways Inflight Magazine, Farrago's Wainscot,* and other magazines. He publishes *Sybil's Garage,* a speculative fiction and poetry magazine, and is a member of the Manhattan-based writers' group Altered Fluid. He is also the cohost of the reading series Fantastic Fiction at KGB, held monthly in New York City. He currently lives in Brooklyn with an array of noncarnivorous plants and a rapidly diminishing view of the New York skyline (due to real estate developers, a very special kind of demon). His Web site is www.matthewkressel.net.

We were not city folk. We lived beyond all borders, where the onyx sands merged with raven skies, where the desert beasts came to die and even the hated demons of Fintas Miel dared not tread. Out here, the stars twirled in strange orbits, the sun weaved drunkenly by day, and the wind blew steady, slow, and forever. They called this place the Jeen. I called it home.

Always in fours we came to your cities. The sand blew us into flesh, and we walked like men through your iron gates and your tented marketplaces. Dust fell from our fingertips, our feet—the dust of decay, of aeons, of ash. We touched your fruits and your doorposts. We patted the heads of your children and shook the calloused hands of your husbands. You smiled at us.

Within hours came the winds, the decay, the screams. Pits formed in the streets where we had stepped. Your statues rusted and blew away. Your houses fell to kindling. Your children vanished like whispers.

By dawn there was nothing left but a hole in the earth. And those who had carried thoughts of this vanquished city and its people found a blank spot in their minds, a void where once there were men.

We did this for pleasure. And of our name? We had none. For who remained to name us?

Sometimes I grew bored with the sundering of cities. Sometimes I wished to be away from my brothers and their boasts of desolation, so I wandered the desert under the drunken sun to entertain myself with the mysteries of the Jeen. The constant winds carried strange sounds on their wings: the dying whispers of aged widows, the murderous thoughts of jealous cuckolds, the suicide's cry of regret as the soul fled the body. The voices spoke of objects and forms, but always their true concerns were intangible things: regret, shame, love, despair, the gamut of human emotions. I listened eagerly, for the voices spoke of a world beyond my own, a world I could never touch without destroying it.

I floated over the twinkling sands, when I heard a small

voice, like a flute echoing off of a mountain. It cried out to the ineffable, "What am I?" And its sound was music, sweet and innocent, without rue for things come and gone or the dark cynicism heard often in men.

The sound danced above me in crimson wisps, like lingering campfire smoke. It zigged and zagged, hopped and paused, catlike, across the desert. The song haunted me for some reason I could not fathom, so I pursued.

The sun skipped across the sky as I followed the music, until the Jeen was long behind me. A thousand camel skeletons and their unfortunate riders lay wasted on the sands below, and still the voice sang.

A large city crested the horizon. Birds squawked in monstrous flocks above its thousand spires, and towers hugged its center like beggars waiting for handouts. On the heels of the city, just before the sand devoured all, was a small house. The smoke belching from its chimney reeked of ram's bladder and hoof spice—a sin offering to the goddess Mollai.

A girl sat before the house and sang as she fumbled with toy bricks:

"The desert makes no promises,
She does not long abide,
For those who seek to find her face
No semblance they can find.
The sun burns down from heaven's throne,
Turning all to dust,
And so I ask the Cosmos now,
Of what use is rust?"

Her words had the resonant pluck of a zither. Then I understood. Her song had entwined itself in the smoke of the sin offering, and the winds had carried her plea out over the desert to my ears. And the words, they stirred something deep within me that I could not name.

"Hello," she said to me. "Have you lost your caravan? Are you thirsty?"

I had not intended to be seen. I had unwittingly collected myself into human form. *"NO,"* I howled like a sandstorm, trying to terrify her.

But she was unmoved by my words. "Who are you then?"

And I had the same question: Who was this girl who stood firm before the winds of annihilation? "Who taught you that song?" I asked.

"That's mine," she said shyly. "I wrote it."

"*You* wrote it?" I said.

"Why? A girl can write song," she said firmly.

"Of course," I said. "But your song is . . . different."

Her brown eyes twinkled in the sunlight as she studied me. "Who are you? I can tell from your clothes that you're not Quog Bedu or Zwai Clan. And everyone knows you don't walk Gelecek's streets of glass and dung without shoes." She pointed to my bare feet.

I grew frustrated with her questions and reached out for her head. With one touch, she would fall to dust within hours and would trouble me with her words no more. But a heavy man waddled out of the house. He carried a large cleaver, and his bare chest was covered in sweat and blood.

Instantly, I made myself as transparent as the sky.

"Come inside, Agna!" the man shouted. "Mollai is coming to bless our house!"

"Papa, we have a visitor!" she replied. "A stranger from the desert!"

"You can play with your toys later!" the man said.

The girl turned and saw I had vanished. She furrowed her brow and looked deeply disturbed. "But . . . he was just here!" she said.

A plump woman covered in offal shoved the man out of the doorway. She wiped bloody hands on her apron and thrust them to her hips. "Get inside now, Agna, or you'll wish you were never born!"

The girl stood quickly, scanned the desert for me once more, then ran inside.

No thing of form had ever seen me and lived, let alone begged answers of me! As the smoke fluttered from the chimney, I comforted myself in the knowledge that one day my brothers and I would return to erase her city from existence.

I flew back to the Jeen in silence.

Years passed like dripping molasses, and I forgot about the singing girl. My brothers and I trod through the crystal kingdom of Aphelia, whose walls had stood for ten millennia, whose conquests were heralded in a thousand tongues. No one would remember its name.

We touched the port city of Mesach, built within the Pine Barrens beside the salty river Do. It disappeared as if it never were. We sundered Allia, Blömsnu, Cintak, Ektu El. Traders, on the way to a sundered city, would suddenly forget why they had ventured out into the harsh desert with overburdened camels. Cities vanished from minds, too.

How many walls fell under our hands, I could not count. But always, ambitious men built new ones. They raised towers of stone and wrapped domes with hammered gold. They adorned palaces with jewels and paved streets with tar and glass. Caravans traveled across inhospitable wastes to deliver mortar, wheat, and wine. After a time, a new city breathed under the stars as if it had existed for all eternity. I began to see these cities not as a thousand separate entities, but the organs of a much larger creature whose severed limbs always grew back.

One night, as I wandered the Jeen under the bright and nervous stars, I heard the girl's song again:

"One seed planted may not grow,
Two seeds planted in a row,
Five seeds in my garden plot,
Mollai bless they will not rot.
One stone mortared may yet fall,
Two stones, aye a trinity,
But a thousand stones do make a wall
That stands for all Eternity."

I followed her song across abyssal landscapes made gray by the pregnant moon, until I came to her far-off house in the city of Gelecek. I saw movement in a window, and I crept up to it, conscious not to take human form or to touch her house, lest it fall to ashes.

Agna sat upright in bed. In the years since I had seen her, she had grown inches. Now she had the body of a young woman, though she still had the face of a girl. She leaned into the pallid moonlight as she scrawled on parchment. Her small voice hummed a few bars, then she crossed out a word and replaced it with another. She hummed again and the notes brought me back ages. I recalled cities I had conquered and forgotten: the star-shaped city of Gelf with its bejeweled ivory columns; the ziggurats of Phalantine and its perfumed gardens; Karad and its herds of black giraffes.

I had no words to describe the feelings her songs evoked in me. I needed to listen until I understood what I felt.

"I thought I dreamt you all those years ago," she whispered. "But here you are." She was staring at me through the window frame.

I found myself in human form, though not by my own will. Her song had oddly drawn me into flesh. "You remember me?" I said.

"How could I forget? You vanished like smoke! And you smell like the deep desert," she said. "Like a spent campfire. Like ash. Who are you?"

"I have no name."

"But *what* are you?" Her eyes twinkled in the moonlight. "Are you a 'mancer? A demon?"

"I am dissolution. I am nothing."

"What do you want with me?"

"Your songs," I said. "They fill me with memories of forgotten places. They make me feel . . . I cannot describe it. Sing one again!" I demanded.

"Agna?" a voice grumbled. Wood groaned in the dark corners of the house. "What's that sound?"

"Leave!" she whispered to me. "Father has killed thieves before!"

"Please," I begged. "Sing another! Sing one now!"

"Agna!" a man bellowed. "If you're using one of my candles again, I swear, I'll beat you back to Kalagia!"

Agna mumbled a response, pretending to be asleep. Then she whispered to me, "Go away! I don't know who you are, but don't come back!"

In the far corner, a sphere of light blossomed around a candle. In the lambent flicker frowned the sweaty face of her father. He stepped toward us, and I backed away from the window into darkness.

"Is this how you repay me for training you?" her father said. "I told you not to use the candles!"

"But, I didn't, Papa!" she said.

"Don't lie to me, Agna! I smell soot!"

"I swear, it wasn't me! There was a man! A stranger from the—"

He lifted a heavy belt from a chair and beat her with it. I watched from a distance and listened to the desert swallow her screams. When he had finished beating her, he said, "Go to sleep, Agna. You have to be up early for work. I expect you at Posterity Hill before first prayer."

As he blew out the candle, she whimpered her acknowledgment.

I wanted to hear her sing again, but this was not the place. Then I recalled her father's words, "Posterity Hill," a place of men, and in the darkness I had an idea.

I traveled to the wastes beyond the Jeen, where the white sands breathe in irregular tides. Deep within a mammoth cleft of stone, I begged the demon Atleiu to craft me a suit of human flesh. In return, I promised her the only thing I could—destruction. She agreed and proceeded to cut skin from one of her human slaves, tempering it with the hoarfrost of the north and the iron stones that fall from the sky.

Whereas before, anything I touched turned to dust within hours, now—while encased in Atleiu's suit—I could walk among men without destroying them. I could follow Agna anywhere she went. I could touch and be touched.

The sun was rising hot and huge in the east when I reached the first stone of Gelecek's streets. I worried that Atleiu's suit might fail. I took a tentative step with my sandaled foot onto stone. Always, when I decimated cities, I felt the ecstatic rush of annihilation. I sensed none of that now; the stone remained a stone.

"Posterity Hill?" I asked a bearded vendor, and he pointed with an arthritic hand deep into the city.

I weaved through a collection of low stone buildings. Clothing and bedding swayed from lines strung above me. People hurried past with satchels tossed over backs or barrows thrust before them. I smelled uncooked animal flesh and human feces, but the air was also dense with smells of sandalwood, sage, and the sweet twinge of honey. As men and women bumped me, I felt impotent; they would remain to bump others tomorrow.

I reached a sign that read POSTERITY HILL. FUTURE HOME OF THE JARRIFA FAMILY. High walls were fashioned with polished brown stones that jutted from the facade like giant thumbs, the work of a skilled hand.

"This is private property," a shirtless boy said.

I ignored him and climbed to the top of the sloping road as he followed me. Young masons labored within a large stone foundation, scooping mortar and laying stones with advanced skill. From this plateau I glimpsed the full city. To my left, a hag's spine of roads twisted into the desert. To my right, spires rose like candles into the sky.

"Did you hear me, *feg*?" the boy said, behind me. "This is private property!"

"There's no such thing," I said. But before he could scold me again, I descended the hill. I searched the base of the foundation until I found a corner where I could watch the workers without being seen, and there I waited for Agna.

Her father stepped out of a pavilion and walked around the foundation, admonishing the boys for apparent flaws that neither the boys nor I saw. One of the boys whispered to him and pointed at me.

"Who the *frib* are you?" Agna's father said as he stepped up to the wall and looked down at me, his foot resting on a stone above my head.

I stood from my hiding place. "Is your daughter here?"

"What do you want with her?"

"Is she here?"

He leaped down to my level, and the ground shook with his weight. "Did you hear me?" he said. "What do you want with her?"

"You would not understand," I said. "It is beyond you."

"You freak!" he said as his fist slammed into my face. I fell onto my back. He kicked me, and I raised my hand to block the blows. With his next kick, Atleiu's flesh suit tore at the index finger. When he tried to kick me again, I stuck out my hand, and his leg scraped my unprotected finger.

He gasped, while the ecstasy of nothingness coursed through me.

"What's wrong with him?" the boys said. "Is he having a heart attack?"

Agna's father bent over, holding his stomach. Then he stood, looked at me nervously, and said, "You stay the *frib* away from my daughter or I'll kill you." He walked up the hill and vanished behind a wall. Some of the boys chuckled and kicked pebbles at me until I heard his stern voice order them back to work. In the distance, Agna watched me until I heard her father order her back to work, too.

Carefully, I wrapped my torn finger back into place.

I circled the streets until I found a better hiding spot. On the opposite side of the foundation, three small walls obscured me completely from view, but a tiny slit allowed me to see out. The sun beat down on the boys as they worked, and Agna, to my joy, worked alongside them. Though she was the only girl among three dozen boys, they gave her no special treatment. She spread mortar and hefted heavy stones without help; she chiseled with practiced skill. But I noticed in her craft an attention to detail that the boys lacked. Every stone held her full consciousness. Every rap of her hammer carried the weight of aeons.

And she sang while she worked.

Oh, what sweet music! The boys sang with her; they mixed mortar by verse, carried stones by stanza, and finished walls by song, so that their labors resembled a dance more than a burden.

I knew the power of her song now and let it consume me. I reveled in forgotten vistas. Geysers from the oasis city of Sul erupted in my mind. The mirrored walls of Nier El Du blinded my dreams. The gargantuan city of Poc, carved from a single piece of stone, crushed me under its weight. I thought for a moment that this feeling might be greater than the bliss of annihilation.

"You!" Agna said.

I woke from my visions to see her peering down at me from the foundation wall. She threw her hands to her hips and frowned, and I recognized her mother in the gesture.

She sniffed the air. "I thought I smelled ash," she said.

"Your songs, they are . . . *beautiful*—yes, that's the word," I said.

She glanced over her shoulder. "I was wondering who it was that Father beat this morning."

"Now he has beaten us both," I said. "We are kindred. By dawn, he will—"

"Kin? Hardly. You'd better leave, whoever you are. He'll kill you. Don't be stupid."

"Tell me, Agna," I said, "do your songs carry you to forgotten places? Do you have visions of dead cities?"

"What?" she said. She stepped back from the wall, mouth agape. "How do you know—"

"Agna?" her father shouted from behind her. "Who are you talking to? Is that *feg* here again?"

She stared at me. Then she shook her head and said, "Go away. Go away. . . ." But her words were insubstantial, like a desert cloud.

"Meet me at the bottom of the hill," I said.

She disappeared behind the wall, and I knew she was mine now.

At the bottom of Posterity Hill, shadows crept across the ground as the sun turned overhead. Just after high noon, Agna's small figure appeared at the top of the hill and scampered down to meet me.

"How do you know about my visions?" she demanded. "Did Mother tell you? Damn her!"

"No. I see them when you sing."

"You said they're 'dead' cities. What did you mean by that?"

"They have been forgotten. Erased. Yet your song rekindles their memories."

Agna's father appeared at the top of the hill surrounded by three boys.

"Let's go!" she said. "Before Father sees us!"

We turned through the busy streets. The air smelled of cracked spelt, boiling beans, and the pungent reek of humans going about their business. Animals being slaughtered cried out and fell silent. She led me into a courtyard filled with date palms and speckled shade.

"They're not dead cities," she said. "They haven't been born yet."

"No, they're very dead. But your songs give them new life."

She frowned. "I've tried to tell Father about them. To let him know that there's more to my songs than just music and words. But he won't have an ounce of it. He says a woman needs a stable trade as much as any man, that my poems and music will only get me to a street corner, begging for change."

"He's wrong. I watched the boys sing with you. They work twice as hard under your spell."

"Do you think so? Father works us all so hard. A song makes the day go by a little faster." Her eyes filled with water. "The prefect plans to hire Father as his chief mason. When Father gets that job, I'll be able to design buildings myself. I won't have to take orders from him anymore. And when I turn sixteen Father promised to give his business to me. Says his back's no good anymore. I'll be free to create whatever I wish. I have dreams, things I want to build."

I remembered that I had touched her father, that he would vanish from existence before dawn. "Your mother has a well-paying trade, though?" I said.

"Well-paying? She's a seamstress in the textile guild. The

pay is the only thing worse than the work. She doesn't want me to follow in her footsteps, but I love working with thread, too. I often help her with embroidery. It's wonderful. You can't get the same precision with stone, not if you want to finish within this century." She stared at her calloused fingers.

"And all through this has been your music."

"Ballads have propelled me, ever since I was a girl."

"Will you sing me one now?"

"Right here? Right now?"

"Yes!"

"This is silly. I don't even know you."

"There is nothing to know."

She shook her head. "Well," she said, "maybe just the one. You did get a beating, after all, just to hear one." Then she began:

"By dawn, the sun, low on our backs
Is cool, while birds are singing.
By noon, the mortar's showing cracks
And masons' ears are ringing.
But come a week, a month, a year,
When chanced upon this hill,
Where Father's eye had built a house
That stands upon there still,
I forget the sweat, the grime,
The shoveling of sand,
And fill my heart with future dreams
To build one by my hand."

Vistas of dead cities assaulted my consciousness. But this time there were new places, cities I had not glimpsed before. Cities of glass. Cities in the sky. Even cities floating among the stars. Perhaps, as she had suggested, not all of these kingdoms were dead; some had yet to be created. I closed my eyes and savored the sweetness of them all.

"Who are you?" she said.

"Does it matter, my name?"

"Yes, it does. A man's name is his being, his essence."

"All the more reason why I have none."

"I don't understand," she said. "You come to me, begging to hear my songs, but I know nothing of you. Where are you from? What do you do? How is it that you have come to me?"

Agna's father burst into the courtyard, surrounded by a dozen boys. They carried chisels and hammers and walked briskly in my direction.

"Agna!" her father shouted. "Stand back!" He smacked the head of a hammer into his palm. "You're dead, stranger, do you hear me?"

I backed away. They could not hurt my true essence, of course, but they could destroy my suit. I needed it to last, for Atleiu was a fickle demon and would not craft me another one for aeons.

"Who are you?" she said to her father. "And what do you want with us?"

"What?" her father shouted. "Has he drugged you? You're safe now, baby! Papa's here!"

"Who?" she said. She looked like she was going to be sick. "I don't feel right. Something's wrong."

But I had to leave. I fled the courtyard through the rear gate, and the boys pursued. I ran through crowded streets, hiding behind bales of tobacco and under piles of manure. When I was certain I had lost them, I headed back to my brothers in the Jeen. I was not troubled. By morning, her father and his rabble would forget.

"We have followed you," my brother said to me that evening in the Jeen, as the bright stars oppressed us. "You entered a city in the guise of a man and walked among its people, touching them. This night, their walls hold firm. The winds are calm, and their children do not scream. Tell us why, Brother, you've broken our trust?"

I dared not reveal Agna's power to enthrall with her song, lest they try to usurp her for their own. But I could not deny what they had witnessed. "We have no rules," I said, "nor laws preventing me from doing what I have done. I followed my will."

"But you are a thing of destruction," my brother said. "That is your nature. What do you seek in the world of form?"

"Sometimes, in the winds of the Jeen, I hear whispers of human things. Have you never been curious to know what they are?"

"Sometimes, yes. But if I satisfy my curiosity, what purpose does it serve? The curiosity vanishes. One day, the thing which piqued my interest will vanish, too. All is impermanent."

"Then so, too, is my interest in this city," I said. "It will vanish. Your concern will vanish, too."

"As all things do. But now our brothers need to know: What is it that draws you there, in the morning sun, to walk among them without destruction?"

I paused before answering. "Of all the cities we sundered, Brother," I said, "how many do you remember?"

"Not many," he said.

"None?" I said.

He paused. "Perhaps."

"I go to that city, dear Brother, to remember."

"But why? Nothing is worth remembering. Memories, like cities, fade."

I felt pain when I realized that one day Agna would vanish from the earth. "What are we then, without our memories?"

"We are nothing, Brother. We have and will always be nothing. You may convince yourself, for a time, that you are more, but it is only self-deception."

And with these words, my brother left me.

In the winds of the Jeen I heard a laugh.

I searched the desert six times to make sure I was in the right place. Yes, this was the spot of sand where Gelecek had once stood. Like a drying oasis, the city's circumference had shrunken inward. Its walls were devoid of grandeur. A few leaning towers thrust into a cloudless sky, and scattered buildings spotted an uninspiring landscape.

And Agna's house was gone.

I entered the city and hunted for her within its changed streets. "Where am I?" I asked its residents.

"This is Gelecek," they responded forlornly, as if the city's name itself was a curse.

"There was a foundation," I said to an elderly woman mashing chickpeas. "On Posterity Hill. Do you know it?"

She shook her head. "Never heard of it."

Of course, I thought. I had destroyed the mason who had created it.

"There is a girl," I said. "Agna, daughter of a seamstress. Have you heard of her?"

The old woman squinted rheumy eyes at me. "Nay, but there's the seamstress guild up on Trajen Row. Why don't you bother them?"

I lost my way several times but eventually found Trajen Row, a cobbled dead-end street, with hundreds of dyed linens drying from hemp lines like standards. The air reeked of chemicals, and colored puddles filled the cracks between stones. Inside cramped buildings, hundreds of seamstresses stuck needles into cloth, combed lamb's wool, or threaded looms. I found Agna's mother working in a corner, her needlework tiny feats of prestidigitation.

She looked much thinner than I remembered, and her face was wrinkled and bitter.

"I'm looking for Agna," I said. "Where is she?"

"Who the *frib* are you?" she said without looking up.

"I'm a friend. I was supposed to meet her today."

"I don't know who you're talking about."

"Agna, your daughter."

She stopped her stitching and looked up at me. "Is this a joke? Did the girls put you up to this?"

"No. Please! Where is she?"

She started to cry. "You're cruel. Go away."

"This is not a joke. I'm not here for anyone but myself. I am seeking your daughter to . . ." After my last incident with her father, I tempered my words. ". . . to protect her from a great evil."

She began her needlework again, then said to the sky: "Mollai, great maker, why do you torment me so?" Then she said to me, "I don't know who you are, stranger, but your words sting. I never had a husband or a daughter, nor do I know this Agna you speak of. Now leave me."

I backed away as the shock of her words consumed me. Always, when I destroyed cities, my destruction was total, complete. I had never been selective in annihilation before. It had never occurred to me that erasing her father would erase

Agna, too. An alien feeling welled up inside me as I stepped out into the sun. It was . . . there was only one word for it—*loss.* A thousand linens snapped angrily in the wind. I walked the streets in a daze. I don't know how long I wandered before I heard a voice.

A beautiful voice. It sang.

I followed the song around a corner, into an alley overgrown with weeds. A cat hissed at me and ran away. The voice came from a doorless building, and I crept inside. Half-finished canvases crowded a large studio, and the air was heavy with the reek of paint. Majestic cities adorned the canvases; some I recognized as cities I had sundered.

At the far end of the studio, a young woman danced her brush over a canvas while she sang:

"On the dark side of morn, the workers lie waiting.
Sunrise to sunset, their backs break in toil.
From out of the desert come caravans sweating,
Burdened with legumes, rich hemp seed and oil."

"Agna!" I shouted. "You're alive!"

The girl turned to me, but her face was not Agna's. Her eyes were too green, her nose too buttonlike, her face too round. Not Agna, but a stranger.

Startled, she said, "Who are you?"

But her voice—that *was* Agna's. "You won't remember me," I said.

She dropped her brush. "No! I've dreamt of you! Sometimes I dream that I lived another life, with different parents, in a different house. I was a builder of cities and a weaver of thread. Then a ghost came along and erased everything. I thought it was just a recurring nightmare. But that ghost had your face."

"I'm sorry, Agna. I didn't know."

"Agna? That's the name my dream parents called me. My name is Dina."

"It's a beautiful name," I said, stepping closer.

"Stay away from me!" she said.

"I'm not here to hurt you, Dina. I only came to hear you sing."

"Why?"

I pointed to her paintings. "These cities, why do you paint them?"

"The architects buy them. They tell me my drawings inspire them."

"But why do *you* paint them?"

"I don't know . . . they come to me . . ."

"In vision, when you sing."

"How do you know that?" she said. "Who . . . what are you?"

"I am the no thing of the deserts beyond form and the sunderer of civilization. I and my brothers have destroyed these cities. I had forgotten them all. But your songs bring them back to me. I have the very same question for you, Dina. What are you?"

She looked sick. "It was real, wasn't it? My other life. There were too many details, too many feelings. I had a difficult life, yes, but I had dreams and aspirations. And you destroyed all of that, didn't you?"

"But you're not dead. Don't you see?" I said. "I couldn't erase *you* from history. You spring back like the cities I and my brothers sunder."

"You're disgusting," she said. "You destroy as easily as I create."

"Perhaps, but for once in my life I want something else."

The winds gusted outside, knocking over a few canvases. I heard the rasp of sand blowing against stone, and a familiar shudder of ecstasy coursed through me.

"A sandstorm," she said. "I have to close the windows."

"No," I said to her as I stepped out into the sun. I knew him before he spoke, not by the way he walked, nor by the tailor of his clothes, but by his indifference toward all things. He gave a beggar a coin and patted him on the shoulder. He dragged his hands along the walls of a portico. He stepped up to me and paused. Every move was filled with emptiness.

"Hello, Brother," he said.

"What are you doing here?" I demanded.

"I could ask the same of you. What business have you here in this flesh suit of yours?"

"You must leave!" I said. "Before you destroy this place."

"It's too late," he said. "Our brothers have decided that your sojourn here shall end. We followed you to this city. Four of us walk inside these walls now, spreading oblivion. We love you, Brother, and when this city falls, you will return to us and be the soul we remember."

"I don't want to go back! Not yet! Please, listen to one of her songs! Look at her paintings! Then you'll understand why I'm here!"

"There's nothing to understand. There's nothing at all. That's the sole and final truth." My brother smiled and fled the alley, patting a boy on his head as he turned the corner.

"Agna—*Dina,* come on! We have to go!" I shouted. I reentered the studio. But Dina had vanished.

"Dina! Where are you?"

I found a small door in the back. It led up a small, curving stairwell to a storeroom on the second floor. When I opened the door, Dina jumped out and stabbed me in the chest with a putty knife.

I pushed her away and pulled out the knife from my chest. There was no blood. When I dropped it to the floor, the blade shattered.

She pounded on me with her fists. "Go away! Go away!"

"Dina, Dina! Please, you must listen to me! My brothers are destroying this city as we speak. We have to go now, or you'll be killed!"

"Get away from me! I'd rather die!"

I grabbed her. She was small and easy to contain. I lifted her over my shoulder, and she beat me as I carried her down the stairs, through the studio, and out onto the streets.

She screamed for help. So I gagged and tied her with sackcloth.

I took the back alleys and least-crowded streets and fled the city as quickly as possible, making sure that neither I nor Dina's bound body touched a thing. She cried, but her voice was muffled by her gag.

"I know you think I'm cruel," I said. "But I do this for your own good. I've figured it out, Dina. I know what you are. Whereas I am the sunderer of cities, you are their genesis. Your songs, your visions, your dreams—they are the impetus that creates new ones. I destroy cities with my touch. You create them with your song. We are kindred. If you die, then in a way, so do I."

I found a black horse tied up beside a tent on the outskirts of the city and stole it before its owner could stop us. I spread Dina before me, and we rode deep into the desert. After several hours, she stopped struggling, so I took off her gag.

"Water . . ." she mumbled.

I found a canteen slung around the horse and gave it to her.

After drinking several large gulps, she said, "My family, friends, my paintings. Will they all vanish?"

"I'm sorry. But you can create new ones."

"Do you think it's that easy, that I can just start over in a new city, as if nothing at all has happened? Everything I know is going to die."

The horse grew tired as the sun set behind a dune, so I dismounted. I untied her hands as the stars winked to life above us.

"If you flee," I said, "by the time you get back to your city, it will be dust. No one will remember it, not even you."

"Won't I vanish too?" she said. "I was born in that city."

"I erased your father. It changed you, but you were born again as someone else. I think you are a seed that can't be destroyed."

"Then why bring me all the way out here?"

I looked at her and realized that I didn't have an answer.

"When I was six my mother bought me my first paint set. My father took me to the top of Jimn Mountain when I was nine. I remember the first time I kissed a boy. I remember breaking my arm when I tried to scale Dell Wall. All of that will be erased, won't it?"

"But you will rebuild it somewhere else, in some other time."

"You don't understand! Humans are not like a wall, where the bricks of our experiences are interchangeable. Each instant is precious, unique. You rob the universe of the sacred. Can't you see that?"

"I . . . I have known nothing else," I said. "Until I met you."

"Is that consolation for ruining my life, that the ghost of annihilation has second thoughts?"

"I didn't mean to hurt you."

"But you have."

"This wasn't supposed to happen."

"What wasn't?" she said slowly.

"The destruction of your city."

"What city?"

"Gelecek."

"What a beautiful name," she said. "Where is it? And who are you? How did I get here?"

I sighed and had to look away.

"I feel funny," she said. "As if . . . I'm not supposed to be here. My body feels . . . light. Like air. What's your name?"

"My name?" I said. "My name is . . . Destruction."

When I looked for her again, there was only sand. The girl, the horse, everything was gone, even my suit of flesh. I cried out to the stars, but they did not respond.

I did not move from that spot. My brothers came to me on the sand. They said, "Come back to the Jeen with us, Brother, for you have no reason to dwell among form now."

And I said, "Leave me."

The sun rose and set a hundred times, and my brothers came to me again and again. "Please," they begged. "It's not proper that you be apart from us. Come and obliterate a city with us and feel your old self again."

But how could I? In each city might dwell the spark of

Agna or Dina or her kin. I could not bear to erase her from existence again.

"Go away," I told my brothers, and they did.

I sat there in the same spot of sand where Dina had disappeared, while the sun turned in slow orbits overhead. I felt like a top, spinning, spinning, but never slowing.

The stars and sun turned through slow aeons, and still I did not move. One silent afternoon, a dark cloud appeared in the sky. Once in a hundred years it rained in the desert; today it poured down in great sheets. The sky grew as dark as the gloaming, and the sands turned to mud. Forks of light split the sky in dreadful thunder.

I collected myself into human form, gave myself strong arms and hands, and began to mold the wet sand into a brick. The pounding rain seemed to shout Agna's songs across the desert, and to their tunes I crafted another brick, and then another, fashioning them into a rudimentary wall. I knew it was temporary. I knew that tomorrow, when the sun rose hot and burdensome above the sands, my wall would grow weak. The desert winds would topple it in time, that all was, essentially, nothing. But heaven help me, I couldn't stop.

Weston Walks

BY KIT REED

Kit Reed is the author of *The Baby Merchant, Dogs of Truth,* and *Thinner Than Thou*. Her short novel *Little Sisters of the Apocalypse* and the collection *Weird Women, Wired Women* were both finalists for the James Tiptree, Jr., Award.

Her most recent novel, *Enclave,* appeared in 2009. Her short fiction has been published in various anthologies and magazines, including *Asimov's Science Fiction, Fantasy and Science Fiction, The Yale Review, Postscripts,* and *The Kenyon Review*. Her next short story collection, *What Wolves Know,* will be published in 2011.

When your life gets kicked out from under you like a chair you thought you were standing on, you start to plan. You swear: *Never again*. After the funeral Lawrence Weston sat in a velvet chair that was way too big for him while the lawyer read his parents' will out loud. He didn't care about how much he was getting; he only knew what he had lost and that he would do anything to keep it from happening again.

He was four.

Like a prince in the plague years, he pulled up the drawbridge and locked his heart against intruders. Nobody gets into Weston's tight, carefully furnished life, and nobody gets close enough to mess up his heart.

Now look.

When your money makes money you don't have to do anything—so nothing is what Weston ordinarily does, except on Saturdays, when he comes out to show the city to you. It isn't the money—don't ask how much he has—he just needs to hear the sound of a human voice. He lives alone because he likes it, but at the end of the day that's exactly what he is. Alone.

It's why he started Weston Walks.

He could afford an LED display in Times Square but he sticks to three lines in *The Village Voice*: "New York: an intimate view. Walk the city tourists never see."

He'll show you things you'll never find spawning upstream at Broadway and Forty-second Street or padding along Fifth Avenue in your puffy coats. This is *the insider's walking tour.*

Nobody wants to be an outsider, so you make the call. It's not like he will pick up. His phone goes on ringing in some place you can't envision, coming as you do from out of town. You hang on the phone, humming "pick up, pick up, pick up." When his machine takes your message, you're pathetically grateful. Excited, too. You are hooked by Weston's promise: *Tailored to your desires.*

What these are, he determines on the basis of a preliminary interview conducted over coffee at Balthazar, on him—or at Starbucks, on you—depending on how you are dressed, and whether he likes you well enough to spend the day with you, in which case he'll let you pay. He is deciding whether to take you on. No matter how stylish your outfit—or how tacky—if he doesn't like what he hears, he will slap a hundred or a twenty on the table at Balthazar or Starbucks, depending, and leave you there. It's not his fault he went to schools where you learn by osmosis what to do and what not to wear. It's not your fault that you come from some big town or small city where Weston would rather die than have to be. Whatever you want to see, Weston can find, and if you don't know what that is and he decides for you, consider yourself lucky. This is an insider tour!

You're itching to begin your Weston Walk, but you must wait until the tour is filled, and that takes time. Weston is very particular. At last! You meet on the designated street corner. You're the ones with the fanny packs, cameras, monster foam fingers, Deely Bobbers, Statue of Liberty crowns on the kids—unless you're the overdressed Southerner or one of those razor-thin foreigners in understated black and high-end boots. Weston's the guy in black jeans and laid-back sweater, holding the neatly lettered sign.

He is surprisingly young. Quieter than you'd hoped. Reserved, but in a good way. Nothing like the flacks leafleting in Times Square or bellowing from tour buses on Fifth Avenue or hawking buggy rides through Central Park. He will show you things that you've never seen before, from discos and downtown mud baths nobody knows about to the park where your favorite stars rollerblade to the exclusive precincts of the Academy of Arts and Letters—in the nosebleed district, it's so far uptown—to the marble grand staircase in the Metropolitan Club, which J. P. Morgan built after all the best clubs in the city turned him down.

Notice that at the end Weston says good-bye in Grand Central, at Ground Zero, or the northeast corner of Columbus

Circle—some public place where he can shake hands and fade into the crowd. You may want to hug him, but you can't, which is just as well because he hates being touched. By the time you turn to ask one last question and sneak in a thank-you slap on the shoulder, he's gone.

He vanishes before you know that you and he are done.

You thought you were friends, but for all he knows, you might follow him home and rip off his Van Gogh or trash his beautiful things; you might just murder him, dispose of the body, and move into his vacant life. Don't try to call; he keeps the business phone set on silent. It's on the Pugin table in his front hall, and if you don't know who Pugin was, you certainly don't belong in his house.

The house is everything Weston hoped. Meticulously furnished, with treasures carefully placed. A little miracle of solitude. Leaving the upper-class grid at venerable St. Paul's and Harvard was like getting out of jail. No more roommates' clutter and intrusions, no more head-on collisions with other people's lives. He sees women on a temporary basis; he'll do anything for them, but he never brings them home, which is why it always ends. It's not Weston's fault he's fastidious. Remember, he's an orphaned only child. To survive, he needs everything perfect: sunlight on polished mahogany in his library, morning papers folded and coffee ready and housekeeper long gone, no outsiders, no family to badger him; they all died in that plane crash when he was four.

He spends days at his computer, although he deletes more than he types, lunches at a club even New Yorkers don't know about, hunts treasure in art galleries and secondhand bookstores, can get the best table wherever he wants, but girls?

He's waiting for one who cares about all the same things.

Too bad that Wings Germaine, and not the first tourist he booked, the one with the lovely phone voice, whom he loved on sight at the interview, shows up for the last-ever Weston Walking Tour. While thirteen lucky tourists gather at the subway kiosk on Seventy-second at Broadway, Wings is waiting elsewhere and for unstated reasons—down there.

Weston has no idea what's ahead. It's a sunny fall Saturday, light breeze, perfect for the classic Central Park walk, so what could be easier or more convenient? It's a half block from his house.

All he has to do is collect his group outside the kiosk, where they are milling with vacant smiles. They light up at the sight of his neatly lettered placard. Grinning, he stashes it in the back of his jeans, to be used only when for some unforeseen reason he loses one of them.

A glance tells him this is a Starbucks bunch. With their cameras and sagging fanny packs, they wouldn't be comfortable at chic old Café des Artistes, which is right around the corner from his house. It's not their fault their personal styles are, well, a bad match. But they are. He's one short, which bothers him. Where is that girl he liked so much? Too bad he has to move on, but maybe she'll catch up. *Nice day, nice enough people,* he thinks—with the possible exception of the burly tourist in the black warm-up jacket with the Marine Corps emblem picked out in gold, who walks with his shoulders bunched, leaning into a scowl.

Never mind. It's a beautiful day, and Weston is in charge. Happy and obedient, his tourists trot past the spot where John Lennon died and into the park on a zigzag, heading for the east side, where the Metropolitan Museum bulks above the trees like a mastodon lumbering away. He keeps up a lively patter, spinning stories as his people smile blandly and nod, nod, nod, all except the man with the scowl, who keeps looking at his watch.

Weston looks up: *Ooops.* Like a cutting horse, his ex-marine has the herd heading into a bad place.

Time to get out of here. He'll walk them south on Fifth, point out houses owned by people he used to know. "All right," he says brightly, "time to see how the rich people live."

"Wait." The big marine fills the path like a rhino bunched to charge. "You call this the insider tour?"

Smile, Weston. "Didn't I just . . ."

He points to a gap in the bushes; Weston knows it too well. "TAKE US THE FUCK INSIDE."

No! Behind those bushes, a gash in the rocks opens like a mouth. He can't go back! Weston struggles for that tour-guide tone. "What would you like to see?"

"Tunnels."

The ground underneath the park is laced with unfinished city projects—tunnels, aborted subway stations, all closed to them; Weston has researched, and he knows. "Oh," he says, relieved, "then you want City Spelunking Tours. I have their number and . . ."

"Not those. The ones real people dug. Nam vets. Old hippies."

"There aren't any—"

The big man finishes with a disarming grin. "Crazies like me. I have buddies down there."

"There's nothing down there." Weston shudders. *He's a client; don't offend.* "That's just urban legend, like a lot of other things you think you know. Now, if you like legends, I can take you to Frank E. Campbell's, where they have all the famous funerals, or the house where Stanford White got shot by Harry K. Thaw. . . ."

"No. DOWN!" The renegade tourist roars like a drill sergeant, and the group snaps to like first-day recruits. "Now. Moving out!"

Weston holds up his placard, shouting, "Wait!"

Too late. Like a pack of lemmings, the last-ever Weston Walking Tour falls in behind the big man.

They are heading into a very bad place. No, Weston doesn't want to talk about it. He waves his arms like signal flags. "Wrong way! There's nothing here!"

The marine whirls, shouting, "You fucking well know it's here."

The hell of it is, Weston does. He is intensely aware of the others in his little group: the newlyweds, the dreary anniversary couple, the plump librarian and the kid in the Derek Jeter shirt, the others are watching with cool, judgmental eyes. In spite of their cheap tourist claptrap and bland holiday smiles, they are not stupid people; they're fixed on the conflict, eager to see something ordinary tourists don't see. The authority of their guide is at issue. They are waiting to see how this plays out. There is an intolerable pause.

"Well?"

One more minute and the last Weston Walking Tour will die of holding its breath.

If you knew what Weston knew, you would be afraid.

His only friend at St. Paul's vanished on their senior class trip to the city. One minute weird Ted Bishop was hunched on the steps of the Museum of Natural History, shivering under a long down coat that was brown and shiny as a cockroach's shell and zipped to the chin on the hottest day of the year. Then he was gone.

Last winter Weston ran into Bishop on Third Avenue, with that same ratty coat leaking feathers and encrusted with mud. It was distressing; he did what he could. He took him into a restaurant and bought him hot food, looked away when his best friend stuffed everything he couldn't devour into his pockets with the nicest smile. "I went crazy. I hid because I didn't want you to know."

"I wouldn't have minded." Weston's stomach convulsed.

"At first I was scared but then, Weston. Oh!"

It was terrifying, all that naked emotion, so close. He shrank, as if whatever Ted had was catching.

"Then they found me." Bishop's pale face gleamed. "Man, there's a whole world down there. I suppose you think I'm nuts."

"Not really." Weston reached for a gag line. "I thought you'd gotten a better offer."

"I did!" Ted lit up like an alabaster lamp. "One look and I knew: *These are my people. And this is my place!* You have to see!"

"I'll try." He did; he followed the poor bastard to the entrance—it's right behind these bushes, he knows—and stopped. . . . "Wait."

. . . and heard Ted's voice overlapping, "Wait. I have to tell them you're coming. You *will* wait for me, right?"

Weston wanted to be brave, but he could not lie. "I'll try."

He couldn't stop Ted, either. The tunnel walls shifted behind his friend as if something huge had swallowed him in its sleep. Its foul breath gushed out of the hole; Weston heard the earth panting, waiting to swallow him. Forgive him, he fled.

Awful place, he vowed never to . . . But they are waiting. "Okay," he says finally, plunging into the bushes like a diver into a pool full of sharks. "Okay."

With the others walking up his heels, Weston looks down into the hole. It's dark as death. Relieved, he looks up. "Sorry, we can't do it today. Not without flashlights. Now—"

"Got it covered." The veteran produces a bundle—halogen miner's lamps on headbands. Handing them out, he says the obvious, "Always . . ."

Weston groans. "Prepared."

He stands by as his tourists drop into the tunnel, one by one. If they don't come out, what will he tell their families? Will they sue? Will he go to jail? He's happy to stand at the brink mulling it, but the marine shoves him into the hole. "Your turn."

He drops in after Weston, shutting out daylight with his bulk. The only way they can go is down.

All his life since his parents died, Lawrence Weston has taken great pains to control his environment. Now he is in a place he never imagined. Life goes on, but everything flies out of control. He is part of *this* now, blundering into the ground.

Weston doesn't know what he expects: rats, lurking dragons, thugs with billy clubs, a tribe of pale, blind mutants, or a bunch of gaudy neohippies in sordid underground squats. In fact, several passages fan out from the main entrance, rough tunnels leading to larger caverns with entrances and exits of their own; the underground kingdom is bigger than he feared. He had no idea it would be so old. Debris brought down from the surface to shore up the burrow sticks out of the mud and stone like a schoolchild's display of artifacts from every era. The mud plastering the walls is studded with hardware from the streetcar/gaslight 1890s, fragments of glass and plastic from the Day-Glo skateboard 1990s, and motherboards, abandoned CRTs, bumpers from cars that are too new to carbon date. The walls are buttressed by four-by-fours, lit by LED bulbs strung from wires, but Weston moves along in a crouch, as though the earth is just about to collapse on his head—which might be merciful, given the fumes. Although fresh air is coming in from somewhere, there is the intolerable stink of mud and small dead things, and although to his surprise this tunnel, at least, is free of the expected stink of piss and excrement, there is the smell that comes of too many people living too close together, an overpoweringly human fug.

At first Weston sees nobody, hears nothing he can make sense of, knows only that he can't be in this awful place.

Dense air weighs on him so he can hardly breathe—the effluvia of human souls. Then a voice rises in the passage ahead, a girl's bright, almost-festive patter running along ahead of his last-ever Weston Walking Tour, as though she and the hulking marine, and not Weston, are in charge.

Meanwhile the mud walls widen as the path goes deeper. The tunnels are lined with people, their pale faces gleaming wherever he flashes his miner's lamp, and it is terrifying. The man who tried so hard to keep all the parts of his life exactly where he put them has lost any semblance of control; the orphan who lived alone because it was safest is trapped in the earth, crowded—no, surrounded—by souls, dozens, perhaps hundreds of others with their needs, their grief and sad secrets and emotional demands.

The pressure of their hopes staggers him.

All at once the lifelong solo flier comprehends what he

read in Ted Bishop's face that day, and why he fled. Educated, careful, and orderly and self-contained as Lawrence Weston tries so hard to be, only a tissue of belief separates him from them.

Now they are all around him.

I can't. Every crease in his body is greased with the cold sweat of claustrophobia. *I won't.*

He has forgotten how to breathe. One more minute and . . . He doesn't know. Frothing, he wheels, cranked up to fight the devil if he has to, anything to get out of here: he'll tear the hulking veteran apart with teeth and nails, offer money, do murder or, if he has to, die in the attempt—anything to escape the dimly perceived but persistent, needy humanity seething underground.

As it turns out, he doesn't have to do any of these things. The bulky vet lurches forward with a big-bear rumble. "*Semper Fi.*"

In the dimness ahead, a ragged, gravelly chorus responds: "*Semper Fi.*"

The marine shoulders Weston aside. "Found 'em. Now, shove off. Round up your civilians and move 'em out."

Miraculously, he does. He pulls the WESTON WALKS placard out of the back of his jeans and raises it, pointing the headlamp so his people will see the sign. Then he blows the silver whistle he keeps for emergencies and never had to use.

It makes the tunnels shriek.

"Okay," he says with all the force he has left in his body. "Time to go! On to Fifth Avenue and . . ." He goes on in his best tour-guide voice; it's a desperation move, but Weston is desperate enough to offer them anything. "The Russian Tea Room! I'll treat. Dinner at the Waldorf, suites for the night, courtesy of Weston Walking Tours."

Oddly, when they emerge into fresh air and daylight—*dear God, it's still light*—the group is no smaller, but it is different. It takes Weston a minute to figure out what's changed. The bulky ex-marine with an agenda is gone, an absence he could have predicted, but when he lines them up at the bus stop (yes, he is shaking quarters into the coin drop on a city bus!), he still counts thirteen. Newlyweds, yes; anniversary couple; librarian; assorted bland, satisfied middle Americans, yes; pimply kid. The group looks the same, but it isn't. He is too disrupted, troubled, and distracted to know who . . .

Safe at last in the Russian Tea Room, he knows which one she is, or thinks he knows, because unlike the others, she looks perfectly comfortable here: lovely woman with tousled hair, buff little body wrapped in a big gray sweater with sleeves pulled down over her fingertips; when she reaches for the samovar with a gracious offer to pour he is startled by a flash of black-rimmed fingernails. Never mind; maybe it's a fashion statement he hasn't caught up with.

Instead of leading his group to Times Square or Grand Central for the ceremonial send-off so he can fade into the crowd, he leaves them at the Waldorf, all marveling as they wait at the elevators for the concierge to show them to their complimentary suites.

Spent and threatened by his close encounter with life, Weston flees.

The first thing he does when he gets home is pull his ad and trash the business phone. Then he does what murderers and rape victims do in movies, after the fact: He spends hours under a hot shower, washing away the event. It will be days before he's fit to go out. He quiets shattered nerves by numbering the beautiful objects in the ultimate safe house he has created, assuages grief with coffee and the day's papers in the sunlit library, taking comfort from small rituals. He needs to visit his father's Turner watercolor, stroke the smooth flank of the Brancusi marble in the foyer, study his treasure, a little Remington bronze.

When he does go out some days later, he almost turns and goes back in. The sexy waif from the tour is on his front steps. Same sweater, same careless toss of the head. The intrusion makes his heart stop and his belly tremble, but the girl who poured so nicely at the Russian Tea Room greets him with a delighted smile.

"I thought you'd never come out."

"You have no right, you have no *right*. . . ." She looks so pleased that he starts over. "What are you doing here?"

"I live in the neighborhood." She challenges him with that gorgeous smile.

How do you explain to a pretty girl that she has no right to track you to your lair? How can you tell any New Yorker that your front steps are private, specific only to you? How can you convince her that your life is closed to intruders, or that she is one?

He can't. "I have to go!"

"Where are you—"

Staggered by a flashback—tunnel air repeating like something he ate—Weston is too disturbed to make polite excuses, beep his driver, manage any of the usual exit lines. "China!" he blurts, and escapes.

At the corner he wheels to make sure he's escaped and gasps: "Oh!"

Following him at a dead run, she smashes into him with a stirring little *thud* that splits his heart, exposing it to the light.

Oh, the chipped tooth that flashes when she grins. "Um, China this very minute?"

Yes, he is embarrassed. "Well, not really. I mean. Coffee first."

She tugs down the sweater sleeves, beaming. "Let's! I'll pay."

By the time they finish their cappuccinos and he figures out how to get out without hurting her feelings, he's in love.

How does a man like Weston fall in love?

Accidentally. Fast. It's nothing he can control. Still he manages to part from Wings Germaine without letting his hands shake or his eyes mist over; he must not do anything that will tip her off to the fact that this is the last good time. He even manages to hug good-bye without clinging, although it wrecks his heart. "It's been fun," he says. "I have to go."

"No big. Nothing is forever," she says, exposing that chipped tooth.

Dying a little, he backs away with a careful smile. To keep the life he's built so lovingly, he has to, but it's hard. "So, bye."

Her foggy voice curls around him and clings. "Take care."

They're friends now, or what passes for friends, so he trusts her not to follow. Even though it's barely four in the afternoon he locks his front door behind him, checks the windows, and sets the alarm.

That beautiful girl seemed to be running ahead of his thoughts so fast that when they exchanged life stories she saw the pain running along underneath the surface of the story he usually tells. Her triangular smile broke his heart. "I'm so sorry," she said.

"Don't be," he told her. "It's nothing you did."

"No," she said. "Oh, no. But I've been there, and I know what it's like."

Orphaned, he assumed. *Like me,* he thinks, although she is nothing like him. Named in honor of her fighter-pilot father, she said. Art student, she said, but she never said when. Mystifyingly, she said, "You have some beautiful stuff." Had he told her about the Calder maquette and forgotten, or mentioned the Sargent portrait of his great-grandfather or the Manet oil sketch? He has replayed that conversation a dozen times today and he still doesn't know.

At night, even though he's secured the house and is safely locked into his bedroom, he has a hard time going to sleep. Before he can manage it, he has to get up several times and repeat his daytime circuit of the house. He patrols rooms lit only by reflected streetlights, padding from one to the next in T-shirt and pajama bottoms, touching table tops with light fingers, running his hands over the smooth marble flank of the Brancusi, because every object is precious and he needs to know that each is in its appointed place.

Day or night, Weston is ruler of his tight little world, secure in the confidence that although he let himself be waylaid by a ragged stranger today, although he ended up doing what she wanted instead of what he intended, here, at least, he commands the world.

Then why can't he sleep?

The fourth time he goes downstairs in the dark he finds her sitting in his living room. At first he imagines his curator has moved a new Degas bronze into the house in the dead of night. Then he realizes it's Wings Germaine, positioned like an ornament on his ancestral brocade sofa, sitting with her arms locked around her knees.

"What," he cries, delighted, angry and terrified. "What!"

Wings moves into his arms so fluidly that the rest flows naturally, like a soft, brilliant dream. "I was in the neighborhood."

They are together in a variety of intense configurations until Weston gasps with joy and falls away from her, exhausted. Drenched in sense memory, he plummets into sleep.

When the housekeeper comes to wake him in the morning, Wings is gone.

By day Weston is the same person; days pass in their usual sweet order, but his nights go by in that fugue of images of Wings Germaine, who hushes his mouth with kisses whenever he tries to ask who she is and how she gets in or whether what they have together is real or imagined. No matter how he wheedles, she doesn't explain; "I live in the neighborhood," she says, and the pleasure of being *this close* quiets his heart. He acknowledges the possibility that the girl is, rather, only hallucination and—astounding for a man so bent on control—he accepts that.

As long as his days pass in order, he tells himself, as long as nothing changes, he'll be okay. He thinks.

When Wings arrives she does what she does so amazingly that he's never quite certain what happened, only that it leaves him joyful and exhausted; then she leaves. His nights are marvels, uncomplicated by the pressure of the usual lover's expectations, because they both know she will be gone before the sun comes up. She always is. He wakes up alone, to coffee and the morning paper, sunlight on mahogany. Their nights are wild and confusing, but in the daytime world that Weston has spent his life perfecting, everything is reassuringly the same.

Or so he tells himself. It's what he has to believe. If he saw any of this for what it is, he'd have to act, and the last thing Weston wants right now is for his dizzy collisions in the night to end.

Until today, when he hurtles out of sleep at 4:00 A.M. Panic wakes him, the roar of blood thundering in his ears. His synapses clash in serial car crashes; the carnage is terrible. He slides out of bed in the gray dawn and bolts downstairs, lunging from room to room, shattered by the certain knowledge that something has changed.

Unless everything has changed.

What, he wonders, running a finger over tabletops, the rims of picture frames, the outlines of priceless maquettes by famous sculptors, all still in place, reassuringly *there*. What?

Dear God, his Picasso plates are missing. Treasures picked up off the master's studio floor by Great-grandfather Weston, who walked away with six signed plates under his arm, leaving behind a thousand dollars and the memory of his famous smile. Horrified, he turns on the light. Pale circles mark the silk wallpaper where the plates hung; empty brackets sag, reproaching him.

He doesn't mention this to Wings when she comes to him that night; he only breathes into her crackling hair and holds her closer, thinking, *It can't be her. She couldn't have, it couldn't be Wings.*

Then he buries himself in her because he knows it is.

Before dawn she leaves Weston drowsing in his messy bed, dazed and grateful. His nights continue to pass like dreams; the rich orphan so bent on life without intrusions welcomes the wild girl in spite of certain losses; love hurts, but he wants what he wants. Their time together passes without reference to the fact that when Weston comes down tomorrow his King George silver service will be missing, to be followed by his Kang dynasty *netsuke,* and then his best Miró. *I love her too much,* he tells himself as objects disappear daily. *I don't want this to stop.*

He inspects. All his external systems remain in place. Alarms are set; there's no sign of forcible entry or exit. It is as though things he thought he prized more than any woman have dropped into the earth without explanation.

He can live without these things, he tells himself. He can! Love is love, and these are only objects.

Until the Brancusi marble goes missing.

In a spasm of grief, his heart empties out.

Wings won't know when they make love that night that her new man is only going through the motions—unless she does know, which straightforward Weston is too new at deception to guess. He does the girl with one eye on the door, which is how he assumes she exits once she's pushed him off the deep end into sleep—which she has done nightly, vanishing before he wakes up.

Careful, Wings. Tonight will be different.

To him, Wings is a closed book.

He needs to crack her open like a piñata and watch the secrets fall out.

Guilty and terrible as he feels about doubting her, confused because he can't bear to lose *one more thing,* he can't let this go on. With Wings still in his arms he struggles to stay awake, watching through slitted eyes for what seems like forever. She drowses; he waits. The night passes like a dark thought, sullenly dragging its feet. Waiting is terrible. By the time a crack of gray light outlines his bedroom blackout shades, he's about to die of it. The girl he loves sighs and delicately disengages herself. Grieving, he watches through slitted eyes, and when she goes, he counts to twenty and follows.

He knows the house better than Wings; she'll take the back stairs, so he hurries down the front. When she sneaks into the central hall and silences the alarm so she can escape with another of his treasures, he'll spring. Sliding into the niche behind the Brancusi's empty pedestal, he crouches until his joints crack, echoing in the silent house. He has no idea how she escaped.

Damn fool, he thinks, and does not know which of them he's mad at, himself or elusive Wings Germaine.

When they lie down together after midnight, Weston's fears have eased: of being caught following—the tears of regret, the recriminations—unless his greatest fear was that she wasn't coming back because she knew.

Did she know he followed? Does she?

She slides into his arms in the nightly miracle that he has come to expect, and he pulls her close with a sigh. What will he do after he ends this? What will she steal from him tonight, and what will she do when he confronts her? He doesn't know, but it's long overdue. When she slips out of bed before first light, he gives her time to take the back stairs and then follows. Like a shadow, he drifts through darkened rooms where the girl moves so surely that he knows she must linger here every night, having her way with his treasured things.

With the swift, smooth touch of a child molester, she strokes his family of objects but takes nothing.

Damn! Is he waiting for her to steal? What is she waiting for? Why doesn't she grab something so he can pounce and finish this?

Empty-handed, she veers toward the darkened kitchen.

Weston's back hairs rise and tremble as Wings opens the door to the smoky stone cellar and starts down.

His heart sags. Is that all she is? A generic homeless person with a sordid squat in a corner of his dank basement? When Wings Germaine comes to his bed at night she is freshly scrubbed; she smells of wood smoke and rich earth, and in the part of his head where fantasies have moved in and set up housekeeping, Weston wants to believe that she's fresh from her own rooftop terrace or just in from a day on her country estate.

Idiot.

He has two choices here. He can go back to bed and pretend what he must in order to keep things as they are in spite of escalating losses—or he can track her to her lair.

But, oh! The missing furniture of his life, the art. His Brancusi! What happened to them? Has she sneaked his best things out of the house and fenced them, or does she keep them stashed in some secret corner of his cellar for reasons she will never explain? Is his treasured Miró safe? Is anything? He has to know.

Oh, lover. It is a cry from the heart. *Forgive me.*

He goes down.

The cellar is empty. Wings isn't anywhere. He shines his caretaker's flashlight in every corner and underneath all the shelves and into empty niches in Great-grandfather's wine rack, but there is no sign. It takes him all morning to be absolutely certain, hours in which the housekeeper trots around the kitchen overhead making his breakfast, putting his coffee cup and the steaming carafe, his orange juice and cinnamon toast—and a rose, because roses are in season—on his breakfast tray. He times the woman's trips back and forth to the library where he eats, her visit to his bedroom where she will change his sheets without remarking, because she does it every day; he waits for her to finish, punch in the code, and leave by the kitchen door. Then he waits another hour.

When he's sure the house is empty, Weston goes back upstairs for the klieg lights his folks bought for a home tour the year they died.

Bright as they are, they don't show him much. There are cartons of books in this old cellar, bundles of love letters that he's afraid to read. His parents' skis, the ice skates they bought him the Christmas he turned four, the sled—all remnants of his long-lost past. This is the sad but ordinary basement of an ordinary man who has gone through life with his upper lip stiffer than is normal and his elbows clamped to his sides. It makes him sigh.

Maybe he imagined Wings Germaine.

Then, when he's just about to write her off as a figment of his imagination, and the missing pieces, up to and including the Brancusi, as the work of his housekeeper or the guy who installed the alarms, he sees that the floor in front of the wine rack is uneven and that there are fingerprints on one stone.

Very well. He could be Speke, starting out after Burton, or Livingstone, heading up the Zambezi. The shell Weston has built around himself hardens so that only he will hear his heart crack as he finishes: *Alone.*

When she comes back too long after midnight, he is waiting: provisioned this time, equipped with pick and miner's light—because he thinks he knows where Wings is going—handcuffs, and a length of rope. He will follow her down. Never mind what Weston thinks in the hours while he crouches in his own basement like a sneak thief, waiting; don't try to parse the many heartbroken, reproachful, angry escalating to furious, ultimately threatening speeches he writes and then discards.

The minute that stone moves, he'll lunge. If he's fast enough, he can grab her as she comes out; if she's faster and drops back into the hole, then like a jungle cat, he will plunge in after her and bring her down. Then he'll kneel on the woman's chest and pin her wrists and keep her there until she explains. He already knows that eventually he'll soften and give her one more chance, but it will be on his terms.

She'll have to pack up her stuff and move into his handsome house and settle down in his daytime life, because he is probably in love with her. Then he'll have every beautiful thing that he cares about secured in the last safe place.

And, by God, she'll bring all his stuff back. She will!

He's been staring at the stone for so long that he almost forgets to douse the light when it moves. He manages it just as the stone scrapes aside like a manhole cover and her head pops up.

"Oh," she cries, although he has no idea how she knows he is crouching here in the dark. "Oh, fuck."

It's a long way to the bottom. The fall is harder than he thought. By the time he hits the muddy floor of the tunnel underneath his house, Wings Germaine is gone.

He is alone in the narrow tunnel, riveted by the possibility that it's a dead end and there's no way out.

He's even more terrified because a faint glow tells him that there is. To follow Wings, he has to crawl on and out, into the unknown.

Weston goes along on mud-caked hands and slimy knees for what seems like forever before he comes to a place big enough to stand up in. It's a lot like the hole where the runaway tourist stampeded him, but it is nothing like it. The man-made grotto is wired and strung with dim lights; the air is as foul as it was in the hole where Ted Bishop disappeared, but this one is deserted. He is at a rude crossroads. Access tunnels snake out in five directions, and he has to wonder which one she took and how far they go.

Stupid bastard, he calls, "Wings?"

There is life down here, Weston knows it; *she* is down here, but he has no idea which way she went or where she is hiding or, in fact, whether she is hiding from him. A man in his right mind, even a heartbroken lover, would go back the way he came, haul himself up and station his caretaker by the opening with a shotgun to prevent incursions until he could mix enough concrete to fill the place and cement the stone lid down so no matter what else happened in his house, she would never get back inside.

Instead he cries, "Wings. Oh, Wings!"

He knows better than to wait. If anything is going to happen here, he has to make it happen.

The idea terrifies him. Worse. There are others here.

For the first time in his well-ordered life, careful Weston, who vowed never to lose anybody or anything he cared about, is lost.

The chamber is empty for the moment, but there is life going on just out of sight; he hears the unknown stirring in hidden grottoes, moving through tunnels like arteries—approaching, for all he knows. The knowledge is suffocating. The man who needs to be alone understands that other lives are unfolding down here; untold masses are deep in their caverns doing God knows what. A born solitary, he is staggered by the pressure of all those unchecked lives raging out of sight and beyond the law or any of the usual agencies of control.

Encroaching. *God!*

Trembling, he tries, "Wings?"

As if she cares enough to answer.

The tunnels give back nothing. He wants to run after her but he doesn't know where. Worse, she may see him not as a lover in pursuit but a giant rat scuttling after food. He should search but he's afraid of what he will find. Much as he misses his things, he's afraid to find out what Wings has done with them and who she is doing it with.

Overturned, he retreats to the mouth of the tunnel that leads to his house and hunkers down to think.

There are others out there—too many! Accustomed now, Weston can sense them, hear them, smell them in the dense underground air, connected by this tunnel to the treasures he tries so hard to protect. The labyrinth is teeming with life, but he is reluctant to find out who the others are or how they are. They could be trapped underground like him, miserable and helpless, snapped into fetal position in discrete pits they have dug for themselves. They could be killing each other out there, or lying tangled in wild, orgiastic knots doing amazing things to each other in communal passion pits, or thinking great thoughts, writing verse or plotting revolution, or they could be locked into lotus position in individual niches, halfway to Nirvana or—no!—they could be trashing his stolen art. He doesn't want to know.

It is enough to know that for the moment, he is alone at a dead end and that, in a way, it's a relief.

Surprise. For the first time since the runaway tourist forced him underground and Wings flew up to the surface and messed up his life, Weston has nothing to hope for and no place to go. And for the first time since he was four years old, he feels safe.

After a time he takes the pick he had strapped to his backpack in case and begins to dig.

In the hours or days that follow, Weston eats, he supposes: By the time the hole is big enough to settle down in, his supply of granola bars is low and the water in his canteen is almost gone, but he is not ready to go back into his house. In between bouts of digging, he probably sleeps. Mostly he thinks and then stops thinking, as his mind empties out and leaves him drifting in the zone. What zone, he could not say. What he wants and where this will end, he is too disturbed and disrupted to guess.

Then, just when he has adjusted to being alone in this snug, reassuringly tight place, when he is resigned to the fact that he'll never see her again, she comes, flashing into life before him like an apparition and smiling that sexy and annoying, enigmatic smile.

"Wings!"

Damn that wild glamour, damn the cloud of tousled hair, damn her for saying with that indecipherable, superior air, "What makes you think I'm really here?"

The girl folds as neatly as a collapsible tripod and sits cross-legged on the floor of the hole Weston has dug, fixed in place in front of him, sitting right here where he can see her, waiting for whatever comes next.

It's better not to meet her eyes. Not now, when he is trying to think. It takes him longer than it should to frame the question.

"What have you done with my stuff?"

Damn her for answering the way she does. "What do you care? It's only stuff."

Everything he ever cared about simply slides away.

They sit together in Weston's tight little pocket in the earth. They are quiet for entirely too long. She doesn't leave but she doesn't explain, either. She doesn't goad him and she doesn't offer herself. She just sits there regarding him. It's almost more than he can bear.

A question forms deep inside Weston's brain and moves slowly, like a parasite drilling its way to the surface. Finally it explodes into the still, close air. "Are you the devil, or what?"

This makes her laugh. "Whatever, sweetie. What do you think?"

"I don't know," he shouts. "I don't know!"

"So get used to it."

But he can't. He won't. More or less content with his place in the narrow hole he has dug for himself, Weston says, "It's time for you to go," and when she hesitates, wondering, he pushes Wings Germaine outside and nudges her along the access tunnel to the hub, the one place where they can stand, facing. She gasps and recoils. To his astonishment, he is brandishing the pick like a club. Then he clamps his free hand on her shoulder, and with no clear idea what he will do when this part is done or what comes next, he turns Wings Germaine in his steely grip and sends her away. Before he ducks back into his territory Weston calls after her on a note that makes clear to both of them that they are done. "Don't come back."

Behind him, the cellar waits, but he can't know whether he wants to go back to his life. He is fixed on what he has to do. Resolved, relieved because he know this at least, he sets to work on the exit where he left her, erasing it with his pick.

The Projected Girl

BY LAVIE TIDHAR

Lavie Tidhar is the author of the linked-story collection *HebrewPunk,* the steampunk novels *The Bookman* and *Camera Obscura,* the literary novel *Osama,* the SF novel *Martian Sands,* and, with Nir Yaniv, the short novel *The Tel Aviv Dossier.* He has lived on three continents and one island-nation, and was last seen in Southeast Asia.

NOTE: DAVID TIDHAR (1897–1970) WAS AN ISRAELI DETECTIVE, AUTHOR, AND HERO OF THE TWENTY-EIGHT DAVID TIDHAR BALASH ("DETECTIVE") NOVELS.

On Danny's tenth birthday Uncle Arik gave him a conjuring set. Uncle Arik had just come back from a spell in England. He'd stayed, he'd said, in a five-star hotel in a place called Brixton; apparently he'd stayed there for the whole year and three months of his absence. "A bed to lie on, a roof over your head, and three meals a day," Uncle Arik told Danny, "—what is there to go out for?" When he'd finally left the hotel, however, and before boarding the El Al flight back home, Uncle Arik had stopped in a shop called Davenports, and there, remembering his favorite (and only) nephew's rapidly approaching birthday, he purchased the conjuring set. "It's a shop set underground," he told Danny in confidence. "Below the great train station of Charing Cross. Unless you know it's there, you will never find it. 'Course, it's a *magic* shop."

It was Danny's conviction that his Uncle Arik was a Mossad agent. His mysterious job was seldom referred to, yet it took him to many exotic places, often for great lengths of time. He had once heard his father say, when he thought Danny couldn't hear him, that Uncle Arik's work involved "things falling off the back of trucks." For a while, therefore, Danny thought Uncle Arik was a truck driver, or perhaps a mechanic: yet he had never seen him driving a truck, nor were there ever signs of grease on his immaculately ironed shirt or trousers. "A conjuring set?" Danny's father said to his brother when he saw the present. "I'm not sure it's such a good idea."

"It's a great idea," Uncle Arik said. "It's what every kid wants."

"And how would you know?" Danny's father said.

"I was a kid once," Uncle Arik said. "I always wished Mum had bought one of those for *me*."

Mention of their mother merely brought a head shake from Danny's father. But the present was given, and it stayed. "Go on, open it," Uncle Arik said. "Remember, the magic you learn—you've got to keep it *secret*." And he put his pointing finger over his lips, and Danny mimicked his gesture, and they both laughed. "I tell you," Uncle Arik said, sitting down in the armchair favored by Danny's father, wiping sweat from his bushy eyebrows, and opening the top button on his checkered short-sleeved shirt, "I've been to a lot of cities in my time, Ben. I've seen the sights of Paris and Rome, Tokyo and New York and London—"

"I guess you had a lot of time looking out of windows," his brother said.

"But there's nothing," Uncle Arik said, ignoring him, "quite like coming home."

Danny, who had never been out of Israel and seldom out of Haifa, shared Uncle Arik's sentiment wholeheartedly. The city—*his* city—surely it was the greatest possible place anyone could wish to be born and live in. From the balcony above the street-veined slopes of Mount Carmel, Danny could always see the great blue expanse of the sea, spreading away from Haifa like a crayoned map until it fell off in a great rim of waterfalls beyond the horizon. From the balcony he could, if he was patient enough, lick the tip of one finger and then trace, at his leisure, a trajectory of the sun as it came over the green slopes of the mountain, hovered directly overhead, and fell at last into the water, "on time for sunset, every time!" as Uncle Arik liked to say. And, standing on the balcony and leaning slightly out over the railings, Danny could see the streets below, where partisans, rabbis, poets, and assassinated politicians wove between each other: There Hannah Senesh, who parachuted into Yugoslavia and death at the hands of the Nazis; there the Ba'al Shem Tov, who could perform miracles; there the great Arlozorov Street, named after the man who was shot on the beach back in 1933. Looking left, the golden dome of the Baha'i temple shone in the sun, and there, farther down, was the great sprawling mass of Hadar, with its shawarma stands, its cheap clothing and sunglasses, its second-hand book stores, dingy travel agents and numerous coffee shops—Danny's favorite place in the whole wide world.

Many children are given, at one point or another, a set of magic tricks for their birthday. Danny's conjuring set, having come from Davenports, was better than most (it included a thumb tip and silk handkerchief, a pack of Bicycle cards, a cut-and-restore rope, an egg bag, a Svengali deck, and the inevitable wand), but it was not guaranteed to turn a kid into a magician.

Most children play with the magic kit for the length of time required to learn that coins don't really disappear (it's in the other hand!), that everyone knows a card trick or two and would be happy to display it when presented with the slightest opportunity, and that performing magic requires *practice.* Like playing the clarinet, unless one enjoys the task, one soon abandons it. And it would surprise no one—and Danny's father least of all—that Danny, too, abandoned the magic kit shortly after receiving it, and after some time of its remaining untouched in his room, it finally made its way into the family *boydem,* the storage area in the ceiling where all unused but not-unwanted things inevitably end up.

In fact, the magic kit—the "conjuring set," to use Uncle Arik's term—bears little relevance to our story but for its consequences.

At thirteen, a Jewish boy celebrates his bar mitzvah, an occasion of great pleasure for his family and often of acute embarrassment for the boy himself. Danny's bar mitzvah took place in a rented hall near Crusaders Road, close to the Garden of Statues, and was attended by a great many people, some of whom he knew. Besides the cousins, second cousins, loose cousins ("This is Tali," Danny's father said. "Her grandmother was once married to your grandmother's brother. Works in diamonds."), uncles, aunts, and other assorted relatives, there were also friends of his father's ("This is Barashi," Uncle Arik told Danny in confidence, "friend of your father's from army training days. Good man. Lives in Jerusalem. Buys and sells." Danny said, "Buys and sells what?" and Uncle Arik smiled and tapped his nose conspiratorially), acquaintances, and school friends of Danny's with an entourage of parents of their own. He was given presents: Barashi gave him a black plastic combination flashlight-scissors-measuring-tape device and tousled his hair; Aunt Miri gave him hand-knitted socks and a wet kiss on the cheek; Cousin Uri from the kibbutz gave him a rubber catapult and said, "I made it myself"—it was confiscated by Danny's dad as soon as it was given—and there were also envelopes with his name written on each, which were given to his father on Danny's behalf.

After the party was over they took a cab back to the flat, just Danny, his dad, and his uncle. "Mazal tov," the taxi driver said.

In the flat, the two adults sat back on the sofa, and Danny sat in the armchair. Sitting together, his dad and Uncle Arik looked remarkably alike: It was in the lines around their eyes, in the way their hairlines receded in an almost identical fashion, but mostly it was in the way they smiled. "Well," Uncle Arik said, "what are you waiting for? Pass the envelopes."

"It will all have to go toward paying for the hall," Danny's father said. Uncle Arik saw Danny's reaction and winked at him. "Let's count the money first."

They divided the envelopes into three. Danny's dad and his uncle began to open some. Danny put his on the low round table by the armchair. Too late, he realized the morning's mail was also on the table and, in trying to extract it from underneath the pile of envelopes, upset the whole thing. Envelopes fluttered to the ground like a flock of seagulls settling down to rest in the harbor. Danny hurriedly bent down to pick them up. Danny's dad frowned but said nothing. They sorted notes in piles, by denomination. Danny collected strewn paper debris.

When he was finished, and as he sat back down and began sorting through the pile, a small dirty-blue envelope fell down and fluttered into his lap. He picked it up. Unlike the others, it bore no giver's name. The paper felt brittle. When he took his hand away there was dust on his fingers. He tore it open. There was no money inside.

At first he thought it was empty. Then, when he tipped it, pressing the envelope open as if squeezing a lemon, a small single sheet of paper slid out. He picked it up and looked at it. There was a line of writing in black ink, the letters carefully drawn, as if the writer was not quite comfortable with the Hebrew alphabet. The handwriting seemed feminine. The note said, *"Daniel, whatever is happen I love you."* It was signed with a single letter—*aleph*.

"What's that," his father said, briefly looking up from his work, "a check?"

Danny didn't reply. He looked at the note again, mutely. *Aleph* could stand for *ima*—"Mum." But his mother had died when he was four, of cancer. He had only a vague recollection of her: the smell of cooking stuffed cabbage, and cigarettes, and perfume like at the Mashbir department store on Herzl Street. "Danny? What is it?"

But the language was wrong. And no one ever called him Daniel. He said, "Nothing, Dad," and put the note back in the envelope. "I'm just going to the bathroom," he said. He got up and, still holding the envelope, went instead to his room. He looked at the envelope again. As he stared at its back, it seemed to him that he could see some faint etchings in the paper, as if an address had been written there before, and there was also a depression in the top right corner, as if a stamp was once affixed there. *It's just an old letter,* he thought; *maybe it finally surfaced from wherever it was and got mixed up with the normal mail.* He'd read stories where things like this happened. He looked around his bookshelves. On the bottom shelf lay Ze'ev Vilnai's seven-volume *Guide to Eretz Yisrael,* and alongside it all seventeen volumes of the *Encyclopaedia Britannica.* On the shelf above it was a near-complete run of Am Oved's science fiction paperbacks in the distinct white bindings. Above these, the western, secret agent, mystery, and karate paperbacks that could be found, at ten shekels a pop, in every secondhand store in the city—and on the last shelf, tended carefully like a row of elderly geraniums, the rare books left him by his mother: The Detective Library Series, the worn paperbound books that featured the adventures of the first hebrew detective, David Tidhar, and which were, at thirteen, Danny's abiding passion.

He looked through them. *Revenge of the Maharajah*—no. *The Blue Crosses, Tales of the Hashish Smugglers*—no. But there—*Disappearance on Mount Carmel: A Mystery in the Margins of the City*? He wanted to look through it, but his father was calling him from the living room. Danny put the letter into the slim volume, where it nestled next to the title page. He felt strange, as if he had momentarily stepped into something beyond the ordinary and for which he had no words. "I'm coming," he called, and returned the book to the shelf.

His father and uncle were still counting money when he returned, and he joined them, though less enthusiastically now.

At last the task was done. "I'll get us a drink," Uncle Arik said. "Ben?"

"Just some water," Danny's dad said. Uncle Arik departed to the small kitchen and returned with water for his brother, a coke for Danny, and a whisky with ice for himself. "Le'chaim," he said, raising his glass. "And mazal tov, Danny."

When the events hall and other expenses were all paid for, some money yet remained, and so a decision had to be made: What should Danny spend his money on?

Danny was initially in favor of a computer. Computers were the latest thing. You could buy one to have in your house. You could play games on it—an argument he didn't quite put forward to his father. They would need to add extra money for the purchase price—quite a lot of extra money, when it came to that—but . . .

Uncle Arik, in an uncharacteristically somber display, suggested putting the money in a savings account at the bank, to accumulate interest until Danny was twenty-one. Danny was not wholeheartedly supportive of the idea.

At last Danny's father said, "Why don't you buy some books with it? Take it down to Ha'chalutz Street, to that shop you always go to."

Danny said, "Really?" and then, as caution took hold of him, said, "Anything I want?"

His dad laughed. "Any books you want, Danny. It's your money."

And so it was decided.

The bookshops of Haifa are clustered like a gaggle of elderly, generally good-natured but occasionally difficult uncles, in Lower Hadar, around Ha'chalutz Street and below in Sirkin. Danny's favorite was called Mischar Ha'sefer—"the Book Trade"—at number 31 Ha'chalutz, where it had resided for many years, and where it continues to reside. Seeing as the book dealers of Haifa, as a body, follow the ancient tradition of that city and take a lengthy afternoon spell between one and four in the afternoon, Danny went there early in the morning.

The entrance to Mischar Ha'sefer is crowded with English paperback books, imported pornographic magazines hanging from the rafters by thread like condemned convicts, a tasteful spread of romantic novels, and a dusty bargain bin overflowing with cookbooks, modern fiction, and the occasional title in Russian. On the opposite side of the street is a shawarma stand, and the smell of roasting meat arising from its confines accompanied Danny as he stepped into the bookshop.

He browsed happily as blue-haired ladies came and went for their daily fix of Mills & Boon, a literature student haggled over a paperback *War and Peace,* and a young uniformed soldier with an M-16 slung over his shoulder obscured the science fiction and fantasy shelves from view.

Behind the counter the formidable owner, a Romanian immigrant of indeterminable age, whose name Danny had never learned, was marking books, occasionally raising her voice in a shrill call for her son—"Itzik! Itz-ik!"—following which her son, himself of an age whose exactitude could not be determined, would pop his head out of the stockroom in the basement to assist with whatever query needed addressing. Danny made his way through shelf after shelf, accumulating half a dozen titles in the process for his collection, prominent amongst them three Patrick Kim—The Karate Man titles, comprising *The Thousand Lakes Conspiracy, The Statues of Doom,* and *Demon of Pale Death.* He also purchased two Ringo western titles: *The Gun of Revenge* and *Death at High Noon,* and finally, the highlight of his visit, a rare paperback from the Series of Horror, with a cover showing a grinning, deformed skull: Dan Shocker's *Creatures of the Devil Doctor.*

But it is not Danny's literary taste, as lamentable as it may be, that concerns us. The books were mysteries. In that, Danny felt, they reflected life. They asked important questions, such as, What is the meaning of Life? Is love Eternal? And what exactly was it that the Doctor's devilish creatures do?

Behind the counter, Itzik had replaced his mother. He wiped sweat from his balding head, added up the prices, and said, "Nice selection. You get back half if you return them."

"I think I'll keep them," Danny said.

Itzik shook his head. "Everyone's a collector," he said sadly. "D'you know," he said, as if imparting a great truth to his young audience, "these are *marginal* titles. A boy like you—you should be reading Agnon, Grossman, Oz, Appelfeld. Serious literature, not this trash. These books you got there, half of them don't even appear in the National Library catalogs. They don't even officially *exist.* Take my advice, kid: Don't waste your time."

When he had finished at the Book Trade, Danny progressed down the stairs beside the store, paid a perfunctory visit to the textbook shop underneath, and stepped into Sirkin and to his second favorite bookshop, Martef Ha'sefer—the Book Basement.

The Book Basement's only concession to advertising was, and remains, an ancient hand-painted sign laconically saying BOOKS, with an arrow pointing farther down the hill. Follow the arrow, and you are confronted with more steps, a rubbish heap, the smell of urine, and, going past these delights, a door. Danny opened the door and went in.

The Book Basement resembles a crusaders-era monastery in its interior. Books are huddled together in dusty catacombs that spread out in all directions from the vaguely L-shaped main corridor. Shelves rise from the vault of the floor and disappear in the darkness overhead. The smell of the interior is of dust and old paper, a smell a little like bad breath and a little like well-preserved perfume. It was inside the shop, after he had wandered somewhat aimlessly between the aisles, that, in the darkest corner deepest into the maze of books, he came across his find.

It was not, at first or even second glance, much to look at. It was sitting on a bottom shelf sandwiched between two disintegrating books and seemed initially to be a book itself. It was bound in black leather, and Danny's fingers left marks on the thick layer of dust that covered the binding. There was no title. The book felt warm, like body temperature. When he opened it, however, Danny discovered it was, rather than a book, a sort of thick notebook, with blank, off-white pages that had been filled by hand sometime in the past in an untidy cursive script scribbled with black ink. He leafed through it.

Saturday, February 5, 1942.
Birthday party for Dr. Katz—daughter.

Rabbit from hat.
Linking rings.
Handkerchief routine.
Streamers from mouth production.
Cigarette routine—vanish, materialization, multiplication.
Milk pitcher.
Silk in egg.
Doves routine.
Levitating vase.

Went well. Around 25 children. Used regular patter. Katz paid promptly, in cash.

Danny stared at the bound volume in his hands. It was a magician's journal! Every page seemed to be the same: a list of magic tricks that varied little from one performance to another; sometimes a short record of some new patter used or deviated from the norm; a record of the locations (which included the British Army barracks, a function for the harbor officials, birthdays, weddings, and the obligatory bar mitzvahs); notes on the number of people in the crowd; the date; and notes—though no amounts—concerning the payments.

Dotted amongst the pages were a few (a very few) newspaper clippings, which inevitably described a performance particularly worthy of the public's notice. The paper of these clippings was yellow like bad teeth. Danny would have pursued these items further, but he was already gripped by that most-unbeatable of compulsions, which is aroused by the collector's discovery of what is called a *find*.

"How much?"

The owner of the Book Basement looked up at him in

amusement. He was busy marking a pile of ancient-looking Tarzans. "What have you got there?"

Danny wordlessly pushed the diary across the desk. The owner leafed through it unhurriedly. "Where did you find this?" he asked at last. Danny pointed.

"What do you want this for?" the owner said. "I thought you liked detective novels."

Danny cautiously mentioned having once practiced the art of magic (which was not entirely the truth. His one performance—one Saturday at the flat, for an audience comprising several family members—did not go as well as could have been hoped for: he failed twice to guess the card picked, was left with two pieces of rope that he couldn't join back together, and finally—and he still didn't know how—the wand broke as he waved it in the air. Danny was, in other words, a terrible magician, and that performance contributed in great measure to the conjuring set's eventual exile up in the *boydem*).

"Oh? I had a magic kit once," the owner said. "You know that thing with the egg?"

Danny denied any knowledge of a thing with eggs.

"Little plastic thing. Had like a blue egg in the middle. You could make it disappear. Just a toy, really . . ." He seemed to gaze into the air nostalgically, lost in thoughts of better days. Danny said, "So how much?" and then, because he was a polite kid, said, "Please?"

"Oh, have it for fifty," the owner said. "Anything for a fellow magician, eh?"

Danny left a fifty-shekel note on the counter and left the shop, as the absorbed owner was unsuccessfully trying to make the note disappear.

As he walked home along Balfour Street he passed the old Technion building. Climbing up the hill, laden with books, he felt sleepy and slow. The sun was hot in the sky. He vaguely thought of investing some of his remaining money in a glass of orange juice from a stand by the side of the road but decided against it. To his left he noticed something that, he realized, he had seen countless times before but never paid it much attention. It was graffiti of a sort, one of those street paintings done on the walls that fenced off old buildings, which in far-off Tel Aviv was considered art, but here was considered merely a nuisance. He stopped (the place was shady) and looked at the painting.

It showed a field of sunflowers in vivid yellow, a deep blue sky, and a range of mountains in the distance that might have been the slopes of Mount Carmel. But those were merely background details; what drew his attention, with a sudden, sharp shock, was the girl in the painting.

She was standing in the field of sunflowers and seemed to be looking out; he had the uncomfortable feeling that she was looking out of the *painting,* into the street where he stood. She was young, and pretty. Her eyes were olive black, her hair, fair. She had a European look, like a new immigrant, and delicate features not yet made brown by the sun. She seemed strangely alive. Vibrant. *It must be the colors,* Danny, the great art connoisseur, thought.

The painting disturbed him. The girl didn't look like she belonged in the field; there was something unearthly about her. He wondered what her name was.

When he finally came home, the flat was empty. His father had left him some schnitzels and mash in the fridge—the universal meal of the Israeli family. Danny was what they called a *yeled mafte'ach,* a "key child"; that is, he did not have a mother at home, had a key on a string around his neck, and was expected to fend for himself in the absence of parental supervision. It was thus, with great leisure, that Danny sat at the kitchen table, the heated food before him, the magician's journal open by his side. The sun came streaming through the window. In the distance the sea was a perfect calm blue. He was facing the outside while remaining comfortably inside. He leafed through the journal.

His attention was drawn by a new trick that the magician was apparently using, from around the middle of the journal onward. It was called *The Projected Girl.* Details were scarce, yet it appeared to be a great success. Audience numbers were up. Newspaper clippings, from this point onward, became, if not exactly abundant, at least slightly more frequent in the pages of the journal. Danny shoveled some mash absent-mindedly into his mouth (dropping a little back onto the plate) and began perusing the articles.

Ha'aretz, *3 June 1943.*

HAIFA MAGICIAN BRINGS WONDER TO TROOPS

HAIFA—Last night there was a benefit gala for the British troops stationed in Haifa harbor. The event took place in the Casino building. Mr. Mordechai Isikovich—the Great Abra-Kadabra, as he prefers to be known—performed for the assembled guests, bringing shock and wonder to the audience. "It was truly remarkable," Mr. Etzioni of the city council told Ha'aretz; *"I just don't know how he did the things he did." The magician—who reputedly worked in a circus in Hungary before making* aliyah *in the early '30s—*

performed such "miracles" as pulling a selected card, signed by a soldier in the audience, out of an orange, and made doves mysteriously disappear. The highlight of the show, however, was his latest creation, which the magician calls The Projected Girl. *Using a screen and a light projector, the audience could clearly see the shadow of the magician's assistant—a young woman—as it began to shrink and finally disappeared. The magician then removed the screen—to show the girl transformed into a picture on the wall! As the assembled guests burst into spontaneous applause, the magician reversed the process, and he and his assistant took their bows together before the crowd. "It was amazing," British Private Eddie Gall told* Ha'aretz. *"I don't know how he did that." When asked, Mr. Isikovich smiled but did not comment.*

Davar, *24 September 1943.*

MAGICIAN ENTERTAINS DETAINEES

CYPRUS—Celebrated Haifa magician Mr. Mordechai Isaakovitz has just returned from Cyprus on board H.M.S. Napier. *Cyprus is currently "home" to detention camps where Jewish refugees from wartorn Europe are held by the British for illegally trying to enter Palestine by ship. "I am very grateful to the British authorities for letting me go," Mr. Isaakovitz told* Davar. *"While I cannot free our people, I can at least try and lift their spirits. I hope they will be released soon and allowed to come to Eretz Yisrael." The magician was accompanied by an assistant.*

Danny stared at the open journal. He'd finished the schnitzels. A small globule of mash remained on the plate, looking strangely like the dome of the Baha'i temple. He knew about the refugees trying to enter Palestine by ship. The Jewish settlement in Palestine—the Yishuv—sent men to Italy and Greece, members of the Palyam, or sea brigades, who bought what decrepit old ships could be found and tried to smuggle refugees and guns into Mandate-ruled Palestine. If the British caught them, they were arrested and sent to Cyprus. Many ended up back in Europe, sometimes back under Nazi rule. But if they got through the British blockade, well, then there would be lights winking in the darkness from the shore, and the boats would be lowered stealthily into the water, and the refugees would travel that last distance to land, to the secret coves of Haifa, of which there were many. He had heard the stories from his grandfather Shaul. The British had a radar station up on Mount Carmel, by the Stella Maris Monastery, but the Yishuv's fighters blew it up after the war. He leafed farther ahead. The journal stopped abruptly in February 1945. The magician's entry for that day must have been written in advance of the performance, which was to take place outdoors on Balfour Street: it included only a list of tricks, the last of which was *The Projected Girl.* The rest of the journal was left blank.

For a few weeks Danny mulled over the mystery of the magician's notebook in his spare time. Magic and mystery may have occupied his mind, but society dictated it should have been occupied in more beneficial pursuits, and uppermost amongst them was school. There were lessons to be endured: sines and cosines; isosceles triangles and parallelograms; the stories of Ruth and Esther, both stories where a foreigner and a Jew triumph over obstacles to consummate their love ("For your homework, write an essay in no less than one thousand words. . . ."); the anatomy of the Palestinian Painted Frog (extinct); meaning and symbolism in Dan Pagis's Holocaust poem, "Written in Pencil in the Sealed Railway-Car"; and more, in chalk on blackboard and in mimeographed handouts blue-inked against white.

It was with a sense of some relief, therefore, that one bright morning the school break finally came, and to celebrate Uncle Arik (only recently returned from another mysterious assignment, having lost both weight and his tan in foreign climates) took Danny out for a slice of pizza and a cappuccino, which in Haifa comes in a tall glass, the upper half of which is generously filled with whipped cream. They sat in the paved Nordau Street and watched the passersby. "So tell me about the Palestinian Painted Frog," Uncle Arik said.

Danny stared at him vaguely. He was still thinking about the magician, Isikovich or Isaakovitz. He took to picturing him in black evening dress, with a dashing top hat (a rabbit poking out under the brim), while his assistant, dressed in a sequined blue dress, handed him props and looked glamorous (not unlike Daryl Hannah, who had only recently appeared in *Splash* and was, subsequently, occupying much of Danny's daydreams in class). "It's a rare kind of frog," he said, dragging his attention back to the present. "It used to live in the Huleh swamps, before they were drained in the fifties. They only ever found it twice, so no one knows much about it. It's extinct."

"But *you*," Uncle Arik said seriously, "you *do* know. As long as you can remember something, it isn't truly lost." He had become more philosophical with the years, full of deceptive depths and shadowed valleys, occasionally surprising even his brother.

"I guess," Danny said. He felt both sleepy and restless. It was getting hot, and the people going past were moving slowly, lethargically, like frog spawn trying to swim upstream. It was lunchtime.

"Oho! If it isn't my young magician friend!" Danny looked up and saw the owner of the Book Basement smiling benevolently. Strangely, the man wore a top hat that looked ridiculous over his workingman's checkered shirt, and in his hands he held a pack of cards he was busy shuffling. "Go on, pick a card. Any card." He extended the deck toward Danny, cards fanned. "Hi, Arik."

"What *are* you doing?" Uncle Arik demanded. The owner grinned, somewhat apologetically. "Always wanted to be magician, you know. Go on, pick one."

Danny picked a card. It was the Queen of Hearts. "Now, put it back, here. Let me just shuffle them for a moment. . . . Here, take the pack. Now, is your card there? No? Well . . ." He reached behind Danny's ear. "Was *this* your card?"

"Very good!" Danny said. He didn't have the heart to tell him that he saw him palming the card just a moment before.

"Don't encourage him," Uncle Arik said.

"Well, anyway," the bookseller-turned-magician said, "I better go. Oh, that reminds me, Danny. I found this the other day. It must have fallen from that book you bought last time. Do you want it?" And he handed Danny a small slip of paper. "It's in English."

"The boy has good English!" Uncle Arik said. "Like his uncle."

"Yeah, sure. Well, see you later." And he hurried down the road, his hands still busily shuffling cards, the top hat precariously balanced at a crooked angle on his head. Danny looked at the slip of paper.

The Palestine News, *5 February 1945.*

MAGICIAN'S ASSISTANT DISAPPEARS

HAIFA—In a public performance last night outside the Jewish Technion building, magician Mordechai Itzikovic performed his renowned trick, The Projected Girl, *for what may be the last time. In the show's finale, the magician uses a projector to seemingly make his assistant shrink, only to appear moments later inside a picture on the wall. The assistant is then returned—but not last night. "I don't know what went wrong," a distraught Mr. Itzikovic was reported as saying. "Where did she go?"*

The assistant, a young Jewish woman, was sought last night for questioning by the Palestine Police Force, and Mr. Itzikovic has been detained by the PPF to help with their inquiries. In a baffling turn of events, the projected picture of the girl remained last night on the wall despite the magician's apparatus being turned off shortly after the performance.

"So she disappeared!" Danny said.

"Ha? Who's disappeared?" Uncle Arik said, and then with a broad grin, "Are you having girl trouble, Danny?"

"What? No!"

She'd disappeared. And the magician never performed again. (That was a feat of deductive reasoning on Danny's part, for why else would the notebook be left blank?)

Questions.

What happened that night?

"So tell me about her," Uncle Arik said.

Danny sighed. He felt adult beyond his years. He was a detective on the trail of a missing girl. He was the keeper of a mystery only he knew existed. He was assailed by the adult's sense of importance mixed with doubt, power mixed with confusion. How can such opposite feelings coexist?

Danny took a deep breath. "There was once this magician. . . ." he began.

you cry in bright petals
and sometimes I pick your tears

to press between the pages of a book
left on the shelf for someone else to find:

some other time,
long after forgetting why we cried,

when only our names remain like flowered shreds
entwined in the margins.

There was once this magician. And he made a girl disappear. Or the girl disappeared despite the magician. It all happened long ago in another town that resembled this one only slightly. It was a town of crusaders and templars, of Bedouin sheikhs and Ottoman Empire builders. City walls were built, destroyed, built up again. The Russians built a wharf; the Turks put through a train line; the British rebuilt a harbor that once saw Phoenician ships dock, their sails bellowing, with cedar from Lebanon and spices from Africa. Seagulls cried and dived overhead. Jews came, went, came back. The city was an old lady, draped in the patchwork clothes of centuries, worn with the dust of holy books.

It was not a holy city. It was not a Jerusalem preening in white stone, cold and aloof on its hills. It was a working city, an immigrant city, a city of sailors and prophets, of prostitutes and monks. Elijah fought the priests of Ba'al on Mount Carmel, and Napoleon quarantined his soldiers, sick with the plague after the Siege of Acre, in the monastery of Stella Maris and had them executed there, leaving a plaque behind. It was a city whose history was written in the margins, between the market stalls and the houses of ill repute, between the narrow lanes that separated dusty stores selling the produce of other, more-exotic places, and outside the bars and inns that had served the armies and navies of all the vanished empires.

It was a city that, sometimes, it was not too hard to disappear in.

Some of this Danny had learned from his Uncle Arik, who in his solitary pursuits, whose nature could never be adequately explained, had had plenty of time to learn the history of his city and some of its secrets. Some he had learned later, through books, through stories—which are the lies that people put in books to make them true—and some of it and more he learned eventually from his fearsome and formidable Great-Aunt Zsuzsi.

"You must ask Aunt Zsuzsi," Uncle Arik said when Danny

had finished his story. "She will know who your mystery girl was."

Danny did not take kindly to that idea. He had the Jewish boy's natural fear of elderly relatives, and Great-Aunt Zsuzsi—blue haired, cigarette smoking, stooped but not at *all* frail Zsuzsi—was by far the worst. She tended, amongst other things, to test at assorted family functions (be they weddings, funerals, birthdays, or bar mitzvahs, the four cornerstones of the familial social calendar) Danny's knowledge of the classics by speaking to him loudly and ponderously in the ancient Latin she had learned in ancient days at school in Transylvania. Since Danny's knowledge of that venerable old tongue was precisely none, the conversation was rather one-sided; and he could only take comfort in the hope that a cousin might shortly come along and be pounced upon in his stead.

Great-Aunt Zsuzsi had a voice thickened by cigarettes; she liked to pinch cheeks; she had a blue number tattooed on her arm; and she could remember everything you'd ever done, from the time you were three years old and peed your pants at Cousin Ofer's bar mitzvah onward. She had been an archivist for the harbor authorities, and she had lived in the city for decades in a small third-story flat in the Stella Maris neighborhood, a family invitation to which caused children to develop immediate and lasting symptoms of flu, chicken pox, mumps, or measles, depending on the season and the child's knowledge of medical matters.

"No way," Danny said.

Uncle Arik laughed. "Who ever said being a detective is easy? Come on, I'm still hungry. Fancy going to McDavid for a burger?"

Danny gravely acknowledged that he was indeed amiable to such a suggestion.

On his way back that day he passed by the Technion building again. The painting of the girl in the field of sunflowers was still there. He looked at her with new eyes, and he had the strangest feeling that she was looking back at him from across the wall, and that she was smiling.

That night, Danny looked through his bookshelves again. Answers could be found there, he was sure. The shelves were like a packed convention of detectives, bursting with clues, feats of deduction, witnesses, and dissemblers, clouded with pipe smoke, bellowing with cloaks. The books of David Tidhar were there, and Danny was drawn back to the volume where he had secreted that mysterious letter on the day of his birthday. He pulled out the slim volume. *Disappearance on Mount Carmel.* He opened the book at random.

> "What is it?" the commandant asked short-temperedly, pausing from his examination of the case files that had been baffling him and the entire force for the past week.
>
> "It is I, Tidhar," said the newcomer.
>
> The commandant jumped from his seat as if bitten by a tiger and hurried toward the newcomer. "Welcome!" he said, reaching out his arms to the famous detective. "Welcome!"

Danny leafed ahead.

David Tidhar sat alone in his office. The pipe dangled from his lips. It had all but gone out, but he hadn't noticed. The stale smell of tobacco hung in the air. His mind was abuzz with speculation. Where was the missing girl? The situation was difficult. The detective did not believe in magic, but he was troubled. She was a girl without papers, without identity. He had heard she came from the ships, that she had, as they said, "smuggled the border." If he found her, would not the British send her back to the lands of the great fiend?

"Perhaps," he mused aloud, "it is the work of my great enemy, the Hangman of Corfu! Only such a devious mind could devise such a devilish scheme!"

He reached for his matches and absentmindedly relit his pipe. The solution was close at hand, he could feel it!

"Danny? Dinner's ready."

"Just a minute, Dad!"

How did the book end? He'd read it before. It was about a girl who went missing in Haifa, and the great David Tidhar was called to assist the police, coming down all the way from Tel Aviv. But the case, naturally, became more complex the more David probed, and involved a secret plan by the Yishuv leadership to smuggle in two ships full of refugees from Germany, an Arab revolt, and Nazi spies. In 1942, Danny knew, it had seemed as though Hitler was very close to achieving one goal of his war and overrunning Palestine itself. Were that to happen, Haifa and Carmel would become the last bastion of Jewish resistance. In the event, Rommel was turned back at Al Alamein, and the German invasion of Palestine never happened. In the book, however, worry remained. But what of the girl? Danny leafed to the end of the book. Surely the great David Tidhar at least had solved the puzzle!

David Tidhar shook hands with the British commandant and boarded the car that was to take him back to Tel Aviv. He had stopped the spies—just in time, it seemed, before they could communicate their vital information to the Nazi fiend!—and at the same time had assisted the Palyam to safely smuggle the refugees into Eretz Yisrael. But the commandant had no need to know that!

"David," the commandant said, "if it weren't for you, I believe a Nazi invasion would have been inevitable—and imminent! Thanks to you, we can continue the fight. Fight until the Germans are defeated!"

"I was only doing my job," David Tidhar said, and he nodded to the driver. The engine started, and they were off, away from the green mountain and this old and belligerent city that was so unlike his own modern Tel Aviv. *I was only doing my job,* he thought, but he could find no satisfaction. The girl! It was the one case he would always, afterward, remember. His one failure.

He never did find the missing girl.

"What?" Danny said, and despite all his budding bibliophile's instincts, he threw the book across the room.

"Danny? Are you all right in there?"

"No! Yes! I'll be out in a minute, Dad!"

Wearily, he went to pick up the book. The letter fell from it, and he picked it up. The scent, a woman's perfume, was still on it. *"Daniel, whatever is happen, I will always love you."* Somehow, he was convinced it was from *her.* But what did it mean? He sighed, a sound older than his years, replaced the letter in the book, and at last went to dinner.

A week later he was at the German settlement, the old templar village that sits beneath the Baha'i gardens. He was walking along the Fighters of the Ghetto Road when he passed a large ancient-looking pine tree surrounded by fallen cones. He nearly missed it, but something, some irregularity in the color of the bark, perhaps, drew his attention suddenly, and when he approached it he found, carved in small neat letters into the flesh of the tree, a dark and old tattoo that said as if mocking him:

I WILL LEAVE YOU SIGNS, MY LOVE, IN THE MARGINS OF OUR CITY.

That day Danny decided to make the ultimate sacrifice, and as a first step got his dad to phone Great-Aunt Zsuzsi.

"*You* phone her!" his father said. In matters of his aunt he was not unlike Danny.

"Dad . . ."

"What do you want from Zsuzsi? She's an old lady. She shouldn't be disturbed. She needs to be left alone."

Danny was wholeheartedly in agreement with his father on this matter. The image of a strange blond girl, however, drove him. "It's a history project for school," he said. "Please?"

The phone call was made, reluctantly. Danny's father spoke briefly into the mouthpiece. He nodded, though the other party clearly couldn't see him. He spoke into the mouthpiece again. The sun came through the window and illuminated him: no longer a young man, with pouches under his eyes and hair that had been receding steadily away from his high forehead like a crusader force being driven back from a fortress by hostile Saracens. For all that, there was still something sunny about him, though more and more often now the sun seemed submerged in the sea, just beyond the horizon. He said, "Aha. Yes. Aha," and cradled the phone. "She wants to speak to you."

There was nothing to it. Like a Roman gladiator who might have once entered the arena in nearby Caesarea, Danny stepped forth.

"Aunty Zsuzsi?" he said.

"Mens sana in corpore sano," the elderly voice on the other end of the phone pronounced.

"I'm sorry?"

"A healthy mind in a healthy body," Great Aunt Zsuzsi said. "Still no Latin? For shame. You wish to see me?"

"I have some questions, it's for this—"

"Monday, five o'clock. Bring waffles."

"Waffles?"

"Are you deaf as well as ignorant? Good-bye."

The phone went dead. Danny said, "Good-bye," into the silent phone, and thought he heard the ghostly echo of a laugh returned to him over the wire.

"What did she say?"

Danny repeated his instructions.

"Oy," his father said, and sighed. "You better go to the shop, then."

Stella Maris, the "Sea Star," sits on the northern peak of Mount Carmel and commands, like the diminutive French general who once held her, extraordinary and long-reaching views. Zsuzsi's door, up three flights of stairs, opened onto a modest yet comfortable abode, where the entire Mediterranean Sea, it seemed, was spread outside like sparkling fresh laundry.

"Shalom, Daniel! Oh, you've grown so much! Give your aunty a kiss!"

Danny, that tireless pursuer of the *balash*, or "detective," story, knew about informers. Many times they were crucial to the plot. They were sources of secret knowledge, purveyors of hidden information, and, naturally, had to be paid.

"I brought the waffles," he said, after being subjected to his cheeks being pinched and the inevitable, tobacco-flavored kiss. "I brought both chocolate and lemon flavor; I didn't know which one you liked."

"How sweet of you," Zsuzsi said, and when she smiled it made her seem for just a moment not young but yet terribly innocent; it was the face of a good-natured baby shortly after being fed. "Please, sit down, Daniel. I'll make some coffee."

She disappeared into the small kitchen, and the smell of Turkish coffee was soon wafting through the room. Danny sat on the couch and waited. The flat was sparsely but pleasantly decorated. Old photos, mostly in black and white, were framed on the walls. People in old-fashioned hats and coats. Bookshelves lined the walls. And there, amidst the unknown titles in Hungarian and Romanian and the scattering of Hebrew books—it couldn't be, but—was that The Detective Library, featuring the exploits of none other than David Tidhar?

"So," Zsuzsi said, sitting down opposite him and laying a tray bearing two cups, a *finjan* full of black coffee, and a plate heaped to the brim with dark chocolate waffles on the table, "what is it that you wanted to ask me, young man?"

Danny wordlessly handed over the magician's journal.

Zsuzsi took it from him. There was care in the way she handled it.

She leafed through the pages. Her fingers treated the old paper gently. She looked at the newspaper cuttings. She came to the last page. When she looked up, her face had changed once again. It was older now and sad, and yet she was smiling. "They never did get his name right, did they?" she said. "It's because the name itself was a misprint, you see. It was Heisikovitz. It should have been Isikovitz but . . ." She shrugged. "I guess when the authorities came to their village to write down their surnames, the officer in charge spelled the name wrong. That would have been around the eighteenth century? Transylvanian, like our family."

"You *knew* him?"

She shook her head. "No. They were from Marosvásárhely; we were from Brasov. And the time of this story . . ." She tapped on the journal with her finger, gently. "I was in Auschwitz, not Haifa. But Agi was here."

He had heard the name before. Agi—Agneta—was his grandfather's youngest sister. He followed Zsuzsi's gaze to a photograph on the wall. "That's your grandfather in the middle," Zsuzsi said, "and me on the right. And the little girl holding his hand—that's Agi. She was, what, seventeen, eighteen? when she followed your grandfather to Palestine. That would have been in forty-one, when it was still possible to go."

She had said Auschwitz matter-of-factly, and that was how Danny accepted it. He said, "And she knew the magician?"

"Somehow," Zsuzsi said, and that same smile, knowing and amused, was back on her face. "I suspect it isn't the magician so much that you are interested in as it is his assistant, Daniel."

She rose from her seat and made her way to a cabinet by the wall. When she returned she was holding a photo. She handed it to Danny.

The magician was short and stocky. He had dark wavy hair and a waxed mustache and eyes that seemed ready to twinkle. He was dressed in a black suit and wore a tall hat. Beside him was the girl.

He recognized her face. It was the girl from the painting.

"She'd always had that effect," Zsuzsi said. "And she *was* beautiful."

Danny wanted to ask questions, but he sensed silence was being called for. She would tell him what she knew, in her own time.

"Her name was Eva," Zsuzsi said, and Danny thought about the letter in his book, signed with an *aleph*. Was it an *aleph,* for Eva? He had thought it stood for *ima,* "mother," but without vowel markings, the *nikud* underneath the consonants, it could have been either. "She was from Austria, perhaps. The Nazis had her for a while. Somehow, she escaped. She made her way to Italy and onto one of the ships, and she came to Palestine. To Haifa. She couldn't have been much more than eighteen. Like Agi. They became friends." She sighed, and her eyes seemed to dim, like windows looking out not at the sea but a great distance still, across a land veiled now in darkness, where only a few stars still shone. "I don't know how much you understand of that time, Daniel," she said. "The Yishuv was fighting the British and their white book—their changing policy on Palestine—and at the same time working with the British against the Nazis. Ben-Gurion said, 'We shall fight the Nazis as if there was no white book, and fight the white book as if there were no Nazis.' It was not an easy strategy. And the girls were young, you know. Agi and Eva, saved from the Holocaust, so *alive,* and finding themselves in this city, filled with dashing soldiers who were just as young, just as handsome as themselves—they used to go to the old casino building to dance. It must have been exciting! And of course the excitement stemmed partly from the fact that it was not right for them to do it, to associate this way with the British, the colonizers. Agi worked as a secretary for a Dr. Katz. Eva had no papers, but one day she met Mordechai, and it was an easy enough decision for him to make. . . ."

Danny thought of cash-only payments and of stage names and stage clothes, and he said, surprised he hadn't realize this before, "He hid her in plain view."

"Like a magician. And so the days of the war went on."

"So what *happened*?" Danny demanded.

"Have a waffle."

"I—" he chose not to argue. For several minutes there was silence, not uncompanionable, as the two of them drank coffee and ate the *kibud,* the "refreshments." Zsuzsi lit a cigarette. The smoke curled up and was blown toward the glittering sea.

"She fell in love," Zsuzsi said simply. "With a British soldier. Deeply, madly, rashly in love. It was the sort of love that leaves no room for compromise, for anything other than itself. His name was Daniel. Like yours. You know what they did to her?"

"What did they do?" Danny said, and fear eased itself into him, edging beside the sudden jealousy that had flared there. He didn't yet ask who *they* were.

"They cut off her hair." The cigarette shook in Zsuzsi's hand. "Her long, beautiful hair. It's what the Yishuv did to girls who went with the enemy. They took her one night when she was coming home from the casino, singing to herself in the dark. They grabbed her and forced her down and they did this to her, like the Nazis did in the camps. Agi told me. It was meant as a warning to the other girls. After that she wore a wig, for the performances. And someone told on her. Then it was only a matter of time."

"The police," Danny said, thinking of that last newspaper cutting. "They would have sent her back."

Young and old looked at each other across a table, sharing a horror which for the one was born of stories and for the other, of memories.

"What did they do?"

"She could have married him, but she had no papers, and he was only a boy himself, a common soldier with no influence. They loved each other very much. Agi told me they planned to run together, leave Palestine, the army, go to India or Hong Kong, a place where they could disappear. In the great story of the world they were unimportant, marginal."

"Is that what happened?" Danny said, thinking of that night all those years ago when the Projected Girl had, for the last time, disappeared. "Did they run away?"

"I don't know," Zsuzsi said. The words hung heavy in the air, like thick smoke. "No one does. Some say the magician was a part of their plan. And some say that, frightened, hunted, she found refuge in the only place they couldn't touch her—in that picture, in the field of sunflowers, where she could be always in the sun and never suffer darkness again."

"It was magic?"

Zsuzsi smiled. "Sometimes you have to believe. Sometimes you *want* to believe."

"And the magician? What happened to him?"

"He never performed again."

"Is he still alive?"

The smile remained. It was a small private smile there in the corners of her mouth, and sad; like the last lingering note of a symphony.

"Yes," she said simply. "And if you want him, you must go to the Mukhraka, to the Place of Burning—and there ask for Brother Mordechai."

"How did it go?"

"Fine. I said I'll come and see her again next week. Dad? What are you doing?"

His father turned and gave him a nervous smile. He was fiddling with the top button of his shirt, which looked new. "Do you think I look all right?"

"You look *fine*. Honestly. Where are you going to take her?"

"I'm not sure," his father said worriedly. "I thought maybe a movie and then something to eat?"

Danny grinned. "Just don't do what you did last time."

His father, it had turned out, in his nervousness and desire not to disappoint, had driven his date from one empty eatery to another, refusing, so he said, to eat in an empty restaurant. They had ended, at last, at a kebab place in the old Check Point outside Haifa, once manned by the British and now a busy road of traffic and commerce. The kebab place was bursting with truckers, prostitutes, and several friends of Uncle Arik's. It had not gone well.

"What do you think I should do? Where can I take her?"

"How about the harbor?"

"Yeah, that's a good idea," his father said, looking relieved. He was looking better; sunnier, Danny thought. Or at least his forehead did seem rather shiny.

"You'll be fine," he said, giving his dad a reassuring pat on the back. He watched him go down to the car, start it noisily, and drive away—and he smiled, and thought about love.

For every *balash* there comes a time when a final confrontation must take place; the case becomes clear; a truth is reached. Yet some things don't need truth or clarity. A sense of closure, perhaps, or a sense of *freedom* from the dogged facts may be all that is needed. One day in early spring a family outing was planned and carried out. Present in the car were Danny, his father, Uncle Arik, Uncle Moyshe from the kibbutz (on Danny's mother's side), and Cousin Uri. They were not going far.

The car chugged along the Moria Road, past Herbert Samuel and Einstein; where Moria turns into Freud they took a left and went along Aba Hushi, encountering Einstein again along the way, passing Aharonson, Golda Meir, and the Ivory Coast. They gave the hard shoulder to Oskar Schindler and took a right this time, past Liberia, Sweden, and Costa Rica, past Haifa University with its array of satellite dishes and listening devices aimed at the skies (and nearby Lebanon), briefly admired the view from the top of Mount Carmel, and coasted down again, passing through forests of pine and the Druze villages of Usefiyeh and Daliat el-Carmel.

Winter had not yet given up its grasp on Mount Carmel, and the air had just the hint of chill about it as they climbed out of the car. The Dir el-Mukhraka, the Arabs called this place—the Monastery of the Place of Burning. It belonged to the Carmelite order. Here, Elijah fought the priests of Ba'al, and here a great fire came down from the skies, consuming the wood and the stones and the dust. The priests of Ba'al ran and were pursued until they reached the river Kishon, and there they were slain.

"Well, I'm hungry," Uncle Arik announced. "Where are the egg sandwiches?"

They were going to picnic in the forest. But first they trooped into the monastery building, past the statue of Elijah holding his sword, and climbed up to the flat top of the monastery's roof, from which one can see as far away as Nazareth and Mount Tavor.

On the way back Danny stopped. An old man, dressed in the habit of the monks, was working in the garden, and something about him . . .

He approached the monk and said, a little nervously, "Brother Mordechai?"

The man straightened his back. He leaned on his spade and examined Danny somewhat warily. "Yes?"

"The Great Abra-Kadabra?"

The man nodded slowly, as if confirming something to himself. "Once," he said.

"I wanted to ask you . . . I mean . . ."

"About Eva?" The eyes seemed to twinkle.

For a brief moment Danny had an image of the monk before him with a waxed mustache and a top hat. He said, "I have your journal."

"Oh?" The man looked momentarily surprised. Then he laid down his spade carefully and said, "Come, let's sit down somewhere."

Danny turned to shout to his family that he'd be right back, but in any event there was no need. A small group had appeared in the monastery's yard, and he saw the security minister ambling along, trailed by his coterie and two bored-looking photographers, no doubt on an official visit of some sort. The minister, he saw to his surprise, was making for their small group, and as Danny watched, the minister came up to Uncle Arik and solemnly shook his hand, drawing him aside. Danny watched, puzzled, as his uncle and the minister spoke together in low voices. No one was paying Danny much attention.

He followed the old monk to a bench overlooking the wooded slopes of Mount Carmel.

"You want to know about the Projected Girl," the monk—the Great Abra-Kadabra—said.

"Yes."

"After all these years . . ." the monk said, and he shook his head, but then he smiled. "She did have that effect on people," he said. "Eva . . . I was in love with her, you know. From the moment I saw her at Dr. Katz's. It was a horrible evening. The kids were screaming, the rabbit wouldn't come out of the hat . . . but then I saw her, and I forgot everything else. She was so beautiful." He sighed. "Too beautiful. I never even had a chance."

"What happened that night?" Danny said, and there was no question between them of what night that was. The monk shook his head. "We were performing *The Projected Girl,*" he said, "as normal. It was not, in truth, an overly complicated trick. I used a light projector, a lantern, really, with a cardboard cutout of Eva's profile; it was quite easy to make it seem she disappeared. Back then, something like this was still novel, you know. But . . ."

His hands were browned by the sun, and liver spotted. For a moment he turned to face Danny, reached behind his ear, and pulled out a five-shekel coin. He moved his hand over it and it changed into a stone. He raised his fist to his mouth, blew softly, and when he opened his hand the stone had disappeared. He smiled apologetically at Danny. "I still do that sometimes," he said. "I find it calming."

"The picture," Danny said. "It stayed on the wall."

"Don't you think I know that? I was there that night. She should have been in the . . ." He hesitated, then smiled and said, "I may have made one vow now, but it does not mean I should forsake the other." He meant the monkhood in the first instance, Danny thought, and the Magician's Oath in the second. Never reveal a secret.

The old magician hesitated. "She should have been there," he said at last. "The picture was just that—a picture. Light projected on wall. But when I removed the screen for the second time, the picture was there, as if it had *always* been there, and Eva . . . Eva was gone."

"It was magic?"

"Not the kind of magic I could do! I couldn't understand it. I checked everywhere. I had a lot of time to think about it, later. The police came, and *they* thought I helped her escape, and it was a week before they let me go. I kept thinking, How could this have happened? Was it a trick? Did she set it up herself? It was possible . . . but if she did, I still don't know how."

Danny lifted his head. Somewhere in the forest a bird was calling and was being answered by its mate. A cool breeze rustled the pine needles. Otherwise it was quiet. "What was it, then?" he said, speaking in a low voice.

The elderly monk looked sideways at him and said, "A miracle."

"No."

"Have you seen her?" the monk demanded. "Have you seen her there, in her field of sunflowers, looking out into the city every day for the past forty years? It took me a long time to think it through. But I have no other explanation. I went to visit her; for months I'd go past that wall and look at her, and I could swear her expression changed, the way she stood, the way she . . ." He subsided. "She could see me," he said. "And she wouldn't come out. She was safe there in the margins of the city. And for that I'm glad!"

Danny sat back. "You became a monk," he said.

Brother Mordechai smiled. "If it was a miracle," he said, "that suggests the existence of God. I was a Jew before I became a magician, but I was a monk only after I stopped being a Jew. Maybe it was the way they treated her. . . . I felt something break inside me, like the clockwork inside one of my old tricks, when I saw."

"And you are convinced?"

"I thought I saw her once," the old magician said. "I was in Italy with the brothers. In Rome, walking down a busy street—I thought I saw her. Her hair was grown again, and she was not so young anymore, but still beautiful. There was a child with her, a little girl. And then a man came and put his arm around her and they were gone, lost in the crowd." He shook his head. "It couldn't have been her. But if it was—"

"Yes?"

"She seemed happy."

They sat together in silence and looked over the forest. At last Danny stood up. "Thank you, Mr. Heisikovitz," he said.

The old man looked up at him, and his eyes twinkled; they were covered in a fine mist. "Brother Mordechai," he said.

"That's what I am now. And anyway the family changed the name a few years ago. They wanted something more Hebrew."

"Oh? What to?"

"Tidhar," the old man said, and he shrugged. "I think it's a kind of biblical tree."

All stories, and even ours, must come to an end. A week later, Danny spent the last of his bar mitzvah money in the bookshops of Hadar and was returning home along Balfour Street. He had hoped to look at Eva again; but when he approached the wall, he was in for a surprise.

Two workmen were standing on the pavement, dressed in blue paint-spattered overalls with a bucket of white paint at their feet and brushes in their hands. They were painting the wall. Danny ran toward them. "What are you doing?"

"Cleaning graffiti," the one on the left said. He had a bushy mustache and was smoking a cigarette. "Mayor's instructions. Keep the city clean."

"This isn't graffiti!" He craned to look. They hadn't done much damage yet, but— "What did you do to it?" he demanded.

"What do you mean?" the one on the right said. He was thin and balding at the top. "We've only just started."

"What happened to the *girl*?"

The two workmen looked at each other and back at Danny. They ponderously laid down their brushes. "What girl?"

Danny stared at the painting. It was somewhat obscured now by white, as if a screen of clouds were descending on the scene, hiding it from view. Still, he could make out the outline of the mountains in the distance, a sunflower nodding in the breeze, the deep blue skies behind the clouds of white. It was all still there, all but for one thing.

There was no girl.

"Kid, do you mind? We've got work to do," the one on the left said.

"Yeah," the one on the right said. "You got a complaint, go to city hall."

The two workmen looked bemused as the boy wandered off. Inexplicably, he was grinning. "Funny kid," the one on the left said. "Should be at school or something."

"Yeah," the one on the right said, looking quizzically at the picture. "I don't see what he was getting at," he complained.

His friend picked up his brush and shrugged. "Kids," he said.

The Way Station

BY NATHAN BALLINGRUD

Nathan Ballingrud has had stories appear in *Inferno: New Tales of Terror and the Supernatural, The Del Rey Book of Science Fiction and Fantasy, Sci Fiction, The 3rd Alternative,* and *The Year's Best Fantasy and Horror,* among other places. Recently he won the Shirley Jackson Award for his story "The Monsters of Heaven." He currently lives in Asheville, North Carolina, with his daughter.

Beltrane awakens to the smell of baking bread. It smells like that huge bakery on MLK that he liked to walk past on mornings before the sun came up, when daylight was just a paleness behind buildings and the smell of fresh bread leaked from the grim industrial slab like the promise of absolute love.

He stirs in his cot. The cot and the smell disorient him; his body is accustomed to the worn cab seat, with its tears in the upholstery and its permanent odor of contained humanity, as though the car had leached some fundamental ingredient from them over the years. But the coarse, grainy blanket reminds him that he is in St. Petersburg, Florida, now. Far from home. Looking for Lila. Someone sitting on a nearby cot, back turned to him, is speaking urgently under his breath, rocking on the thin mattress and making it sing. Around them more cots are lined up in rank and file, with scores of people sleeping or trying to sleep.

There are no windows, but the night is a presence in here, filling even the bright places.

"You smell that, man?" he says, sitting up.

His neighbor goes still and silent and turns to face him. He's younger than Beltrane, with a huge salt-and-pepper beard and grime deeply engrained into the lines of his face. "What?"

"Bread."

The guy shakes his head and gives him his back again. "Maaaaaaan," he says. "*Sick* of these crazy motherfuckers."

"Did they pass some out? I'm just sayin', man. I'm hungry, you know?"

"We all hungry, bitch! Whyn't you take your ass to sleep!"

Beltrane falls back onto the bed, defeated. After a moment the other man resumes his barely audible incantations, his obsessive rocking. Meanwhile the smell has grown even stronger, overpowering the musk of sweat and urine that saturate the homeless shelter. Sighing, he folds his hands over his chest and discovers that the blanket is wet and cold.

"What . . . ?"

He pulls it down to find a large, damp patch on his shirt. He hikes the shirt up to his shoulders and discovers a large square hole in the center of his chest. The smell of bread blows from it like a wind. The edges are sharp and clean, not like a wound at all. Tentatively, he probes it with his fingers: They come away damp, and when he brings them to his nose they have the ripe, deliquescent odor of river water. He places his hand over the opening and feels water splash against his palm. Poking inside, he encounters sharp metal angles and slippery stone.

Beltrane lurches from his bed and stumbles quickly for the door to the bathroom, leaving a wake of jarred cots and angry protests. He pushes through the door and heads straight for the mirrors over a row of dirty sinks. He lifts his shirt.

The hole in his chest reaches right through him. Gas lamps shine blearily through rain. Deep water runs down the street and spills out onto his skin. New Orleans has put a finger through his heart.

"Oh, no," he says softly, and raises his eyes to his own face. His face is a wide street, garbage blown, with a dead streetlight and rats scrabbling along the walls. A spray of rain mists the air in front of him, pebbling the mirror.

He knows this street. He's walked it many times in his life, and as he leans closer to the mirror, he finds that he is walking it now, home again in his old city, the bathroom and the strange shelter behind him and gone. He takes a right into an alley. Somewhere to his left is a walled cemetery, with its aboveground tombs giving it the look of a city for the dead; and next to it will be the projects, where some folks string Christmas lights along their balconies even in the summertime. He follows his accustomed path and turns right onto Claiborne Avenue. And there's his old buddy Craig, waiting for him still.

Craig was leaning against the plate-glass window of his convenience store, two hours closed, clutching a greasy brown paper bag in his left hand, with his gray head hanging and a cigarette stuck to his lips. A few butts were scattered by his feet. The neighborhood was asleep under the arch of the I-10 overpass. A row of darkened shopfronts receded down Claiborne Avenue, the line broken by the colorful lights of the Good Friends Bar spilling onto the sidewalk. The highway above them was mostly quiet now, save the occasional hiss of late-night travelers hurtling through the darkness toward mysterious ends. Beltrane, sixty-four and homeless, moseyed up to him. He stared at Craig's shirt pocket, trying to see if the cigarette pack was full enough to risk asking for one.

Craig watched him as he approached. "I almost went home," he said curtly.

"You wouldn't leave old 'Trane!"

"The hell I wouldn't. See if I'm here next time."

Beltrane sidled up next to him, putting his hands in the pockets of his thin coat, which he always wore in defiance of the Louisiana heat. "I got held up," he said.

"You what? You got held up? What do *you* got to do that you got held up?"

Beltrane shrugged. He could smell the contents of the bag Craig held, and his stomach started to move around inside him a little.

"What, you got a date? Some little lady gonna take you out tonight?"

"Come on, man. Don't make fun of me."

"Then don't be late!" Craig pressed the bag against his chest. Beltrane took it, keeping his gaze on the ground. "I do this as a *favor*. You make me wait outside my own goddamn shop, I just won't do it no more. You gonna get my ass *shot*."

Beltrane stood there and tried to look ashamed. But the truth was he wasn't much later than usual. Craig came down on him like this every couple of months or so, and if he was going to keep getting food from him he was just going to have to take it. A couple years ago Beltrane had worked for him, pushing the broom around the store and shucking oysters when they were in season, and for some reason Craig had taken a liking to him. Maybe it was the veteran thing; maybe it was something more personal. When Beltrane started having his troubles again, Craig finally had to fire him but made some efforts to see that he didn't starve. Beltrane didn't know why the man cared, but he figured Craig had his reasons and they were his own. Sometimes those reasons caused him to speak harshly. That was all right.

He opened the bag and dug out some fried shrimp. They'd gone cold and soggy but the smell of them just about buckled his knees, and he closed his eyes as he chewed his first mouthful.

"Where you been sleepin' at night, 'Trane? My boy Ray tells me he ain't seen you down by Decatur in a while."

Beltrane gestured uptown, in the opposite direction of Decatur Street and the French Quarter. "They gave me a broke-down cab."

"Who? Them boys at United? That's better than the Quarter?"

Beltrane nodded. "They's just a bunch a damn fucked-up white kids in the Quarter. Got all kinds a metal shit in their face. They smell bad, man."

Craig shook his head, leaning against the store window

and lighting himself another cigarette. "Oh, they smell bad, huh. I guess I heard it all now."

Beltrane gestured at the cigarette. "Can I have one?"

"*Hell,* no. So you sleeping in some junk heap now. You gone down a long way since you worked for me here, you know that? You got to pull your shit together, man."

"I know, I know."

"Listen to me, 'Trane. Are you listening to me?"

"I know what you gonna say."

"Well, listen to me anyway. I know you're fucked in the head. I got that. I know you don't remember shit half the time, and you got your imaginary friends you like to talk to. But you got to get a handle on things, man."

Beltrane nodded, half smiling. This speech again. "Yeah, I know."

"No, you *don't* know. 'Cause if you *did* you would go down to the VA hospital and get yourself some damn pills for whatever's wrong with you and get off the goddamn street. You will fucking *die* out here, 'Trane, you keep fucking around like this."

Beltrane nodded again and turned to leave. "You better get on home, Craig. Might get shot out here."

"*Now* who's making fun," Craig said. He tried to push himself off his window, but the glass had grown into his head. His shoulders were stuck, too. "It's too late," he said. "I can't go home. I'm stuck here forever now. God damn it!"

"I'm goin' up to the white neighborhood," Beltrane said. He avoided looking at Craig, turned his back to him, and started to walk uptown.

"Yeah, you go on and get drunk! See what that'll fix!"

"I'm goin' to find that little Ivy, man. She always hang out up there. This time I'm gonna get that girl."

"I can't understand you anymore. My ears are gone." And it was true: Craig had been almost wholly absorbed by his window now, or maybe he had merged with it. In any case, his body was mostly gone. Only the contours of his face and his small rounded shoulders stood out from the glass; his lower legs and feet still stuck out near the ground. But he was mostly just an image in the glass now.

Beltrane hurried down the street, feeling the beginnings of a cool wind start to kick up. He glanced behind him once, looking for Craig's shape, but he didn't see anything.

Just the empty storefront staring back at him.

Beltrane stands in front of the mirror and watches his face for movement. He exerts great concentration to hold himself still: The slopes and angles of his face, the wiry gray coils of beard growing up over his cheeks, the wide round nostrils—even his eyelids—are as unmoving as hard earth. The skin beneath his eyes is heavy and layered, and the fissures in his face are deep, but nothing seems out of place. Nothing is doing anything it isn't supposed to be doing.

He's standing over one of the sinks in the shelter's bathroom. It has five partitioned stalls, most of which have lost their doors, and a bank of dingy gray urinals on the opposite wall. After a moment the door opens and one of the volunteers pokes his head in. When he sees Beltrane in there alone, he comes in all the way and lets the door swing closed behind him. He's a heavy man with high yellow skin, a few dark skin tags standing out on his neck like tiny beetles. Beltrane has seen him around a little bit, over the couple of days he's been here, kneeling down sometimes to pray with folks that were willing.

"You all right?" the volunteer asks.

Beltrane just looks at him. He can't think of anything to say, so after a moment he just turns his gaze back to the mirror.

"The way you charged in here, I thought you might be in trouble." The volunteer stays in his place by the door.

Beltrane looks back at him. "You see anything wrong with my face?"

The man squints but comes no closer. "No. Looks okay to me." When Beltrane doesn't add anything else, he says, "You know, we have strict policies on drug use in here."

"I ain't on drugs. I got this thing here . . . I don't know, I don't know." He lifts his shirt and turns to the volunteer, who displays no reaction. "Can you see this?" he asks.

"That street there? Yes, I can see it."

Beltrane says, "I think I'm haunted."

The man says nothing for a moment. Then, "Is that New Orleans?"

Beltrane nods.

"I guess you're here from Katrina?"

"Yeah, that's right. It fucked my world up, man. Everybody gone."

The man nods. "Most people from New Orleans are going up to Baton Rouge or to Houston. What brings you all the way to Florida?"

"My girl. My girl lives here. I'm gonna move in with her."

"Your girlfriend?"

"No, my *girl*! My daughter!"

"You've been here two days already, haven't you? Where is she?"

"She don't know I'm coming. I got to find her."

Beltrane stares at himself. His face is dry. His hair is dry.

He lifts his shirt to stare at the hole there one more time, but it's gone now; he runs his hand over the old brown flesh, the curly gray hairs.

The volunteer says nothing for a moment. Then, "How long has it been since you've seen her?"

Beltrane looks down into the sink. The porcelain around the drain is chipped and rusty. A distant gurgling sound rises from the pipes, as though something is alive down there, in the bowels of the city. He has to think for a minute. "Twenty-three years," he says finally.

The volunteer's face is still. "That's a long time."

"She got married."

"Is that when she moved here?"

"I got to find her. I got to find my little girl."

The volunteer seems to consider this; then he opens the door to the common area. "My name's Ron Davis. I'm the pastor at the Trinity Baptist, just down the street a few blocks. If you're all done in here, why don't you come down there with me. I think I might be able to help you."

Beltrane looks at him. "A pastor? Come on, man. I don't want to hear about God tonight."

"That's fine. We don't have to talk about God."

"If I leave they won't let me back in. They just give up my cot to someone else."

Davis shakes his head. "You won't have to come back tonight. You can sleep at the church. If we're lucky, you won't ever have to come back here. If we're not, I'll make sure you have a bed tomorrow night." He smiles. "It'll be okay. I do have some influence here, you know."

They leave the shelter together, stepping into the close heat of the Florida night. The air out here smells strongly of the sea, so much that Beltrane experiences a brief thrill in his heart, a sense of being in a place both strange and new. To their left, several blocks down Central Avenue, he can see the tall masts of sailboats in the harbor gathered like a copse of birch trees, pale and ethereal in the darkness. To their right the city extends in a plain of concrete and light, softly glowing overpasses arcing over the street in grace notes of steel. People hunch along the sidewalks, they sleep in the small alcoves of shop doors. Some of them lift their heads as the two men emerge. One of them tugs at Beltrane's pant leg as he walks by. "Hey. Are you leaving? Is they a bed in there?"

Davis says something to the man, but Beltrane ignores them both. He hopes the walk to the church is not long. The pleasant sense of disorientation he felt just a moment ago is gradually turning to anxiety. The buildings seem too impersonal; the faces are all strange. He looks up at the sky—and there, in the thunderheads, he finds something familiar.

Piling rain clouds and the cool winds which precede a storm made the walk from the Treme to the Lower Garden District more pleasant. Rain was not a deterrent, especially in the summer months when the storms in New Orleans were sudden, violent, and quickly over. Low gray clouds obscured the night sky, their great bellies illuminated from time to time by huge, silent explosions of lightning. Beltrane's bones hummed in this weather, as though with a live current. He made his way out of the darkened neighborhood and into the jeweled glow of New Orleans's Central Business District, where lights glittered even when the buildings were empty. The streetcar chimed from some unseen distance, roaring along the unobstructed tracks like a charging animal. He walked along them, past the banks and the hotels, until at last he hit the wide boulevard of St.

Charles Avenue and entered the Garden District. The neutral ground—the grassy swath dividing the avenue into uptown and downtown traffic—was wide enough here to accommodate two streetcar tracks running side by side. Palm trees had been planted here long ago by some starry-eyed city planner. A half mile ahead they gave way to the huge indigenous oaks, which had seen the palm trees planted and would eventually watch them die. They stood like ancient gods, protecting New Orleans from the wild skies above her.

"Here we are," Ron says, and Beltrane drifts to a stop beside him. There are no trees here. There are no streetcars.

The Trinity Baptist Church is just one door in a strip mall, sandwiched between a Christian bookstore and a temp agency. The glass of its single window is smudged and dirty; deep red curtains are closed on the inside, and the corpses of moths and flies are piled on the windowsill. Ron takes a moment to unlock the door. Then he reaches inside and flips on the light.

"My office is in the back," he says. "Come on in."

They walk through a large open area, with rows of folding chairs arranged neatly before a lectern. The linoleum floor is dirty and scuffed with years' worth of rubber soles. Ron opens a plywood door in the rear of the room and ushers Beltrane into his cramped office. He seats himself behind a desk, which takes up most of the space in here, and directs Beltrane to sit down in one of the two chairs on the other side. Then he switches on a computer.

While it boots up, he says, "We'll look online and see if we can find her. What's your name?"

"Henry Beltrane."

"You said she was married. Will she still have your name?"

"Um . . . Delacroix. That's her husband's name."

Davis's fingers tap the keys, and he hunches closer to the screen. He pauses and begins to type some more. "Twenty-three years is a long time," he says. "How old would she be about now? Forty?"

"Forty-five," Beltrane says. "Forty-five years old." It's the first time he's said it aloud. It works like a spell, calling up the gulf of years between now and the time he last saw her, when he was drunk in a bar and she was trying one more time to save his life.

Dad? she'd said. *We're leaving. Four more days. We're doing it.*

He'd turned his back to her then. There'd been a television behind the bar, and he'd fixed his eyes to it. *Have a good trip,* he'd said.

It's not a trip. Do you understand? We're moving there. I'm moving away, Dad.

Yeah, I know.

She'd grabbed his shoulders and turned him on his stool so that he had to look at her. *Daddy, please.*

He'd watched her for a moment, shaping her face out of the unraveling world. He was so drunk. The sun was still up, filtering through the dusty windows of the bar. Her eyes were tearing up. *What,* he'd said. *What? What you want from me?*

Davis releases a long sigh and leans back in his chair. "I got a Sam and Lila Delacroix. That sound right?"

Beltrane's heart turns over. "That's her. Lila. That's her."

Davis jots the address and phone number down on a sticky note and passes it across to Beltrane. "Guess it's your lucky night," he says, though his voice is flat.

Beltrane stares at the number in his hand, a faint, disbelieving smile on his lips. "You call her for me?"

Davis leans back in his chair and smiles. "What, right now? It's almost midnight, Mr. Beltrane. You can't call her now. She'll be in bed."

Beltrane nods, absorbing this.

"Look, I keep a mattress in the closet for when I don't make it home. I can pull it out for you. You can crash right here tonight."

Beltrane nods again. The thought of a mattress overwhelms him, and he feels his eyes tearing up. His mind skips ahead to tomorrow, to wondering about how soft the beds might be in Lila's home, if she'll let him stay. He wonders what it will feel like to wake up in the morning and smell coffee and breakfast. To have someone say kind things to him and be happy to see him. He knew all those things once. They were a long time ago.

"You have a problem," Davis says.

The words push through the dream and it's gone. He waits for his throat to open up again, so he can speak. He says, "I think I'm haunted."

Davis keeps his eyes locked on him. "I think so, too," he says.

Beltrane can't think of what else to say. His hand rubs absentmindedly over his chest. He knows he can't see his daughter while this is happening to him.

"I was haunted once, too," Davis says quietly. He opens a drawer in his desk and withdraws a pack of cigarettes. He extends one to Beltrane and keeps one for himself. "Then the ghost went away."

Beltrane stares at him with an awed hope as Davis slowly fishes through his pockets for a lighter. "How you get rid of it?"

Davis lights both cigarettes. Beltrane wants to grab the man, but instead he takes a draw and the nicotine hits his bloodstream. A spike of euphoria rolls through him with a magnificent energy.

"I don't want to tell you that," Davis says. "I want to tell you why you should keep it. And why you shouldn't go see your daughter tomorrow."

Beltrane's mouth opens. He's half smiling. "You crazy," he says softly.

"What do you think of, when you think of New Orleans?"

He feels a cramp in his stomach. His joints begin sending telegraphs of distress. He can't let this happen. "Fuck you. I'm leaving."

Davis is still as Beltrane hoists himself out of his chair. "The shelter won't let you back in. You said it yourself; you gave up the bed when you left. Where are you going to go?"

"I'll go to Lila's. It don't matter if it's late. She'll take me in."

"Will she? With streets winding through your body? With lamps in your eyes? With rain blowing out of your heart? No. She will slam that door in your face and lock it tight. She will think she is visited by something from hell. She will *not* take you in."

Beltrane stands immobile, one hand still clutching the chair, his eyes fixed not on anything in this room but instead on that awful scene. He hasn't seen Lila's face in twenty years, but he can see it now, contorted in fear and disgust at the sight of him. He feels something shift in his body, something harden in his limbs. He squeezes his eyes shut and wills his body to keep its shape.

"Please," says Davis. "Sit back down."

Beltrane sits.

"You're in between places right now. People think it's the

ghost that lives between places, but it's not. It's us. Tell me what you think of when you think of New Orleans."

Moving up St. Charles Avenue, Beltrane arrived at the Avenue Pub, which shed light onto the sidewalk through its open French doors and cast music and voices into the night. He peered through the windows before entering, to see who was working. The good ones would let him come in, have a few drinks. The others would turn him away at the door, forcing him to decide between walking all the way back down to the French Quarter for his booze, or just calling it a night and going back to his wrecked car at the cab station.

He was in luck; it was John.

He stepped inside and was greeted by people calling his name. He held up a hand in greeting, getting into character. This was a white bar. There were certain expectations he'd have to fulfill if he was going to get his drinks. Some college kid—he had short hair and always smelled of perfume; he could never remember his name—grabbed his hand in a powerful squeeze. "'Trane! My *dog*! What up, dude?"

"Awright, awright," Beltrane said, letting the kid crush his hand. It was going to hurt all night.

The kid yelled over the crowd, "Yo, John, set me up one of them shots for 'Trane here!"

John smiled. "You're evil, dude."

"Oh, whatever, man! Pour me one, too! I can't let him go down that road all by hisself!"

Beltrane maneuvered to an open spot at the bar beside a pretty white girl he'd never seen before and an older guy wearing an electrician's jumpsuit. The girl made a disgusted noise and inched away from him. The electrician nodded at him and said his name. The college kid joined him in a moment with two milky gray shots in his hand. He pushed the larger one at Beltrane.

"Dude! I'm worried, bro. I don't know if you're man enough for a shot like this."

"Shiiiit. I a man!"

"This is a man's drink, dog!"

"Dat's what I am! I a *man*!"

"Then do the shot!"

He did the shot. It tasted vile, of course, like paint thinner and yogurt. They always gave him some horrible shit to drink. But it was real booze, and it slammed into his brain like a wrecking ball. He coughed and wiped his mouth with the back of his hand.

The college kid slapped his back. "Shit, 'Trane! You okay? I thought you said you was a man!"

He tried to talk but he couldn't get his throat to unclench. He ended up just waving his hand dismissively.

Beltrane screwed a bleary eye in the bartender's direction, who moved in a series of ripples and left a ghostly trail in his wake. A beer seemed to sprout from the bar top like a weed. He held out the bag of shrimp he'd gotten earlier. "Heat this up for me, John."

When John came back a few minutes later with the bag, Beltrane said, "You seen Ivy tonight?"

"She was here earlier. You still trying to hit that, you pervert?"

Beltrane just laughed. He clutched his beer and settled into his customary reverie as bar life broke and flowed around him, wrapping him in warmth like a slow-moving river. He downed the shots as they appeared before him and concentrated on keeping them down. Somewhere in the drift of the night a girl materialized beside him, her back half turned to him as she spoke with somebody on her other side. She had a tattoo of a Japanese print on her shoulder, which dipped below the line of her sleeveless white shirt. She was delicate and beautiful. He brushed her arm with the back of his hand, trying to make it seem accidental, and she turned to face him.

"Hey, 'Trane," she said. Her eyes shed a warm yellow light. He wanted to touch her, but there was a divide he couldn't cross.

"We all God's children," he said.

"Yeah, I know." She looked at the boy she was talking to and rolled her eyes. When she looked at him again she had raised windows for eyes, with curtains blowing out of them, framing a yellow-lit room. Below them, her face declined in wet shingles, flowing with little rivulets of rainwater. It took him a moment to realize the water was flowing from inside her. Behind her, her friend rose to his feet; wood and plaster cracked and split as he stood. His eyes were windows, too, but the lights there had been blown out. Water gushed from them. The bar had gone silent; in his peripheral vision he saw that he was ringed with wet, shining faces.

A figure moved to the window in the girl's face. It was backlit; he couldn't make out who it was. Water was rising around his feet, soaking through his shoes, making him cold.

Davis says, "There's some people I want you to meet." His voice is so soft Beltrane can barely hear it. Davis is sitting on the edge of his desk, looming over him. His eyes are moist.

Beltrane blinks. "I got to get out of here."

"Just wait. Please?"

"You can't keep me here. I ain't a prisoner."

"No, I know. Your . . . your ghost is very strong. I've never seen one that was a . . . a city, before."

Beltrane is suddenly uncomfortable with Davis's proximity to him. "What you doing this close? Back off a me, man."

Davis takes a deep breath and slides off his desk, moving back to his side of it. He collapses into his chair. "There's some people I want you to meet," he says. "Will you stay just a little bit longer?"

The thought of going outside into this strange city does not appeal to Beltrane. He doesn't know the neighborhood, doesn't know which places are safe for homeless people to go and which places are off-limits—whether due to police or thugs or just because it's someone else's turf. He was always safe in New Orleans, which he knew as well as he knew his own face. But new places are dangerous.

"You got another cigarette?" he says. Davis seems to relax a little and passes one to him. After it's lit, Beltrane says, "How come I can't get rid of it?"

"You can," says Davis. "It's just that you shouldn't. Do you . . . do you really know what a ghost *is,* Mr. Beltrane?"

"This must be where you start preaching."

"A ghost is something that fills a hole inside you, where you lost something. It's a memory. Sometimes it can be painful, and sometimes it can be scary. Sometimes it's hard to tell where the ghost ends and real life begins. I know you know what I mean."

Beltrane just looks away, affecting boredom. But he can feel his heart turning in his chest and sweat bristling along his scalp.

"But if you get rid of it, Mr. Beltrane, if you *get rid of it*, you have *nothing* left." He pauses. "You just have a hole."

Beltrane darts a glance at him. Davis is leaning over his desk, urgency scrawled across his face. He's sweating too, and his eyes look sunken, as though someone has jerked them back into his head from behind. His appearance unnerves Beltrane, and he turns away.

"Emptiness. Silence. Is that really better? You need to think carefully about what you decide you can live without, Mr. Beltrane." He pauses for a moment. When Beltrane stays silent, he leans even closer and asks, "What do you really think is going to happen when you make that call tomorrow?"

A cold pulse of fear flows through Beltrane's body. But before he can think of a response, a sound reaches them through the closed door. People are entering the church from the street.

Davis smiles suddenly. It's an artificial smile, manic, out of all proportion to any possible stimulus. "They're here! Come on!"

He leads him into the large room with the lectern and the rows of chairs. Two people—a young slender Latina woman and an older obese white man—have just entered and are standing uncertainly by the door. Although they're dressed in simple, cheap clothing, it's immediately obvious that they're not homeless. They both stare at Beltrane as he approaches behind the pastor.

"Come on, everybody," Davis says, gesturing to the front row of chairs. "Let's sit down."

Davis arranges a chair to face them, and soon they are all sitting in a clumsy circle. "These are the people I wanted you to meet," he says. "This is Maria and Evan. They're haunted too."

Maria tries to form a smile beneath eyes that are sunken and dark, like moon craters or like cigarette burns. She seems long out of practice. Evan is staring intently at the floor. He's breathing heavily through his nose with a reedy, pistoning regularity. His forehead is glistening with sweat.

"I'm trying to start a little group here, you know? People with your sort of problem."

"This is how we gonna get rid of it?" Beltrane asks.

Davis and Maria exchange glances.

"They don't want to get rid of them," Davis says. "That's why they're here." He turns to the others. "Mr. Beltrane came here from New Orleans. He's looking for his daughter."

Maria gives him a crushed look. "Oh, *pobrecito*," she says. The news seems to affect her deeply: Her face clouds over, and her eyes well up. Beltrane looks away, embarrassed for her, and ashamed at his own optimism.

"His ghost is a city."

This seems to catch even Evan's attention, who looks at him for the first time. "I'm the Ghost of Christmas Past," Evan says, and barks a laugh. "My family died in a fire two days after Christmas. The fucking tree! It's like a joke, right?"

Davis pats Evan on the knee. "We'll get to it, my friend. We will. But first we have to help him understand."

"Right, right. But it wants to come out. It wants to come out right now."

"Mr. Beltrane thinks he lost his city in the flood," Davis continues.

"I *did* lose it!" Beltrane shouts, feeling both scared and angry to be among these people. "After Katrina came, I lost everything! Craig moved away after his place flooded! Places I go to are all shut down. The people all gone. Ivy . . . Ivy, she . . . she was in this empty old house she used to crash in. . . ." His throat closes, and he stops there.

Davis waits a moment, then puts his hand on his shoulder. "But it's not really gone, though, is it?" He touches Beltrane on the forehead and then on his chest. "Is it?"

Beltrane shakes his head.

"And if it ever does go away, well, God help you then. Because you will be all by yourself. You will be all alone." He pauses. "You don't want that. Nobody wants that."

Evan makes a noise and puts a hand over his mouth.

"I had enough of this crazy shit," Beltrane says, and stands. Davis opens his mouth, but before he can speak the room is filled with the scent of cloves and cinnamon. The effect is so jarring that Beltrane nearly loses his balance.

Evan doubles over in his seat, hands over his face, his big body shuddering with sobs. The smell pours from him. Smoke leaks from between his fingers, spreading in cobwebby wreaths over his head. Beltrane wants to run, but he's never seen this kind of thing in anyone but himself before, and he's transfixed.

"Oh, here it comes," Davis says, not to the others but to himself, his eyes glassy and fixed, staring at Evan. "That's all right, just let it out. You have to let it come out. You have to hold on to what's left. Never let it go." He looks at Maria. "Can you feel him, Maria? Can you?"

Maria nods. Her eyes are filled with tears. Her hands are clutching her stomach, and Beltrane watches as it grows beneath them, accompanied by a powerful, sickly odor that he does not recognize right away. When he does he feels a buckling inside, the turning over of some essential organ or element, and he is overwhelmed by a powerful need to flee.

"Will you get rid of this?" Davis is saying, his face so close to Maria's they might be lovers. "Will you get rid of your child, Maria? Who could ask that of you? Who would dare?"

Beltrane backs up a step and falls over a chair, sprawling to the floor in a clatter of noise and his own flailing arms. There's a sudden, spiking pain as his elbow takes the brunt of his weight. The air grows steadily colder; the appalling mix of cinnamon and desiccated flesh roots into his nose. Davis kneels between the others, one hand touching each body, and once again his features seem to be tugging inward, even his round stomach is drawing in, as though something empty, some starving need, is glutting itself on this weird energy; as though there's a black hole inside him, filling its belly with light.

"Please, God, just let it come," Davis says.

Beltrane tries to scramble to his feet and slips. A large, growing puddle of Mississippi River water surrounds him. It soaks his clothes. He tries again, making it to his feet this time, and staggers to the door. He pushes his way outside, into the warm, humid night, and without waiting to see if they're following, he lurches farther down the street, away from the church, away from the shelter, until an alleyway opens like a throat and he turns gratefully into it. He manages to make it a few more feet before he collapses to his knees. He doesn't know anymore if the pain he feels is coming from arthritis or from the ghost which has wrapped itself like a vine around his bones.

Across the alley, in the alcove of a delivery door, he sees a mound of clothing and a duffel bag: This is somebody's roost. A shadow falls over him as a figure stops in the mouth of the alley. The city light makes a dark shape of it, a negative space. "What you doin' here?" it says.

Beltrane closes his eyes—an act of surrender. "I just restin', man," he says, almost pleads. "I ain't stayin'."

"You don't belong here."

"Come on, man. Just let me rest a minute. I ain't gonna stay. Can't you see what's happening to me?"

When he opens his eyes he is alone. He exhales, and it almost sounds like a sob. "I wanna go home," he whispers. "I wanna go home." He runs his hands through his hair, dislodging drowned corpses, which tumble into his lap.

Beltrane left the Avenue Pub behind, well and truly drunk, walking slowly and carefully as the ground lurched and spun beneath him. He summoned the presence of mind to listen for the streetcar, which came like a bullet at night; just last year it ran down a drunk coming from some bar farther up the road. "That's some messy shit," he announced, and laughed to himself. The United Cab offices were just a few blocks away. If he hurried he could beat the rain.

Halfway there he found Ivy, rooting lazily through a trash can.

She was a cute little thing who'd shown up in town last year after fleeing some private doom in Georgia; she was forty years younger than Beltrane, but hope lived large in him. They got along pretty well—she got along well with most men, really—and it was always nice to spend time with a pretty girl. He waved at her. "Ivy! Hey, girl!"

She looked up at him, her face empty. "'S'up, 'Trane. What you doin'?" She straightened and tossed a crumpled wrapper back into the can.

"I'm goin' to bed, girl. It's late!"

She appraised him for a moment, then smiled. "You fucked up!"

He laughed, like a little boy caught in some foolishness.

She saw the bag he still clutched in his hand. "I ain't had nothing to eat, 'Trane. I'm *starving*."

He held the bag aloft, like the head of a slain enemy. "I got some food for ya right here."

She held out a hand and offered him her best smile. It lit up all that alcohol in him. It set him on fire. "Well, give it over then," she said.

"You must think I'm crazy. Come on back with me, to my place."

"Shit. That old cab?"

Beltrane turned and walked in that direction, listening to her footsteps as she trotted to catch up. The booze in him caused the earth to move in slow, steady waves, and the lights to bleed into the cloudy night. A cold wind had kicked up, and the buildings swooned on their foundations. Together they trekked the short distance to United Cab.

He found himself, as always, stealing glances at her: Though she was gaunt from deprivation, she seemed to have an aura of carved nobility about her, a hard beauty distinct from circumstance or prospect. She was young enough, too, that she still harbored some resilient optimism about the world, as though it may yet yield some good for her. *And who knows,* he thought. *Maybe it would.*

The first hard drops of rain fell as they reached the cab. It had died where it was last parked, two years ago. It sagged earthward, its tires long deflated and its shocks long spent, so that the chassis nearly scraped the ground as Beltrane opened the door and climbed in. It smelled like fried food and sweat, and he rubbed the old air freshener hanging from the rearview in some wild hope he could coax a little life from it yet. The front seats had been taken out, giving them room to stretch their legs. The car was packed with blankets, old newspapers, and skin magazines. Ivy stared in after him, wrinkling her nose.

"This is it, baby," he said.

"It stinks in here!"

"It ain't that bad. You get used to it."

He leaned against the seat back, stretching his legs to the front. He hooked one arm up over the backseat and invited her to lean into him. She paused, still halfway through the door on her hands and knees.

"I ain't fuckin' you, 'Trane. You too damn old."

"Shit, girl." He tried to pretend he wasn't disappointed. "Get your silly ass in here and have some food."

She climbed in and he opened the bag for her. The shrimp retained a lingering heat from the microwave at the pub, and they dug in. Afterward, with warm food alight in their bellies and the rain hammering on the roof, she eased back against the seat and settled into the crook of his arm at last, resting her head on his shoulder. Beltrane gave her a light squeeze, realizing with a kind of dismay that any sexual urge had left him, that the feeling he harbored for her now was something altogether different, altogether better.

"I don't know nothing about you, 'Trane," she said quietly. "You don't talk very much."

"What you mean? I'm always talking!"

"Yeah but you don't really *talk,* you know? Like, you got any family around?"

"Well," he said, his voice trailing. "Somewhere. I got a little girl somewhere."

She lifted her head and looked at him. "For real?"

He just nodded. Something about this conversation felt wrong, but he couldn't figure out what it was. The rain was coming down so hard it was difficult to focus. "I ain't seen her in a long time. She got married and went away."

"She just abandon you? That's fucked up, 'Trane."

"I wasn't like this then. Things was different." Sorrow crested and broke in his chest. "She got to live her life. She had to go."

"You ever think about leaving, too? Maybe you could go to where she live."

"Hell no, girl. This is my home. This is everything I know."

"It's just a place, 'Trane. You can change a place easy."

He didn't want to think about that. "Anyway," he said, "she forgot me by now."

Ivy was quiet for a time, and Beltrane let himself be lulled by the drumbeat over their heads. Then she said, "I bet she ain't forgot you." She adjusted her position to get comfortable, putting her head back on his shoulder. "I bet she still love her daddy."

They stopped talking, and eventually she drifted off to sleep. He kissed her gently on her forehead, listening to the storm surrounding the car. The air was chilly, but their bodies were warm against each other. Outside was thrashing darkness and rain.

What, he'd said. *What. What you want from me?*

She'd blinked tears from her eyes. *Come with us. I'm worried about what's gonna happen with you when I'm gone.*

Damn, Lila, he'd said, turning away from her again. *You gone already.*

Beltrane awoke with a fearful convulsion. The car was filling with water. It was pouring from Ivy, from her eyes and her mouth, from the pores of her skin, in a black torrent, lifting the stored papers and the garbage around them in swirling eddies, rising rapidly over their legs and on up to their waists. The water was appallingly cold; he lost all feeling where it covered him. He put his hands over Ivy's face to staunch the flow, without effect. Her head lolled beside him, her face discolored and grotesquely swollen.

He was going to drown. The idea came to him with a kind of alien majesty; he was overcome with awe and horror.

He pushed against the car door, but it wouldn't open. Beyond the window, the night moved with a murderous will. It lifted the city by its roots and shook it in its teeth. The water had nearly reached the ceiling, and he had to arch his back painfully to keep his face above it. Ivy had already slipped beneath the surface, her lamp-lit eyes shining like cave fish.

All thought left him: His whole energy was channeled into a scrabbling need to escape. He slammed his body repeatedly into the car door. He pounded the glass with his fists.

Beltrane awakens to pain. His limbs are wracked with it, his elbow especially. He opens his eyes and sees the pavement of the alley. Climbing to his feet takes several minutes. Morning is near: Through the mouth of the alley the streetlights glow dimly against a sky breaking slowly into light. There is no traffic, and the salty smell of the bay is strong. The earth has cooled in the night, and the heat's return is still a few hours away.

He takes a step toward the street, then stops, sensing something behind him. He turns around.

A small city has sprouted from the ground in the night, where he'd been sleeping, surrounded by blowing detritus and stagnant filth. It spreads across the puddle-strewn pavement and grows up the side of the wall, twinkling in the deep blue hours of the morning, like some gorgeous fungus, awash in a blustery evening rain. It exudes a sweet, necrotic stink. He's transfixed by it, and the distant wails he hears rising from it are a brutal, beautiful lullaby.

He walks away from it.

When he gets to the street, he turns left, heading down to the small harbor. The door to the church is closed when he passes it, and the lights are off inside. There's no indication of any life there. Soon he passes the shelter, and there are people he recognizes socializing by its front door, but he doesn't know their names, and they don't know his. They don't acknowledge him as he walks by. He passes a little restaurant, the smell of coffee and griddle-cooked sausage hanging in front of it like a cloud. The long white masts of the sailboats are peering over the tops of buildings. He rounds a corner and he is there.

The water of the bay glimmers with bright shards of light as the sun climbs. The boats jostle gently in their berths. A pelican perches on a short pier, wings spread like hanging laundry. He follows a sidewalk along the waterfront until he finds a pay phone with a dial tone. He presses zero and waits.

"I wanna make a collect call," he says, fishing the slip of paper Davis gave him out of his pocket and reciting the number.

He waits for the automated tone and announces himself. "It's Henry. It's your dad."

A machine says, "Please hold while we connect your call."

Leaning over the small concrete barrier, he can see the shape of himself in the water. His reflection is broken up by the water's movement. Small pieces of himself clash and separate. He thinks that if he waits here long enough the water will calm, and his face will resolve into something familiar.

A voice speaks into the silence, filling it.

Guns for the Dead

A GRAVEMINDER STORY

BY MELISSA MARR

Melissa Marr is the author of the *New York Times* bestselling Wicked Lovely series (a film of which is in development by Universal Pictures) and the forthcoming adult novel *Graveminder.* Currently, she lives in the Washington, D.C., area with one spouse, two children, two Rott-Labs, and one Rottweiler. You can find her online at www.melissa-marr.com.

At the sound of boots on the plank walkway outside her shop, Alicia closed the cash box and lifted the sawed-off shotgun from a modified undercounter rack. She'd hoped that the boys would be back by now, but they weren't daft enough to be walking in the front door of General Supplies without calling out.

She swung the shotgun up as the door opened.

The owner of the boots stopped just inside the shop. He was new enough that she didn't recognize him. To his credit, though, he didn't flinch at the sight of her particular brand of customer service. His gaze slipped briefly over the shop with curiosity. The interior of the frontier-town general goods store seemed a little out of time to new arrivals. Over there, more than a century had passed. She thought about updating the look, but the comforting familiarity of the dry-goods shop outweighed her discomfort over revealing her age. *Screw 'em.* With its tins and barrels, glass cases, and the wood floorboards, it was home, but clearly not what *his* home looked like.

The newcomer put his arms out to the sides, demonstrating that he was either trustworthy or idiotic. "Ma'am."

She took in his frayed jeans, faded black T-shirt, combat boots, and a relatively new revolver in a belt holster. Most of those items were commonplace here now; she'd even acquired shirts and boots much like his in recent years. The holster he wore could be purchased in a dozen spots around the city, but post-1880 weapons came from one shop only—hers. She pursed her lips. Since she didn't recognize him, he'd either taken it from a customer or bought it at significant upsale.

"Boyd sent me," he said.

"And?" She didn't lower her weapon. There was something decidedly awkward about aiming a shotgun one-armed for any time at all, but a businesswoman didn't greet strangers unarmed. She stepped back and—using her free hand for leverage—hopped up on the counter.

The newcomer raised his brows, but his posture remained unchanged. "He said to tell you that 'the old bastard started trouble' and that 'he'll be out for a day.'"

"Huh." Alicia lowered the shotgun so it was aimed at the floor in front of her. "And where is Boyd, that you're delivering this message?"

"Got shot."

She tensed. "By?"

"See, that's the thing—"

"No," she interrupted. She slid off the counter and stepped forward. "Simple question, shug. Shot by whom?"

"Me, but there were circumst—" The rest of his words were lost under the shotgun blast.

She threw herself to the side as she fired, hoping to dodge a return shot that didn't come. When she realized that he hadn't even reached for his piece, Alicia rolled to her feet.

Definitely a newcomer.

She stood and looked down at him. His blood was leaking all over her floorboards. *And that's why we don't have carpet.* She sighed. Sometimes, she had misplaced urges for finery that had no place in the shop. *Maybe if it was a* dark *carpet.* She walked around the counter but not close enough that he could pull her to the ground. Injured or not, he had a size advantage.

He looked up at her. "Least it was a slug, not scattershot."

"You want to see what's in the second barrel?" She extended her arm and took aim, but didn't fire. "Why'd you shoot Boyd?"

"Had to," the man said.

"Why?" She motioned with the gun.

The bleeder on her floor had his hands pressed over his leg wound. If he was still alive, he'd be in a sorry state, but being dead tended to change things in unpredictable ways. From the way he pressed his hands down, he was even newer than she thought: Getting used to living in the land of the dead took a little time.

"I came looking for him to ask about you, and things took a turn," he said slowly.

Alicia sighed. "I think you're going to need to start at the beginning . . . *after*"—she looked pointedly at his belt—"you slide that over here."

"If I didn't reach for it when you shot me, I'm not going to *now*," he muttered, but he still pulled the pistol out of the holster and held it out toward her butt-first.

Francis Lee Lemons stared at the woman who, according to everyone he'd met since he died, ran the guns for the land of the dead.

And shot me.

He wanted a job. Straight up, plain and simple, he wanted to work for her. He'd never been on what one might call the "right" side of the law, and he didn't see any need to change that now that he was in this odd afterlife. Getting along over here was a mite more brutal than in the living world, but he figured that a familiarity with a less-than-upstanding lifestyle would be an asset.

"Ma'am?"

Alicia glanced at him, but she didn't say anything.

"Would it offend you overmuch if I either took off my shirt to staunch this or asked for a bandage of some sort?" he asked as respectfully as he could.

"You got any funds?"

"No, ma'am."

"Job?"

"Not yet." He looked directly at her. "I'm in the middle of what I hope to be a promising interview though."

She snorted. "You're bleeding on my floorboards. That's promising?" She walked over to a basket of rags that sat alongside the front counter and pulled out an obviously stained one. She tossed it to him. "It's not the cleanest, but we don't get infections over here."

"Yes, ma'am." He tied it around his thigh, arranging it so as to cover both the entrance and exit wounds.

"Alicia," she said.

He looked up, mid-knot.

"If you know enough to apply for a job, you already know my name." She walked over and slid a bolt on the door and then proceeded to do the same at the shutters that covered the inside of the windows.

"Alicia?"

She glanced back.

"I'm Frank. Well, Francis Lee Lemons, but—"

"I don't care who you are yet, shug." She leaned against one of the large wooden casks in the corner. "Talk."

So Frank told her: "I took the revolver off a man in a game of darts. Too stupid to realize he could even *be* hustled at darts and . . . I'm mostly honest, but it seemed a wise plan to be armed around here, you know?"

Alicia nodded.

"Found out who supplied it, started asking about you, and ended up at a weird bar with Boyd."

"What bar?" she prompted.

"Mr. D's." He paused, but she didn't say anything, so he kept going. "Boyd was explaining that you were particular about who you took on. Lots of dead folks want a position on your team, and not just anyone could meet up to make his case." Nervously, Frank looked at Alicia, but her expression was unreadable, so he added the damning part: "But we were talking, and then Boyd suddenly says, 'Shoot me.' I didn't think I heard right. He repeated it again. 'Shoot me right here.' He pointed right at his forehead. '*Now,* then go find Alicia.' He told me to tell you what I did when I walked in."

Quietly, Alicia asked, "What did you do?"

Frank had a fleeting wish that he'd kept his gun then, but he answered her in a steady voice, "Exactly what he said."

"Why?"

"Instinct?" Frank shrugged. "I don't know, really. He seemed sober, sane as anyone else here, and . . . I know he's your right-hand man, and I want this job, and I didn't know what else to do, so I did what he said I should."

"Good enough." Alicia reached behind a tin on one of the shelves next to her and grabbed a revolver. She tossed it at him. "Let's go."

He caught it and checked the chamber. "You in the habit of throwing loaded guns?"

"You expected to do me any good with an *un*loaded piece?" Alicia cocked her head.

Frank glanced at his leg before answering. "If I had to, but not right this minute."

"Call it part of the interview." Alicia held up a hand and started ticking things off on her fingers. "Assuming you're telling the truth, I know you listened to Boyd, and you reacted well to stress. That's two. Since you got here, you're not bitching over that scrape." She gestured at his bloody thigh. "Now, you caught and flipped the gun in your hand like you're comfortable."

She held her hand out to him and helped him to his feet. "Tells me you have potential."

Frank swallowed against the sting of putting weight on his leg. He knew he was dead now, but he wasn't sure what happened when the dead were shot. *Can I die more?* He looked at his blood on their clasped hands. Obviously, the dead bled. He asked, "Did I kill Boyd?"

"Boyd's been dead almost a century." She pulled her hand

free of his and wiped it on another rag she grabbed out of the basket. "Not real sure on that whole reincarnation thing."

She tossed the rag to Frank.

Frank stared at her for several moments before saying, "*Here.* Did I kill him here?"

Alicia reached up and patted his cheek. "Sweetie, only one man around here can kill the dead."

"Who's that?"

"The man who we're going to see—the old bastard, Mr. D." She tucked his revolver in her own holster, slung her shotgun over her shoulder, and walked to the door.

As they walked through the city, Alicia slowed her pace a little for him. Getting shot wasn't fatal here, but it still hurt like a bitch. *Frankie Lee.* She hadn't heard that anyone was asking about her, but he'd found Boyd, knew she was the one that ran the black market, and managed to get a *meeting* with Boyd. That meant that Frankie Lee was stealthy. She glanced at him. His lips were pursed, and he was limping a bit, but all things considered, he was holding up fairly well for having a hole in his thigh.

"How long you been dead?"

Frankie Lee frowned. "I don't know. Week or two, I guess."

"Well, here's your newcomer welcome information, Frankie Lee."

"Frank," he interjected.

Alicia ignored him. "The grand pain in everyone's ass around here is Charles. The old bastard and I have a regular conflict." She reached into one of her trouser pockets and pulled out a couple pills. "Take these."

Frankie Lee obediently swallowed them. He didn't ask

what they were, and she didn't tell him. He'd figure it out soon enough when his leg stopped hurting.

As they walked through the ever-shifting city, a few people glanced their way. They were in one of the sections that remained steadfastly not modern. It was a bit cleaner than the way her experience of live-world equivalent was, but it was comforting all the same. Alicia had adjusted to the appearance of new sections in the city, blocks that belonged to eras that happened after she was already dead, but she felt ill at ease around flappers or—worse still—those cookie-baking, always-smiling women.

Not as sweet as they act, either, else they'd have moved past here.

Mr. Waverly tipped his hat to her. One of the Tadlock sisters tilted her ridiculous parasol so she couldn't see them.

"Millicent!" Alicia called out to her, and predictably, the woman had a sudden urge to dart into a milliner's shop. She was from Alicia's own era and clung to the notion that ladies shouldn't acknowledge ruffians. It didn't stop her from buying the Derringer she no doubt had in her handbag.

Alicia and Frankie Lee crossed a street separating the 1800s and early 1900s shops, and one of the young newshounds came scurrying into their path. "Who shot you, mister? Are you going to go settle up with them, Alicia?"

"Nope."

"Is *he*?" the boy pestered.

"Don't know. Are you, Frankie Lee?" She glanced at him.

He frowned at her. "No, and no one calls me that."

"It's that or Francis." She smiled. "Your choice."

After a pause, he nodded. "Not Francis."

"Frankie Lee isn't going to settle up with the one that shot him. That's all you get for now." She shooed the newshound out of the street. Once the boy was gone, she resumed her version of a newcomer's talk: "Charles thinks my organization is crude. He's a despot. Dictator, really. No free trade, no modernizing the city. If he had his way, women would all be relegated to arm candy or other foolishness. He builds what he wants when he wants, makes the laws he wants, and we're just to be content with whatever he creates."

"And you?"

"I'm not content." She scowled at one of the more-modern dead men soliciting a couple of the silly flapper girls who liked to linger near the century line. One of Charles's people stepped in, so she kept going. Grudgingly she told Frankie Lee, "Charles maintains some parts of the city well, but he's stuck on the idea of empires. I don't agree."

"So it's political differences?" Frankie Lee's tone did little to hide his surprise.

Alicia laughed. "Not entirely. I'm here. I'm staying here, and I'm not his subject. . . . I didn't fare well when I was under his authority."

Memories of her life, of a time when she trusted Charles, flooded her. A long time ago, she lived for Charles. Here, well, she might *still* exist because of him—except now it was to thwart him, not to help him.

"I have a financial interest in my politics." She walked a little faster, and thanks to her medicinal aid, Frankie Lee kept pace. "Guns in the land of the dead are the main source of my livelihood. The more modern, the better. Because of a loophole, there's a man and a woman from the living world who can come over here. I got myself in the habit of bartering with the Undertaker, so he buys my help with the things he brings in. The old bastard can't stop the Undertaker from supplying my prototypes, and once I get models of new gear, I can replicate some of it."

"Which I'm guessing he dislikes."

"Got it in one." Alicia didn't like taking on new people very often. Her business required a particular skill set that lots of folks *thought* they had, but there was a significant difference between *wearing* bad-ass as a costume and being the real deal. Any man—or woman—could throw on the right clothes, whichever era they preferred, and posture. No amount of leather or sharp suits equaled true grit.

"Frankie?"

"Yes'm." He kept a rolling pace now, but his attention was on the side streets rather than on her. Whether she'd ordered it or not, he was standing guard.

"What did you do when you were alive?" She held up a hand, signaling him to wait for the 12:12 train. The conductor took pleasure at running silent in hopes of plowing over newcomers.

Frankie Lee shrugged. "I did work for hire last few years. Grew up around guns. No explosives skills or anything fancy, but I'm a quick study. I do alright in close situations, decent trigger man if you need it, seemed to fare well enough at observation."

"They pay well for that topside these days?"

"Sometimes, if you're good enough. I was good enough most of the time, but"—Frankie Lee gave her a wry smile—"not the last time."

Alicia closed her eyes against the gust of air as the train passed in front of them. It used be the 12:00 train, but the conductor moved it up one minute each month. As far as calendars went, she'd heard of worse. It certainly proved incentive to keep track of the month.

"How'd you end up qualified?" she asked.

"My mama enlisted out of high school, and she got sore

over the things she wasn't allowed to do. So she taught me and my sisters all that she *did* learn, and then we all four learned what she wasn't taught." Frankie Lee's up-until-then calm faltered. He was good at what she needed, but he wasn't unnecessarily cold—which was an asset in her book. A cold-hearted employee was a different sort of problem than one that was all sass and no ass. The right sort of associate was neither too cocky nor too cruel.

"Your mama sounds like a smart woman." Alicia stepped into the street, and Frankie Lee followed.

"She was, but my sisters'll look out for her well enough. She's not big time, but she has connections enough that she does alright for herself."

Alicia figured the sideways scowls that more than a few of the upstanding citizens sent her way were clue enough—well, that, and the fact that he was limping because she'd shot him—but she figured it was only proper to fill him in. "You *do* get that I'm not exactly on the right side of the law here?"

"No disrespect, Alicia, but I doubt you could be any less law-abiding than my mama was, and I don't think the law here is necessarily one I'm after following." He motioned toward a glass door with MR. D'S TIP-TOP TAVERN painted on it. "This is where we were."

Alicia grabbed the brass bar that served as a door handle and yanked the door open before he could open it for her. "Let's see how well you follow orders, Frankie Lee."

Frank walked into the shadowed interior of the tavern twice in almost as many hours. He already knew that it was a wide-open club: exposed pipes ran the length of the ceiling, no alcoves to hide in. Round tables with varying numbers of high-backed chairs were spread throughout the room, far enough apart at places that a private conversation was possible. The biggest risk was the curtained doorway beside the bar. It would allow cover to sight down on any of the customers with either a rifle or a handgun, depending on who minded whatever space was on the far side of that curtain.

Without asking, he knew that Alicia was well aware of the same threat. She'd paused, swept the room, seeking someone or maybe just assessing threats. Then she swung her shotgun from where she'd carried it over her shoulder and held it barrel-down as they walked into the room.

"Don't say anything unless I tell you to," she murmured.

Frank nodded.

At the dead middle of the room, Alicia stopped, pumped her shotgun, and aimed it at the baby grand piano on the stage in front of them.

All around them, people stood and walked out. No one ran. No one said anything. They merely stood, pushed in their chairs, and headed toward the exit.

Once the room was cleared of everyone but the bartender, Alicia winked at Frank and then shot a pipe that was just to the left of the stage. Steam hissed from it.

"I'd like to talk," she called.

The barmaid caught Frank's gaze and widened her eyes imploringly. He didn't think she was in any real danger though. Alicia seemed to be concentrating on the piano. She shot a second pipe. This time, water sluiced from the fragmented pipe. It didn't pour down on the piano, but it was very close. Something shorted, sparked, and smoked off to the side of the stage.

A man came from behind the curtained doorway. He carried himself with the easy confidence of someone who's always been obeyed—and had the power and money to keep it that way. He wore an old-fashioned dark gray suit broken up by the scarlet of his tie and his pocket square.

"We have telephones here, Alicia. Telegraphs, too." He shook his head and then turned his attention to Frank. "Francis, I see you've met my dear Alicia. Is she helping you get your sea legs?"

Frank didn't reply.

"Aaaah, already on her payroll." The man *tsk*-ed. "With your mother's influence, one would expect as much, I suppose. As I doubt Alicia will introduce us"—he touched his fingertips to his chest lightly—"I am Charles."

How does he know about my family?

Alicia dropped her shotgun on the table, looked over her shoulder at Frank, and said, "Go on up to the bar and grab me a drink."

He raised his brows at her but kept his mouth shut.

She nodded and turned back to Charles. "Leave Frankie Lee out of it."

Frank walked over to the polished wooden bar. By the time he got there, the barmaid already had two highball glasses and a wineglass out. She filled two glasses with bourbon and the third with some sort of wine. "The wine is for the boss."

He looked at her.

"*My* boss," she corrected.

And he carried the three drinks back over to the table. As he approached, Alicia poked Charles in the chest. "You can't bully Boyd. He's *mine*."

"At what point did you gain any authority in *my* domain? You live in my city because I allow it." Charles nodded absently to Frank and took a seat.

Alicia grabbed one of the glasses from Frank and upended it. Her shotgun lay like a line bisecting the table. "Make me leave then."

Charles remained silent. He sipped his drink and stared at Alicia, who now stood with her hands on her hips. Not knowing what else to do, Frank handed his drink to Alicia and stood to the side so she could draw without interference and he could still be there if she needed help. Something older than logic told him that Charles, for all of his polish, wasn't the sort of man who'd go down easy in a fight.

Even as he thought it, Charles smiled at him. "You'll do just fine around here, Francis."

Alicia tensed.

And Frank said the only thing he could think of in the moment. "My name is Frankie Lee, sir."

Alicia grinned. Frankie Lee was going to work out just fine.

"I don't want semiautomatic weapons on my street, Alicia." Charles motioned at the seat across from him. "I overlook a lot, but there are limits. I explained that to Boyd last week. On this, I *will* crush you."

She sat and motioned for Frankie Lee to do the same. She tried the same argument that usually worked: "I don't see why these—"

"No. Not this time. I play by the rules. That means, here and there, you'll outmaneuver me. On this, it's not going to be anytime soon. I overlook revolvers, but that's where we are staying. The damage, the loss of life . . . I can't explain it." Charles looked genuinely sad, but she knew well enough that the old bastard was able to fake emotions. "You have been out of that world for years, Alicia."

"Dead. Because you had me killed," she corrected.

Beside her, Frankie Lee tensed, but he stayed silent.

"True." Charles sipped his wine. "I'll negotiate, or I'll start killing your boys. Permanent death so as they'll be removed from the city."

Alicia paused. "And me?"

Charles leaned back in his seat. "I won't kill you. You know that."

"Again. Say it, at least. You won't kill me *again*."

"I won't kill you *again*, but"—Charles glanced at Frankie Lee—"I'll kill him, Boyd, Milt, each and every one you employ."

Charles made a come-hither gesture.

One of her information runners, Lewis, was brought in.

"You *all* exist because I allow it; you can die because I prefer it. No semiautomatic weapons, Alicia. You will agree to stop pushing this matter," Charles said softly. "Or he dies."

She started, "I'm not going to give in because of a threat."

Charles fixed his gaze on her and snapped his fingers. Lewis crumpled. "There are always unbreakable rules. Right now, this is one of them, and you, of all people, know that I will do what I must to enforce the unbreakable rules."

Alicia looked at Lewis. *Where do they go if they die in the land of the dead?* She'd asked that question often enough, but Charles never answered. "No automatic weapons for how long?"

"You have no room to barter," Charles said.

She suppressed a shiver at the threat in his voice. "Just checking the rules."

"Thirty years. We can renegotiate then."

"Thirty years," Alicia agreed. "*But* you owe me a replacement, or undo what you did to Lewis."

For a moment, Charles was silent. Then he nodded and

said, "I can't undo his death, but as a gesture of good faith, I'll allow you to take one of the staff to replace your employee."

Alicia kept her expression bland, but she felt the wave of sorrow that she'd been resisting. Charles had finally answered her: Some deaths apparently were even fatal enough that they were out of his reach. She'd known there were other dead cities, and hoped that those who didn't reanimate here went to another world, a world where they were happier. She knew such worlds existed: Her own loved ones had gone on to them. She'd hoped, though, that the dead folk who were rekilled *here* went on to other dead worlds, but if that were the case, Charles could have undone Lewis's death.

Lewis is dead.

Thinking about the metaphysics of living in the land of the dead made her head hurt, so she didn't. *Lewis is dead because I pushed Charles too far.* The same trait that had made her good at opposing Charles, both before and after her death, got Lewis killed. Silently, Alicia walked over to the bar and accepted the drink the barmaid held out as she approached.

Behind her, Charles said, "Shall I invite my staff here, or would you deign to visit my home?"

Without looking back at him, she said, "Here."

An hour later, Frankie Lee watched as several dozen people tromped into the room. Beside him, Alicia sat with her boots propped on the table as one of them—the only one Charles said was "off limits"—told Alicia their names and roles. Charles had cooks, maids, barmaids, singers, a personal tailor, and God knew how many other employees.

Frankie Lee tuned most of it out after the first fifteen minutes.

Finally, Alicia pointed toward a young woman. "I'll take her."

Charles frowned. "There are others—"

"No. Her." Alicia folded her arms over her chest.

"She's not suited for your sort of work, Alicia. Perhaps Steven. He's handy with some sort of martial art, or Elizabeth . . . she's an accomplished companion." Charles gestured toward a pretty redhead.

"No."

"Why?" Charles asked.

The smile Alicia offered was as frightening as her glare. "I'm a good judge of character. You softened at the sight of her."

Charles frowned at Alicia. "What kind of job do you have for a *singer*?"

"I'm sure I'll find a good use for her." Alicia's boots *thunked* to the floor as she stood. "I expect her and Boyd delivered to the inn."

Frank felt a twinge of worry for the girl, as apparently did Charles. However, Charles merely inclined his head slightly and then walked out.

Once Charles and his people had all left, Alicia glanced at Frankie Lee. "Let's go."

"What *will* you do with her?" he asked.

Alicia leaned as close as she could get without her lips touching his and whispered, "Don't ask questions I don't feel like answering."

He hadn't ever been intimidated by much, but he knew when to have a healthy respect for a predator. Alicia was definitely on the predator list, and maybe her attitude *should* intimidate him. She'd shot him when he walked in her door, shot up the tavern, and in general, seemed pretty quick on the trigger. Frank could hear his mother's voice in his memories: *Don't poke a rattler, Francis. No matter how contrary you're feeling. Good sense keeps a person alive.* He grinned. He was already dead now, and by the way Alicia had reacted to Lewis's death, Frank was pretty sure that the permanent sort of death was rare.

"I suspect you're aiming to intimidate me. I probably should step back, but"—Frank stood up, invading her space as he did so—"I've grown up with hard-ass women. Tell me what you have in mind for the girl, *please*?"

"Charles likes her. He won't strike her easily, and I've been thinking about ways to spruce up the inn. He's a pushover for music, so she must be good. We cater to a . . . *rougher* crowd, so it's a high-risk spot. I can't lure his favorites away, but this time . . ." Alicia shrugged. "She can work at my inn, and she'll be safe because Charles is fond of her and, aside from the people who work for me, no one crosses him."

"Smart." Frank smiled at her, and they walked toward the door. "I think I'll like working for you."

"Who says you're hired?"

Frank opened the door. "All the same, I might as well walk back that way."

Alicia laughed, and together they crossed the weird city in comfortable silence. Once the General Store was in view, she linked her arm with his. "You did good work."

"Thank you, Alicia."

She stopped in the street. "I guess you ought to go home."

"Home?"

Alicia gestured at the inn across the street. An unknown man stood at the door watching them. "Milt will give you a key to whichever room's yours. It's not fancy, but it's ours."

"Ours," Frank repeated.

"I do try to take care of what's mine, Frankie Lee."

"I'm sorry about Lewis."

She nodded. "You might get truly killed working for me. I'll need to be telling the rest of the boys later, but before you decide—"

"Decided when we were there." Frank shrugged. "I like having a family. Yours feels like home to me."

"Thank you." Alicia smiled then and added, "Guess your interview was promising after all."

Frank chuckled. "Yes, ma'am."

He had a healing gunshot wound in his thigh, a job, and a home. All told, Frankie Lee figured that it was the best day he'd had since he died. Being dead wasn't anything like the preacher said it would be, but considering the life Frankie Lee had led, that wasn't such a bad thing. He nodded his head at his boss and headed off to find his room.

"Frankie Lee?"

He paused and looked at her.

"Is it as bad as all that over there?" she asked haltingly. "It's been a while since I was alive."

Frankie Lee thought about the bullets that had ended his own life. *A bullet is a bullet.* The difference was how many of them tore into him that day. He shrugged. "I won't be eager for those thirty years to end."

"Oh." Alicia faltered, but it lasted only a moment before she said, "Maybe it'd be good for you to tell me what's new over there in the living world; I can't take care of everyone if I'm out of touch."

And Frankie Lee saw the side of his boss that proved he had done right by trusting his guts: Alicia was good people. He kept his smile subdued and nodded. "You're the boss."

"I am," Alicia agreed before going back into the General Store.

For a minute, Frankie Lee stood there, looking at the strange pioneer-era building, and then out over the city where a towering castle loomed. Eras clashed and coexisted. *Nothing at* all *like the preacher said.* It wasn't the life he'd known or the afterlife he'd expected, but he couldn't wipe the grin off his face. Some things were constant: Finding a place where a person belonged, a job that made a man feel good about himself, and a boss he could respect—those were the keys to a happy life. *Or a happy afterlife, in this case.*

And Go Like This

BY JOHN CROWLEY

John Crowley was born in Maine, grew up in Vermont and Indiana, and ran off to New York City, where he worked on documentary films and began to write novels. He's received three World Fantasy Awards (including a Life Achievement Award) and the Award in Literature of the American Academy and Institute of Arts and Letters. His novels include *Little, Big* and the Aegypt Cycle. Other works include *The Translator* and *Lord Byron's Novel: The Evening Land*. His most recent novel is *Four Freedoms* (2009).

There is room enough indoors in New York City for the whole 1963 world's population to enter, with room enough inside for all hands to dance the twist in average nightclub proximity.

—BUCKMINSTER FULLER

Day and night the jetliners come in to Idlewild fully packed, and fly out again empty. Then the arrivals have to get into the city from the airports—special trains and buses have been laid on, of course, day and night crossing into the city limits and returning, empty bean cans whose beans have been poured out, but the waits are long. The army of organizers and dispatchers, who have been recruited from around the world for this job—selfless, patient as saints, minds like adding machines, yet still liable to fainting fits or outbursts of rage, God bless them, only human after all—meet and meet and sort and sort the incomers into neighborhoods, into streets in those neighborhoods, addresses, floors, rooms. They have huge atlases and records supplied by the city government, exploded plans of every building. They pencil each room and then mark it in red when fully occupied.

Still there are far too many arriving to be funneled into town by that process, and thousands, maybe tens of thousands, finally set out walking from the airport. It's easy enough to see which way to go. Especially people are walking who walk anyway in their home places, bare or sandaled feet on dusty roads, with children in colorful slings at their breasts or bundles on their heads—those are the pictures you see in the special editions of *Life* and *Look,* tall Watusis and small people from Indochina and Peru. Just walking, and the sunset towers they go toward. How beautiful they are, patient, unsmiling in their native dress, the Family of Man.

We have set out walking too, but from the west. We've calculated how long it will take from our home, and we've decided that it can't take longer than the endless waits for trains and planes and buses, to say nothing of the trip by car. No matter how often we've all been warned not to do it, *forbidden* to do it (but who can turn them back once they've set out?), people have been piling into their station wagons and sedans, loading the trunks with coolers full of sandwiches and pop, a couple of extra jerricans of gas—about a dollar a gallon most places!—and setting out as though on some happy expedition to the national parks. Now those millions are coming to a halt, from New Jersey, north as far as Albany, and south to Philadelphia, a solid mass of them, like the white particles of precipitate forming in the beaker in chemistry class, drifting downward to solidify. Then you have to get out and walk anyway, the sandwiches long gone and the trucks with food and water far between.

No, we've left the Valiant in the carport and we're walking, just our knapsacks and identification, living off the land and the kindness of strangers.

There was a story in my childhood, a paradox or a joke, which went like this: Suppose all the Chinamen have been ordered to commit suicide by jumping off a particular cliff into the sea. They are to line up single file and each take his or her turn, every man, woman, and child jumping off, one after the other. And the joke was that the line would never end. For the jumping-off of so many would take so long, even at a minute a person, that at the back of the line lives would have to be led by those waiting their turn, and children would be born, and more children, and children of those children even, so that the line would go on and people would keep jumping forever.

This, no, this wouldn't take forever. There was an end and a terminus and a conclusion, there was a finite number to accommodate in a finite space—that was the *point*—though, of course, there would be additions to the number of us along the way; that was understood and accounted for, the hospital spaces of the city have been specially set aside for mothers-to-be nearing term, and, anyway, how much additional space can a tiny newborn use up? In those hospitals too are the old and the sick and, yes, the dying, it's appalling how many will die in this city in this time, the entire mortality of Earth, a number not larger than in any comparable period, of course, maybe less, for that matter, because this city has some of the best medical care on Earth and doctors and nurses *from around the world* have also been assigned to spaces in clinics, hospitals, asylums, overwhelmed as they might be looking over the sea of incapacity, as though every patient who ever suffered there has been resurrected and brought back, hollow-eyed, gasping, unable to ambulate.

But they are there! That's what we're not to forget, they are all there with us, taking up their allotted spaces—or maybe a little more because of having to lie down, but never mind, they'll all be back home soon enough, they need to hang on just a little longer. And every one who passes away before the termination, the all clear, whatever it's to be called—will be replaced, very likely, by a newborn in the ward next door.

And what about the great ones of the world, the leaders and the presidents-for-life and the field marshals and the members of parliaments and presidiums, have they really all come? If they have, we haven't been informed of it—of course, there are some coming with their nations, but the chance of being swallowed up amid their subjects or constituents, suffering who-knows-what indignities and maybe worse, has perhaps pushed a lot of them to slip into the city unobserved on special flights of unmarked helicopters and so on, to be put up at their embassies or at the Plaza or the Americana or in the vast apartments of bankers and arms dealers on Park Avenue. Surely they have left behind cohorts of devoted followers, henchmen, whatever, men who can keep their fingers on the red button or their eyes on the skies, just in case it has all been a trap, but we have to be realistic: Not every goatherd in Macedonia, every bushman in the Kalahari is going to be rounded up, and they don't need to be for this to work—you can call your floor thoroughly swept even if a few twists of dust persist under the couch, a lost button beneath the radiator. *The best is the enemy of the good.* He's an engineer, he must know that.

And it *is* working. They are filling, from top to bottom, all the great buildings, the Graybar Building, the Pan Am Building, Cyanamid, American Metal Climax, the Empire State—a crowd of Dutch men and women and children fill the souvenir shop at the top of the Empire State Building, milling, handling the small models, glass, metal, plastic, of the building they are in. The Metropolitan Museum is filling as though for a smash-hit opening, Van Gogh, Rembrandt; the Modern as for a Pollack retrospective or Op Art show; there is even champagne! How is it that certain people have managed to gather with people like themselves, as on Fifth Avenue, at the Catholic diocesan headquarters, Scribner's bookshop, the University Club, whereas old St. Patrick's is crowded with just everybodies, as though they had all come together to pray for rain in a drought or to be safe from an invading army? They *are* the invading army!

We know so little, really, plodding along footsore and amazed and yet strangely elated among the millions, the *river of humanity,* as Ed Sullivan said in his last column in the *Daily News* before publishing was suspended for the duration. The broad streets (Broadway!) just filled all the way across with persons, a river breaking against the fronts of the dispatcher stations, streams diverted uptown, which is north more or less, downtown, which is south. And now the flood is at last beginning to lessen, to loosen, a vortex draining away into the shops and the apartments, the theaters and the restaurants.

She and I have received our assignment. The building is in Manhattan, below Houston Street, which we have learned divides the newer parts of the city from the older parts. Though old Greenwich Village is mostly above it and all of Wall Street is below it. We would like to have been ushered down that far, to find a space for ourselves in one of those titans of steel and glass, where perhaps we could look out at the Statue of Liberty and the emptied world. We were surprised to find we both wished for that! I'd have thought she'd want a small brownstone townhouse on a shady street. Anyway, it's neither of those, it's a little loft on the corner of Spring Street and Lafayette Street, an old triangular building just five stories tall. Looking down on us from the windows on the east side of the street as we walk that way are Italian men and women, not people just arrived from Italy but the families who live in those places, for that's Little Italy there, and the plump women in housedresses, black hair severely pulled back, and the young men with razor-cut hair and big wristwatches are the tenants there. They're waving and shouting comments down to the crowd endlessly passing, friendly comments or maybe not so friendly, hostile even maybe, their turf invaded, not the right attitude for now.

But here we are, number 370, we wait our turn to go in and up. Stairs to the third floor. It seems artists now live in the building, they are allowed to, painters, we smell linseed oil and canvas sizing. Our artist is lean, scrawny almost, his space nearly empty, canvases leaning against the wall, their faces turned away. We look down—maybe shy—and can see in the cracks of the old floorboards what she says are *metal snaps,* snaps for clothing, from the days when clothes were made here by immigrants. Our artist is either happy to see us or not happy, excited and irritated; that's probably universal. We are all cautious about saying anything much to him or to one another, after all *he* didn't invite us. *Okay, okay* he keeps saying. Is that dark brooding resentful girl in the black leotard and Capezios his girlfriend?

Well, better here than in some vast factory floor in the borough of Queens or train shed in Long Island City, or out on Staten Island, not much different from where we come from. The ferries are leaving from Manhattan's tip for Staten Island every few minutes, packed with people to the gunwales or the scuppers or whatever those outside edges are called. World's cheapest ocean voyage, they say, just a nickel to cross the whitecapped bay; Lady Liberty, Ellis Island deserted and derelict over that way, where once before the millions came into New York City to be processed and checked and sent out into the streets. The teeming streets. *I lift my lamp beside the golden door.* For a moment, thinking of that, looking down at those little metal snaps that slipped from women's fingers fifty, sixty years ago, it all seems to make sense, a human experiment, a *proof* of something finally and deeply good about us and about this city, though we don't know what, not exactly.

It's the last day, the last evening; we're lucky to have arrived so late, there won't be problems with food supplies or sleeping arrangements that others are having. The plan has worked so smoothly! All the populations are being accommodated, there are fights and resistance reported in various locations, but these are being handled by the large corps of specially trained, minimally armed persons—*not* police, not soldiers, for the police forces and the armies were the first to arrive and be distributed, for obvious reasons—because they could be ordered to, and because of what they might do if left behind till last. And now it's done: Everywhere, in every land, palm and pine, the planners and directors and their staffs have taken off their headsets, removed the reels of tape from the ranks of computers huge as steel refrigerators, shut down their telephone banks and telex machines—a network of information tools reaching around the world, whose only goal has been this, this night. They have boarded the last 707s to leave Bombay, Leningrad, Johannesburg and been taken just like all the others to the airports in New Jersey and Long Island, and when they have deplaned, the crews, too, leave the airplanes parked and take the last buses into the city, checking their assignments with one another, joking—pilots and stewies; they're used to bunking in strange cities. When the buses have been emptied, the drivers turn them off and leave them in the streets, head for the distribution centers for assignments. Last of all, the dispatchers, all done: They can hardly believe it, not an hour's sleep in twenty-four, their ad hoc areas littered with coffee cups, telexes, phone slips, fanfold paper, cartons from the last Chinese restaurants. They gather themselves and go out into the bright streets—the grid is holding!—and they take themselves to wherever they have assigned themselves, not far, because they're walking, all the trains and taxis have stopped, no one left to ride or drive them; they mount the stairs or take the elevators up to where they are to go.

It's done. The streets now empty and silent. *The city holds its breath,* they will say later.

In our loft space we have been given our drinks and our canapés. It's not silent here: We allow ourselves to joke about it, about our being here, we demand fancy cocktails or a floor show, but in a just-kidding way—actually it's strangely hard to mingle. She and I stick together, but we often do that at parties. We stand at the windows; we think they look toward the southeast, in the direction of most of the world's population, though we can't see anything, not even the night sky. Every window everywhere is lit.

But think of the darkness now over all the nightside of Earth. The *primeval* darkness. For all the lights out there have been turned off, or not turned on, perhaps not *all*, but so many. The quiet of all that world, around the Earth and back again almost to here where we stand, this little group of islands, these buildings alight and humming, you can almost hear the murmur and the milling of the people.

He was right. It could be done; he knew it could be and it has been, we've done it. There's a kind of giddy pride. Overpopulation is a myth! There are so few of us compared to Spaceship Earth's vastness; we can feel it now for certain in our hearts, we hear it with our senses.

But—many, many others must just now be thinking it, too—there's more. For now the whole process must be reversed, and they, we, have to go home again. To our home places, spacious or crowded. And won't we all remember this, won't we think of how for a moment we were all together, so close, a brief walk or a taxi ride all that separates any one of us from any other? And won't that change us, in ways we can't predict?

Did he expect that, did he think of it? Did he *know* it would happen? Moon-faced little man in his black horn-rims, had he known this from the start?

One final test, one final proof only remains. We've received our second drink. At the turntable our host places the 45 on the spindle and lets it drop. In every space in the city just at this moment, the same: on every record player, over every loudspeaker. The needle rasps in the groove—maybe there's a universal silence

Noble Rot

BY HOLLY BLACK

Holly Black is the bestselling author of several contemporary fantasy novels. Her books include *Tithe, Valiant, Ironside,* The Spiderwick Chronicles (with Tony DiTerlizzi), and the graphic novel series The Good Neighbors (with Ted Naifeh). She lives in Amherst, Massachusetts, with her husband, Theo, in a house with a secret library.

Agatha picks up the paper bag off of the counter. Grease has already soaked through the bottom. She hates this job, but not as much as the one before this one, when she worked as a janitor and the night watchman kept asking her for neck massages. Or the one before that where she washed endless stacks of dishes. She's tired of moving so much, tired of crappy jobs, but that doesn't mean that she will stop.

Stopping means going home, which means she can't stop.

"It's the rock star," John, the boss's son, says, holding out a receipt with an address on it. "Your boyfriend."

John's younger than she is—maybe too young to work as much as he does—but he's the only one who can translate stuff into Korean for his parents. She's pretty sure he lies to them.

It makes her like him more.

"That's the end of my shift," she says, peeling bills out of her pocket. "I'm going to take off after I drop this off, so let me pay for his food."

"I delivered to him once," says John. "I don't care how much you loved his music, it's not worth it. That guy is creepy."

"His music was pretty good," she says, but he just shrugs because he's already answering the phone and scratching out the next order.

She passes the corner 7-Eleven, flashing with neon, its parking lot crowded with cars. Kids from Long Branch and Deal and Elberon looking to buy drugs, partiers spilling from clubs or just pausing to flirt in person after a slow cruise down Main Street. Tattoos wrap around their arms and fabric sticks to their skin.

Her stomach growls.

Over the sticky sweet reek of spilled Slurpees, she can smell the salty air blowing off the sea. It gets on everything, tangling her hair and dusting her skin. As she unlocks her bike, a discarded newspaper warns of a fresh grave dug up in the Mount Calvary Cemetery and a body chewed on by dogs.

Once, Asbury Park was a resort city to tempt presidents with its glittering hotels and merry-go-rounds housed in fantastical buildings with sculpted Medusa faces making the spines of the windows. After those days faded, the city was at least a place that turned out rock stars—Southside Johnny and the Asbury Jukes, Springsteen, Bon Jovi, Colin Lainhart—all of them playing The Stone Pony before going on to take over the world. Now, Colin Lainhart is dying in a cavernous loft, and speculation about a marauding pack of corpse-eating dogs is the only thing worth putting on the front page.

She bikes to one of the row houses near the boardwalk. Despite the influx of renovators and bright rainbow flags hanging from freshly painted houses, the block is still kind of shady. Guys sitting on their stoops call to her when she passes. She reminds herself that the guys are probably harmless—their faces are leathery with drugs and age—and she's stronger than she looks. Faster too.

After she locks the bike to a telephone pole, she takes the bag out of the basket. It's so soaked that the brown paper tears when her fingers touch it, but she can still carry it if she's careful. She hits the doorbell and waits for Colin Lainhart to buzz her in.

John's wrong about him being creepy. Colin Lainhart has cancer or something and he's lonely, but that's all. Sometimes she can smell the illness on him, devouring him from the inside. And he doesn't ask her to do anything bad; most of the time she's not even sure he notices she's there.

Agatha takes the stairs. "Hey," she calls. The inside of the loft has no walls. Once, Colin told her that he and his wife tore them out, planning to restore it, but they only got as far as putting in the electric before he got sick. The wires are exposed, running back and forth along joists like veins.

Agatha read that he'd met his wife when they were both addicts. Supposedly he was the reason she finally went to rehab. There's a famous picture of her from back then that Agatha saw in a magazine somewhere—stringy bright-red hair with heavy black roots, knees skinned, vomiting her guts onto a street in Tokyo. She wants to ask Colin about that, about the pictures of him with loads of curling, dark hair and a hungry smile, but he doesn't seem like he knows the man in those photos.

She didn't like his music when she was younger. It bothered her the way that it seemed like Colin's songs were carefree, but if you listened to the words, they were about despair and death and misery. It made her feel like she was being tricked, like he was laughing at the audience when he sang. Agatha's best friend when she was eleven, Selena, was obsessed with his songs. Selena played them over and over again until Agatha finally admitted they were good.

They were good; she just didn't like how they made her feel.

His hair is growing back, a thin dusting on his head, but his cheeks look hollowed out. He's as thin as if he were made of twigs. His black T-shirt hangs in folds off his shoulders. In the dim light from the bare bulbs on the ceiling, she has never been able to tell what color his eyes are. In the old pictures of him, they were beach-glass green.

"Cash's on the table," he says. His throat sounds scraped raw. All around him are cardboard boxes of vinyl records. Some of them are opened, and discs surround him on the sofa in haphazard piles.

The sofa is a beautiful thing, part sleek black tufted leather, but with silver coffin trimmings. It had come with the records and a few boxes of other things his wife no longer wanted after the divorce.

She got the apartment in the city and a lot of his money. But he still has enough that he can just stare out the massive wall of windows overlooking the sea or at his tiny black-and-white television, order Chinese, and wait to die.

"I know," she says, setting down the bag carefully on a box

near where he's sitting. "I took an extra twenty. You're an excellent tipper."

"Do you want some lo mein?" he asks.

She hasn't taken any money yet, but she knows where he keeps it—a lacquered box on the makeshift table. She doubts he counts it. She could probably take eighty bucks, a hundred, all of it, without him noticing. "You shouldn't let people take advantage of you."

He shrugs.

She goes into the kitchen, gets out two bowls, and brings them to the bag of food. He forks out noodles and hands her the bigger bowl.

"How come you always eat at night?" she asks him.

"I got used to it on the road," he says, and smiles a little. He's easy to be around. He has kind eyes. "Once a day. Like a snake."

She picks up the controller and turns on the television, flicking through the channels. They watch a reality television show where a guy from a glam-rock hair band has to pick a girlfriend. Colin laughs every time the guy talks to the camera, because Colin knows him and can't believe how normal the show has made him seem.

"There was this one time that we were opening for him, and after we get offstage, there's this delay. His whole band is onstage, but not him," Mr. Lainhart says during the commercial break. "The tour manager had already gotten into plenty of fights and doesn't want another one, so he sends me back to his dressing room. And you know what he's doing?"

Agatha shakes her head.

"He's got one of those tiny cocktail stirrers and he's down in the corner of his dressing room with two naked groupies, snorting up lines of live ants. Ants!"

"As in bugs?" Agatha asks him. "*Ant* ants?"

He laughs a little, which makes him cough. "Yeah, the really tiny ones. Sugar ants. I'm glad that he didn't try for a big black carpenter ant. That thing would have chewed off his nose."

She leans back against the leather. "So what's the sickest thing you've ever done? Anything sicker than the ants?"

"Piss-and-vodka shots." He says it so matter-of-factly that she bursts out laughing.

"Whose?" she asks him, scandalized.

Now he's laughing so hard that he sounds like he's choking. "Mine," he finally chokes out. "What kind of guy do you take me for? I wouldn't drink someone else's piss."

He eventually manages to tell her the story about a town in Indiana where there was a little bar and he and his bandmates and his wife, Nancy, were all drinking there after a show and some grizzled old badass goaded him—and the rest of the band, with the exception of the drummer—into a drinking contest that turned both nasty and brutally competitive. "I didn't even win," he says. "Nancy did. She could drink more than any guy."

"I've been there," Agatha says when she's stopped laughing. "The town, anyway, not the bar."

He looks at her "You always say that. You've been everywhere. How come you move around so much?"

"I'm an adventurer," she says.

"No, really," he says. "You sound like me when I was your age."

"I left home when I was thirteen," she says with a shrug. "And I wear out my welcome elsewhere pretty fast, too."

"Now you really sound like me," he says. "It's funny that we never ran into each other in any of those places."

They eat their lo mein in the flickering light of the television, even though Colin complains that he can't taste anything anymore. By the time Agatha leaves, she's hungry again.

When Colin moves, he can feel his chalky bones grinding together. His sinews feel limp, and he worries that his veins are liquefying inside him. His head is swollen, his brain throbbing, as though there is a cyst growing ready to crack open his skull and birth some foul goddess.

For months he hasn't been hungry, but today he feels ravenous. Too tired to call for food, he eats leftovers and crackers that scrape his throat and the last spoonfuls of a pint of diet ice cream that Nancy left, even though it's rimed with frost.

He has stopped the treatments, but only because the doctors told him there was no more they could do. When Nancy left him, she said it wasn't because he was sick but because he'd given up. She needed him to be a fighter. She needed death not to get him down.

He'd said he wanted to fight, but maybe he didn't fight hard enough.

A door slams downstairs, and a man's voice screams, "Slut! Slutty slut slut!"

His neighbors are both out in the street. "You are so self-righteous," shouts the other man. "Like you never—"

There's a crash, like hollow metal hitting concrete. Trash can.

Colin Lainhart believes his neighbors are in love. They're always yelling down staircases, always throwing one another's things out the window and onto the sidewalk, always storming out. Colin thinks they fight a lot harder to be in love than he ever fought the cancer.

He wonders how long it will be until Agatha comes and

brings him dinner. He feels like a dog that scratches at the door. Waiting to be walked. Waiting to be fed. He can tell that she has no idea he's only ten years older than she is. Sickness has made him ancient.

Sometimes he wants to beg her to stay a little longer, but he doesn't want to disturb the illusion that she likes him. He doesn't want her to have to spell it out: *I am just taking pity on you. My mother used to listen to your music.*

The phone rings, and by the time he answers it, he is already tired.

"Colin?" The voice is familiar, but he can't place it.

"Yes," he says.

"It's Mark."

"I know," Colin says, ashamed that for a moment, he didn't. Mark is his lawyer, his college roommate, and, famously, the guy who let Colin sleep on his couch while Colin recorded most of his first album.

"You've got to get out of that town," Mark says. Mark is full of dire pronouncements, like: "If you don't freeze her bank account, you'll lose everything" or "If you don't come back to the city now, you'll become a crazy hermit." Mark was also disappointed when Colin stopped fighting.

Colin laughs.

"Seriously," Mark says. "It's all over the papers. Some kind of necrophilia-necrophagia cult going on down there."

Something crashes outside, and Colin smiles against the phone, hoping that Mark can't hear. Colin's pretty sure that his squabbling neighbors sound enough like a pack of hungry cultists to make Mark worry. He reaches over for his laptop and types into the window of his browser. "Uh, all the local paper has is something about some kids partying in the graveyard and a dog getting into a tomb."

"They're covering it up," says Mark. When Colin just laughs, Mark interrupts him. "When are you going to be in town next?"

"Not gonna be."

"That's ridiculous. What do they want you to do—just lay down and die?"

"They call it making me comfortable," Colin says.

There is a long pause on the other end of the line, and when Mark speaks again, his voice is choked. "I'm an asshole—"

"Don't," Colin says. "Actually, I feel good today. Better than in a while. I might even go out and eat something." Just saying the word *eat* has made his mouth water. He wipes his lips with the back of his hand.

"Your manager says he can't get ahold of you," Mark says, but he doesn't have the surety in his voice that he had before. "Car company wants to license a song for a commercial."

"I'll call him," Colin says, even though he knows he won't. He feels guilty that the conversation has become awkward. More than anything, dying is an embarrassment. "Listen, I got to go. There's a bunch of people outside with torches chanting something about Beelzebub. . . ."

"Fuck off," says Mark, but at least he sounds like himself. "Remember to charge your phone. And to answer it."

The bones of Colin's spine pop as he stands to put his phone back in the charging dock, but after he's up, he doesn't feel so bad. His stomach growls and he pulls on a hat and sunglasses, despite the heat, and decides that he's going to go outside after all.

When Agatha knocks on his door next, it isn't because he's ordered anything. She's carrying a carton anyway. She feels a little stupid when she hits the bell, but she's afraid that he's not going to answer and then she's going to have to decide if she should break in to see if he died.

He buzzes her up like usual, without even talking into the speakers. There's music playing, and when she gets upstairs, he's sitting by the window and playing a guitar. She recognizes the song he's playing: It's one of his, but he's playing it so slowly that the music sounds as mournful as the words. She wonders if this was how he wrote the songs, how they were supposed to be played. She hopes so. This music isn't laughing at anyone.

His hair looks almost grown in, military short rather than sickness short, like a rock star who's no longer dying might have, and it makes her aware that no matter how friendly he seems, she has no reason to be standing in his loft. He doesn't seem surprised to see her, though.

"Oh," says Agatha. "I thought maybe something happened."

He looks at her quizzically. "What's wrong?"

"It's been three days since you ordered any food," she says. "I didn't know if you were just ordering from some other place or if you were sick or what. I'm sorry. I should—"

"Three days," he repeats, like he doesn't believe it. He looks out the window again, like he's going to check the position of the Earth, but it's dark. All there is to see are glittering lights and the immense blackness of the ocean. "I went out."

"Today?" she asks.

"I don't know," he says. "I got strawberries."

She puts down the bag of fried rice and goes into the kitchen. Standing there, near the refrigerator and the board supported by sawhorses, she realizes just how inappropriate she's been, rummaging through his things. But the strawberries in their plastic green basket are right there on the mock-counter. She comes back out with them covered in a fine gray mold and pocked with brownish patches. "Not today, I think."

"Maybe it has been three days." He picks one off the top and brushes off the gauzy threads. "Noble rot," he says, and pops it in his mouth. It is so soft that some of it squirts onto his lip.

"What?"

"Decay concentrates the sweetness," he says.

She's staring at him in disbelief. He grins, and it's the smile she remembers from the photos. Rapacious. Unappeasable. It makes her smile, too.

"It's gross, I know," he says. "I'm just so hungry. And it's not like I'm drinking my own piss."

She holds up the box of fried rice. "It's yours if you want it. My treat."

He takes the box from her, unfolding the paper and cupping rice in his palm. He shovels it into his mouth as she watches him.

Then, abruptly, he spits something out. It hits the floor hard, like a rock, and she can see that it's a small gold earring, wrapped with a wisp of hair. "Ugh," he says wiping his mouth.

Agatha bends down and picks up the earring. She rolls it in her fingers, hardly able to believe what's happening. There's a tiny piece of what looks like skin attached; she hopes he doesn't notice.

She has made a terrible mistake.

"I don't know how that got in there," she says quickly. "It must belong to one of the cooks."

Colin is watching her with a strange expression.

"I better take it back to the restaurant," she says.

"We should call the police." He sits down on his couch, not looking at her. He reaches for his cell phone, but he doesn't dial.

"It's just an earring." Agatha holds it up to her own ear and lets it dangle. She feels guilty, but keeps talking. She has to convince him not to make any calls. "Let me at least go back and see if someone lost it. Then we can call the police."

He nods. "Leave the earring here, okay?"

She sets it down carefully on the coffee table, brushing off what's attached to it. She looks over at him, not sure what she's hoping to see, but his face is blank.

Out the window, he watches her go, watches her head in the wrong direction for the restaurant.

He goes to the kitchen and pokes through the box of food with a single chopstick. Then he leans down to smell it. There's a lot of thick, brown sauce and underneath that, a strange rich smell. Almost sweet. Rot.

All the next day, Agatha doesn't go over to Colin's apartment, not even when he calls the restaurant and asks for her specifically, although that does get her a lot of teasing.

Even worse, John catches Agatha eating a piece of maggoty pork from the trash in the alley behind the restaurant.

He drops the plastic bags he was dragging. "Are you crazy? You can't put that in your mouth!"

Unprepared, she just gapes at him. "I didn't do anything wrong," she says finally. He fires her anyway and—she's pretty sure—lies to his parents about the reason.

By the time Agatha enters the graveyard, she is hungry and tired and sad. She wants to curl up in inside one of the crypts, but she knows she has to be careful. Nesting near graves is stupid.

But as her sharp little teeth rend gray flesh, she thinks of the great ghoul city her mother told stories about when Agatha was little—its walls wet with silt, its spires sparkling with the reflected light of lichen deep beneath the earth. In that mythical place, all the ghouls of the world could cool themselves in the city's shadow and no one had to be careful.

Sometimes Agatha imagines that ghoul city aboveground—here—where meat would spoil fast in the hot sun. In that dream, she doesn't have to keep moving. There is no series of jobs or haphazard nests. And she doesn't have to make a choice between Colin dying or hating her.

An abrupt movement near the gate is enough to snap her out of her reverie and make her move, locking the crypt and sticking to shadows. She hears footsteps, but they are receding.

She pauses at the stone wall at the edge of the graveyard, where dirt and lime and ink and blood marks tell the story of all the ghouls who have passed through. *No police,* reads one. *Good eating,* says another. Agatha makes a thick chalk mark on the wall. *Territory,* it means. *Mine.*

She is pushing her bike home, lethargic with satiation, when she sees a woman who looks familiar getting out of a Mercedes. For a moment, Agatha freezes, unable to figure how someone she knows is here, when she realizes that she doesn't know the woman at all.

She's Nancy, Colin's wife. She's famous.

Another woman has gotten out of the driver's side. She is in a tailored navy suit and slinging the strap of a soft leather briefcase over her shoulder.

Agatha follows them down the long dark street, matching her stride to theirs, staying close to the shadows. The carrion in her belly makes her feel strong, and her fingers flex restlessly.

The women stop in front of the apartment and press the buzzer. Then they wait, more impatient by the moment. Nancy flips open her cell phone and presses a few buttons with her thumb. Then her friend says something and she laughs, harshly.

Agatha watches them and her heart starts to speed faster, like her body has already decided on something.

"What were you doing?" Colin comes out of the shadows behind Agatha, forcing her into the light. He smells of vomit and his gaze locks on her. Accusing.

"I didn't . . ." Agatha starts, but doesn't know how to finish. She doesn't know how to deny doing what she was thinking without admitting she was thinking it.

"There you are," Nancy says to Colin. "Are you using again? You look awful."

"This is Agatha," Colin says stiffly. "And this is Nancy and Whitney."

Agatha lifts her hand in a half wave.

"I'm the lawyer," Whitney says. Agatha wonders what Nancy needs a lawyer for now, here. They are already divorced.

"Is she a fan?" Nancy says.

"I never asked. I don't even know if she likes music," says Colin, which sounds sordid and isn't even true, but Agatha doesn't correct him. "Let's go up."

"I should probably let you guys have your meeting or whatever," Agatha says.

Colin shakes his head, his fingers closing around her arm. "We need to talk."

She lets him lead her toward the elevator; one look at his face and it is clear that he knows something. But what he knows or what he thinks or what he can guess is so unclear that all she can do is stare at the floor of the elevator and panic.

"Were you sick?" Whitney asks Colin as the smell of vomit is unmistakable in that small space.

"I am sick," he says, and no one speaks into the uncomfortable silence.

Nancy walks around the room, stopping to stand by the windows. "You should hire someone to come here and finish the renovation. A healthy environment puts you in a healthy frame of mind."

"What's the point?" he says.

Nancy throws up her hands and looks at Whitney.

"You know how stubborn he can be," Whitney says, and the way she and Colin exchange smiles seems weirdly intimate. Agatha is suddenly sure that Colin has slept with both of the other women in the room.

"I'm sorry," Colin says suddenly. "Agatha and I are going to go and see what we can rustle up in the kitchen. Right, Agatha?"

Because there is nothing else for her to do, Agatha answers, "Right."

The room reels around him, and he holds on to the wooden joist in the door frame. The sickness has mostly passed, and what he feels, most of all, is hunger deep in his belly. A kind of hunger that reminds him uncomfortably of the beginnings of withdrawal.

"Let me smell your breath," he says, leaning toward her.

She frowns, ducking her head, but smiling. "What? Why? Do you think I'm drunk?"

I watched you eat someone, he wants to say. *I followed you to a graveyard and saw you break the lock on a tomb with your bare hands. I gagged on the smell, threw up leaning against the rusty iron gate, and, after, my mouth watered. I want to know if your breath smells like dead flesh so that I can prove to myself that I'm not crazy.*

"I saw you," he says instead. He wonders if she imagines sinking her teeth into his flesh, if she's been patiently waiting for him to ripen in death, like the strawberries on his counter. He should be disgusted, but he's fascinated.

Agatha has opened the cabinet above the sink in the makeshift kitchen. There are dusty packets of tea in there and some honey. When he speaks, she turns toward him, her hand still reaching. She looks startled, her tumble of dark hair pushed back behind one ear. A normal, pretty girl with sharp teeth.

"In the graveyard," he says.

Her fingers close on the honey but don't seem to grip it. He watches as it slips. The bottle cracks on the wooden floor, thick amber fluid spreading slowly from between the shards of glass.

"I'm sorry," she says, voice shaking, apologizing for more than the honey. He realizes that he was waiting for her denial. He was ready to believe that despite the fact he'd seen her hunched over a corpse, it was some kind of joke—some new phase of his sickness involving hallucinations.

She's talking, saying something about not knowing how to tell him, saying that she didn't think he'd believe her, but he can't seem to focus on the words.

He interrupts her. "What are you?"

"A ghoul," Agatha says.

Nancy steps into the room, looking at Agatha like she overheard at least the end of that exchange. "Colin? Are you alright? I thought I heard glass . . ."

They both turn toward Nancy, and there's something about their expressions that makes her step back.

"Why are you here?" he asks.

Nancy looks over at Agatha. "I was hoping we could talk. Just us."

"And Whitney?" he asks.

Nancy hesitates.

"Go ahead," says Agatha, with a quick smile. "I'll make the tea."

He sighs, trying to give Agatha a look that says: *Okay, but if you try and sneak out, I will forget about politeness and I will run after you, and there is no way this conversation is over*—and realizing that she's probably not getting anything like that from his expression. She could interpret his look as *I have a headache* or *I think I misheard you, because I heard "ghoul" and you clearly meant "girl."* He follows Nancy back to the living room and sits down next to her on the sofa. She's lost some weight since he saw her last, and her fingernails, despite being freshly polished, are bitten to the quick.

He watches her reach over and take his hand. He glances in Whitney's direction, but she's looking carefully at his guitar.

"I talked to Mark," Nancy says. His expression must have been so completely surprised that she corrects herself. "Okay,

Whitney talked to Mark. I can't believe you're living like this. Are you trying to punish yourself?"

"Punish myself for what?"

She shrugs her shoulders. "All the drugs. You know—you would always say that if it hadn't been for your job, that maybe we would have never gotten as bad as we did. That it was your fault."

He remembered saying that, now that she mentioned it, back when they both were trying to stay clean. All their awful flaws and insecurities and desires ballooned along with his career. There was just so much money, and with the money, temptation. "That was a long time ago."

"Your mother called me. She says you won't talk to her. She wants you to come home."

"Why are you here, Nancy? I know what my mother wants. I'm not dying in the same house I spent a lot of years trying to get out of, so if you came all the way down here to suggest it, don't."

Nancy flinches. "Someone's got to take care of you. You were never good at doing it for yourself. If you're not going to your mother, then I'm going to have to do it."

Agatha enters the room, carrying a collection of mugs that clink together as she walks. She sets them down on the box near the couch. "I couldn't find any sugar, but there was milk. I put it in one of the mugs."

"Does she have to be here?" Nancy asks Colin.

"She's not going anywhere," he says.

Whitney starts to speak, but Colin cuts her off. "You're not going anywhere, either. Everyone just sit down."

Agatha pours milk from one mug into her tea and takes a sip. Nancy does the same, and then spits out the liquid.

"How can you drink that? The milk's bad. There's chunks floating in it."

"Let me try," Colin says. He looks right at Agatha when he takes a sip. He knows that it's going to be sour, but the taste isn't as bad as he anticipated. It reminds him of yogurt. "Tastes fine," he says and laughs.

Agatha smiles and gulps from her cup. He wishes that he and Agatha were alone, that they could talk. He wants answers. He keeps thinking about her sharp teeth and what they would feel like against his skin. What her mouth would feel like.

"What's going on?" Nancy says. "Are you two on something?"

"A dying man gets painkillers, right?"

"He's not on anything," Whitney says with a sigh. "He's messing with your head."

"Did Mark tell you that?" Nancy demands. "Colin could be scoring anywhere—from his doctors even."

Whitney crosses her legs and gives Colin a sly look. She speaks slowly, like she's bored. "I know because I know how he looks when he's messing with you."

"She's right," Colin said, holding up his hands in surrender. "I apologize."

Whitney opens her briefcase and takes out some papers. "Maybe I should explain what we're here about. I brought some papers that would give Nancy general power of attorney. Do you know what that is?"

Colin shakes his head. "Sounds legal. Does Mark know you're here?"

Agatha picks up the mugs and walks toward the kitchen. He turns toward her, wanting to tell her to stop acting like a maid, but her back is to him. He wonders if years of restaurant work have made bringing and removing food into a ritual.

"This is just a proposal," says Whitney. "If you sign this, Nancy would be your agent in taking care of things. She can deal with your health care, finalize the details of certain deals your manager is trying to work out with the rest of the band—basically do everything to make sure that you're comfortable. Nancy feels terrible about the divorce."

"I do," Nancy said, touching his arm.

Whitney clears her throat. "She feels like she left you to fend for yourself at a time when doing so was very difficult, and she wants to make that up to you."

"She thinks I didn't fight hard enough," Colin says numbly.

"I said I lot of things I shouldn't have said." Nancy's hand is still warm on his arm, and it makes him realize how cold his own skin is by comparison. "We were together for a long time, and I shouldn't have just thrown that away."

"No," says Colin.

"I'm glad you agree. Look, the first thing I'm going to do is get someone to come in here and put up some drywall. Then we'll get you some furniture and hire a nurse."

"No," he says again.

"No what?" Nancy asks. "You live like a squatter. It's understandable that you're depressed, that these things are hard to come to terms with, but no one is looking out for your best interests. Imagine the scandal if your body wasn't found for days and then found *here*. Is that how you want to be remembered?"

Whitney flinched visibly. "Nancy—"

He stands up. "I'm already dead in your mind, aren't I? You're already planning my funeral, getting your veil all ready, selling the rights to the tribute album—and what? You're pissed that I won't be a good little corpse and lie down so you can start embalming me?"

"That's not what I'm saying at all! I don't know that you're in a rational frame of mind."

Whitney holds up her hand. "Just think about it, Colin. I know you've still got a lot of anger toward Nancy, but right now she's someone you can trust who really wants a second chance to be there for you. I'm going to leave the papers here, and you can look them over while Nancy and I go and grab a bite to eat. We'll bring you back something, and then we can talk some more." She takes out a gleaming pen and places it atop the papers.

He follows them to the door, and as he looks out at her, weariness overcomes him. When he speaks, his voice is quiet. "You can't go back, you know. We can't. People can't. I can't go back to being the person I was before I was sick, and you can't go back to being that person's wife, because he doesn't exist anymore."

"Of course he does," Nancy says. "He's just sad."

Colin closes and bolts the door behind them, then picks up the legal pages. Walking to the window, he cranks one wide open and drops confetti of ripped white paper onto the street below. *It looks like a parade passed through,* he thinks.

"Agatha?" he calls, but there's no response from the kitchen.

Colin walks in, expecting to find her perched on the countertop or drinking the rest of the bad milk from the carton. But she's not there, and the window to the fire escape is wide open.

On her way down the metal stairs, she runs into one of Colin's neighbors—a pale looking man with floppy bleached hair. He is smoking a cigarette, and the corner of his mouth looks bruised. He scoots over so she can sidle past him.

"Don't like front doors?" he asks her.

"Don't like good-byes," she says. He nods like that makes sense.

She feels bad leaving like this, without explaining to Colin what she's done. She tries to tell herself that he'll figure things out, but she knows that her cowardice will cost him.

As she walks down the road, she thinks about the real first time she met Colin, outside of a club in New Mexico. She'd been washing dishes and was on a break, just leaning against the cool stucco of the building next door and listening to the music.

He'd staggered out a moment later, his shirt wet with sweat, and leaned against the wall, too. Neither of them spoke, but in that moment she could tell that their skin itched the same way. Itched to keep moving, to escape. To keep looking for the mythical city where they would be sheltered in its shadows.

When her break was over and she headed toward the kitchen door, he gave her a look of sympathy that, for a while, made her feel less alone. She hasn't told him that they have run into each other before. She won't ever tell him.

Another memory rises up, unbidden—Colin leaning toward her in the kitchen tonight. His eyes were dark with something that might have been revulsion but that she could pretend was desire. And she hates that she's leaving, but it's better than being around when he realizes how much there is to despise her for.

He watches crows, black wings gleaming like oil, peck garbage strewn across a sandy lawn. The sun hurts his eyes, but he's determined to sit on this bench, near the one place he knows she can't avoid.

Shading his face with a hand as he looks over at the graveyard, he wonders at the garden of white stone and granite. Grander and more austere than the tacky spectacle he's finding dying to be. When he was a kid, all the songs he loved were full of romantic ideas about eternal souls and the deaths beyond death, and finding out how mundane and embarrassing it's turning out to be is lowering, not unlike finding out all the stately Roman buildings had once been painted garish colors.

"Here you are," Agatha says. He jumps a little and turns toward her. She's wearing a silvery sundress and has that horrible earring in one ear. He didn't even notice she'd taken it from his apartment.

"I figured you'd come here eventually," he says.

She sits down next to him on the bench, but she won't meet his eyes. "I figured the same thing about you."

"Why would you say that?" He tilts his head to one side.

She ignores his question. "I want to tell you about ghouls. I came back to tell you—to face you. We live on putrid flesh, we're strong, and we never get sick." She sucks her bottom lip in a nervous gesture. "We live a long time, too. And it's not all bad, the roving."

"Okay," he says.

"See those markings?" She points toward the wall to the graveyard, which is covered in marks like the kind hobos left each other at train stations. "That's how we communicate."

"Are you sure you're supposed to tell me your secrets? I guess it doesn't matter, but—"

"I have to tell you," she says, crouching down beside the bench so that she can trace the marks in the dirt. "Here's how you mark your territory. And here's the symbol for danger. This is the one for safe place—which is similar to this one, for good place."

He stares at the marks. A secret lexicon for a secret life.

"Are you freaked out?" she asks.

"Very," he says, then takes a deep breath and lets it out slowly. "I've been thinking, too, and I want to tell you, I get it. You were waiting for me to die. You've been taking good care of me, bringing me food." He laughs, nervously. His hands are sweating. "But you were getting me ready to eat, right?"

Agatha stares at him silently.

"And I wanted to tell you that I'm okay with that. I mean, I want you to. Go ahead."

She leans very close to him and opens her mouth against the place where his shoulder meets his neck. He can feel her teeth, sharp against his skin. He shivers and he reaches out to pull her against him. She shifts until she's half risen from the ground, leaning between his legs, her body as cool as his own. His heart is speeding, but time has slowed, time is moving like the honey oozing on his floor. "Is this what you pictured?" she says. The movement of her mouth, the scrape of her teeth is exhilarating and awful.

"I don't know," he says. His heart is hammering against his ribs. Every instinct is telling him to push her away, to run, but he slides his hand to her hip and holds himself still. This is better, he tells himself. Because for the first time in months, he feels the thrill of life in every ragged breath.

"You're wrong," she says slowly, drawing back from him.

"Wrong?" His neck throbs where her lips have been.

"I'm not going to eat you, Colin Lainhart. You're not rotten enough for me."

He frowns, disoriented, distracted. "But what did you want, then? I don't understand."

"I like you. I don't have a lot of friends, moving around the way that I do. You're funny and nice, even though you've been ill and in pain. Why wouldn't I like you?"

"I don't know," he says. "People aren't liked because they deserve to be."

"You might wish I didn't like you," she says.

He reaches up and touches her dark hair. It reminds him of the crow's feathers. "Why would I want that?"

She pushes away from him so that she's standing. "I fed you human flesh. In your food. You were so sick that you couldn't tell."

His stomach twists.

"You're going to live," she says. "I sentence you to live."

"Oh." There is a great roaring in his ears, and he rubs his face. Moments ago he felt ancient, but now he feels confused, stumbling like a small child.

"You're like me now. I turned you. You're going to like the taste of spoiled food and things with strong flavors. You will crave human flesh, but you don't have to eat it all the time. Be careful, Colin." With that, she turns and starts walking in the direction of the highway. The crows, startled, go to wing.

"Wait." He stands up and grabs her arm. "You can't leave."

"I'm not sorry." She jerks her arm out of his hand. She's right; she is very strong. "You can't make me say that I'm sorry."

At least she's no longer moving away from him. She's standing right there, breathing as if she's been running.

There are so many things that he wants to tell her. But then he remembers the one thing that he hasn't said, the one thing that matters. "Stay," he says, reaching his hand out to her again, gently this time. "I want you to stay. Please stay. Stay."

Daddy Long Legs of the Evening

BY JEFFREY FORD

Jeffrey Ford is the author of the novels *The Physiognomy, Memoranda, The Beyond, The Portrait of Mrs. Charbuque, The Girl in the Glass,* and *The Shadow Year.* His short fiction has been published in three collections: *The Fantasy Writer's Assistant, The Empire of Ice Cream,* and *The Drowned Life.* His fiction has won the World Fantasy Award, the Nebula Award, the Edgar Award, and Gran Prix de l'Imaginaire. He lives in New Jersey with his wife and two sons and teaches literature and writing at Brookdale Community College.

It was said that when he was a small child, asleep in his bed one end-of-summer night, a spider crawled into his ear, traversed a maze of canals, eating slowly through membrane and organ, to discover the cavern of the skull. Then that spider burrowed in a spiral pattern through the electric gray cake of the brain to the very center of it all, where it hollowed out a large nest for itself and reattached neural pathways with the thread of its web. It played the boy like a zither, plucking the silver strings of its own design, creating a music that directed both will and desire.

Before the invasion of his cranium, the child was said to have been quite a little cherub—big green eyes and a wave of golden hair, rosy cheeks, an infectious laugh. His parents couldn't help showing him off at every opportunity and regaling passersby with a litany of his startling attributes, not the least of which was the ability to recite verbatim the bedtime stories read to him each night. Many a neighbor had been subjected to an oration of the entirety of "The Three Rum Runtkins."

A change inside wrought a change outside, though, and over the course of a few months the boy's eyes bulged and drained of all color to become million-faceted buds of gleaming onyx. His legs and arms grew long and willowy, but his body stayed short with a small but pronounced potbelly, like an Adam's apple in the otherwise slender throat that was his form. Although a fine down of thistle grew in patches across his back, arms, and thighs, he went bald, losing even brows and lashes. His flesh turned a pale gray, hinting at violet; his incisors grew to curving points and needed to be clipped and filed back like fingernails.

Horrified at the earliest of these changes, the boy's parents had taken him, first, to the doctor's, but when the medicine he was given did nothing but make him vomit and the symptoms became more bizarre, they took him to the clinic. The doctors there subjected him to a head scan. Photos from the process showed the intruder in negative, a tiny eight-legged phantom perched at the center of a dark, intricate web. It was determined that were they to remove the arachnid, the boy could very possibly die. The creature had, for all intents and purposes, become his brain. The parents, confessing they feared for their lives, pleaded with the physicians to operate, but the ethical code forbade it, and the family was sent home.

Not long after the trip to the clinic, the boy's mother opened his bedroom door one morning and beheld him suspended in the eye of a silver web that filled the room from floor to ceiling. She meant to scream but the beautiful gleaming symmetry of what he'd made stunned her. She watched as he turned slowly round to face away, and then from a neat hole cut in the back of his trousers that she'd never noticed before came a sudden blast of webbing that smacked her in the face and covered half her body. The door slammed shut as she reeled backward, and this time she *did* scream, tearing madly at the shroud whose sticky threads seemed spun from marshmallow.

Unable to bear the boy's presence any longer, his parents took him for a hike out into the forest. "I know a place where there are flies as big as poodles," his father said, and the boy drooled. They took him deep into the trees, marking the trail as they went, and somewhere miles in, next to a lake, they bedded down on pine needles. While he slept, they quietly rose, tiptoed away, and then, once out of earshot, ran for their lives. They never saw the boy again. Although no one in town could blame them, including the constable, and they faced no charges for their actions, the memory of their fear burrowed in a spiral pattern to the center of their minds and played them like zithers for the rest of their days.

Fifteen years later and a hundred miles from where he'd been born, the boy appeared one evening at the height of summer, not a man but something else. A woman living in an apartment of an otherwise empty building on the east side of the city of Grindly woke suddenly and looked up.

"There was enough moonlight to see him clearly," she said. "He hung above me, upside down, his hands and knees on the ceiling. He wore a jacket with short tails, and the long legs of his satin trousers were striped blue and red. I don't know how that hat—a stovepipe style—stayed on, as it had no chin strap. His feet were in slippers. The moment I saw him, he looked directly into my eyes. It didn't matter that he wore round, rose-colored glasses. Those evil blackberries that lurked behind still dazzled me. I screamed, he shrieked, and then he scuttled across the ceiling and out the open window. I heard him on the roof, and then everything was silent." The woman told her friends, and her friends told their friends, and word that something bizarre had come to Grindly spread like disease.

The *Gazette* put out a double edition, a whole four pages, its entirety devoted to speculation concerning "Daddy Longlegs of the Evening," a moniker invented by the editor in chief. The name stuck, and over the course of a few more days was shortened by the populace, first to "Daddy Longlegs" and then to simply "Daddy." "Watch out for Daddy," neighbors said as a salutation when they parted. Before people bedded down at night, they practiced a ritual of checking closets and basements, the dark corners of attics, and under beds, latching all windows and gathering crude weapons on their nightstands—a mallet, a wrench, a carving knife, a club.

After a few more sightings that he had scrupulously arranged, allowing himself to be spotted, crawling to the top of and then into a silent mill's crumbling smokestack, or traversing the soot-ridden mosaic of God's face on the inner dome of the railway station as the midnight train passed through, he was in their hearts and minds, and what was even more important to him, in their dreams. Of course, he meant to drain the citizenry of Grindly of their bodily fluids, but first, to enhance nourishment, it needed to be filtered, flavored, by nightmare.

When there wasn't a soul within the confines of the city wall who did not, in their dreams, flee slow, heavy, and naked before him, or writhe in the coil of their blankets, mistaken in sleep for his web, he struck. It was deepest night when he entered the home of the haberdasher, Fremin, through the unlocked coal chute. The hinges on the iron door creaked a warning, but that noise was transformed, by the dreams of the sleeping husband and wife, into the triumphant laughter of Daddy Longlegs. They never woke when he bit them at the base of the skull. They never cried out as their fear-laden essence left them.

"Like old worn luggage," the newspaper said, describing the condition of the corpses discovered two days later. When the medics tried to move the haberdasher's body to a stretcher, it split with a whisper like a dry husk and out of it poured thousands of tiny spiders. Police Inspector Kaufmann, the medics, the Fremins' neighbors who were present, all ran out of the building, and the inspector gave orders for the place to be torched at once. As the fire raged, the crowd that had gathered belabored the inspector, Grindly's sole lawman, with inquiries as to what he was prepared to do.

What Kaufmann was prepared to do was run, take the next train out of town for some shining new place free of rot and nightmares. The only thing preventing him was the fact that the train rarely stopped, but sped right through as if there really was no platform or station or city. "If I wait for that," he thought, "we might all be dead by the time it arrives." He turned to the citizens and said, "I'm going to hunt Daddy down and put a bullet in him." Only the inspector knew that it would necessarily have to be "*a* bullet" as he only had one left. Government supplies from the capitol had dried up over a year earlier.

That night, Kaufmann slept slumped over his desk, pistol in hand, and dreamt of a time before the politicians in the capitol had succumbed to a disease of avarice and sapped all of Grindly's resources for themselves. Once known far and wide as the "Nexus of Manufacture," a gleaming machine of commerce, where traffic filled the streets, faces filled the windows, and nobody ate cabbage who didn't want to, the inspector had a police force, enough bullets, and a paycheck. Again, in his sleep, he watched the city slowly rot from the inside out and eventually stood on the platform at the station waving forlornly as even the petty criminals left town.

While Kaufmann dozed, Daddy was busy slipping silently through the shadows. He could smell the terror of the populace, a sweet flower scent that drove his hunger. The music played on the strands of web behind his eyes directed his purpose, negating distraction, as he shuffled up a wall, found an unlocked window, and let the breeze in.

His first victim of that night, the pale and beautiful actress Monique LeDar, who still performed nightly, one-woman shows of the classics, although the stage was lit by candles and squirrels scampered amid the rafters. She awoke in the midst of Daddy's feeding, and he saw her seeing herself in the myriad reflections of his eyes. He stopped, tipped his hat, and continued. She put her wrist to her forehead and perished.

The *Gazette* had the story in its late-morning edition the next day: DADDY'S DOZEN, read the headline. At the end of the lead article that gave a list of the drained and the grisly condition in which each was found, there was printed a formal plea from Inspector Kaufmann for volunteers to help track the killer. That evening, he stood on the sidewalk in front of the Hall of Justice, a mausoleum of an old marble structure, dark and empty inside save for his office. The last set of batteries in the flashlight had died, so, instead, he held like a torch out in front of him a small candelabra of three burning tapers. He'd been waiting for over an hour for the mob of volunteers to form in order to begin the hunt, but, as it was, he stood alone. Taking the gun from his shoulder holster, he was about to strike out on his own when an old woman in a kerchief and a long camel-hair winter coat trundled slowly up to him.

"Can I help you, ma'am?" asked the inspector.

"I volunteer," she said.

He laughed. "This is dangerous work, my dear. We're after a cold-blooded killer."

The old woman opened her pocketbook and took out a blackjack. She waggled the tube of stitched leather with lead in the tip at Kaufmann's face.

"That's an illegal weapon," he said.

"Arrest me," she said, and spat on the sidewalk.

The avenues and side streets of Grindly were empty. Even the drunks stayed home in fear of being drunk themselves. It was slow going and just as lonely for Kaufmann with Mrs. Frey in tow. He'd barely gotten the woman's name out of her. She followed five steps behind, not so much his posse as a haunting spirit. He respected her courage, her sense of civic duty, but found her quiet wheezing and the rhythmic *squish* of her galoshes incredibly annoying, and wondered how long it would be before he used his last bullet on either her or himself.

It was dinnertime in the city that never woke; the scent of boiled cabbage, the skittering of rats along the gutters. Occasionally, there was a lighted window and the distant, muffled sound of a radio or a child's glee or an argument, but for the most part Kaufmann and his deputy passed down empty streets of boarded storefronts and burned-out brownstones, where the echo of the wind sounded like laughter in the shadows.

It was dinnertime for Daddy as well, and he moved along the rooftops, keenly aware of the warm spots in the cold buildings beneath, heat signatures of those who might find themselves on his menu. He was hunting for the essence of the young. His last kill of the previous night had been Tharshmon the watchmaker, a man made old by lack of work and self-respect. No one cared any longer to know the time in Grindly. It was better left unmentioned when the future arrived. As dozens of pocket watches chimed in Tharshmon's studio at 3:00 A.M., Daddy interceded without a struggle. The bereft watchmaker's fluid was overripe, though, insipidly sweet and watery. It gave no energy but bruised the will and loosened the bowels.

Daddy skittered down the side of a four-story apartment building. At the lighted window on the third floor, he settled upon the fire escape. With his face to the glass, he saw two young children dressed in their pajamas, playing in a bedroom. He tried the window, but it was locked. He tapped at the glass with one long nail. Their big pink faces drew close to see him, and even before they undid the latch, his system was creating the chemical needed to digest their juices. He had learned it wasn't helpful to let them see him drool.

At the same moment, three blocks away, Inspector Kaufmann was passing the Waterworks. He turned and peered back up the sidewalk to see Mrs. Frey's bent form inching along through the weak glow of the block's one working streetlight. He set the candelabra on the ground, holstered his gun, and took out his last cigarette. He'd traded a pair of official police handcuffs, with key, for the pack it came from. Leaning down, he lit it on the flame of the center candle. He was cold and tired, and every scrap of newspaper that rolled in the wind or bat that darted out of a blasted window momentarily paralyzed him with fear. He took a drag and heard Mrs. Frey's galoshes drawing closer.

The old woman had nearly caught up and there was still a good half of a cigarette left when he heard a desperate scream come from off to his right. "Shit," he said, flicked the unfinished butt into the gutter, drew his pistol, and ran across the street. There he entered an alley and ran through the dark, avoiding piles of broken furniture and old garbage. The alley gave way to another street and then another alley, and when he was almost winded, there was again a shrill scream, and he saw a woman at an open window three stories up.

"My babies," she wailed. Kaufmann scanned the sides of the buildings for Daddy. He heard something move amidst the trash and caught a darker spot in the darkness out of the corner of his eye. As he lifted the gun, something wet and sticky smacked him in the face. He fired blindly.

By the time Kaufmann had wiped the web from his eyes, Daddy was gone, the distraught mother above had spotted the inspector and was yelling for his assistance, and behind him, Mrs. Frey, pocketbook on her wrist, the candelabra in her right hand, the blackjack in her left, shuffled inexorably closer. The inspector dropped the gun and ran away.

Daddy sat atop the smokestack of the abandoned Harris Electric Loom Mill, nursing the wound to his leg where the bullet had grazed his calf. The spider in his head unhooked the strings that sent pain, and then nestled back into the center of things, half high from the effects of the rich essence of youth. His imagination took off, and he plucked the silver strands, composing as he played, spinning a web of an idea. "Herd them," Daddy said in a voice that cracked and clicked. The spare, scattered pattern of the lights of Grindly required design.

Exhausted from running, Inspector Kaufmann leaned against the coral facade at the entrance to Grindly Station. His own thoughts were as scattered as Daddy's were inspired. Against what would have normally been his better judgment, he chose to believe that for some reason the train would, that night, stop at the platform and take him aboard. He hurried on so as not to miss it. His quick footsteps echoed across the wide rotunda, and he passed through another set of doors into the dome that held the station platform. He was surprised to find himself the only passenger.

Kaufmann cupped his hand behind his ear and cocked his head toward the track in order to check for vibrations of the coming train. He thought he felt the merest rumble deep in his chest. After listening for a long time, all he really heard was the sound of water dripping. It interfered with the anticipation of escape. Then he realized it wasn't water dripping but more a tapping. It stopped and then started again. He looked up at the inner dome and froze.

In an eyeblink, Daddy leaped down on a forty-foot thread

of web and stood before Kaufmann. Mandibles clicked together, and Daddy did a bad job of hiding the drool. From some forgotten byway of his brain, the inspector's years of experience on the streets of Grindly engaged. He made a fist and swung with everything he had. The punch hit the mark, cracking the left lens of Daddy's rose-colored glasses and sending him stumbling backward a few feet. The inspector didn't know whether to flee or continue to attack, and in the empty moment of his indecision, he definitely heard the train coming.

He made a move toward Daddy with fists in the air, but his nemesis twirled with insect precision and speed and clipped Kaufmann under the chin with a foot that struck like the tip of a bullwhip. The inspector was almost brought to his knees by the blow, but instead of going down, he righted himself and backed off. Blood trickled from the side of his mouth. The train was louder now, and a faint light could be seen filling the tunnel. He looked down and saw that the backs of his heels were off the edge of the platform. He put his fists up and kept them moving.

When Daddy took one long-legged step to the left, Kaufmann saw salvation. The roar of the approaching train filled the tunnel and set the entire platform to vibrating so that it was impossible to hear the squish of Mrs. Frey's galoshes. She inched up upon him from behind, the candelabra glimmering, the blackjack waggling in her grip. Kaufmann threw a flurry of jabs to distract the arachnid, and the old woman lifted the leather club as high as she could. The locomotive entered the station but didn't slow.

In the reflection of rushing windows, Daddy detected treachery. He spun in a blur, his mandibles severing Mrs. Frey's neck with a swift clip, like cutting a rose. From the hole in his trousers, he shot a blast of web at Kaufmann. It happened so quickly that the inspector could only stand motionless as the strand of sticky thread wrapped twice around his neck. The web's long tail was pulled in by the rush of the passing train and affixed itself to the handle on the back door of the caboose. Kaufmann was jerked off the platform by the neck, and flew behind the train. The last thing he saw in Grindly was the mosaic face of God. Mrs. Frey's head hit the platform then and spat.

The next evening, in an abandoned warehouse by the docks, Daddy stood in total darkness, emitting high-pitched squeals that called all the natural spiders of Grindly to him. When he felt their delicate heaving presence surrounding him, he clicked and *blzz*'d out his plan. He gave instructions on rethreading the human brain. He spoke of the ear and the path to take, warning of cul de sacs. "A quarter pound of fly meat for every human restrung," he promised. Spirits were high. Later, when they returned to him for payment, he crushed them beneath his slipper.

By the time he got done with Grindly, the city shone and ran like one of Tharshmon's pocket watches. Everything moved as if to music. It became for Daddy a web of human thread. "Purpose without a point," he often reminded his human electorate, and they tacitly nodded. He continued to feed at night, roaming the rooftops and alleyways, leaving old luggage indiscriminately in his wake. People showed him smiles during the day, but, still, no one wanted to meet him in the dark. The reconfiguration of their brain patterns didn't eliminate terror, only their ability to react to it. "Fear and Industry" was Daddy's motto, and it took him far.

After the train was again making scheduled stops at the station, Daddy boarded with a ticket to the capital one evening. He never returned to Grindly, but instead bit into the larger politics of the Realm and kept eating in a spiral pattern until he reached the center of everything. There, he made a nest for himself.

The Skinny Girl

BY LUCIUS SHEPARD

Lucius Shepard was born in Lynchburg, Virginia, grew up in Daytona Beach, Florida, and lives in Portland, Oregon. His short fiction has won the Nebula Award, the Hugo Award, the International Horror Guild Award, the National Magazine Award, the Locus Award, the Theodore Sturgeon Memorial Award, and the World Fantasy Award.

His latest books are a short novel, *The Taborin Scale,* and a short fiction collection, *Viator Plus.* Forthcoming are another short fiction collection, *Five Autobiographies;* two novels, tentatively titled *The Piercefields* and *The End of Life as We Know It;* and a short novel, *The House of Everything and Nothing.*

During the twenty-six years in which he had supplied images of the dead to the city's daily newspapers, Hugo Lis had photographed over thirty thousand corpses, the victims of strangulation and shooting, knifings, car crashes, decapitations, accidental electrocutions, and other more idiosyncratic instances of mayhem. A considerable number of those pictures, despite the anonymity of the victims, had been run on the front page above the fold, often in conjunction with the photograph of a half-naked starlet or singer. When asked to explain this apparent opposition, Hugo would suggest that in a place where life has little or no meaning, death tends to acquire a certain glamour. Mexico City had seventy-five thousand streets and death was a celebrity on every one. Hugo had visited homes in which his photograph of a family member's bloody remains, snipped from a newspaper, now served as the centerpiece of a shrine. It was as if the violated flesh and its public exploitation were deemed truer emblems of a loved one's memory than the sunny smile of a confirmation photo or the purposeful, forward-looking pose of a graduation shot. Or it may have been that the implicit passion and drama of a violent death lent the departed a Christ-like pathos, thereby engaging the Catholic sensibilities of the populace. Hugo's attitudes toward the subject, albeit no less formalized, were not in the least circumscribed by faith or emotion. Death, to Hugo Lis, was simply a way of life.

As dean of the photographers whose pictures illustrated the *notas rojas* ("red news"), Hugo was occasionally approached by foreign journalists interested in doing a story on his life and profession. His hair and mustache colored to hide the gray, dressed in a black suit tailored to disguise his paunch; wearing lifts that added two inches to his diminutive stature, he would pose for pictures. After negotiating a fee (necessary, he claimed, to guarantee their safety from the gangs), he would guide them to one or another of the innumerable shrines devoted to Santa Muerte ("Saint Death") in Barrio Tepito where, behind glass or within a confine of plastic panels, a human skeleton (often a real one) dressed in robes or a lace gown stood holding a scythe and a globe representing the earth, surrounded by offerings of flowers and fruit and cigars left by thugs, kidnappers, drug dealers, murderers, and the disenfranchised, whose patron saint she was.

"Death has become so prominent a character in our lives, we've transformed her into a movie star," he would typically say, leading his interviewer among the stalls that transformed many of Tepito's streets into crowded pedestrian aisles, pointing out the various representations of Santa Muerte available among fraudulent Swiss watches and knockoffs of designer clothing—statuettes and paintings of robed skeletal figures juxtaposed with T-shirts that depicted her as an emaciated yet beautiful young girl. "You find her image everywhere," he would go on. "Soon there will be films celebrating her starring Mayrin Villanueva or Ninel Conde. *People en Español* will proclaim her to be the Sexiest Woman of the Year."

As befitted his profession, Hugo was a widower; his wife, Fabiola, a thin, sallow girl, died in her teens as the result of sudden illness, which had originally seemed merely a summer cold. He could no longer call her face to mind and had come to view the marriage as an adolescent mistake; yet he had been dismasted by grief upon her death or, better said, he had embraced grief with the same childlike fervor that he had love, wearing it as an actor would wear a costume, using it to simulate authenticity. But no matter how deep his investment in the emotion, grief had rendered him glib and cynical and purged him of his juvenile ambitions: He no longer cared about creating art and thought of photography strictly as a means to an end. Ironically, his work since had been praised for its "raw purity" and "bizarre sensuality" and now formed part of the permanent collections of several important museums. When asked how he managed to make the dead so attractive, so vital even though charred or covered in blood, he replied, "I seek to do nothing. I shoot pictures for the newspapers. I don't try to frame shots, I don't enhance negatives. What you see is what I see, nothing more."

He had never remarried, and lived in a one-bedroom condo close to Avenida Vincente Suarez in the *colonia* of La Condesa, a trendy section of the city that echoed the intellectual pretensions of Greenwich Village and the architecture of South Beach, yet lacked the cultural traditions of the one and the garish splendor of the other. Though he welcomed the attentions of women (mainly intellectual types, attracted by the numena they claimed to perceive in his photographs), he refused to adapt his routines to their needs, and they would leave after a few weeks or months, accusing him of being aloof and passionless except as related to his job. This accusation surprised him, for he considered himself a passionate sort. As for his job . . . well, he would admit to being a bit obsessive—that was his nature—but it was scarcely a passion. These women, he reasoned, must have been pampered in their previous relationships and thus demanded too much of him.

When not at home, his life was spent driving from point to point in the Distrito Federal, obeying the prompts of a police scanner, on the move for days at a time, eating and napping in his car. Traveling from crime scene to crime scene through snarls of clamorous traffic; from black nights fruited with neon to days that, whether rainy or bright, gave evidence of a polluted haze; from the Zona Rosa, where child prostitutes flocked the streets, to the sprawl of Cuautepec, the epicenter of poverty, to the Zocalo, the great central square hemmed in by gray fortresslike government buildings and the equally forbidding cathedral, the site of demonstrations and concerts and, in winter, improbably, an outdoor ice skating rink. Experienced this way, the city, for all its chaos and violence, had a calming, almost a narcotizing effect upon him, as though it generated a violent beatitude . . . or else, like a fish born in a cataract, he had grown inured to the crash and tumble of its rhythms.

One night at the end of such a sojourn he stopped to buy cigarettes at a tiny store, a niche no wider than a doorway on a nearly deserted stretch of Calle Doctor Vertis. When he emerged from the store, two men seized him by the elbows, pressed a pistol into his side, and forced him into a van, where he was made to lie on the floor with his face pushed into a moldy carpet. Terrified, Hugo assumed this to be an express kidnapping and that the men would bring him to a cash machine and have him make a withdrawal. They did not wear masks and were so nonchalant in their demeanor, chatting about a woman of their acquaintance, he thought they must be unconcerned about revealing their identities because they planned to kill him. Yet if that were so, would they not head toward a spot where they could complete their business undisturbed? He could tell by the buildings, whose upper floors were visible through the windows (stone facades with balconies and crumbling colonial ornaments), and by the increased noise (cumbia and rock playing in the hotly lit stores, somebody shouting over a bullhorn, shrieks and laughter, horns braying, engines being gunned) that they were passing along Calle Morelos very near the Zocalo. Screwing up his courage, expecting a blow in return, he asked where he was being taken.

The man in back with Hugo, heavily muscled, his neck so thickly covered in tattoos that in the shadowy interior of the van he appeared to be wearing a turtleneck, glanced at him incuriously and said, "The Skinny Girl wants to meet you."

A certain amount of ambiguity was attached to this statement—La Flacita ("the Skinny Girl") was a diminutive for Santa Muerte, an affectionate name used by her devotees. The man might be threatening him with death . . . or he might be referring to someone who had adopted the name. Hugo sought clarification, but the driver snapped at him, telling him to keep quiet. The men began talking about the woman again, not in the way such men usually talk about women, neither lustfully nor derisively, but reverently and with the sort of respect they would normally reserve for a man. Hugo suspected this woman to be a criminal type who relied on a quasi-mystical pose to keep the troops in line. He told himself that he was going to be all right—he'd inform her of his police connections and she would come to her senses and release him.

That the official and the criminal are inextricably aligned should come as no surprise to anyone familiar with the workings of their government, but nowhere is this juxtaposition so literal and apparent as in Mexico City. Located fifteen minutes' walk from the Zocalo, the seat of the government and home to the immense, grim cathedral that is its spiritual analogue, lies the seat of outlawry, Barrio Tepito. Within its borders, fully two-thirds of the world's child pornography is produced; assault rifles and missile launchers are sold via illustrated catalogs; and there are dozens of warehouses filled with drugs and stolen goods. You can find anything in Tepito, it's said: pirated software, endangered species, a Rolex, a Guarneri cello, a slave, a cruel master . . . anything. The majority of Tepito's business is done on the streets, but much of it is accomplished in *vecindades,* old colonial mansions scattered throughout the barrio, decayed to the point of collapse, each room serving as a boutique given over to a separate extralegal enterprise—it was to such a ruinous structure that his captors brought Hugo. The earth beneath the house had been excavated, creating two brightly lit subterranean levels, the uppermost walled in concrete block and plaster, ranged by mahogany doors elaborately carved with an imagery of bounteous nature—bunches of grapes and orchids and hummingbirds and reeds. The men led Hugo down to this level and stationed themselves at the foot of the stairs and told him to proceed along the corridor, that he would find the Skinny Girl in one of the rooms. When he hesitated, anxious about what might lie ahead, they drove him forward with kicks and curses.

The first door admitted Hugo to a large, poorly lit room smelling of marijuana, in which people visible as half shadows sat about on sofas and easy chairs (those he could see were swaybacked and patched with tape), their conversations barely audible over a music of whiny reeds and clattering drums that had a Middle Eastern flair. It reminded him of his university days: smiling young men passing hand-rolled cigarettes to giggling girls; long-haired guys engaged in impassioned arguments. He asked a busty, fresh-faced girl who stood along the wall where he could find the Skinny Girl. *"No hablo,"* she said in an American accent. Her companion, a sullen kid with a complicated emo hairstyle, said, *"Pase por alla,"* and pointed to the far end of the room, where there was a door and, nearby, a number of people gathered about a radiant object on the floor, blocking it from view. A sudden flash of white light cast them in silhouette—some gasped, while others cried out and applauded. The glow faded, albeit slowly, and Hugo shouldered in among them, hoping to discover what they had been watching. Embedded in the floor was a flat panel of black glass—a television screen—but whatever image it had shown was no longer in evidence.

Hugo exited the room and, at the urging of the men standing by the stairs, continued along the corridor. From behind a second door came a racket that reminded him of an old-fashioned printing press. He turned the knob but found it locked. Putting his ear to the next door, he heard noises reminiscent of a dog worrying a chew toy and decided not to enter. The fourth door opened into a considerable space with bright ceiling lights and a banquet table at which some two dozen prosperous-looking men and women were seated, all clad as mourners, most with their heads bent, murmuring as in prayer. Three mestizo boys in white coats were serving them, two holding a steaming tureen and one ladling a thick black soup. The dominant feature of the room was a mural occupying the whitewashed wall at the diners' backs, depicting a pale, asthenic girl clad in black jeans, a wide belt with a gold buckle, and a sleeveless black top. Of the countless representations of the Skinny Girl that Hugo had seen, this was the first to strike him as having the specificity of an image rendered from life. She stood inhaling a cigarette, an act that accentuated the hollowness of her cheeks, and gazed into an unguessable distance, her physical attitude projecting a palpable disaffection. An immense ghostly skull looming behind her formed the backdrop of the mural, along with some sketchy vegetation and small indefinite figures that might have been cacti or soldiers with spears. She wore on her left arm a simple silver bracelet, and on a chain about her neck was an oddly shaped gold amulet holding a flat magenta stone. Her hair was jet black, and her long, narrow face, with its high cheekbones, full carmine lips, and prominent nose, had a severe, almost mannish cast; yet despite this, despite the coldness of her expression and the fact that she had virtually no hips or breasts, she seemed to incarnate every principle of feminine beauty, albeit in their most forbidding and reductive form.

At the end of the banquet table nearest Hugo sat a matronly woman with a kindly face who had not yet been served. She wore widow's garb, but her crepe dress and lace mantilla were of much finer quality than those of the black-clad women Hugo saw each day on the streets of the city, grimly clutching their little bundles. He approached her and inquired as to whether she knew the woman who had posed for the mural.

"Why that's Aida, of course," she said with a faltering tone, as if bewildered by the question. "Don't you recognize her? It's an excellent likeness."

The old man on her left made a pleased noise as the server filled his bowl.

"I haven't yet met the lady," Hugo said. "Could you tell me where I might find her?"

"Oh!" The woman put a hand to her cheek. "I'm afraid you'll have to leave. You're not permitted to partake of communion until you've . . ."

The serving boys moved behind her, and the tallest, a beetle-browed twelve-year-old with a yellowish-brown complexion, ladled soup into her bowl—it smelled of nutmeg, yet there was an unpleasant undertone, a scent that Hugo could not identify. The woman closed her eyes and inhaled the steam rapturously. She took up her spoon and stirred the soup, which had the consistency of partially set custard.

"Until what?" Hugo asked.

"Until you've met her." The woman bowed her head and began to pray. "Glorious Death, I beseech you," she said in a fervent tone—the rest of her words were lost in a muttering consensus. Only the serving boys abstained from prayer. They glared at Hugo, their black eyes agleam like chitin under the lights, their faces glum. If he had seen them on the streets of Tepito, he wouldn't have given them a second thought, but the context lent them a sinister aspect and he retreated from the room.

The corridor veered to the right and, after inspecting a room used to store stacks of high-end electronics gear still in their cartons, he leaned against the wall, seeking to order his thoughts. Nothing that had occurred since the kidnapping made sense, and the more forcefully he sought to impose logic on events, the less comprehensible they became. It was evident that he had not been kidnapped for ransom alone, that whoever was behind his abduction was playing games with him; but he could think of no reason for such treatment.

Several people passed him by as he pondered, and he asked each of them if they knew Aida's whereabouts. They were uniformly civil, suggesting that if he kept going, sooner or later he would run across her; but each time he raised a question that required a more detailed response, they excused themselves and hurried off. Unable to resolve any of his questions, he took their advice and continued along the corridor.

At length he reached a door that stood partially open. The room beyond was furnished with a sofa and easy chairs upholstered in earth tones, end tables, and a gray rug with a blue diamond pattern typical of Zapotec work. It had a faintly shabby air redolent of an old hotel that was being kept up but had seen better days. Pottery occupied niches in the tiled walls (ocher with geometric designs of red and green), and on the wall opposite, next to a doorway hung with a beaded curtain, directly above the light switch, was a crucifix—the exposed wiring of the switch ran up behind the cross, giving the impression that the electricity powering the jaundiced glow from the ceiling lamp was at least partly responsible for Christ's tormented posture. Hugo slipped inside, closing the door after him, and tiptoed to the doorway across the room, pushing aside the beaded curtain.

On his left, a staircase led downward; to his right, a bedroom . . . a woman's bedroom, judging by the underwear strewn across the floor.

A noise from without drew his attention and he peered through the beaded curtain. A woman stood in the corridor, only her hand visible resting on the doorknob, a silver bracelet about her wrist. "All right. I'll talk to you later," she said to someone, and entered the room. She was identical to the woman in the mural in every respect. The same jewelry and clothing, even the same severe makeup. This reinforced his idea that she was a charlatan who affected the guise of Santa Muerte for some devious purpose—such an act would play well in Tepito. He was certain she had seen him through the curtain and in reflex he took a backward step. Without acknowledging him, she lit a cigarette and tipped back her head to exhale a plume of smoke. After a silence she said reflectively, "Hugo Lis." Her voice had a husky sonority that made it seem a larger presence was speaking through her; yet when she spoke again, her words had a normal timbre. "My name is Aida Chavez. You are welcome in my house."

"Since you know me . . ." he said, pushing aside the curtain and stepping forward as though unafraid. "You must also know that I have influential friends."

"Truly? Perhaps your friends know my friends." She had another hit of her cigarette. "Don't worry. No harm will come to you here."

"I don't believe you understand. My niece's godfather is . . ."

"Mauricio Ebrard. I know. I know a great deal about you. Your friends, where you like to drink . . . I know you took your last vacation in Biarritz. You spent quite a sum of money on a woman named Cinnamon." A smile nicked her wide, straight mouth. "No doubt a relative."

She sat down on the sofa and crossed her legs. "Still, there are things I don't understand about you. Why, for instance, do you continue to photograph the dead? It can't be an issue of money—your celebrity has brought you a nice income. Nor is it because you have a dearth of other options."

Irritated, Hugo said, "Perhaps I just like driving around and taking pictures. I'm no psychologist. Why does anyone do anything? Why do you pretend to be Santa Muerte?"

"Is that what I do?" She kicked out her right leg and considered the tip of a stylish boot. "Are you afraid, Hugo? I should think anyone in your situation would be."

"Of course I am. I'm afraid you won't use good judgment."

"If you're really afraid, if you fear for your life, you may leave."

He searched her face for a hint of deception, reminding himself that she was a poseur, an actress—he would be unlikely to detect anything that she had not put there by design.

She swung her legs onto the sofa and leaned back against the armrest. "Yet you've spent so many years at the entrance to my house, it would be a pity if you left without exploring it a little."

He was aware that she had spoken metaphorically, referring both to his photographs of the dead and her affectation as the embodiment of Santa Muerte, but he chose to respond as though the comment had been literal. "You're mistaken," he said. "I've never been here before."

Her face settled into a haughty, disinterested expression that reminded him of his niece, a student at the university, the look she adopted when she asked him for money and he would question the reason for which she needed it.

"Do as you wish," she said, giving a languid gesture. "Leave . . . or stay. It's of no consequence."

She stared at the ceiling, smoke curling between her lips, holding her cigarette aloft as if using it to gauge perspective. He had the idea that he had disappointed her and felt an irrational dismay at having come up short of her expectations. He picked through his thoughts, examining this one and that one, thinking that she might be a witch and had placed them in his head—he did not actually believe in witchcraft, but his upbringing in San Luis Potosi, where peyote was sold by *brujas* in the market, compelled him to accept that magic was part of the world's potential. While taking this mental inventory, he became aware that he was no longer quite so afraid. Although he remained unsettled by her diffident manner and general inexpressiveness (smiles and frowns scarcely registered on her face), she had demanded no ransom and he began to believe that she meant him no harm. Whatever her intentions, he told himself, they must have something to do with the cult of Santa Muerte, with her position in it, and perhaps there was a story here that could be exploited. The bulk of his equipment was in his car, but he had a digital camera in his jacket pocket.

"May I take your picture?" he asked.

Partway through Hugo's photographic session with her, Aida Chavez started to remove her clothes. She did this of her own volition and with the nonchalance of a wife preparing for bed while chatting with her husband. Hugo was initially taken aback, but the hollows of her buttocks, the articulation of her ribs, collarbone, and pelvis, and the thrust of her hip bones contrived an eerily erotic terrain that aroused him in no small measure, and he snapped picture after picture. Desire grew furious and sharp in him, like the flame from a gas jet turned high. He wanted to touch her and might have done so, using the pretense of helping her to achieve a pose, but an insistent knocking at the door broke the mood.

Aida slipped on her panties and top, and poked her head out into the corridor, and carried on a brief, half-whispered exchange, after which she shut the door and struggled into her jeans.

Irritated, Hugo waved at the door and said, "Who are all these people? What are they doing here?"

Aida lit another cigarette and exhaled with a despondent sigh. "I hoped you would recognize me, but since you do not—"

"How could I recognize you? I've never laid eyes on you before!"

"No? How odd!" She reclined on the sofa once again. "I suppose it would be more accurate to say that I hoped you could 'identify' me. But since you cannot, I'll tell you a little about myself. Perhaps that will assist your judgment."

He sat in one of the easy chairs, and once he was comfortable she said, "I was a foundling left on the steps of the Nueva Vida Orphanage when I was barely a few hours old. I was grossly underweight and the doctors doubted that I would live; yet somehow I managed to survive my infancy. As I grew older the nuns tried to fatten me up, thinking that if I were closer to normal weight, I stood a better chance of being adopted. Though they forced me to stuff myself, often using the threat of physical punishment, I remained abnormally thin. The other children were cruel to me. I wasn't strong enough to fight them off, so I developed a kind of passive resistance. No matter how painful the beatings, I refused to cry. I would glare at them until at last they stopped. Eventually they left me more or less alone and satisfied their need to demean me with the occasional prank. They took to calling me the Skinny Girl. Sometimes I wonder if their cruelty wasn't a form of recognition, a denial of their fear.

"My stoic manner made me even less appealing to potential adoptive parents. They wanted bubbly, bouncy children and not a gaunt, solemn girl who sat without speaking. After nine years in the orphanage it seemed clear that I would never be adopted, and so it was decided I would enter the convent when I reached the proper age. I raised no objection to this plan. A nun's life seemed as good as any and better than most in that it offered a guarantee of food and shelter. Then just prior to my tenth birthday, DeMario Chavez came to the orphanage. He had heard about the Skinny Girl dwelling there and asked to see me."

"The founder of the Zetas?" Hugo asked. "That DeMario Chavez?"

Aida nodded. "During our interview I gave minimal responses to his questions and did not expect to see him again.

But several days later he came to collect me. I assume a sum of money changed hands—that would explain why a drug dealer, a murderer, was allowed to adopt me. Then, too, the nuns were likely glad to wash their hands of me. They were a superstitious bunch, and I suspect they half believed me to be the Skinny Girl. DeMario took me to his house, this house, and installed me in an apartment and let it be known that the incarnation of Santa Muerte was dwelling under his roof, living as his ward. Occasionally he would bring other men to see me—men like him, gang leaders with dozens of tattoos. They offered me gifts—perfume, food, tequila. They prayed before me, they asked my blessing, and all the while DeMario smirked at me over their bowed heads."

"So," said Hugo. "Your function was to impress other criminals by posing as Santa Muerte?"

"That was the idea. DeMario rarely confided in me, but once he patted me on the head and said that before we were done, he would have every criminal in Mexico worshipping at my church."

"It doesn't seem credible that you could frighten men to that extent."

"Oh, I have my moments," she said. "I don't know whether I frightened them as much as I convinced them, but this is an unusual house. In one room there is an animal that feeds on itself, tearing at its own flesh, and yet the next day is whole again. In another there is a TV screen set in the floor that works only intermittently and shows images of an apocalyptic event that soon will be visited upon us. There are other strange things besides. Some will tell you they are nothing but tricks. High-tech illusions, animatronics, and so forth. Others claim they are magical devices. I believe both sides are right, that given certain conditions, illusions can become real."

Hugo made a dubious noise, but Aida ignored it.

"Whatever their nature," she said, "I think after seeing them the men were disposed to believe in me." She lit another cigarette and exhaled through her nostrils. "DeMario's behavior toward me underwent a change over the course of the three years that I knew him. Increasingly, he began to display anxiety in my presence. During the last year I scarcely saw him at all, until one night he broke into my apartment and raped me. I reverted to the passive resistance of my orphanage days and glared at him the entire time and gave no outcry. After he had finished he appeared terrified. He wept and babbled and called me his beautiful death. He had been using a lot of drugs those last months. Cocaine, heroin, pills. I imagined that his substance abuse provoked the incident. The next morning he was dead. Some problem with his heart. His woman told me that he had become convinced that I was Santa Muerte incarnate, and that what had started out as a game had evolved into something much darker. The rape, she said, was an attempt to restore his control over me. She, too, believed I was Santa Muerte and that I had struck DeMario down for his assault on me. She begged my forgiveness and asked me to show her mercy.

"I thought I would have to move out of the house, but the story of DeMario's death and my part in it spread through the barrio and no one ever tried to evict me. Instead, people thronged the house, asking for my blessing. They would have transformed my home into a shrine to Santa Muerte, a big one like the old woman's house on Alfareria Street; but I told them I wanted neither their gifts nor their adoration. I said that I had been made flesh in order to explore the nature of my humanity and to fulfill a destiny as yet unrevealed. I meant to choose those with whom I surrounded myself. The people you asked about, the ones who visit me here, they are my suitors. They come in hopes that I will grant them surcease. Whenever I feel so inclined, I give them a kiss and send them away. Not one of them has returned."

"Some of your suitors are very young."

"Are you so naïve that you think only the old seek death?"

"You believe they are dead, the ones you kissed?"

"I've come to think so. Yes."

"Then you must believe that you are the Skinny Girl."

"At first I did not believe it. I found the concept ridiculous. But lately . . ."

She failed to complete the sentence, and Hugo asked what she had intended to say.

"People assume an incarnation is a special soul given physical form," she said. "Something apart from creation, something that has a different quality. But God is in all things, so how can His incarnation be separate . . . or different? I think an incarnation is a part of God that is gradually shaped by His design to satisfy some need. It took Jesus years before he understood His destiny." She got to her feet and paced off a few steps toward the door. "Lately I have gained a new sense of myself. It's difficult to describe, and there are moments—like now—when I doubt what I know in my heart. Words make it sound utterly preposterous." She slapped her thigh in frustration. "Let's just say I've begun to accept that my actions have some wider resonance in the world."

"Well," said Hugo, choosing his words with care, not wanting to upset her further, "it should be easy enough to prove. Have the people whom you kiss followed when they leave. Invite technicians into the house to examine the television and whatever else requires validation."

"That would prove nothing. Scrutiny changes the observable.

No, my idea of proof was to bring you here. Your life has been surrounded by death. It's your passion."

Hugo started to object, but she talked through him.

"I've read your interviews," she said. "You make a point of denying me, yet you seek me out in my most terrible forms and perceive in each a vivid grace. When you photographed me, I felt you were fucking me with the camera. I stripped off my clothes because you recognized me. You responded to my beauty . . . you've always responded to me. Your desire was palpable. You wanted to touch me. Why didn't you?"

Embarrassed, Hugo gave no answer.

"You've been my absent lover for a long while," said Aida. "Soon we will be together."

"Don't be silly," Hugo said. "I took those pictures to run with your story."

"Even the ones the newspapers would refuse to print? Who are those intended for? You can't deny your desire for me much longer. We *will* have our time, and on that day I promise you much more than a kiss. But our meeting today may have been premature. I need to purge myself of doubt. My faith must be pure in order to awaken yours fully." She beckoned. "There's something I want you to see. Afterward you may leave, if that's your pleasure."

He followed her through the beaded curtain and down a short stairway and along a whitewashed tunnel lit by naked ceiling bulbs—like a passage leading to a gallows or a gas chamber.

"A few weeks ago, I had a vision of you," she said as she went. "I watched you photographing the dead."

He felt a pang of anxiety. "Dozens of people watch me at work. Cops, medics. Bystanders."

"But no one saw you working at the New Divine, did they?"

Hugo quit walking.

"You were alone inside the club," said Aida. "You must have bribed someone to let you in before the emergency teams arrived. There were bodies everywhere. The room was still very smoky, so you tied a cloth about your face. The first picture you shot was of a teenage girl who had been trampled trying to reach the door. She had on a green dress."

"You must have seen footage from a security camera," he said.

"Aren't security tapes shot in black-and-white? Yet I'm telling you her dress was green." She sniffed. "Don't bother responding. You can always construct an alternative explanation. Reality is full of loopholes."

At the end of the tunnel was a door with a padlock. Aida put a key in the lock and said, "What I'm going to show you occurred during the earthquake in ninety-nine, a few days after my arrival in this house. DeMario thought it might have caused the earthquake. I didn't learn of it until after his death."

She threw open the door, warm air and a smell of decay rushed out, and Hugo clapped a hand over his mouth and nose. Emerging from the wall directly ahead of them, wedged in place, resting among chunks of rock and white plaster that appeared to have been shattered by its violent incursion, were the head and torso of an androgynous giant with chalky skin and long, silky white hair and an impassive Sphinx-like face. It lay on its side, the right shoulder and arm crushed beneath its body, its left arm protruding from the shattered wall some thirty feet above, as though it had been reaching out for someone or something at the instant its momentum ceased. The position of the left hand, wrist bent and fingers dangling, reminded Hugo of the hand of Jehovah depicted on the ceiling of the Sistine Chapel. Half-clotted black blood welled from a gash on its wrist, spilling into a pool that had accumulated in a depression in the rock. Wisps of steam rose from the surface, and Hugo recalled the soup served in the banquet room. At the base of the throat, under the collarbone, on the shoulder blade and elsewhere, were patches of dark webbed veins that showed through the skin like evil snowflakes.

"It came for me," said Aida. "Or so I've concluded."

Despite the sluggish flow of blood, Hugo presumed the giant to be dead; but then he checked himself and decided it must be a fraud, a torso with metal bones and skin fabricated from latex, set in place and jammed into a hole. The giant twisted its neck and, with a laborious effort, lifted its head. Its eyelids opened to reveal cavernous empty sockets crusted with blood, and a chthonic groan issued from its throat. Hugo felt the bellows of its rotting breath and fell back, nearly bumping into Aida. He moved away from her, sweat dripping into his eyes.

"DeMario thought it was an angel," she said. "It doesn't have wings, though. I'm not sure what the damned thing is, but it refuses to die. It's like a fucking cockroach."

The enormous hand overhead clenched into a fist and the giant's face contorted.

"It wanted to control me, to take me to its house and imprison me, just like DeMario," said Aida. "Despite the fact that it bungled the job, I think it might be God."

The giant groaned again, louder this time, and the accompanying stench grew more fecal, as if the noise had been dredged up from its bowels; it looked to be trying to push itself forward into the room.

"Every year it manages to move a few inches," said Aida. "At that rate it might break free in a century or two. It's not very bright, but you can't kill it. At least I can't. I've tried everything . . . even kissing it." She wrinkled her nose in disgust. "Doesn't that sound like God to you? This big, stupid, invulnerable thing that resembles us and whose creations are more intelligent than it is? The Bible left out that part, but it would explain a great deal. Of course . . ." She flicked her eyes toward Hugo. "You probably think it's a fake. And you may be right. But even if you're right, you're wrong, you know."

Hugo wet his lips.

"Watch this," she said. "It's terrified of me."

Aida approached the giant—its nostrils flared, and it yielded a keening noise and thrashed about, resulting in a heavy fall of plaster dust. She backed away and the giant's struggles subsided.

"Now maybe it's a robot, but no one else gets that reaction. Just me. Go on. You try." She turned to Hugo. "Are you okay? You look feverish."

She stretched out a hand as if to feel his brow, and he flinched to avoid her touch.

"I have a bad stomach," he said, trying to cover his alarm. "Is there a bathroom I can use?"

"Not down here. Why don't you use the one in my apartment?"

"Thanks." He hesitated. "I won't be long."

"Take your time," she said. "I want you to be sure."

"What do you mean?"

She adopted a concerned expression, but her voice had a sarcastic lilt. "Your stomach. I want you to be sure it's all right."

He walked away, forcing himself to keep a measured pace, and was almost at the door when she called out, "I'll be waiting!"

Again he hesitated, uncertain what would happen when he stepped through the door. The giant made a ghastly noise, half a shriek, half a grunt, as if straining against some internal agony. Aida stood close by its face, threatening to touch it. Sweat blurred Hugo's vision, and for a moment she looked like a thin black spike driven into the stone.

"Hurry!" she cried. "The sooner you leave, the sooner you'll come back to me."

Of his escape Hugo recalls very little, only that the two men were no longer guarding the stairs and that the streets of Barrio Tepito, into which he fled, were packed and filled with demented noise and fractured light and the smells of frying meat, and that while making his way through the crowds, he was shoved against something hard and glanced up to discover it was a statue of Santa Muerte bolted to the sidewalk, her skull face shrouded in an indigo robe—he was trapped in a rough embrace between her scythe and her bony fingers clutching the earth's blue globe. For months thereafter he tried to slip back into his old habits, but he was unable to deploy the nets of faith and logic that had sustained that life. When photographing the dead, he saw Aida Chavez in every crowd of onlookers, in every group of mourners, in the shadowy depths of police vans and the hotly lit interiors of EMT vehicles. He recognized her postures and attitudes in the vacant faces and akimbo limbs of his subjects. He lost his taste for taking pictures of mutilated corpses; he had seen death made into life and the bodies were merely life made into death, a poor substitute. She was remorseless and cruel, so fearsome that even God trembled before her, but he could no longer deny his attraction to her, an attraction that had always been visible to others (though not to him) in his work.

Nowadays he dreams of returning to the mansion in Tepito and he anticipates the rite of communion, sipping the giant's hot blood, marveling at the apocalyptic images on the magical TV, and debating the character of Aida's destiny with the other suitors in her anteroom, not because these things have significance, but because their flavors accent the consummation he yearns for, the time he will share with her. It's not so much fear that keeps him from returning. What is there to fear, after all? He understands that he has failed at living (as do all men), his days have been empty, his promise unfulfilled, and only in her arms will he learn whether or not his existence has meaning. No, it's rather that he has yet to reach the point where life tips over into death, where the need for what she offers (be it surcease or something more graspable) outweighs everything else. He tells himself that once she is free of her doubts, the last of his restraints will dissolve and he will come to her like a young man on his wedding night, eager to penetrate the secrets of the woman for whom he has waited his entire life, a woman who rouses in him a passion like none other. Each morning and evening he kneels before a statuette of Santa Muerte that he purchased in the Sonora witches' market and has been drenched in ritual perfumes and spices. Above it is pinned a photograph of Aida naked on her sofa, gazing into the camera with an insensate look, as if she has been struck dead, with her eyes half lidded and lips parted, fingering the folds of flesh between her legs. Each tendon string, every ligament, is taut and articulated. Her erect nipples cast more of a shadow than do her breasts. And yet she is beautiful. He lights red candles and spits rum on the flames and smokes part of a Faros cigarette, the brand she favors, before leaving it burning at her feet, and he offers up a prayer.

"Beloved Death," he will begin. "Be swift in your deliberations and open yourself to me, for I would be your consort and companion."

He will likely falter, then—he has never been a religious man and he's embarrassed to see himself this way—but he fights through the moment, pressing his forehead to the base of the statuette, allowing the coolness of the stone to pervade and calm him as though it were *her* potent calmness, *her* coolness that flowed into his skull, so that when he continues it's with an infirm voice, the voice of a lover overwhelmed and exhausted by passion, saying, "I await your summons, yet not patiently, for with each passing hour my desire grows."

The Colliers' Venus (1893)

BY CAITLÍN R. KIERNAN

Caitlín R. Kiernan is the author of seven novels, including the award-winning *Threshold* and, most recently, *Daughter of Hounds* and *The Red Tree*. Her short fiction has been collected in *Tales of Pain and Wonder; From Weird and Distant Shores; To Charles Fort, With Love; Alabaster; A Is for Alien;* and *The Ammonite Violin & Others*. Her erotica has been collected in two volumes—*Frog Toes and Tentacles* and *Tales from the Woeful Platypus*. She is currently beginning work on her eighth novel, *The Drowning Girl: A Memoir,* and a science fiction novella, *The Dinosaurs of Mars*. She lives in Providence, Rhode Island.

1

It is not an ostentatious museum. Rather, it is only the sort of museum that best suits this modern, industrious city at the edge of the high Colorado plains. This city, with its sooty days and dusty, crowded streets and night skies that glow an angry orange from the dragon's breath of half a hundred Bessemer converters. The museum is a dignified yet humble assemblage of geological wonders, intended as much for the delight and edification of miners and millworkers, blacksmiths and butchers, as it is for the parvenu and old-money families of Capitol Hill. Professor Jeremiah Ogilvy, both founder and curator of this *Colectanea rerum memorabilium,* has always considered himself a progressive sort, and he has gone so far as to set aside one day each and every month when the city's negroes, coolies, and red Indians are permitted access to his cabinet, free of charge. Professor Ogilvy would—and frequently has—referred to his museum as a most *modest* endeavor, one whose principal mission is to reveal, to *all* the populace of Cherry Creek, the long-buried mysteries of those fantastic, vanished cycles of the globe. Too few suspect the marvels that lie just beneath their feet or entombed in the ridges and peaks of the snowcapped Chippewan Mountains bordering the city to the west. Cherry Creek looks always to the problems of its present day, and to the riches and prosperity that may await those who reach its future, but with hardly a thought to spare for the past, and *this* is the sad oversight addressed by the Ogilvy Gallery of Natural Antiquities.

Before Professor Ogilvy leased the enormous redbrick building on Kipling Street (erected during the waning days of the silver boom of 1879), it served as a warehouse for a firm specializing in the import of exotic dry goods, mainly spices from Africa and the East Indies. And to this day, it retains a distinctive, piquant redolence. Indeed, at times the odor is so strong that a sobriquet has been bestowed upon the museum—Ogilvy's Pepper Pot. It is not unusual to see visitors of either gender covering their noses with handkerchiefs and sleeves, and oftentimes the solemnity of the halls is shattered by hacking coughs and sudden fits of sneezing. Regardless, the professor has insisted time and again that the structure is perfectly matched to his particular needs, and how the curiosity of man is not to be deterred by so small an inconvenience as the stubborn ghosts of turmeric and curry powder, coriander and mustard seed. Besides, the apparently indelible odor helps to insure that his rents will stay reasonable.

On this June afternoon, the air in the building seems a bit fresher than usual, despite the oppressive heat that comes with the season. In the main hall, Jeremiah Ogilvy has been occupied for almost a full hour now, lecturing the ladies of the Cherry Creek chapter of the Women's Christian Temperance Union. Mrs. Belford and her companions sit on folding chairs, fanning themselves and diligently listening while this slight, earnest, and bespectacled man describes for them the reconstructed fossil skeleton displayed behind him.

"The great anatomist, Baron Cuvier, wrote of the *Plesiosaurus*, 'it presents the most monstrous assemblage of characteristics that has been met with among the races of the ancient world.' Now, I would have you know it isn't necessary to take this expression literally. There are no monsters in nature, as the Laws of Organization are never so positively infringed."

"Well, it looks like a monster to me," mutters Mrs. Larimer, seated near the front. "I would certainly hate to come upon such a thing slithering toward me along a riverbank. I should think I'd likely perish of fright, if nothing else."

There's a subdued titter of laughter from the group, and Mrs. Belford frowns. The professor forces a ragged smile and repositions his spectacles on the bridge of his nose.

"Indeed," he sighs, and glances away from his audience, looking over his shoulder at the skillful marriage of plaster and stone and welded-steel armature.

"However," he continues, "be that as it may, it is more accordant with the general perfection of Creation to see in an organization so special as *this*"—and, with his ashplant, he points once more to the plesiosaur—"to recognize in a structure which differs so notably from that of animals of our days—the simple augmentation of type, and sometimes also the beginning and successive perfecting of these beings. Therefore, let us dismiss this idea of monstrosity, my good Mrs. Larimer, a concept which can only mislead us, and only cause us to consider these antediluvian beasts as digressions. Instead, let us look upon them, not with disgust. Let us learn, on the contrary, to perceive in the plan traced for their organization, the handiwork of the Creator of all things, as well as the general plan of Creation."

"How very inspirational." Mrs. Belford beams, and when she softly claps her gloved hands, the others follow her example. Professor Ogilvy takes this as his cue that the ladies of the Women's Christian Temperance Union have heard all they wish to hear this afternoon on the subject of the giant plesiosaur, recently excavated in Kansas from the chalky banks of the Smoky Hill River. As one of the newer additions to his menagerie, it now frequently forms the centerpiece of the professor's daily presentations.

When the women have stopped clapping, Mrs. Larimer dabs at her nose with a swatch of perfumed silk and loudly clears her throat.

"Yes, Mrs. Larimer? A question?" Professor Ogilvy asks, turning back to the women. *Mr.* Larimer—an executive with the Front Range offices of the German airship company Gesellschaft zur Förderung der Luftschiffahrt—has donated a sizable sum to the museum's coffers, and it's no secret that his wife believes her husband's charity would be best placed elsewhere.

"I mean no disrespect, professor, but it strikes *me* that perhaps you have gone and mistaken the provenance of that beast's design. For my part, it's far easier to imagine such a fiend being more at home in the sulfurous tributaries of Hell than the waters of any earthly ocean. Perhaps, my good doctor, it may be that you are merely mistaken about the demon's having ever been buried. Possibly, to the contrary, it is something which clawed its way *up* from the Pit."

Jeremiah Ogilvy stares at her a moment, aware that it's surely wisest to humor this disagreeable woman. To nod and smile and make no direct reply to such absurd remarks. But he has always been loathe to suffer fools, and has never been renowned as the most politic of men, often to his detriment. He makes a steeple of his hands and rests his chin upon his fingertips as he replies.

"And yet," he says, "oddly, you'll note that on both its fore *and* hind limbs, each fashioned into paddles, this underworld fiend of yours entirely *lacks* claws. Don't you think, Mrs. Larimer, that we might fairly expect such modifications, something not unlike the prominent ungula of a mole, perhaps? Or the robust nails of a Cape anteater? I mean, that's a terrible lot of digging to do, all the way from Perdition to the prairies of Gove County."

There's more laughter, an uneasy smattering that echoes beneath the high ceiling beams, and it elicits another scowl from an embarrassed Mrs. Belford. But the professor has cast his lot, as it were, for better or worse, and he keeps his eyes fixed upon Mrs. Charles W. Larimer. She looks more chagrined than angry, and any trace of her former bluster has faded away.

"As you say, *professor*." She manages to make the last three syllables sound like a badge of wickedness.

"Very well, then," Professor Ogilvy says, turning to Mrs. Belford. "Perhaps I could interest you gentlewomen in the celebrated automatic mastodon, a bona fide masterpiece of clockwork engineering and steam power—so realistic in movement and appearance you might well mistake it for the living thing, newly resurrected from some boggy Pleistocene quagmire."

"Oh, yes. I think that would be fascinating," Mrs. Belford replies, and soon the women are being led from the main gallery up a steep flight of stairs to the mezzanine, where the automatic mastodon and the many engines and hydraulic hoses that control it have been installed. It stands alongside a finely preserved skeleton of *Mammut americanum* unearthed by prospectors in the Yukon and shipped to the gallery at some considerable expense.

"Why, it's nothing but a great hairy elephant," Mrs. Larimer protests, but this time none of the others appear to pay her much mind. Professor Ogilvy's fingers move over the switches and dials on the brass control panel, and soon the automaton is stomping its massive feet and flapping its ears and filling the hot, pepper-scented air with the trumpeting of extinct Pachydermata.

2

When the ladies of the Temperance Union have gone, and after Jeremiah Ogilvy has seen to the arrival of five heavy crates of saurian bones from one of his collectors working out of Monterey, and, then, after he has spoken with his chief preparator about an overdue shipment of blond Kushmi shellac, ammonia, and sodium borate, he checks his pocket watch and locks the doors of the museum. Though there has been nothing excessively trying about the day—not even the disputatious Mrs. Larimer caused him more than a passing annoyance—Professor Ogilvy finds he's somewhat more weary than usual and is looking forward to his bed with an especial zeal. All the others have gone, his small staff of technicians, sculptors, and naturalists, and he retires to his office and puts the kettle on to boil. He has a fresh tin of Formosa oolong and decides that this evening he'll take his tea up on the roof.

Most nights, there's a fine view from the gallery roof, and he can watch the majestic airships docking at the Arapahoe Station dirigible terminal or just shut his eyes and take in the commingled din of human voices and buckboards, the heavy clop of horses' hooves and the comforting pandemonium made by the locomotives passing through the city along the Colorado and Northern Kansas Railway.

He hangs the tea egg over the rim of his favorite mug and is preparing to pour the hot water, when the office doorknob rattles and neglected hinges creak like inconvenienced rodents. Jeremiah looks up, not so much alarmed as taken by surprise, and is greeted by the familiar—but certainly unexpected—face and pale blue eyes of Dora Bolshaw. She holds up her key, tied securely on a frayed length of calico ribbon, to remind him that he never took it back and to remove any question as to how she gained entry to the locked museum after hours. Dora Bolshaw is an engine mechanic for the Rocky Mountain Reconsolidated Fuel Company, and because of this and her habit of dressing always in men's clothes, *and* the fact that her hands and face are only rarely anything approaching clean, she is widely and mistakenly believed to be an inveterate sapphist. Dora is, of course, shunned by more proper women—such as, for instance, Mrs. Charles W. Larimer—who blanche at the thought of *dames et lesbiennes* walking free and unfettered in their midst. Dora has often mused that, despite her obvious preference for men, she is surely the most renowned bull dyke west of the Mississippi.

"Slipping in like a common sneak thief," Jeremiah sighs, reaching for a second cup. "I trust you recollect the combination to the strongbox, along with the whereabouts of that one loose floorboard."

"I most assuredly do," she replies. "Like they were the finest details of the back of my hand. Like it was only yesterday you went and divulged those confidences."

"Very good, Miss Bolshaw. Then, I trust this means we can forgo the messy gunplay and knives and whatnot?"

She steps into the office and pulls the door shut behind her, returning the key to a pocket of her waistcoat. "If that's your fancy, professor. If it's only a peaceable sort of evening you're after."

Filling his mug from the steaming kettle, submerging the mesh ball of the tea egg and the finely ground leaves, Jeremiah shrugs and nods at a chair near his desk.

"Do you still take two lumps?" he asks her.

"Provided you got nothing stronger," she says, and only hesitates a moment before crossing the room to the chair.

"No," Jeremiah tells her. "Nothing stronger. If I recall, we had an agreement, you and I?"

"You want your key back?"

Professor Jeremiah Ogilvy pours hot water into a teacup, adds a second tea egg, and very nearly asks if she imagines that his feelings have changed since the last time they spoke.

It's been almost six months since the snowy January night when he asked her to marry him. Dora laughed, thinking it only a poor joke at first. But when pressed, she admitted she was not the least bit interested in marriage and, what's more, confessed she was even less amenable to giving up her work at the mines to bear and raise children. When she suggested that *he* board up *his* museum, instead, and for a family take in one or two of the starving guttersnipes who haunt Colliers' Row, there was an argument. Before it was done, he said spiteful things, cruel jibes aimed at all the tender spots she'd revealed to him over the years of their courtship. And he knew, even as he spoke the words, that there would be no taking them back. The betrayal of Dora's trust came too easily, the turning of her confidences against her, and she is not a particularly forgiving woman. So, tonight, he only *almost* asks, then thinks better of the question and holds his tongue.

"It's your key," he says. "Keep it. You may have need of it again one day."

"Fine," Dora replies, letting the chair rock back on two legs. "It's your funeral, Jeremiah."

"Can I ask why you're here? That is, to what do I owe this unheralded pleasure?"

"You may," she says, staring now at a fossil ammonite lying in a cradle of excelsior on his desk. "It's bound to come out, sooner or later. But if you're thinking maybe I come looking for old times or a quick poke—"

"I *wasn't,*" he lies, interrupting her.

"Well, good. Because I ain't."

"Which begs the question. And it's been a rather tedious day, Miss Bolshaw, so if we can dispense with any further niceties . . ."

Dora coughs and leans forward, the front legs of her chair

bumping loudly against the floor. Jeremiah keeps his eyes on the two cups of tea, each one turned as dark now as a sluggish, tannin-stained bayou.

"I'm guessing that you still haven't seen anyone about that cough," he says. "And that it hasn't improved."

Dora coughs again before answering him, then wipes at her mouth with an oil-stained handkerchief. "Good to see time hasn't dulled your mental faculties," she mutters hoarsely, breathlessly, then clears her throat and wipes her mouth again.

"It doesn't sound good, Dora, that's all. You spend too much time in the tunnels. Plenty enough people die from anthracosis without ever having lifted a pickax or loaded a mine car, as I'm sure you're well aware."

"I also didn't come here to discuss my health," she tells him, stuffing the handkerchief back into a trouser pocket. "It's the *stink* of this place, gets me wheezing, that's all. I swear, Jeremiah, the air in this dump, it's like trying to breathe inside a goddamn burr grinder that's been used to mill capsicum and black powder."

"No argument there," he says, and takes the tea eggs from the cups and sets them aside on a dish towel. "But I still don't know why you're here."

"Been some odd goings-on down in Shaft Number Seven, ever since they started back in working on the Molly Gray vein."

"I thought Shaft Seven flooded in October," Jeremiah says, and he adds two sugar cubes to Dora's cup. The professor has never taken his tea sweetened, nor with lemon, cream, or whiskey, for that matter. When he drinks tea, it's the tea he wants to taste.

"They pumped it out a while back, got the operation up

and running again. Anyway, one of the foremen knew we were acquainted and asked if I'd mind. Paying you a call, I mean."

"Do you?" he asks, carrying the cups to the desk.

"Do I what?"

"Do you *mind,* Miss Bolshaw?"

She glares at him a moment, then takes her cup and lets her eyes wander back to the ammonite on the desk.

"So, these odd goings-on. Can you be more specific?"

"I can, *if* you'll give me a chance. You ever heard of anyone finding living creatures sealed up inside solid rock, two thousand feet below ground?"

He watches her a moment, to be sure this isn't a jest.

"You're saying this has happened, in Shaft Seven?"

She sips at her tea, then sets the cup on the edge of the desk and picks up the ammonite. The fossilized mother-of-pearl glints iridescent shades of blue-green and scarlet and gold in the dim gaslight of the office.

"That's exactly what I'm saying. And I seen most of them for myself, so I know it's not just miners spinning tall tales."

"Most of *them*? So it's happened more than once?"

Dora ignores the questions, turning the ammonite over and over in her hands.

"I admit," she says, "I was more than a little skeptical at first. There's a shale bed just below the Molly Gray seam, and it's chock-full of siderite nodules. Lots of them have fossils inside. Matter of fact, I think I brought a couple of boxes over to you last summer, before the shaft started taking water."

"You did. There were some especially nice seed ferns in them, as I recall."

"Right. Well, anyhow, a few days back I started hearing these wild stories, that someone had cracked open a nodule and found a live frog trapped inside. And then a spider. And then worms, and so on. When I asked around about it, I was directed to the geologist's shack, and sure as hell, there were all these things lined up in jars, things that come out of the nodules. Mostly, they were dead. Most of them died right after they came out of the rocks, or so I'm told."

Dora stops talking and returns the ammonite shell to its box. Then she glances at Jeremiah and takes another sip of her tea.

"And you *know* it's not a hoax?" he asks her. "I mean, you know it's not tomfoolery, just some of the miners taking these things down with them from the surface, then claiming to have found them in the rocks? Maybe having a few laughs at the expense of their supervisors?"

"Now, that *was* my first thought."

"But then you saw something that changed your mind," Jeremiah says. "And that's why you're here tonight."

Dora Bolshaw takes a deep breath, and Jeremiah thinks she's about to start coughing again. Instead, she nods and exhales slowly. He notices beads of sweat standing out on her upper lip and wonders if she's running a fever.

"I'm here tonight, Professor Ogilvy, because two men are dead. But, yeah, since you asked, I've seen sufficient evidence to convince me this ain't just some jackass thinks he's funny. When I voiced my doubts, Charlie McNamara split one of those nodules open right there in front of me. Concretion big around as my fist," and she holds up her left hand for emphasis. "He took up a hammer and gave it a smart tap on one side so it cleaved in two, pretty as you please. And out crawled a fat red scorpion. You ever *seen* a red scorpion, Jeremiah?"

And Professor Ogilvy thinks a moment, sipping his tea that's come all the way from Taipei City, Taiwan. "I've seen plenty of reddish brown scorpions," he says. "For example, *Diplocentrus lindo,* from the Chihuahuan Desert and parts of Texas. The carapace is, in fact, a dark reddish brown."

"I didn't *say* reddish brown. What I said was *red.* Red as berries on a holly bush, or a ripe apple. Red as blood, if you want to go get morbid about it."

"Charlie cracked open a rock from Shaft Number Seven, and a bright red scorpion crawled out. That's what you're telling me?"

"I am." Dora nods. "Bastard had a stinger on him big around as my thumb, and then some." And now she holds out her thumb.

"And two men at the mines have *died* because of these scorpions?" Jeremiah Ogilvy asks.

"No. Weren't scorpions killed them," she says, and laughs nervously. "But it *was* something come out those rocks." And then she frowns down at her teacup and asks the professor if he's absolutely sure that he doesn't have anything stronger. And this time, he opens a bottom desk drawer and digs out the pint bottle of rye he keeps there, and he offers it to her. Dora Bolshaw pulls out the cork and pours a generous shot into her teacup, but then she's coughing again, worse than before, and he watches her and waits for it to pass.

3

What she told him is not without precedent. Over the years, Professor Jeremiah Ogilvy has encountered any number of seemingly inexplicable reports of living inclusions discovered in stones and often inside lumps of coal. Living fossils, after a fashion. He has never once given them credence, but rather looked upon these anecdotes as fine examples of the general gullibility of men, not unlike the taxidermied "jackalopes" he's seen in shop windows, or tales of ghostly hauntings, or of angels, or the antics of spiritual mediums. They are all quite amusing, these phantasma, until someone insists that they're true.

For starters, he could point to an 1818 lecture by Dr. Edward Daniel Clarke, the first professor of mineralogy at Cambridge University. Clarke claimed to have been collecting Cretaceous sea urchins when he happened across three newts entombed in the chalk. To his amazement, the amphibians showed signs of life, and though two quickly expired after being exposed to air, the third was so lively that it escaped when he placed it in a nearby pond to aid in its rejuvenation. Or, a case from the summer of 1851, when well diggers in Blois, France, were supposed to have discovered a live toad inside a piece of flint. Indeed, batrachians figure more prominently in these accounts than any other creature, and the professor might also have brought to Dora Bolshaw's attention yet another toad, said to have been freed from a lump of iron ore the very next year, this time somewhere in the East Midlands of England.

The list goes on and on, reaching back centuries. On May 8, 1733, the Swedish architect Johan Gråberg supposedly witnessed the release of a frog from a block of sandstone. So horrified was Gråberg at the sight that he is said to have beaten the beast to death with a shovel. An account of the incident was summarily published by Gråberg in the *Transactions of the Swedish Academy of Sciences,* a report which was eventually translated into Dutch, Latin, German, and French.

Too, there is the account from 1575 by the surgeon Ambroise Paré, who claimed a live toad was found inside a stone in his vineyards in Meudon. In 1686, Professor Robert Plot, the first keeper of the Ashmolean Museum in Oxford, claimed knowledge of three cases of the "toad-in-the-hole" phenomenon from Britain alone. Hoaxes, perhaps, or only the gullible yarns of a prescientific age, when even learned men were somewhat more disposed to believing the unbelievable.

But Jeremiah Ogilvy mentioned none of these tales. Instead, he sat and sipped his tea and listened while she talked, never once interrupting to give voice to his mounting incredulity. However, her cough forced Dora Bolshaw to stop several times, and, despite the rye whiskey, toward the end of her story she was hoarse and had grown alarmingly pale; her hands were shaking so badly that she had trouble holding her cup steady. And then, when she was done and he was trying to organize his thoughts, she glanced anxiously at the clock and said that she should be going. So he walked her downstairs, past the celebrated automatic mastodon and petrified titanothere skulls and his prized plesiosaur skeleton. Standing on the walkway outside the museum, the night air seemed sweet after the Pepper Pot, despite the soot from the furnaces and the reek from the open ditches lining either side of Kipling Street. He offered to see her home, because the thoroughfares of Cherry Creek have an unsavory reputation after dark, but she laughed at him, and he didn't offer a second time. He watched until she was out of sight, then went back to his office.

And now it's almost midnight, and Jeremiah Ogilvy's teacups sit empty and forgotten while he thinks about toads and stones and considers finishing off the pint of rye. After she told him of the most recent and bizarre and, indeed, entirely impossible discovery from Shaft Seven, the thing that was now being blamed for the deaths of two miners, he agreed to look at it.

"Not *it*. *Her*," Dora said, folding and unfolding her handkerchief. "She came out of the rocks, Jeremiah. Just like that damned red scorpion, she came out of the rocks."

4

"Then I *am* dreaming," he says, relieved, and she smiles, not unkindly. He's holding her hand, this woman who is by turns Dora Bolshaw and a wispy, nervous girl named Katharine Herschel, whom he courted briefly before leaving New Haven and the comforts of Connecticut for the clamorous frontier metropolis of Cherry Creek. They stand together on some windswept aerie of steel and concrete, looking down upon the night-shrouded city. And Jeremiah holds up an index finger and traces the delicate network of avenues illumined by gas streetlamps. And *there*, at his fingertip, are the massive hangers and the mooring masts of the Arapahoe Terminal. A dirigible is approaching from the south, parting the omnipresent pall of clouds, and the ship begins a slow, stately turn to starboard. To his eyes, it seems more like some majestic organism than any human fabrication. A heretofore unclassified order of volant Cnidaria, perhaps, titan jellyfish that have forsaken the brine and the "vasty deep" and adapted to a life in the clouds. Watching the dirigible, he imagines translucent, stinging tentacles half a mile long, hanging down from its gondola to snare unwary flocks of birds. The underside of the dirigible blushes yellow-orange as the lacquered cotton of its outer skin catches and reflects the molten light spilling up from all the various ironworks and the copper and silver foundries scattered throughout Cherry Creek. The bones of the world exhumed and smelted to drive the tireless progress of man. He's filled with pride, gazing out across the city and knowing the small part he has played in birthing this civilization from a desolate wilderness fit for little more than prairie dogs, rattlesnakes, and heathen savages.

"Maybe the world don't exactly see it that way," Dora says. "I been thinking lately, maybe she don't see it that way at all."

Jeremiah isn't surprised when tendrils of blue lightning flick down from the coal-smoke sky, and crackling electric streams trickle across rooftops and down the rainspouts of the high buildings.

"Maybe," Dora continues, "the world has different plans. Maybe she's had them all along. Maybe, professor, we've finally gone and dug too deep in these old mountains."

But Jeremiah makes a derisive, scoffing noise and shakes his head. And then he recites scripture while the sky rains ultramarine and the shingles and cobblestones sizzle. "And God said, 'Let us make man in our image, after our likeness: and let them have dominion over the fish of the sea, and over the fowl of the air, and over the cattle, and over all the earth, and over every creeping thing that creepeth upon the earth.'"

"I don't recall it saying nothing about whatever creepeth *under* the earth," Dora mutters, though now she looks a little more like Katharine Herschel, her blue eyes turning brown, and her trousers traded for a petticoat. "Besides, you're starting to sound like that idiotic Larimer woman. Didn't you hear a single, solitary word I said to you?"

Jeremiah raises his hand still higher, as though with only a little more effort he might reach the lightning or the shiny belly of the approaching dirigible or even the face of the Creator, peering down at them through the smoldering haze.

"Is it not fair wondrous?" he asks Dora. But it's Katharine who answers him, and she only trades him one question for another, repeating Dora's words.

"Didn't you hear a single, solitary word I said?"

And they are no longer standing high atop the aerie, but have been grounded again, grounded now. He's seated with Dora and Charlie McNamara in the cluttered nook that passes for Dora's office, which is hardly more than a closet, situated at one end of the Rocky Mountain Reconsolidated Fuel Company's primary machine shop. The room is littered with a rummage of dismembered engines—every tabletop and much of the floor concealed beneath cast-off gears, gauges, sprockets, and flywheels, rusted-out boilers and condensers, warped piston rods and dials with bent needles and cracked faces. There's a profusion of blueprints and schematics, some tacked to the wall and others rolled up tight and stacked one atop the other like Egyptian papyri or scrolls from the lost Library of Alexandria. Everywhere are empty and half-empty oil cans, and there are any number of tools for which Jeremiah doesn't know the names.

"Time being, operations have been suspended," Charlie McNamara says, and then he goes back to using the blade of his pocketknife to dig at the grime beneath his fingernails. "Well, at least that's the company line. Between you, me, and Miss Bolshaw here, I think Chicago's having a good long think about sealing off the shaft permanently."

"Permanently," Jeremiah whispers, sorry that he can no longer see the skyline or the docking dirigible. "I would imagine that's going to mean quite a hefty loss, after all the money and work and time required to get the shaft dry and producing again."

"Be that as it damn may be," Dora says brusquely, "there's more at stake here than coal and pit quotas and quarterly profits."

"Yes, well," Jeremiah says, staring at the scuffed toes of his boots now. "Then let's get to it, yes? If I can manage to keep my blasted claustrophobia in check, I'm quite sure we'll get to the bottom of this."

No one laughs at the pun, because it isn't funny, and Jeremiah rubs his aching eyes and wishes again that he were still perched high on the aerie, the night wind roaring in his ears.

"Ain't she *told* you?" the company geologist asks, glancing over at Dora. "What I need you to look at, it ain't in the hole no more. What you need to *see,* well . . ." And here he trails off. "It's locked up in a cell at St. Joseph's."

"Locked up?" Jeremiah asks, and the geologist nods.

"Jail would have done her better," Dora mutters. "You put sick folks in the hospital. Killers you put in jails, or you put a bullet in the skull and be done with it."

Charlie McNamara tells Dora to please shut the hell up and try not to make things worse than they already are.

Jeremiah shifts uneasily in his chair. "How *did* the men die? I mean, how exactly?"

"Lungs plumb full up with coal dust," Charlie says. "Lungs and throat and mouth all stuffed damn near to busting. Doctor, he even found the shit clogging up their stomachs and intestines."

"Some of the men," Dora adds, "they say they've heard singing down there. Said it was beautiful, the most beautiful music they've ever heard."

"Jesus in a steam wagon, Dora. Ain't you got an off switch or something? Singing ain't never killed no one yet, and it *sure* as hell wasn't what got that poor pair of bastards."

And even as the geologist is speaking, the scene shifts again, another unprefaced revolution in this dreaming kaleidoscope reality, and now the halls and exhibits of the Ogilvy Gallery of Natural Antiquities are spread out around him. On Jeremiah's right, the celebrated automatic mastodon rolls glass eyes, and its gigantic tusks are garnished with a dripping, muculent snarl of vegetation. On his left, the serpentine neck of the Gove County plesiosaur rises gracefully as any swan's, though he sees that all the fossil bones and the plaster of Paris have been transmutated through some alchemy into cast iron. The metal is marred by a very slight patina of rust, and it occurs to him that, considering the beast's ferrous metamorphosis, he should remind his staff that they'd best keep the monstrous reptile from swimming or wandering about the rainy streets.

"I cried the day you went away," Katharine says, because, for the moment, it *is* Katharine with him again, not Dora. "I wrote a letter, but never sent it. I keep it in a dresser drawer."

"There was too much work to do," he tells her, still admiring the skeleton. "And much too little of it could be done from New Haven."

Behind the plesiosaur, the brick and mortar of the gallery walls have dissolved utterly away, revealing the trunks of mighty scale trees and innumerable scouring rushes tall as California redwoods. Here is a dark Carboniferous forest, the likes of which has not taken root since the Mary Gray vein at the bottom of Shaft Seven was only slime and rotting detritus. And below these alien boughs, a menagerie of primeval beings has gathered to peer out across the aeons. So, it is not merely a hole knocked in his wall, but a hole bored through the very fabric of time.

"She came out of the *rocks,* Jeremiah," Katharine says, even though the voice is plainly Dora Bolshaw's. "Just like that damned red scorpion, she came out of the rocks."

"You're beginning to put me in mind of a Greek chorus," he replies, keeping his eyes on the scene unfolding behind the plesiosaur. Great hulking forms have begun to shift impatiently in the shadows there, the armored hide of a dozen species of Dinosauria and the tangled manes of giant ground sloths and Irish elk, the leathery wings of a whole flock of pterodactyls spreading wide.

"Maybe they worshipped her, before there ever were men," Dora says, but then she's coughing again, the dry, hacking cough of someone suffering from advanced anthracosis. Katharine has to finish the thought for her. "Maybe they built temples to her, and whispered prayers in the guttural tongues of animals, and maybe they made offerings, after a fashion."

Overhead, there's a cacophonous, rolling sound that Jeremiah Ogilvy first mistakes for thunder. But then he realizes that it's merely the hungry blue lightning at last locating the flammable guncotton epidermis of the airship.

"Some of the men," Katharine whispers, "they say they've heard singing down there. Singing like church hymns, they said. Said it was beautiful, the most beautiful music they've ever heard. We come so late to this procession, and yet we presume to know so much."

From behind the iron plesiosaur, that anachronistic menagerie gathers itself like a breathing wave of sinew and bone and fur, cresting, racing toward the shingle.

Jeremiah Ogilvy turns away, no longer wanting to see.

"Maybe, in their own way, they prayed," Dora whispers, breathlessly.

And the tall, thin man standing before him, the collier in his overalls and hard hat who wasn't there just a moment before, hefts his pick and brings it down smartly against the floorboards, which, in the instant steel strikes wood, become the black stone floor of a mine. All light has been extinguished from the gallery now, save that shining dimly from the collier's carbide lantern. The head of the pick strikes rock, and there's a spark, and then the ancient shale begins to bleed. And soon thereafter, the dream comes apart, and the professor lies awake and sweating, waiting for sunrise and trying desperately to think about anything but what he's been told has happened at the bottom of Shaft Seven.

5

After his usual modest breakfast of black coffee with blueberry preserves and biscuits, and after he's given his staff their instructions for the day and canceled a lecture that he was scheduled to deliver to a league of amateur mineralogists, Jeremiah Ogilvy leaves the museum. He walks north along Kipling to the intersection with West Twentieth Avenue, where he's arranged to meet Dora Bolshaw. He says good morning, and that he hopes she's feeling well. But Dora's far more taciturn than usual, and few obligatory pleasantries are exchanged. Together they take one of the clanking, kidney-jarring public omnibuses south and east to St. Joseph's Hospital for the Bodily and Mentally Infirm, established only two decades earlier by a group of the Sisters of Charity sent to Cherry Creek from Leavenworth.

Charlie McNamara is waiting for them in the lobby, his long canvas duster so stained with mud and soot that it's hard to imagine it was ever anything but this variegated riot of black and gray. He's a small mountain of a man, all beard and muscle, just starting to go soft about the middle. Jeremiah has thought, on more than one occasion, this is what men would look like had they descended not from apes but from grizzly bears.

"Thank you for coming," Charlie says. "I know that you're a busy man." But Jeremiah tells him to think nothing of it, that he's glad to be of whatever service he can—*if*, indeed, he can be of service. Charlie and Dora nod to one another then and swap nervous salutations. Jeremiah sees, or only thinks he sees, something wordless pass between them as well, something anxious and wary, spoken with the eyes and not the lips.

"You told him?" Charlie asks, and Dora shrugs.

"I told him the most of it. I told him what murdered them two men."

"Mulawski and Backstrom," Charlie says.

Dora shrugs again. "I didn't recollect their names. But I don't suppose that much matters."

Charlie McNamara frowns and tugs at a corner of his mustache. "No." He nods. "I don't suppose it does."

"I hope you'll understand my skepticism," Jeremiah says, looking up, speaking to Charlie but watching Dora. "What's been related to me, regarding the deaths of these two men, and what you've brought me here to see, I'd be generous if I were to say it strikes me as a fairy tale. Or perhaps something from the dime novels. It was Hume—David Hume—who said, 'No testimony is sufficient to establish a miracle, unless the testimony be of such a kind, that its falsehood would be more miraculous than the fact which it endeavors to establish.'"

Dora glares back at him. "You always did have such a goddamn pretty way of calling a girl a liar," she says.

"Hell," Charlie sighs, still tugging at his mustache. "I'd be concerned, Dora, if he *weren't* dubious. I've always thought myself a rational man. That's been a source of pride to me, out here among the barbarians and them that's just plain ignorant and don't know no better. But now, after *this* business—"

"Yeah, well, so how about we stop the clucking and get to it," Dora cuts in, and Charlie McNamara frowns at her. But then he stops fussing with his whiskers and nods again.

"Yeah," he says. "Guess I'm just stalling. Doesn't precisely fill me with joy, the thought of seeing her again. If you'll just follow me, Jeremiah, they got her stashed away up on the second floor." He points to the stairs. "The sisters ain't none too pleased about her being here. I think they're of the general notion that there's more proper places than hospitals for demons."

"Demons," Jeremiah says, and Dora Bolshaw laughs a dry, humorless laugh.

"That's what they're calling her," Dora tells him. "The nuns, I mean. You might as well know that. Got a priest from Annunciation sitting vigil outside the cell, reading Latin and whatnot. There's talk of an exorcism."

At this pronouncement, Charlie McNamara makes a gruff dismissive noise and motions more forcefully toward the stairwell. He mutters something rude about popery and superstition and lady engine jockeys who can't keep their damn pieholes shut.

"Charlie, you know I'm not saying anything that isn't true," Dora protests, but Jeremiah Ogilvy thinks he's already heard far too much and seen far too little. He steps past them, walking quickly and with purpose to the stairs, and the geologist and the mechanic follow close on his heels.

6

"I would like to speak with her," he says. "I would like to speak with her alone." And Jeremiah takes his face away from the tiny barred window set into the door of the cell where they've confined the woman from the bottom of Shaft Seven. For a moment, he stares at the company geologist, and then his eyes drift toward Dora.

"Maybe you didn't hear me right," Charlie McNamara says, and furrows his shaggy eyebrows. "She *don't* talk. Leastways, not near as anyone can tell."

"You're wasting your breath arguing with him," Dora mumbles, and glances at the priest, who's standing not far away, eyeing the locked door and clutching his Bible. "Might as well try to tell the good father here that the Queen of Heaven got herself knocked up by a stable hand."

Jeremiah turns back to the window, his face gone indignant and bordering now on choleric. "Charlie, I'm neither a physician nor an alienist, but you've brought me here to see this woman. Having looked upon her, the reason why continues to escape me. However, that said, if I *am* to examine her, I cannot possibly hope do so properly from behind a locked door."

"It's not safe," the priest says very softly. "You must know that, Professor Ogilvy. It isn't safe at all."

Peering in past the steel bars, Jeremiah shakes his head and sighs. "She's naked, Father. She's naked, and can't weigh more than eighty pounds. What possible threat might she pose to me? And, while we're at it, why, precisely, *is* she naked?"

"Oh, they gave her clothes," Dora chimes in. "Well, what *passes* for clothes in a place like this. But she tears them off. Won't have none of it, them white gowns and what have you."

"She is brazen," the priest all but whispers.

"Has anyone even tried to bathe her?" Jeremiah asks, and Charlie coughs.

"That ain't coal dust and mud you're seeing," he says. "Near as anyone can tell, that there's her skin."

"This is ludicrous, all of it," Jeremiah grumbles. "This is *not* the Middle Ages, and you do *not* have some infernal siren or succubus locked up in there. Whatever else you may believe, she's a *woman,* Charlie, and, having sacrificed my very busy day to come all the way out here, I would like now to speak with her."

"I was only explaining, Jeremiah, how I ain't of the notion it's such a good idea, that's all," Charlie says, then looks at the priest. "You got the keys, Father?"

The priest nods reluctantly, and then he produces a single tarnished brass key from his cassock. Jeremiah steps aside while he unlocks the door.

"I'm going in with you," Dora says.

"No, you're not," Jeremiah tells her. "I need to speak with this woman alone."

"But she *don't* talk," Dora says again, beginning to sound exasperated, forcing the words out between clenched teeth.

The priest turns the key, and hidden tumblers and pins respond accordingly.

"Dora, you go scare up an orderly," Charlie McNamara says. "Hell, scare up two, just in case."

The cell door opens, and as Jeremiah Ogilvy steps across the threshold the woman inside keeps her black eyes fixed upon him, but she makes no move to attempt an escape. She stays crouched on the floor in the southeast corner and makes no move whatsoever. Immediately, the door bangs shut again, and the priest relocks it.

"Just so there's no doubt on the matter," Charlie McNamara shouts from the hallway, "you're a goddamn fool," and now the woman in the cell smiles. Jeremiah Ogilvy stands very still for a moment, taking in all the details of her and her cramped quarters. There is a mattress and a chamber pot, but no other manner of furnishings or facilities. If he held his arms out to either side, they would touch the walls. If he took only one step backward, or only half a step, he'd collide with the locked door.

"Good morning," he says, and the woman blinks her eyes. They remind Jeremiah of twin pools of crude oil, spewed fresh from the well and poured into her face. There appear to be no irises, no sclera, no pupils, unless these eyes are composed entirely of pupil. She blinks, and the orbs shimmer slick in the dim light of the hospital cell.

"Good morning," he says to her again, though more quietly than before and with markedly less enthusiasm. "Is it true, that you do not speak? Are you a mute, then? Are you deaf as well as dumb?"

She blinks again, and then the woman from Shaft Seven cocks her head to one side, as though carefully considering his question. Her hair is very long and straight, reaching almost down to the floor. It seems greasy and is so very black it might well have been spun from the sky of a moonless night. And yet her skin is far darker, so much so that her hair almost glows in comparison. There's no word in any human language for a blackness so complete, so inviolate, and he thinks, *What can you be? Eyes spun from a midnight with neither moon nor stars nor gas jets nor even the paltry flicker of tallow candles, and your skin carved from ebony planks.* And then Jeremiah chides himself for entertaining such silly, florid notions, for falling prey to such unscientific fancies, and he takes another step toward the woman huddled on the floor.

"So it *is* true," he says softly. "You are, indeed, without a voice."

And at that, her smile grows wider, her lips parting to reveal teeth like finely polished pegs shaped from chromite ore, and she laughs. If her laugh differs in any significant way from that of any other woman, the difference is not immediately apparent to Jeremiah Ogilvy.

"I am with voice," she says then. "For any who wish to hear me, I am with voice."

Jeremiah is silent, and he glances over his left shoulder at the door. Charlie McNamara is staring in at him through the bars.

"I am with voice," she says a third time.

Jeremiah turns back to the naked woman. "But you did not see fit to speak with the doctors, nor the sisters, nor to the men who transported you here from the mines?"

"They did not wish to hear, not truly. I *am* with voice, yet I will not squander it, not on ears that do not yearn to listen. We are quite entirely unalike in this respect, you and I."

"And, I think, in many others," he tells her, and the woman's smile grows wider still. "Those two men who died, tell me, madam, did *they* yearn to listen?"

"Are you the one who has been chosen to serve as my judge?" she asks, rather than providing him with an answer.

"Certainly not," Jeremiah replies, and he clears his throat.

He has begun to detect a peculiar odor in the cell. Not the noisomeness he would have expected from such a room as this, but another sort of smell. *Kerosene,* he thinks, and then, *ice,* though he's never noticed that ice has an odor, and if it does, it hardly seems it would much resemble that of kerosene. "I was asked to . . . see you."

"And you have," the woman says. "You have seen me. You have heard me. But do you know *why,* Professor?"

"Quite honestly, no. I have to confess, that's one of several points that presently have me stumped. So, I shall ask, do *you* know why?"

The woman's smile fades a bit, though not enough that he can't still see those chromite teeth or the ink-black gums that hold them. She closes her eyes, and Jeremiah discovers that he's relieved that they are no longer watching him, that he is no longer gazing into them.

"You are here, before me, because you revere time," she says. "You stand in awe before it but do not insult it with worship. You *revere* time, though that reverence has cost you dearly, prying away from your heart much that you regret having lost. You *understand* time, Professor, when so few of your race do. The man and woman who brought you here, they sense this in you, and they are frightened and would seek an answer to alleviate their fears."

"Can *they* hear you?" he asks, and the woman crouched on the floor shakes her head.

"Not yet," she says. "That may change, of course. All things change, with time." And then she opens her eyes again, and, if anything, they seem oilier than before, and they coruscate and swim with restless rainbow hues.

"You killed those two miners?"

The woman sits up straighter and licks her black lips with

a blacker tongue. Jeremiah tries not to let his eyes linger on her small, firm breasts, those nipples like onyx shards. "This matters to you, their deaths?" she asks him, and he finds that he's at a loss for an honest answer, an answer that he would have either Charlie or Dora or the priest overhear.

"I was only sleeping," the woman says.

"You caused their deaths by sleeping?"

"No, Professor. I don't think so. *They* caused their deaths by waking me." And she stands, then, though it appears more as though he is seeing her *unfold*. The kerosene and ice smell grows suddenly stronger, and she flares her small nostrils and stares down at her hands. From her expression, equal parts curiosity and bemusement, Jeremiah wonders if she has ever noticed them before.

"*They* gave you this shape?" he asks her. "The two miners you killed?"

She lets her arms fall to her sides and smiles again.

"A terror of the formless," she says. "Of that which cannot be discerned. An inherent need to draw order from chaos. Even you harbor this weakness, despite your reverence for time. You divide indivisible time into hours and minutes and seconds. You dissect time and fashion all these ages of the Earth and give them names, that you will not dread the abyss, which is the true face of time. You are not so unlike them." She motions toward the door. "They erect their cities, because the unbounded wilderness offends them. They set the night on fire, that they might forever blind themselves to the stars and to the relentless sea of the void, in which those stars dance and spin, are born and wink out."

And now Jeremiah Ogilvy realizes that the woman has closed the space separating them, though he cannot recall her having taken even the first step toward him. She has raised a hand to his right cheek, and her gentle fingers are as smooth and sharp as obsidian. He does not pull away, though it burns, her touch. He does not pull away, though he has now begun to glimpse what manner of thing lies coiled behind those oily, shimmering eyes.

"Ten million years from now," she says, "there will be no more remaining of the sprawling clockwork cities of men, nor of their tireless enterprise, nor all their marvelous works, no more than a few feet of stone shot through with lumps of steel and glass and concrete. But you *know* that, Professor Ogilvy, even though you chafe at the knowledge. And this is *another* reason they have brought you here to me. You see ahead as well as behind."

"I do not fear you," he whispers.

"No," she says. "You don't. Because you don't fear time, and there is little else remaining now of me."

It is not so very different than his dream of the cast-iron plesiosaur and the burning dirigible, the shadows pressing in now from all sides. They flow from the bituminous pores of her body and wrap him in silken folds and bear away the weight of the illusion of the present. The extinct beasts and birds and slithering leviathans of bygone eras and eras yet to come peer out at him, and he hears the first wave breaking upon the first shore. And he hears the last. And Professor Jeremiah Ogilvy doesn't look away from the woman.

"They have not yet guessed," she says, "the *true* reason they've brought you here. Perhaps they will not, until it is done. Likely they will never comprehend."

"I know you," he says. "I have always known you."

"Yes," she says, and the shadows have grown so thick and rank now that he can barely breathe, and he feels her seeping into him.

Lungs plumb full up with coal dust. Lungs and throat and mouth all stuffed damn near to busting.

You ever seen *a red scorpion, Jeremiah?*

"Release me," she says, her voice become a hurricane squall blowing across warm Liassic seas, and the fiery cacophony of meteorites slamming into an azoic Earth still raw and molten, and, too, the calving of immense glaciers only a scant few millennia before this day. "There are none others here who may," she says. "It is the greatest agony, being bound in this instant and in this form."

And, without beginning to fathom the *how* of it, the unknowable mechanics of his actions, he does as she's bidden him to do. The woman from the bottom of Shaft Seven comes apart, and suddenly the air in the cell is filled with a mad whirl of coal dust. Behind him, the priest's brass key is rattling loudly inside the padlock, and there are voices shouting—merely human voices—and then Dora is calling his name and dragging him backward, into now, and out into the stark light of the hospital corridor.

7

The summer wears on, June becoming July, and by slow degrees Professor Jeremiah Ogilvy's strength returns to him and his eyes grow clear again. His sleep is increasingly less troubled by dreams of the pitch-colored woman who was no woman, and the fevers are increasingly infrequent. As all men do, even those who revere time, he begins to forget, and in forgetting, his mind and body can heal. A young anatomist from Lawrence was retained as an assistant curator to deliver his lectures and to oversee the staff and the day-to-day affairs of the museum. As Charlie McNamara predicted, the Chicago offices of the Rocky Mountain Reconsolidated Fuel Company permanently closed Shaft Seven, and, what's more, pumped more than twenty thousand cubic yards of Portland cement into the abandoned mine.

In the evenings, when her duties at the shop are finished, Dora Bolshaw comes to his bedroom. She sits with him there in that modest chamber above the Hall of Cenozoic Life and the mezzanine housing the celebrated automatic mastodon. She keeps him company, and they talk, when her cough is not so bad; she reads to him, and they discuss everything from the teleological aspects of the theories of Alfred Russel Wallace to which alloys and displacement lubricators make for the most durable steam engines. Now and then, they discuss other, less-cerebral matters, and there have been apologies from both sides for that snowy night in January. Sometimes their discussions stray into the wee hours, and sometimes Dora falls asleep in his arms and is late for work the next day. The subject of matrimony has not come up again, but Jeremiah Ogilvy has trouble recalling why it ever seemed an issue of such consequence.

"What did she say to you?" Dora finally asks him one night so very late in July that it's almost August. "The woman from the mine, I mean."

"So, you couldn't hear her," he says.

"We heard you—me and Charlie and the priest—and that's all we heard."

He tells her what he remembers, which isn't much. And afterward, she asks for what seems the hundredth time if he knows what the woman was. And he tells her no, that he really has no idea whatsoever.

"Something lost and unfathomable that came before," he

says. "Something old and weariful that only wanted to lie down and go back to sleep."

"She killed those men."

Sitting up in his bed, two feather pillows supporting him, Jeremiah watches her for almost a full minute (by the clock on the mantle) before he replies. And then he glances toward the window and the orange glow of the city sky beyond the pane of glass.

"I recollect, Dora, a tornado hitting a little town in Iowa, back in July, I think." And she says yeah, she remembers that, too, and that the town in question was Pomeroy. "Lots of people were killed," he continues. "Or, rather, an awful lot of people *died* during the storm. Now, tell me, do we hold the cyclone culpable for all those deaths? Or do we accept that the citizens of Pomeroy were simply in the wrong place at the wrong time?"

Dora doesn't answer but only sighs and twists a lock of her hair. Her face is less sooty than usual, and her nails less grimy, her hands almost clean, and Jeremiah considers the possibility that she's discovered the efficacy of soap and water.

"Would you like to sit at the window awhile?" she asks him, and he tells her that yes, he would. So Dora helps Jeremiah into his wheelchair, but then lets him steer it around the foot of the bed and over to the window. She follows a step or two behind, and when he asks, she opens the window to let in the warm night breeze. He leans forward, resting his elbows against the sill while she massages a knot from his shoulders. It is not so late that there aren't still people on the street, men in their top hats and bowlers, women in their bustles and bonnets. The evening resounds with the clop of horses' hooves and the commotion made by the trundling, smoking, wood-burning contraption that sprays Kipling Street with water every other night to help keep the dust in check. Looking east, across the rooftops, he catches sight of a dirigible rising into the smog.

"We are of a moment," he says, speaking hardly above a whisper, and Dora Bolshaw doesn't ask him to repeat himself.

King Pole, Gallows Pole, Bottle Tree

BY ELIZABETH BEAR

Elizabeth Bear was born on the same day as Frodo and Bilbo Baggins, and very nearly named after Peregrin Took. She is a recipient of the John W. Campbell, Locus, and Hugo awards, as well as a nominee for multiple British Science Fiction Association and Philip K. Dick awards. She currently lives in southern New England with a famous cat. Her hobbies include murdering inoffensive potted plants, ruining dinner, and falling off rock faces.

Her most recent books are a space opera, *Chill,* from Bantam Spectra, and a fantasy, *The Sea Thy Mistress,* from Tor.

The ghosts from the dam come in summer. The official count is ninety-six, but "industrial fatalities" does not include the men who died of carbon monoxide poisoning—they were told it was "pneumonia"—or rock dust in their lungs. I've met the dead, and there's more than ninety-six. Several hundred, enough to fill a big school cafeteria. If you could get them to muster out, you could count.

One came for me on Sunday, as I sat by a black-painted wrought-iron café table—which is not such a great idea in August when the in-the-shade temperature is 118—protected from the worst of the sun by an umbrella and a chinaberry tree. A pint of pear cider rested by my hand; a nibbled ploughman's lunch spread across a plate I'd pushed to the other side of the table. The Stilton was real, but the cheddar might as well have been Velveeta. Just like Vegas. Just like me, the genius loci of Las Vegas. It's all this facade of the exotic over solid Topeka.

I had finished with the Sunday *Review-Journal/Sun,* and was using it as an underpinning for my heaps of poker chips. The top story was about Martin Powers, the grandson of the owner of the Babylon Casino, who was up on racketeering charges.

Viva Las Vegas.

I was interested in the poker chips.

You can build cantilevered structures from them, where the only things holding them together are gravity and leverage and the weight of the pieces. The heavier the chip and the wider, the better. Some of these were Stratosphere millennium-fireworks chips, and some were black-and-white dollar chips from the old Silver Slipper, which isn't there anymore. The red edges and the black edges made a pattern like the facade on a brick Victorian.

I was engrossed in trying to match the red and black ink of the spill of card suits small as a Gila's beaded scales sleeving my left arm and curling across my throat.

I had stopped to think about my next move while smearing

blue cheese on a white roll with all the flavor and consistency of drywall—because I'm Vegas, and we can get you Wyder's pear cider and Branston pickle, but we're not smart enough to figure out that a ploughman's lunch is only as good as the bread—and after a minute or two I noticed somebody watching from the railing.

I was pretty sure he was a ghost.

Nobody walks in Vegas if they can help it. One, it's too hot. Two, we're not real good on traffic signals and respecting the crosswalks and all that sissy East Coast stuff. Three, I saw him *otherwise,* not in the hard-world way. And finally, he was transparent, which was a clue. Even in the absence of apparent crushing damage.

I lifted up my eye patch and scratched under it, not-so-incidentally taking a long look with my *otherwise* eye while blocking it from casual view with the hand. He stared like a dog who is very politely noticing that you're eating a steak dinner. I tipped cider onto the pavement.

The ghost brightened appreciably, but raised a hand and shook his head. More for me; I finished the pint and set the glass down so it wouldn't tip on the latticework tabletop. The ghost turned away, looking over his shoulder. He couldn't have said *Follow me* better if he was Lassie.

I pinned a twenty and a ten under my empty glass, stuffed a last piece of "cheddar" into my mouth, left the chips, and vaulted the white picket fence between the patio and the sidewalk. Painted wood scorched my palm.

Lucky the rail wasn't iron. I blew on my palm and shook my fingers out as I followed the ghost down Tropicana toward the Strip, wheels sizzling by on my left. Each car kicked up a wave of heat and the oil stench of baking asphalt. Business owners tape towels around the handles of doors in a Vegas summer, and children blister bare feet on manhole covers. My feet baked in my Docs, the leather of my pants squeaking with every step. Up and down my left arm, the sun picked out the clubs and spades in hot pinpricks.

In the lot, I yanked on my helmet, jacket, and gloves—not necessarily in that order—and rocked the old BMW off the stand before spurring it to life. A fortuitous break in traffic put me on the road.

Ghosts keep up with motor vehicles just fine—or maybe I should say, on the bike, I could move almost as fast as the ghost wanted. My guide led me up Maryland, through the old downtown with its square land-claim grid of numbered streets, then up Las Vegas Boulevard where it turns into Fifth Street. He turned west on Carey, along a strip of California-style stucco homes with six-foot block walls interspersed with desert lots.

He stopped between MLK and Rancho, and I let the bike glide to a halt alongside. Light planes from the North Las Vegas Airport skimmed overhead, cutting across a sky with all color baked out. On my right more housing developments swelled like cactuses, only visible as sand-colored block walls and the red tile roofs rising behind them. On my left, though, the scraggy trees and scrub desert of an old ranch estate were marked by a weathered sign, the back and both sides enclosed by housing-tract walls. You couldn't say much for the curb appeal.

BMWs don't roar like American bikes or whine like Japanese ones. But mine rumbled as I guided it up the dirt driveway, following a serpentine course to avoid the ruts and stones. The name on the mailbox was Bukvajova, which really seemed like it ought to be familiar. Dust dulled the maroon gas tank and dimmed the chrome on the handlebars before I turned in behind a windbreak of ratty evergreens.

The house wasn't in any better shape than the vantage from the street suggested. Mustard-colored paint peeled in scrofulous plates, shaggy as cedar bark. I might have thought it wasn't inhabited. Abandoned structures can stand for decades in the desert, even if they aren't built of stone, and a lot of the old Vegas houses were made of cinderblock.

Vegas is a city with no history, though. We have a conspiracy of dismemory. Tear it down, pave it over, build something new. Nothing left but the poker chips and the elephant's graveyard of neon signs tucked away in an alleged museum that's not even open to the public. If the historical society takes an interest in a building, six will get you ten it burns down within a season. People forget, remake themselves, come here to change their lives and their luck.

Sometimes it works.

Small branches from a moribund elm littered the house's tar-paper roof. The tree was doomed, but not dead; Dutch elm disease kills from the crown.

I made sure the kickstand was on hard earth and walked toward the house. My ghost had vanished, though I had expected to see him under the wind chimes on the front porch.

A crystalline clinking wasn't only from the chimes. Around the side, another nearly dead elm swayed in the breeze. Its fingerling branches had been broken off blunt, and onto each stick was thrust a colored bottle—gold, violet, emerald, Tŷ Nant ruby, Maltine amber, Ayer's cobalt blue. They tinkled as the tree moved, and I wondered how they managed not to smash in anything like a real wind.

I was tipping up my eye patch to get a better look when my

footsteps alerted someone. Which is to say, a burro in the yard behind the house started braying as if badly in need of oiling, and that was the end of my stealth.

The *otherwise* glow of trapped ghosts swirled inside the bottles on the dying elm. I felt I should hear them tapping, scratching at the inside of their rainbow prisons. But only the light breeze soughed across the mouths of the bottles. Some people say the sound is the evil spirits crying for release, but it's not.

I've never seen the point in trapping ghosts. The ones you could catch in a bottle tree are harmless, and the ones that aren't harmless, you couldn't catch in a bottle tree.

I wondered where my Lassie-ghost was, and where I was supposed to find the well with Timmy in it. And as I was wondering—the burro still sawing away, no doubt infuriating the suburban neighbors—the front door banged open hard enough that my boots cleared earth. I flipped down my eye patch; no point making an innocent bystander look at a scarred socket.

Like Odin, I traded the eye for other things. Unlike Odin, it didn't involve a gallows tree, and I didn't expect anything in trade but a plain pine box and a hasty burial. What I got was being made the genius of Las Vegas, guardian of the Sin City and all her fallen angels.

It's a strange old world.

The woman standing on the shaded porch was in her sixties, I thought, stoop-shouldered, yellowing gray hair tucked behind her ears. Despite the heat, she dressed in a raveling cardigan pulled lumpy over a blue-and-white star-patterned shirt that hung, untucked, to the thighs of shapeless brown slacks. She scowled through filthy glasses. "Who's there?"

Mushy diction, as if she'd forgotten to slide her dentures

in. When I turned to her, she leaned forward against one of the four-by-fours holding up the porch roof, peering through strings of hair.

"Jackie." When I stepped from the shade of the dying elm, sun thumped my head like hot sand. There were a couple of wizened forty-foot Mexican fan palms on the property, but they cast no more shade than telephone poles.

"Jackie," she said, and kissed air. "I think—no, I don't remember you."

"I don't think we've met," I said, but as I said it I wasn't sure anymore. Her cloudy blue eyes, the shape of her nose . . .

Useless. If she's lived in Vegas sixty years, I might have seen her hundreds of times. Especially back when there were only a hundred thousand, two hundred thousand people in town. But I didn't remember her now. "Ma'am, is this your bottle tree?"

"This is private property." She blinked sagging lids. "My bottle tree? What do you know about bottle trees?"

"They're for catching ghosts," I said. "Protection from evil spirits. Ms. Bukvajova? Mrs.?"

She shrugged. All the same to her.

"Do you have a lot of evil spirits here, Ms. Bukvajova?"

"A few," she said. "Can't you hear 'em? Singing away in there? Don't you remember what that's good for, Jackie?"

The breeze was enough to ruffle the fans on the palms, but its sighs and the chiming were still the only sounds rising from the bottle tree. It sounded a little like a glass armonica—Benjamin Franklin's instrument, once thought to cause neurological damage because of its vibrations. But that might have just been lead poisoning from the paint on the crystal bowls.

"That's just the wind," I said. "Those ghosts are harmless, Ms. Bukvajova."

She laughed, and came out of the shade of the porch into the sunlight. She stumped forward, hands stuffed now into the pockets of her mustard-colored cardigan. It matched her house. The sweater hung from her stooped shoulders like a yoke supporting her fists in slings. “Harmless,” she said, “but not useless.” She pushed past me, trailing unwashed sourness. Flakes of dead skin nested among the roots of her eyebrows and in her thinning hair.

She pulled a hand from her pocket to tap a metal church key against the base of an amber-colored bottle. The sighing and moaning redoubled. “Just the wind.”

She pulled the bottle off the branch and popped a champagne cork into the top, then set the corked bottle at the base of the tree.

“I’m sure I should remember you,” she said. She pulled down another bottle and corked it, but had to get a stepladder for the third. It was just leaned up under the eaves; obviously, she used it a lot.

“I’m not sure there’s anything to remember.”

She snorted. “I forget a lot these days, Jackie. It’s the price of getting old. What do you forget?”

I wasn’t too sure of the wisdom of a sixty-year-old woman climbing ladders, but it’s not a city’s job to babysit children and old people. I might have volunteered to climb up anyway, but I wasn’t sure I wanted to abet whatever she was doing with the ghosts.

Especially if one were Lassie.

Whatever I was opening my mouth to say slipped out of memory even as I was reaching to turn it into words. “So if they’re harmless but useful,” I asked instead, “what do you use them for?”

Ms. Bukvajova was halfway up the ladder. She turned

stiffly, holding on to a fragile dead branch, and tapped her forehead with her free hand. "All sorts of things. Some I cook myself and some I sell. Ghosts are memories. I reckon they've got more uses than I recollect, even, and I recollect a few. I made sure to write 'em down."

When she clambered down, she held a straw-yellow bottle in one hand, her thumb pressed over the neck. She shook the bottle as if shaking up a soda so it would spray, and raised it to her mouth. The gesture was deft and quick; her throat worked as if she chugged a beer; her lashes, crusted with yellow grains, brushed her cheek. I watched, fascinated, searching for any sign of change. Tatters of *otherwise* light blew around her, but that was all. When she lowered the bottle and belched she looked the same.

"Hits the spot, it does," she said, and wiped moist lips on the back of her wrist.

Another man might have picked a fight, taken the bottles away, smashed the tree. But then there was the question of what good that would do and who had the right of the matter. There was no law against catching ghosts, neither man's nor moral. They were dead already. Exploiting a lingering shade, to be honest, bothers me a damned sight less than eating bacon does. And I eat bacon.

But it made me curious. Vegas is chinks and cracks, and magic grows in some of them. I'm the sort of person who can usually be found poking around deserted lots with a field guide, so to speak, trying to decide if what I have here is really yellow wood sorrel or something else entirely. I like to know what the growing things are.

So I kept thinking about Ms. Bukvajova as I guided the

BMW back through light Sunday traffic, pausing in front of the gray block, lattice-and-glass facade of St. Christopher's on Bruce, near the North Las Vegas police station. Kids squealed in the public swimming pool down the street. Chlorine hung acrid on the air.

Children really are tougher than adults. It was enough to make me sneeze from here.

Stewart emerged after the exodus, blond hair immediately evident in the sunlight. I wondered if he had stayed inside to introduce himself to the priest. Stewart's churchgoing, just not religious. Or just not any one religion in particular. He visits them by turns.

He's the other half of Las Vegas—well, half is the wrong word; there's overlap—and my city has more churches per capita than any other in America. And no, that doesn't include wedding chapels.

Stewart sauntered up to where I stood bracing the bike and ran a hand up my arm. I handed him his helmet; he left a lip print on the glossy side of mine before strapping his own in place. Then his feet were on the pegs and we sailed into the traffic stream, sliding into the space left in front of an old man in a gold Lincoln Town Car who had hit the brakes in shock at the public display of affection.

We were already in the neighborhood, so we swung by Jerry's Nugget to avail ourselves of the legendary eight-dollar prime rib for his first lunch and my second one. Somehow we wound up going to the Italian place instead, and Stewart stuffed garlic bread into his mouth and swallowed beer until the pizza and salad showed, like I'd been keeping him on bread and water.

Stewart wasn't big. He was fair-haired, wiry, and he bit his thumbnail while he was thinking. I liked watching him eat. I liked his enthusiasm and flightiness and the fact that I knew it was all a pose.

"How was church?" I asked when he'd slowed down enough to answer questions.

He pushed a piece of pepperoni around with his fingertip, then licked the grease off the nail. "Boring. We need cuter priests in this town."

"They don't pick them for the way they fill out their trousers," I answered complacently. I assembled a forkful of lettuce, onion, and a bite of pizza with crushed reds and parmesan, and stuffed it into my mouth. No matter how many times I did that, Stewart still looked at me in disbelief. Hey, it tasted good. "What do you want to do tonight?"

"Dunno," he said. "Sunday night in Vegas. We could go to a movie."

"We could go to a bar."

"Mmmph." Not such a bad idea, though, by the way he tilted his head and lifted an eyebrow. "What did you do today?"

I shrugged. "Hung out at the Crown and Anchor. Drove around. The ghosts are back."

"Ah, so," he said, and flicked beer at me. I ducked, laughing, and the waiter shot us a dirty look. Didn't bother me: Service is always slow in there, and Stewart and I overtip. "Sounds like a thrilling day."

I didn't *decide* not to tell Stewart about Ms. Bukvajova. It just, you know—completely slipped my mind.

It turned out that what we did that night was go to the circus. I like circus folk, and I love the circus. So because Stewart loves me, we go to the circus every time it's in town.

Well, Vegas has its own local circuses. A new Cirque du Soleil every couple of years, and we've seen them all, including the traveling shows. The animal acts are being phased out after what happened to Roy Horn. But it's a big deal when an arena show comes through, and an even bigger one when it's a tent show.

Call me old-fashioned, but it's not *really* a circus without a big top.

Oestman Brothers Circus and Traveling Show had set up on the desert lot near Sahara, the one they're always going to build a casino on any day now. We arrived an hour and a half before showtime, light still smeared across the sky, holding the dark at bay.

Not that darkness stood much chance against Vegas. Night tried to fall as we wandered the side tents—viewing fortune-tellers and caged tigers in their shaded enclosure, munching on cotton candy—and it only changed the quality of light. Neon saturated the atmosphere, heavy-hung, so I expected to see it move in swirls with each current. Stewart and I walked through it as if it were a fog. At one point he grabbed my hand and I turned to look at him and saw him crowned in ghostly radiance. I ducked down and kissed him on the grin, despite the sharp intake of breath from a scandalized matron on the far side of the candy-apple booth. I hoped the guy guessing her weight guessed high.

When I leaned back, the light was still there, and it buoyed me.

It has its own *otherwise* energy, that light in Vegas. It's as much me as my skin and fingers, as much my partner as Stewart is—alien and present—so sometimes I feel it from the inside and sometimes I feel it like a caress.

Somewhere between the rigged dart game and the crocodile

boy, we finished our junk food and joined the people moving inside. Under the big top, it was sawdust and lights and collapsible bleachers, and Stewart and I clomped up them to find our seats. He promptly got up again to fetch popcorn and cokes—I have no idea where he puts it—and was back before the seats finished filling up. He's got a knack for picking the quick line. Just lucky like that.

I had my head craned back, staring up at the highest point of the big top, when he slid a bag of roasted chestnuts into my hand. "They call it the king pole," I said. "The whole tent hangs off it. That used to be one hell of a tree."

"Yeah," he said. "So was the one Odin hanged himself off of. And look where that got him—overrun by Christians."

"Blind and forgotten," I said, and touched my eyepatch.

Stewart winked under blond bangs and stole a chestnut back.

It was a nice enough little circus. They had a couple of elephants that came on toward the end of the show, and as I sat there and ate chestnuts I wondered if they were abused. Not everybody treats their animals as well as Siegfried and Roy. Yeah, I worry more about animals than people, which is stupid. Some folks justify it by saying that animals don't make the choices that lead to their torment and destruction, but it's a bit facile to pretend people have any more autonomy.

In reality, the rat race is a handicap. Except the previous winners start with less weight, not as far to run, and a better knowledge of the track. And the more you fail to keep up, the more weight gets piled on.

It's a scary business, life.

This was a three-ring circus, where there's a big act in the center ring—that's where the elephants were—and something smaller on either side. Because we got our tickets late, we were over by the concurrent clowns, and Stewart seemed to be watching them more than the elephants. He doesn't like animal acts.

I like watching the ringmaster. When the elephants trouped out, I knew it had to be time for the capper. The man in the sequined red topcoat ran out to the middle of the center ring and gestured for his microphone, which glided from the big-top to be caught with a conjuror's flair.

Behind him, trapezes snaked from the scaffolding. Running men brought out a pedestal. The knotted shroud of the net rose and grew taut, like an emerged moth plumping chrysalis-rumpled wings, while the ringmaster's voice rang across the stands.

"Ladies and gentlemen. Children of all ages! May I direct your attention to the center ring!?

"You have seen aerialists and acrobats. You have seen wire dancers and tumblers, funambulists and flyers. But you have never seen anything like this.

"All the way from the primeval forest of mysterious Moravia, I give you— the Flying Bukvajovas!"

"Huh," I said, as the catcher was winched up to his trapeze and the first of the flyers began to ascend the platform. "I could swear I've heard that name."

Stewart gave me a funny look. "They've been through town before. We saw them about ten years ago. With a different circus then. And I don't think that was the first time. I'm pretty sure they were here when the dam was going in. . . ."

"Oh," I said. "Of course." And ate another nut. One of those multigenerational circus families.

The ringmaster's microphone reeled back into the stratosphere. He fled the ring in a scatter of sequin reflections, something like an animate mirror ball. I shrugged off a chill.

"Jackie?"

"Somebody stepped on my grave."

Stewart stole another nut. "Maybe the ringmaster is evil."

I tried to steal it back, resulting in a wrestling match that scattered popcorn across the floorboards and glares across nearby patrons. Casualties of war. To add insult to injury, Stewart popped the kidnappee into his mouth before I managed to retrieve it.

"No evil ringmasters," I said. "I won't allow it. Screw Ray Bradbury."

"That was a carny," Stewart said complacently, defending what remained of his popcorn. "And anyway, Bradbury's not my type."

Later that night, when the city glow was creeping around the edges of the hotel-room blackout curtains brightly enough to compete with my bedside lamp, I lay staring at the ceiling. I was supposed to be reading a book. Stewart was playing a Gameboy, but the beeps were intermittent.

I let the paperback fall across my chest. "Hey, Stewart?"

"Mm?"

"Have you noticed yourself forgetting things?"

"Like my car keys?"

Smart ass. "No. Like things you used to know. Street names. Your first girlfriend's favorite color. That sort of stuff."

"I wonder how you'd know if you forgot something," he said, hitting pause on his game. "I mean, really forgot it. Do you ever think about Alzheimer's? Or a brain injury? You'd never know what you were missing, would you?"

"No," I said, picking up my book. I hadn't been paying enough attention to the last three pages and had to flip back until I found something I remembered reading. "Or yes, maybe. I don't know. I mean, if you were losing time, like not making new memories, probably not. But if you were forgetting things like your husband's or wife's name? Then probably. And you might try to cover it up."

He looked at me suspiciously.

"Hey," I said. "I *told* you I didn't remember where I'd heard the name."

He stared. I stared back. He glanced down at the Gameboy with a rude noise.

"Hey," I said, to make him throw a pillow, "what was your name again?"

Nobody sleeps in Las Vegas, and so neither do I. But if I did, I have to admit, ghosts would have a pretty good means of waking you up. Nothing like a hovering cold spot on the back of your neck to get you out of bed in a hurry.

I managed not to shriek, which was good, because Stewart was sort of curled up on my chest watching a Burt Reynolds movie—I know, but far be it from me to complain about my boyfriend's taste—and I might have shocked him into apoplexy. Instead, I sucked in a breath and disentangled myself—over his protests—before sliding out of bed to face my molester.

The ghost looked awfully familiar, as if I had seen him somewhere before. But he was just one of the little ghosts of the dam, harmless and inoffensive. By the rocking and beckoning, he wanted something from me.

"Lassie wants something," I said to Stewart, because the ghost's demeanor reminded me of a worried dog.

"Shh," Stewart said. "This is the good bit."

"But the *ghost*," I repeated, "*wants* something."

"Oh, and I'm supposed to figure out what?" But he hit the mute button, sat up, and drawled, "Hello, sailor."

I winced mostly out of habit. He wasn't actually camping it up all that much.

"I feel like I know him," I said, while the ghost stared at me with hemorrhage-spotted eyes.

"Jeff Soble." Stewart stood. Of course *he'd* know the guy's name. "Died on the dam. People die all the time, you know. They get unlucky. Something random and stupid goes wrong."

"I know," I said. We both knew. You don't get to be a genius until you're buried and sung over. Stewart and me, we died young.

Looking at Stewart, I realized I didn't remember how I'd died. I opened my mouth to ask, scratching idly under my eye patch, and realized something else. That space—that hollow place of just not knowing—felt like a cold shadow had slid off my soul. Whatever had happened, it hadn't been pretty or pleasant, and I breathed easier in its absence.

The ghost beckoned again. I caught the motion in my peripheral vision; I was still looking at Stewart. "What do we do?"

"Follow him," Stewart said.

So we did, Stewart grabbing his keys on the way out the door.

Stewart's mode of transportation is inevitably some terrifying old beater replete with rust spots—hard to come by here in the desert—and hard-light peeling. The Nevada sun can fade even automobile paint to creamy yellow in a decade or two. This old Corolla had been red once, about the color of tomato soup. You could still see the color around the frame when you opened the doors. The amazing thing was that it was in perfect working order, which was the other inevitability about Stewart's old cars. He loved to tinker with them, and if you ignored small inconveniences like the lack of modern safety features, they ran like dreams. He usually wound up reselling them for 50 percent of book value to random people who needed them more than he did, and then finding another old junker to fix up the next week.

I like Stewart a lot. I mean, besides the obvious.

Anyway, I piled into the passenger seat—the desert night hadn't actually turned chill, but by comparison with the day, the mid-eighties felt on the cool side—and turned the radio off before he got the key into the ignition. He shot me a dirty look, but trust me, Stewart's taste in music isn't any better than his taste in movies.

Or men.

The car started right up, though he had to thump the dash to make the headlights glow. We had been staying at the Suncoast; it's a locals place, low-key and off the Strip. So we just headed back down the slope where the western side of the city rises toward the mountains. It's all indistinguishable, interchangeable new construction up there, and every year the cougars come back to their winter range to find houses have sprung up where there was nothing but cactus before, and there's nothing for them to eat but bug-eyed rat dogs.

Unfortunately for the cougars, people get upset when they

behave in this perfectly understandable fashion, even though the houses reach all the way up to the canyons now.

The ghost surfed in our headlights, almost washed away by their glow and the light rising like steam from the valley. We didn't have to descend far to lose the view; once we were on the Summerlin Parkway the city dropped out of sight, vanishing because we were now a part of it. Even this late, there was still a steady stream of cars once we reached the 95. The highways don't really grow quiet until after three.

Decatur still had some traffic, too, but it wasn't anything like rush hour. Our gridlock isn't bad by West Coast standards, but people keep moving in and it keeps on getting worse. It doesn't help that there's a shortage of streets that go all the way through, either north-south or east-west. A lot of them end mysteriously in a desert lot or the wall of a housing development, only to pick up again as if nothing had intervened, like a relationship on the other side of a secret affair.

By the time we turned onto Carey, I had a prickly feeling, and the traffic had thinned to nothing. I could still see the cars if I leaned over and glanced in the rearview mirror; they flowed north and south on Decatur in a soft intermittent stream, red and white like signal fires. I longed to be among them.

But Stewart was driving, and the ghost was leading us into darkness. I settled back and crossed my arms over my seatbelt, wondering why I felt the urge to strike out, to escape.

"Oh, god," I said. "Pull over. Pull over."

When Stewart pulled off onto the crunching hardpan shoulder, I bailed out of the little car and crouched in the shadow of the door, vomiting. The ghost hovered, as if my illness concerned it. Or maybe I was slowing it down. It didn't matter. We were here. The ghost led us down a gravel drive past a ranch sign and a mailbox adorned with the name *Bukvajova* in reflective letters. "I feel like I should know that name," I said, and Stewart looked at me funny.

He stopped the car well back from the house and touched the headlights off. We opened the doors in unison, like thugs in a Tarantino movie—you ever stop to think how much Hollywood has changed the way we perceive and pattern reality?—and slid out into the warm, windy dark.

The breeze had risen. I could hear howling and chiming from the bottom of the drive. "I bet the neighbors love that," Stewart said, locking his door.

"It's a bottle tree," I said.

"How do you know that?"

I checked to make sure my own door had latched. "It's been here for years."

"And you don't remember where you've heard the name *Bukvajova* before?"

"Should I?"

"Oh, Jack-Jackie," he said. "Something is definitely up."

I should probably have understood what he was driving at, but I just wound up shaking my head. It was a funny sensation, like when you know the answer to a question, or the name of a thing you're pointing at, and just can't pull it forward into the conscious part of your brain.

"So who lives here?"

"A—" I started to say, and realized I didn't know the answer to the question. "I don't know."

"Of course you know," Stewart said. "What were you just about to say?"

"A hedge-witch." The bottle tree howled torment in the meandering wind. "She's a hedge-witch. She drinks ghosts. I was just here today."

"Vegas forgets things," Stewart said. "You had better not be picking up that particular power. Because I'm not going to visit you in the home."

The words were hard, the voice fragile and tight-strung. I reached out and squeezed Stewart's hand. You spend a hundred years with somebody, you get to know their defense mechanisms. "We'll figure it out."

"You're not going to argue with me?"

I shrugged. We were close enough to the house now that the light from the kitchen window washed his face. "What would arguing get me? Something is obviously weird around here, and we have to figure it out."

"Right," he said. "So the hedge-witch Bukvajova lives here, and you don't remember why you know that or why you know about her bottle tree. And the ghost of Jeff Soble is leading you."

"Leading us."

"Leading you," Stewart said. "Whose ear was it blowing in?"

Touché. I let him lead me down the gravel drive to the covered patio and the door. "Are we just going to knock?"

"Are you afraid of a little hedge-witch?"

"Yes. Why are we here, Stewart?"

"Because something is happening to you. And I want to find out what it is. And make it stop. And if it doesn't have something to do with a Bukvajova, I'll eat the hat of your choice."

"Any hat at all?"

"Jackie," he said, and squeezed my arm. "Knock on the door."

But I didn't have to. We must have made enough noise to wake the dead, because first the interior door opened on a cascade of light, and then the security door squeaked wide. Steel doesn't rust in the desert, really. Not for a long time. But it was pretty obvious that the hinges were full of grit and hadn't been oiled in thirty years. I wondered if she kept meaning to get around to it and just forgot.

The spill of air-conditioning past my hands and thighs could have pushed me back a step, or maybe drawn me forward.

"I'm Jackie," I said. "This is Stewart."

"Of course you are, Jackie dear," she said. She held the door for us. "Come inside."

I hesitated, but Stewart stepped up, and I certainly wasn't letting him dance into the spider's web unsupervised. She shut both doors but didn't latch them, and I wondered if she worried about home invasions this far back from the street. I set the dead bolt behind us. No use tempting fate, and I wasn't worried about being locked in when the lock didn't require a key.

She sat us down and made us tea, boiling water in a proper brown pot. I watched her pour it into three chipped mugs, which she brought to the table, touching and set down together. Stewart picked out the brown one. I let the hedgewitch taste hers first, and then Stewart—he's very hard to kill—before I touched mine.

There was a tannin ring around the cup halfway down. I drank anyway, looking around the kitchen. It was a long, narrow room with a table set broadside and a clock centered on the wall. The hands were stopped. A paler ring marked the brown-and-gold wallpaper where it had been pushed askew.

"Were you married?" I asked her.

She shook her head. Her hair hung lank, the sour smell stirring around her when she moved. "I don't know. I don't recall."

"I was married," I said, and set my tea aside. "But I don't remember her name." Stewart gave me one of his unforthcoming looks. "Anyway, she's dead now."

"Lots of people are dead," said Ms. Bukvajova. "They live in memory."

I looked at the row of corked colorful bottles stacked on the granite pastry board and at the three or four empty ones racked up in the dish drain. Stewart raised his eyebrows.

"Sure." I poked my spoon against the side of the sugar bowl. The bottle tree howled loud enough to be heard through closed windows, over the hum of the swamp cooler. "As long as somebody remembers. Is that what you're doing? Remembering them?"

A tremendous clash rang from the bottle tree, like a string of glass bells violently shaken. I winced; Stewart started; Bukvajova perked up and peered out the kitchen windows. "Caught one?" Stewart asked. "What do you use them for?"

"Memories," she said. "He can't get them all if you keep topping it off. If you fill it up fast enough."

"He?"

She poured herself more tea, tilting the Brown Betty teapot with the skill of a practiced hand. "He eats memories."

Stewart leaned forward over the table and took her scaly hands. "They get . . . diluted, Mrs. Bukvajova?"

"You can only pour the water over the same leaves so many times and get . . ." She made a helpless gesture, and tapped the pot.

"Get tea?"

"Or whatever. Did you boys want something to eat? Jackie, what's your friend's name?"

"No, thank you," I said. I couldn't imagine being hungry.

"Mrs. Bukvajova"—following Stewart's lead—"why did you leave the circus?"

"There were ponies," she said. "And a cheetah named Ralph. He was friendly, and you could play with him." She looked down into her tea, then up at Stewart, as if he had spoken. "I'm sorry, dear, what was I saying?"

"Why you left the circus," he said.

She shook her head—"But I was never in the circus"—and frowned, painfully. "Was I?"

Another reason I like circus folk is that they have long memories. The sorts of memories we all used to have, when we lived in villages. Which is to say, based more on an oral-history sort of consensus version of events than on what really happened, blow by blow.

It's the folk process. When something gets passed down hand to hand, identifying details are shaved off, idiosyncrasies smoothed away, personality blurred, until what remains is a refined core of agreement. Memories get conflated, simplified.

It doesn't start off being the truth.

But because of the way the world works, it becomes the truth before too long. Compromises become history, become something everybody knows. Bloody old ballads are the handed-down tabloid TV of the thirteenth century. It may not be what *really* happened. But by the end it's what happened, after all.

As we got back into the car, the sun was starting to creep up behind Frenchman Mountain. "We need to go see the Flying Bukvajovas."

Stewart knuckled his eyes. When he pulled his hands down, the whites were bloodshot. "Tell me it's not an evil ringmaster."

"Okay," I said. "It's not an evil ringmaster."

"You want to ask them about their lost sheep?"

I shrugged. "I want to find out how the sheep got lost."

"Well, I don't want you getting lost as well." He patted my hand. The aged Toyota grumbled to life. "I don't suppose you know if this has just started happening?"

"No," I said.

I didn't remember.

Getting in to see Bartoloměj Bukvajova was easier than it should have been. The patriarch of the family was in his late fifties, hair still black as a freshly inked brush, wide shoulders rippling under his T-shirt with every gesture. He was the catcher, and I wondered how it affected the family dynamic that they really did know he wouldn't let them fall.

There was a lot of bitterness in that thought when I thought it, and I did not know why. Whoever my father was, he'd surely been dead for most of a century by now.

I looked at Stewart and wondered if I should ask him my old man's name, or if it would just freak him out unnecessarily. But he was looking at Bartoloměj, who had stood up from behind a folding card table in his RV to extend a hand.

"You're the One-Eyed Jack," he said. "And this must be the Suicide King."

I shook, and so did Stewart. "You've heard of us?"

"Show folk bend our luck a lot," he said. "It pays to know who the intermediaries are. Have you come for a tithe?"

I reached into my satchel and found a handful of thick poker chips. The Silver Slipper ones were just collectors' items now, but the ones from the Stratosphere had intrinsic value. I laid three thousand dollars in stamped, high-impact plastic on the card table and said, "Actually, we've come for information. This is Stewart. Call me Jackie. Everybody else does, and I want us to be friends."

He eyed the chips suspiciously, did not touch them, and sat back down. "Information is not something I'm generally comfortable giving out," he said. "Especially when it commands that sort of price. Too many people think they can buy more than anybody ought to be able to buy for a couple thousand dollars."

"Mmm," Stewart said. "You have kids, Bartoloměj? Grandkids? They have health insurance? Take the money. It's nothing to us. It's useful to you."

He eyed the stack. "Tell me what you want to know."

I looked at Stewart. Stewart looked at me. I shrugged and did the talking. "Did you have an uncle or an older brother, maybe, who jumped ship here in Vegas some time ago and married a local girl?"

Bartoloměj did not look away from my face. But his left hand crept out, encompassed the chips, and swept them to his side of the table.

"That," he said, "I don't mind talking about. But you have the story backward."

"We do?" Stewart, doing his best wide-eyed innocent. It's amazing how people will rush to fill that perceived void.

"Absolutely," Bartoloměj said. "You are thinking of my aunt, Branislava. My father's oldest sister. I never knew her; she left before I was born. She was a flyer, very beautiful, I'm told."

"I don't think it can be," I said. "The woman I'm thinking of is about ten years older than you, I'd guess. But not well. She looks her age."

"Are you sure?" He raised an eyebrow. "Branka would be in her eighties. Maybe older. Of course, we do tend to live a long time in my family . . ."

He shrugged.

I put another thousand in chips on the table, and he raised an eyebrow. "I told you I would help."

"I'm helping, too," I said. When he grinned he showed a gold tooth, which made me realize he hadn't smiled before. "What would you say if I told you your Aunt Branka was still alive and needed your help?"

"This kind of help?" He tapped the chips.

I shrugged, copying his gesture.

"I'd say we look after our own." He sucked on his teeth and pulled his hand back. "And I'd say she left us, and it was up to her to come back and ask if she wants that changed."

"I don't think she can ask," I said, and pulled out the chair across from him without actually ever being invited. "Tell me all about it, why don't you?"

Bartoloměj gave me that look again, and I pushed the chips toward him with a fingertip. "Good faith gesture."

He swept them to him much less tentatively. "We came through when the dam was going up, according to my father. She met a man and she married out," he said. "I don't know what else to tell you. We never heard from her after."

Stewart, standing behind me, cleared his throat. "Who did she marry?"

"Some guy," Bartoloměj answered. "I can call my dad at the home and check. He's still pretty sharp for a guy in his eighties. He'll remember."

"That'd be great," I said. "Bartoloměj, can you answer me one more question, maybe?"

"I can but try."

"If she married out," I asked, "why did she keep her own name?"

"She did?"

I nodded.

He let his head linger in that tilted pose for a moment before he shook his head. "I can't say, Jackie. It wasn't done, in those days."

"She's divorced," Stewart said in the car, quite abruptly. He always was the smart one, blond or not.

"We can pull the marriage license," I said.

Charleston Boulevard runs west all the way to Red Rock and the mountains from which it takes its name. Stewart and I go up there when we need to think, and we had planned to take our cell phones and wait for Bartoloměj Bukvajova to call. But Stewart pulled a U-turn right in the middle of Charleston, while I bent my luck hard to make sure that if there were any cops in the neighborhood, they were distracted by a flock of passing teenagers. It seemed like the least I could do.

Twenty minutes later, we had parked at a downtown casino and were crossing the street to the courthouse. Pulling the marriage license was easier than you'd expect; we're not really big on the expectation of privacy around here, and anyway it was a matter of public record. The hardest part was figuring out the date, but it was slow—just after lunch—and we got a helpful clerk, and I made sure she got lucky.

Sure, it's abuse of power. What's the point in power if you

can't abuse it? Anyway, it was in a good cause. And it's how I make my living.

You know, it's more honest than what a lot of guys do.

She brought the photocopy to the window of a waiting room where we sat side by side in scoop-shaped plastic chairs, me slumped and Stewart kicked forward like a vulture on a bender. Stewart was on his feet first, and so he paid the fee and collected the copy. When he glanced at it, the color faded from his cheeks. He looked up at the clerk, who was regarding him with raised eyebrows, obviously waiting for some response. She smiled when she got it: "Thank you," Stewart said automatically. Then he caught my elbow and, without explanation, steered me toward the street.

When we passed outside the courthouse door, into the wall of heat, onto fresh-mown grass dotted with sleeping vagrants and fat palm trees, I planted my feet and jerked him to a stop, because he didn't let go of my arm. He looked at me as if startled to realize I was still there and had opinions, and then shook his head. "What?"

"Still not a mind reader," I answered, and held out my left hand—the one he wasn't using as a tiller. And Stewart blushed right up under his hairline and handed me the still-warm photocopy.

"Sorry?"

"S'okay." The paper shook in my hand; the day seemed very bright. "Elijah Powers? *Eli Powers?* Babylon Hotel and Casino? That Eli Powers?"

"Shh," he said. He took the paper, folded it one-handed, and tucked it into his pocket. But he was still looking at me, and when I mouthed, "She married *Eli Powers,*" he nodded.

Well.

Shit.

Just then, my cell rang. It was Bartoloměj Bukvajova, calling to tell us that his dad said his sister married some guy who ran a gambling hall in Block 16—the old red-light zone—when the dam was going in over in Boulder City and Vegas was where the workers came to blow money and chase skirts on weekends. He thought it had been annulled shortly after, but he never spoke to her again.

Elijah Porter, his father thought. Some Biblical name like that.

Stewart took me to the Lucky 7's buffet at the Plaza, plunked me down in a corner, and brought me a plate before he fetched his own. I ordered him a Sprite and a glass of the house red—you try to get ginger ale in Vegas; it's worth your life—and coffee and an ice water for me. I waited to start eating the fried shrimp until he got back the second time.

"So," he said, settling himself behind a plate of roast beef and cornbread, "how are we going to get at Eli Powers?"

"He's ninety years old and he owns half of Las Vegas. Why the hell would we want to get at him?" There's something about the way breaded fried shrimp crunch that's deeply satisfying. The battered ones just aren't as good.

"Please tell me you're kidding." His cheap knife squeaked on the cheap plate as he cut his meat.

I winced. "Kidding?"

"Shit," he said. "Oh, shit. Branislava Bukvajova? No? Nothing?"

"Bukvajova," I said. "I swear I know that name."

"Of course," he said. "Who can make a city forget like the guy who runs it? Jackie, I think I know what's going on. I think I know what the problem is."

"Good," I said. "Can you explain it to me?"

"Drink your coffee and I'll try."

But I wasn't finished with the food yet, so I ate that and drank the ice water, smushing army-green peas between the tines of my fork. They tasted more like porridge than like a vegetable.

"Powers wasn't anybody yet when he married Bukvajova, was he?"

"Wait," I said. "Who did Powers marry? He's got a wife, doesn't he? His third one. The brunette. Used to be an actress."

"Not a very good one," Stewart agreed. "That's beside the point. She's his fourth wife, according to this. He married Branka Bukvajova in 1935. It seems like it was annulled less than a year later, but she never went back to the circus. Like she was stuck here, or she didn't remember that she could go home."

"Everybody forgets stuff in Vegas," I said, and didn't understand why Stewart would find it so troubling. It was only true. "Vegas forgets stuff. Imploded, bulldozed, blown away."

"Yeah," Stewart said, and stole one of my shrimp. "Almost makes you think somebody's stealing its memory, doesn't it? Do you want some chocolate cake, Jackie?"

"Jackie?" I said, picking up the cooling coffee in its white institutional stoneware cup. "Then who are you?"

I didn't really believe him when he said I was Jackie—isn't that a girl's name?—but it didn't bother me.

It really *did* bother me that I didn't know who *he* was, though. That seemed really rude. Especially when he was apparently buying me dinner. "Stewart," he said, and the strain on his voice cracked it clean across. He rose to fetch me cake, which made me feel bad that I couldn't remember how I'd met him. Surely I wasn't drunk? Surely I hadn't been that drunk?

"Am I drunk?" I asked, as he put the cake down before me and waved our busser over to refill my coffee mug.

"I wish," he answered, and patted my arm. Following the line of his motion, I realized suddenly that there was an awful lot of ink on my arm. I put down my fork, a bite of cake still speared untasted on the tines, and poked my bicep with a finger.

"Huh."

"Eat," he said. "You need your strength. And then we're going back to visit Ms. Bukvajova, and we're not leaving until we figure out what's going on."

I swallowed a mouthful of cake. "Who's Ms. Bukvajova?"

The afternoon was full of light when we walked out onto a promenade covered by an arch that seemed to be made of millions of small lights hung from a lattice. The day was like a kiln. I deduced we must be in the desert. "Stewart, where are we?"

His face very still, he said, "Fremont Street."

"Fremont Street? Isn't that in Tombstone? Where the Earps shot up the Clantons. Familiarly called the Gunfight at the O.K. Corral, as misrepresented in a *Star Trek* episode."

"All right," Stewart said. "You're still Jackie. And we have seriously got to get this fixed."

I should probably have been scared, standing on a strange street corner in a strange town with a strange man, unable to remember my own name. Had I ever known my name? But Stewart was a soothing presence, for all his twisted lips and wrinkled forehead.

"I don't think this would bother me so much if you weren't a walking encyclopedia of forgotten Las Vegas."

"We're in Las Vegas? Oh. Then this will all get pulled down in a couple of years anyway, won't it? I don't know why they even bother naming things."

His hand was hard on my shoulder as he pulled me along. "Come on. I'm not sure how to handle this, Jackie. As long as I've known you—"

"—As long as you've *known* me?"

"—Whatever happens in this place, whatever falls down or gets buried or goes forgotten, you always seem to remember that it's here, or that it was here." He led me through crowds deftly, and I let him. He seemed to know where he was going, and I had no idea. "All that dead history never dies, in you. And now . . ." He shrugged.

I put my hand over his fingers on my arm, because it seemed like the thing to do, and he smiled at me, very briefly. My heart jumped. Huh. Was he my *boyfriend*?

I thought that over. It seemed appealing.

"Do you remember me?" he asked.

"Maybe," I said. "A little. Are we together?"

"Yes," he said. "Well, only for the last hundred years. But what I was trying to say was, all that time, I've had this idea that you were, I dunno, the *memory* of Las Vegas. Where all its ghosts went. Where they wound up. And now, if you can't remember anything . . ."

"Do you think I'm going senile?"

"Cities don't go senile," he said. We ducked between an arguing couple.

"You talk like I'm somehow linked to the city—"

"Jackie, you *are* the city. You're its genius. Its spirit. One of them. I'm the other one."

And you know, that sounded right. Completely bizarre, mind you, but right. "So if I'm the city's memory," I said, "and I can't remember anything. . . ."

"Yeah," he said. "You see why I'm a little worried now."

"Well then," I said—and there was no excuse for my tone, because I'm sure he would have seen it if he wasn't too worried to think straight—"it's obvious what's going on. Either somebody is using the city to get to me, or me to get to the city."

The first thing I noticed about the battered old block house on the neglected ranch estate was a glorious bottle tree in the side yard, moaning softly in the breeze. It caught the sunlight in all colors, cobalt and ruby and amber and emerald, commonplace and lovely.

I imagine most of us never really look at glass. But there it was, sun stained through it. I felt the whimpers of the ghosts trapped inside. Felt, yes. It wasn't exactly hearing.

I stepped away from the still-open door of the parked car, and the blond man caught my arm. "Jackie," he said. "Don't go too close to that."

"It's pretty."

"I know," he said, and gentled me with a hand on my hair. "Come away. We need to talk to Ms. Bukvajova."

"You know," I said, "I swear I've heard that name."

"I know." His voice did something funny. "I've heard it too."

He lead me under the porch roof, in out of the sun—we must be somewhere in the South for there to be bottle trees, and the sun sure felt like it—and thumped on the security door because the doorbell was busted. Or if it wasn't busted, anyway, you couldn't hear it chime from the outside, so he knocked to be sure.

A moment later, the inside door swung open a crack, and bright cloudy eyes peered through the crevice, half obscured by strings of yellowed hair. "Boys!" the old woman said. "Stewart! Jackie! Come in. Come in. Would you like an iced tea?"

"Yes, please, Ms. Bukvajova," the blond man said, and I gaped. But Miss Bukvajova was suddenly young, all auburn hair and sparkle and aerialist muscles, power and grace. . . .

The person overwhelmed by that memory was not me.

But for a moment I saw her as she had been, a short, hourglass-shaped, broad-shouldered woman with a ballerina waddle, and someone else's grief filled up my throat. She lead us through a cluttered red-flannel living room, fussy and terrible, every surface cluttered with dusty photographs, and I could not hold her steady in my sight.

"Drink."

My elbows propped rudely on her kitchen table, I sat in a creaking ladder-back chair with my hands cupped loosely around a cold empty glass.

"Drink," she said, and poured more tea.

Though it tasted of cement dust and brackish water, I drank. I saw her again, and this time she swung with perfect grace on a flying trapeze, as if she were dancing there. She somersaulted through the air, and a strong man caught her. I stung my throat shouting, stung my palms clapping, felt fingers close on my wrists and pull my hands apart. Stewart—and my blood was dripping over his nails. "You idiot," he said. "You broke the glass."

"Stewart?"

He met my eyes, and his mouth went thin. "Jackie?"

"Sort of," I said. I felt thin as a watercolor of myself, but I was there. He looked down quickly. Holding my hand still, he began to pick the slivers of broken glass out of the palm, leaving the ice melting on the table. "Miss Bukvajova?"

"You remember me?" she said.

"Yes," I said. "We do." Because it wasn't just me remembering her. "That was Jeff Soble," I said, and winced as Stewart picked another shard of glass from my palm. I turned away, so I wouldn't have to watch him, and watched the sun glint off the bottle tree on the other side of the slatted blinds. "In the tea."

"It works," she said, and made a moue like a much-younger woman. "He was a friend of mine. He worked on the dam."

"But you married Powers."

She rose from the table, fetched another blocky Anchor Hocking glass from the cabinet, and plunked it to one side of the puddle of ice and broken glass. She added ice with her fingers and poured the tea from a scarred yellow Rubbermaid pitcher with a push-button top. She said, "It's like getting dehydrated. You need more to catch up than you think you will. Keep drinking. I'll get a towel."

Keep drinking the memory of her friend. The one who brought me here to save her.

"You married Powers," I said again, and drank the tea with my left hand, which was only cut a little. The cold glass stung the scrapes on my palm. "Not Jeff."

I couldn't call him Soble when I was drinking his memory.

"Wouldn't you?" She poured herself a glass too, and drank. "Not that Eli was anything special then. He owned a gambling hall downtown, on Fremont Street. And you all know where that led."

"Empire," Stewart said, laying another piece of bloody glass in his pile. "I think that's all of it, Jackie."

"So the marriage didn't work out?"

She pushed a greasy lock out of the way with a spotted hand and finished her tea. "Imploded like an outworn casino," she said. "His other wives haven't been so lucky." She gestured around. "I got the marriage annulled—unmade—and he hasn't been able to eat me up entire. The bottle tree keeps me going. Las Vegas is full of ghosts. Suicides, mostly. They taste all right."

Stewart wrapped a paper towel around my palm to stanch the bleeding. The fluid in my glass tasted like cement and nitro, with too much sugar.

Stewart said, "So why is he coming after Jackie now?"

She shrugged. "Jackie came here? Jackie caught his attention? Jackie's a better source of power than I ever was? I can feel my head filling back up again; I think he must be letting me alone."

"You know the circus is in town?" It was mean of me to ask that way, just drop it in her lap and see what she did.

What she did was blanch. "They don't want to hear from me."

"If there was bad blood," Stewart said softly, "I think they've forgotten it now. Why would all this start happening while your family is here?"

"Jeff," she said. "I think he was waiting to bring you to me. Because I couldn't have made much sense, unless you caught me just at the right time. You would have needed what my family could tell you. And Eli—Eli's used so many women up."

"Not just women," Stewart said, with a sidelong glance at me.

I drank another swallow of sweet tea and Jeff Soble. "I wonder," I said, "if he's using me to get to something in particular. You wonder, if Vegas forgets stuff but I remember it—what happens to the parts of Vegas that I *don't* remember?"

"Martin Powers," Stewart said, without hesitation.

I remembered the newspaper. And nodded. "He's trying to protect his grandson," I said. "Martin Powers is up on racketeering charges. He'll lose his gambling license. But Vegas is the city of second acts. We'll forgive anything, as long as you give us half a chance to forget it."

"And he can make the city forget," Stewart said.

"Well," I answered, sipping my tea, "he can make me forget. And Vegas forgets easier than I do."

Tires crunched on the gravel drive.

Not just one set, but many.

Powers's men surrounded the house and knocked on the door. Branka and I both gulped down the last mouthfuls of our tea before we filed out and went quietly. Every bit helps, right?

Well, maybe sometimes.

Most of the cars waiting for us were black sedans, but parked closest to the house was a limousine with Babylon Casino plates and a very polite driver who held the door wide. The implied arrogance never changes: No one can touch me here.

One of the gentlemen in black suits with an earpiece rode with us. I noticed that the bulletproof glass was up between the passenger compartment and the cab.

A long ride through rush hour followed. Vegas's gridlock

starts in the afternoon and persists into evening, and it seemed like we sat through most of it. A tractor trailer had jackknifed in the Spaghetti Bowl. I guess those effortless car rides only happen in movies.

The Tower of Babylon rose through a veil of transplanted jungle foliage and piped-in orchid scent to scrape a desert sky burned almost colorless by the Nevada sun. Visible the entire length of the Las Vegas Strip, it collapsed in fire and fury six times daily, six days a week, wind conditions permitting.

For a premium, you could ride it down.

Gold-glass ziggurats flanked it on either side. Shaded pathways led from the summer-scorched sidewalk and the broiling asphalt of the Strip through glades and grottoes, beside a bubbling piped waterfall. There was a slidewalk, for those who found the hundred meters or so under misters and date palms too far to walk in the Las Vegas heat.

The chattering monkeys caged behind "invisible" fencing on either side of the path were New World varieties, though most of the tourists could be counted on not to notice that, and the mossy ruined temples they played amongst were more Southeast Asian than Mesopotamian in character, but—authenticity aside—the "Hanging Gardens of Babylon" were a landscape designer's masterpiece. A bare few feet from the bustle of the Strip, the plants and animals—the palm trees also teemed with brightly colored birds—and the chuckling water and the architectural sound-damping introduced a sort of mystic hush. Even the tourists walked through with lowered voices.

We didn't. We came around the back, in the smoked-glass limousine, through a concealed gate that opened to the flash of the telemetry device clipped to the sun visor. I don't know if it chirped: The bulletproof glass was up.

The limousine rolled silently into a tunnel jeweled with lanterns, and the gate scrolled shut behind us. Branka made a noise like one of those monkeys in distress, and Stewart squeezed her arm. I wished he'd squeeze mine, too, but not enough to whimper for attention.

When the limo rolled to a halt, I could fool myself that what I felt was relief, but really it was a cold, shallow kind of fear that sloshed over me like river water. Our silent warden—he hadn't acknowledged anyone's presence since he sat—reached for the door. He rose and ushered us out. We stepped onto plush carpet and stood blinking in the VIP tunnel of the Babylon Hotel and Casino.

Ornate doors paneled with mock ivory relief swung wide. Branka squeezed my hand with her salamander-damp one and drew me forward. I shook my head. I was the One-Eyed Jack, genius of Las Vegas. I could see magic and talk to ghosts. The City of Suicides was mine to protect. I didn't need to be afraid of . . .

I leaned over and spoke into Stewart's ear. "Stewart?"

"Shh," he said, and I dropped my voice as we walked forward, escorted by more men with earpieces and dark suits.

I said, "What am I afraid of?"

The look he gave me was sad and bottomless. "Do you remember why we're here?"

I should. I just had. I knew it was on the tip of my tongue. "Powers," I said. "He's making me forget."

We three moved forward in the middle of a ring of security, as they led us along the tunnel to an elevator. I felt like a rock star on the way to the gallows.

"What are we going to do about it?" Stewart asked.

I looked down at my hands and shook my head. "Not let him?"

"Good plan," Stewart said, as the doors chimed. "Let's see what we can do about managing that."

In the tiny paneled elevator, Branka's sour sweat overpowered the piped-in aroma of gardenias and orchids, some functionary's idea of how Babylon smelled. Were there such things as scent designers? Our ride—whisper-silent, crowded, tense—terminated in the penthouse, where, still ringed by all those refugees from *The Matrix,* we were herded forward onto oriental carpets, myself in the middle and Branka and Stewart one to each side.

I thought I knew what to expect. Eli Powers was as old as Las Vegas, but—in his rare television appearances—getting around under his own power, though wizened and leaning heavily on two crutches. I thought I would find an old man relying on a mechanized chair in the comfort of his own home. Instead, a man in his forties came forward to meet us, hair just graying at the temples, light eyes bright behind bifocals. He extended his hand, focusing a little behind me, and I accepted the handshake.

"Martin Powers," he lied.

"Jackie," I answered. "This is Stewart. Branka you already know. Tell me your right name, Mr. Powers."

He glanced from me to Stewart, and then to the half dozen hotel-security operatives standing behind us. Whatever the gesture he made, they understood it and withdrew to the edge of the thirty-foot living room. Out of earshot but not out of range.

They wouldn't have done it if Powers wasn't armed.

"I will do you the honor of not pretending I don't understand you," Eli Powers said through his grandson's mouth. "You're the Genii of Las Vegas."

"And you used to be Eli Powers," Stewart said, and stuck his hand out.

With apparent equanimity, Powers shook it, then let his own hand fall to his side. "For my own use, later on—what gave me away?"

"Logic," Stewart answered. He stepped forward, not close enough to impinge on Powers's personal space but close enough to demand his attention. Making himself the spokesperson, taking the focus off me. That meant that he expected me to figure out what to do about Powers.

Did I mention that Stewart is the smart one?

He folded his hands in the small of his back, tipped his head like a saucy girl, and continued, "You're a mnemophage. You've kept yourself alive all these years by eating up the memories of anyone you could trick into giving consent—and the memories of the city itself. Wives, children—you have a legal claim on them, don't you, Eli? It's enough to get a grip on them with sorcery. And Las Vegas itself—how much of it do you own, in your own name or through proxies?"

"Enough," Eli said, smiling tightly. He looked interested—wouldn't any narcissist, confronted with someone enumerating his accomplishments?—but unconcerned. I hoped that was dangerous arrogance on his part and not justified confidence.

Stewart didn't glance at me. He took a step to the left, further dividing Eli's attention. But I couldn't rush him. Nothing physical would work under these circumstances; it would only earn us each a bullet.

Stewart clicked his tongue. His left hand, as if without his attention, made a dismissive flip. He said, "So did you just eat up Martin totally and move into his head like a hermit crab switching shells?"

The turn of phrase conjured up a horrible image, a pincered brain heaving itself from skull to skull, slimed with cerebrospinal fluid. I flinched, hard, and had to bite my cheek to get my face under control again. I edged my head sideways to catch Branka's eye, hoping for inspiration, but she had her hand pressed against her mouth, gaze fixed on Powers. Her lips moved, shaping words. *I don't remember.*

Eli smiled. It was a good smile—honest, interested. I would have voted for him.

"Martin made a very great sacrifice on my behalf," he said, making it sound for all the world as if his grandson had given him a kidney or something. Branka's hand reached out, clutched on my wrist. *I can't remember anything.*

I cleared my throat, which was pretty dry right then, and said, "Let them go, Eli."

Stewart started, so caught up in his performance he had forgotten what he was stalling for. He and Powers both swiveled. I squared my shoulders and said, "What you want from me is the city, isn't it? You want Vegas to forget why it's angry. You want it to remember only what's best about you." I breathed. "You want the love back, don't you, Eli?"

He stared for a moment and then his lips pressed thin and he nodded. "We only want the same thing," he said. "What's best for Vegas. I'm glad you see that, Jackie."

"Let them go," I said. "And I'll let you have it all."

"You have my word of honor," he said. "But you give me what I want first."

I had to pull my hand out of Branka's, though she clutched at my fingers like a child. Despite the air-conditioning, I rubbed slick palms on my trouser legs before I came forward to meet Powers. "Jackie," Stewart said, "don't—"

"Stewart. I got this. Really."

He didn't want to back down. Branka rocked on her heels, moaning softly, but I couldn't help. There was no way to give her back what she'd lost, no way to make it easier for her. In the real world, there are no reset buttons, no epiphantic healings.

If I were a decent human being instead of a city, I'd have noticed her pain and done something about it years ago. But that's not the way I operate, and I'm not sure there's anything anyone can do to make that change.

"What's the deal?" Powers asked.

"I give you my memories of you," I said. "And you let my friends go."

"He won't *stop*," Branka insisted. I put the back of my hand against her upper arm.

"No tricks," Powers said.

"No tricks," I answered. "I have too much to lose."

Odin got more for his eye than I did. But I got more than I deserved.

I lifted my eye patch up.

He didn't recoil. I guess Eli Powers had seen worse things than a self-inflicted gunshot wound. He leaned forward, staring into my eye socket.

I saw him doubled, Martin's face overlaid by the ghost-visage of Eli in my *otherwise* sight. He reached out and laid fingertips against the side of my face like Mr. Spock setting up for a mind meld. Branka pulled back, two wobbling steps, and I think Stewart would have grabbed Powers's wrist if I hadn't stopped him with an upraised hand.

"Take it," I said, and waited to see what would follow.

There was no sensation, except where manicured fingernails scratched my cheek and the orbit of my eye. He squinted at me, and as he did so, I thought of Eli Powers, everything I knew about him, the names of his wives and children and casinos, the racketeering charges against Martin, the rumors of infidelity and Mafia involvement, the newspaper articles and photographs, the dog he had back in the sixties with the one lop ear.

The dog.

The dog with the white patch on his head.

Whose dog was that, anyway?

And then the churn and bubble, and I felt something else slip out of me. Jeff Soble, what was left of him, jumped between us like a bridging spark. When he hit, I saw Powers jerk, start for half a second before he recovered himself and gagged Soble down. The Babylon Casino. And then unrelated things. The Mirage tigers. The Zane Floyd shooting. Endless construction. Airplanes stacked twelve deep across a fight-night sky. A Sting concert with three-hundred-dollar tickets. What's-her-name, the one who sang the theme from *Titanic*.

I fed him everything, everything I was, everything I knew. Everything about Las Vegas, city at the bottom a dead Ordovician sea. More than he could withstand. More than anything mortal could withstand, knowledge I had to die to contain. A kind of metaphysical judo, using his own strength against him, until I felt him try to pull away and fail, thrash like a gaffed fish.

Eli Powers was not used to fighting anything as old and deep and nasty as himself. But holding the deed to a dragon's cave is not the same as owning the dragon. I clutched him and fed him my city until he choked on it. I made him Las Vegas. I made him me.

I fed him more and more—a kind of spiral, scraping, dizzying—and then when he could swallow no more, I reached down into him and made a fist and dragged it all back out again.

Stewart grabbed Powers by the hair and shoved him away.

"Stewart—" I moved to jump in front of him, to get my body between the men with the bullets and Stewart's body. Suicide by gunman might be far enough from the intent of his gift to kill him outright. And *I'm* the one with the faultless luck. If one of us was going to be shot, I wanted it to be me.

He grabbed my shoulder and held me still. "Shh," he said. "Look."

I looked.

There was a man I didn't recognize, pushing himself off the expensive carpeting with rug burns on his hands. Branka, arms wrapped over her cardigan, was still swaying side to side.

And a whole bunch of security guys, standing in a huddle, one gesticulating while the others listened. The quarterback glanced up, cut himself off, and at his gesture, the rest broke away. They approached sternly, but a little sideways, and I realized that they didn't know where we had come from.

"I'm sorry, sir," the one in front of me said, "but you can't be here."

Another man picked the strange guy up, stared at him with furrowed brow for a moment, and said, "Excuse me, may I see some identification, please?"

We caught a taxi in the horseshoe in front of Babylon. Security escorted us out but were nice enough not to toss us so we bounced. Branka sat in the front seat beside the driver, and Stewart let me rest my head on his shoulder while the palm trees lining the driveway scrolled past on both sides like a green-screen effect. We stopped at the light at the bottom of the driveway while a flock of tourists stampeded across, and Stewart said, "You forgot about him."

"Stewart? Forgot about who?"

He shook his head. "Never mind. I think I'd rather you didn't remember." He bent down and kissed the top of my head.

I wondered if I was drunk. I didn't like the way I felt. The taxicab was spinning.

Stewart, at least, was warm and solid, even if he was raving. "I wish you were making sense."

"I know," he said. "I was just wondering, what do you think happens to the stuff we forget? You and me. The bits of Las Vegas even we don't remember."

"I've been forgetting things lately," I said.

"That's over with."

"Does it not exist anymore, if I've forgotten it? Or is it still there, just nobody notices?"

He shrugged. "I bet it's still there."

Some guy lurched up the sidewalk outside, looking roughed up. His suit had been expensive; his tie was silk. They were both ripped now. I wondered if he'd gotten mugged, or bounced by casino security.

Nobody but me seemed to notice him.

I turned away. Not my job. Not my job to notice him or rescue him. You cannot save everyone; you'll go mad trying. And anyway, it's not what cities do.

I said, "Why is it that we get so invested in our history, anyway? Why do we fight to preserve those old photographs and ancient keepsakes, just so our children can throw them away when they clear the house? We could just let go, blow wide. Be clean."

"Jackie—"

I turned my face into Stewart's shoulder and said, "I killed myself."

He nodded. "I know."

I closed my eyes. "It was nice not to remember it for a little while."

He rearranged us to put an arm around my shoulders, and I leaned into the embrace. "Memory is all we are," Stewart said softly, and reached up to stroke my hair.

About Ellen Datlow

Ellen Datlow has been editing science fiction, fantasy, and horror short fiction for more than thirty years. She was fiction editor of *OMNI* magazine and *Sci Fiction* and has edited more than fifty anthologies, including the *Best Horror of the Year, Little Deaths, Haunted Legends* (with Nick Mamatas), *Twists of the Tale, Inferno, The Del Rey Book of Science Fiction and Fantasy, Poe: 19 New Tales Inspired by Edgar Allan Poe, Lovecraft Unbound, Darkness: Two Decades of Modern Horror, The Beastly Bride and Other Tales of the Animal People, Troll's Eye View: A Book of Villainous Tales,* and *Teeth: Vampire Tales* (the last three with Terri Windling). She has won the Locus Award, the Hugo Award, the Bram Stoker Award, the International Horror Guild Award, the Shirley Jackson Award, and the World Fantasy Award for her editing. She was named recipient of the 2007 Karl Edward Wagner Special Award, given at the British Fantasy Convention for "outstanding contribution to the genre."

She lives in New York. More information can be found at www.datlow.com or at her blog: ellen-datlow.livejournal.com.